Finding the One

FINDING THE ONE

THE RIVER RAIN SERIES
BOOK SEVEN

KRISTEN ASHLEY

Finding the One
A River Rain Novel
By Kristen Ashley

Copyright 2025 Kristen Ashley
ISBN: 978-1-963135-94-7

Published by Blue Box Press, an imprint of Evil Eye Concepts, Incorporated

BOOK DESCRIPTION

Finding the One
A River Rain Novel, Book 7
By Kristen Ashley

Their parents being family friends, American/English aristocrat, Blake Sharp, and Scottish playboy Alasdair Wallace were thrust together all through their childhoods.

Blake thought Dair was a filthy, obnoxious, little boy bully.

Dair thought Blake was a spoiled, prissy wee miss.

Then Blake grew up to be a beautiful, loving woman who took care of everyone and made amazing pistachio muffins. And Dair grew up to be a protective, fun-loving, hard-living professional rugby player.

In the meantime, they'd both been deeply betrayed by lovers.

When their paths cross again, Blake is still reeling from her fiancé's treachery and what she learned about herself during it.

Dair thinks he's recovered from a marriage to a woman who was not at all what she seemed, and now he's smitten by the woman Blake has become.

So smitten, he has every intention of exploring what they can grow to be together.

But their combined family history is filled with secrets and lies. Secrets and lies that explode in their faces.

And while they deal with that, ghosts from the past rise up and threaten to haunt their future.

Is what they built together strong enough to hold true?

Or will their personal demons tear them apart?

ABOUT KRISTEN ASHLEY

Kristen Ashley is the *New York Times* bestselling author of over one hundred romance novels including the *Rock Chick*, *Colorado Mountain*, *Dream Man*, *Chaos*, *Unfinished Heroes*, *The 'Burg*, *Magdalene*, *Fantasyland*, *The Three*, *Ghost and Reincarnation*, *Moonlight and Motor Oil*, *Dream Team*, *River Rain*, *Misted Pines*, *Avenging Angels* and *Honey* series along with several standalone novels. She's a hybrid author, publishing titles both independently and traditionally, her books have been translated in fourteen languages and she's sold over five million books.

Kristen's novel, *Law Man*, won the *RT Book Reviews* Reviewer's Choice Award for best Romantic Suspense. Her independently published title *Hold On* was nominated for *RT Book Reviews* best Independent Contemporary Romance and her traditionally published title *Breathe* was nominated for best Contemporary Romance. Kristen's titles *Motorcycle Man*, *The Will*, *Ride Steady* (which won the Reader's Choice award from *Romance Reviews*) and *The Hookup* all made the final rounds for Goodreads Choice Awards in the Romance category.

Kristen, born in Gary and raised in Brownsburg, Indiana, was a fourth-generation graduate of Purdue University. Since, she has lived in Denver, the West Country of England, and now she resides in Phoenix. She worked as a charity executive for eighteen years prior to beginning her independent publishing career. She currently writes full-time.

Although romance is her genre, the prevailing themes running through all of Kristen's novels are friendship, family and a strong sisterhood. To this end, and as a way to thank her readers for their support, Kristen has created the Rock Chick Nation, a series of programs that are designed to give back to her readers and promote a strong female community.

The mission of the Rock Chick Nation is to live your best life, be true to your true self, recognize your beauty and take your sister's back whether they're friends and family or if they're thousands of miles away and you don't know who they are. The programs of the RC Nation include: Rock Chick Rendezvous, Rock Chick Recharges, and Rock Chick Rewards. Kristen's Rock Chick Rewards have donated over $200,000 to charity and this number continues to rise.

You can read more about Kristen, her titles and the Rock Chick Nation at KristenAshley.net.

ALSO FROM KRISTEN ASHLEY

Rock Chick Series
Rock Chick
Rock Chick Rescue
Rock Chick Redemption
Rock Chick Renegade
Rock Chick Revenge
Rock Chick Reckoning
Rock Chick Regret
Rock Chick Revolution
Rock Chick Reawakening
Rock Chick Reborn
Rock Chick Rematch

Avenging Angels Series
Avenging Angel
Avenging Angels: Back in the Saddle
Avenging Angels: Tenderfoot

The 'Burg Series
For You
At Peace
Golden Trail
Games of the Heart
The Promise
Hold On

The Chaos Series
Own the Wind
Fire Inside
Ride Steady
Walk Through Fire
A Christmas to Remember
Rough Ride
Wild Like the Wind
Free

Wild Fire
Wild Wind

The Colorado Mountain Series
The Gamble
Sweet Dreams
Lady Luck
Breathe
Jagged
Kaleidoscope
Bounty

Dream Man Series
Mystery Man
Wild Man
Law Man
Motorcycle Man
Quiet Man

Dream Team Series
Dream Maker
Dream Chaser
Dream Spinner
Dream Keeper
Dream Bites Cookbook

The Fantasyland Series
Wildest Dreams
The Golden Dynasty
Fantastical
Broken Dove
Midnight Soul
Gossamer in the Darkness

The Honey Series
The Deep End
The Farthest Edge
The Greatest Risk

The Magdalene Series
The Will
Soaring
The Time in Between

Moonlight and Motor Oil Series
The Hookup
The Slow Burn

River Rain Series
After the Climb
Chasing Serenity
Taking the Leap
Making the Match
Fighting the Pull
Sharing the Miracle
Embracing the Change
Finding the One

The Three Series
Until the Sun Falls from the Sky
With Everything I Am
Wild and Free

The Unfinished Hero Series
Knight
Creed
Raid
Deacon
Sebring

Ghosts and Reincarnation Series
Sommersgate House
Lacybourne Manor
Penmort Castle
Fairytale Come Alive
Lucky Stars

The Rising Series
The Beginning of Everything
The Plan Commences
The Dawn of the End
The Rising

Wild West MC Series
Still Standing
Smoke and Steel
Smooth Sailing

Misted Pines Series
The Girl in the Mist
The Girl in the Woods
The Woman by the Lake
The Woman Left Behind

The Mathilda Series
Mathilda SuperWitch
Mathilda SuperWitch, The Rise of the Dark Lord

Other Titles by Kristen Ashley
Loose Ends: Volume One
Heaven and Hell
Play It Safe
Three Wishes
Complicated
Loose Ends
Fast Lane
Perfect Together
Too Good to Be True

DEDICATION

To the memory of Melisse Shapiro.
You came up with Dair,
but you didn't live to see him make the page.
Even so…
I hope I did you proud.

AUTHOR'S NOTE

Before you dive into Blake and Dair's story, I'm going to give you some insight into the writing process.

Shortly, you'll discover that Blake's hero is Scottish.

Very much so.

To that end, I didn't want him to lose that important aspect of who he is in a reader's reading of his book.

However, as I struggled through the first chapters by typing his dialogue how it would sound with his accent, in all my read-throughs, I found it difficult to follow. His voice was in my head while writing, but I couldn't find it in my head while reading.

I've had the occasion when reading other books to have this same distraction.

And no writer wants her readers to be distracted when they'd much prefer the reader fall into the story.

That said, a Scotsman is going to talk like a Scotsman.

I asked my publishers to read the first few chapters of the book in order to find some kind of happy medium. Make sure the reader hears Dair, be true to this Scotsman, but not lose you while you're reading.

To that end, Dair uses words like "ye" (you), "ken" (know), "dinnae" (don't), "didnae" (didn't) and some other Scottish or British language and slang.

If you aren't British/Scottish, it might help in reading to note that "pissed" is another term for "drunk" (to mean "angry," the language used is "pissed off") and "haver" means "babble" or "talk nonsense."

But I didn't go whole hog peppering his voice with a phonetically typed Scottish accent. I also didn't use those words if they disturbed the flow of what he was saying (or what any of his family was saying) while a reader was reading it. And I abandoned it entirely when we're in his thoughts.

I hope I found the happy medium for Dair to be true to who he is, and you get that too, without losing you along the way.

With that said, I mostly hope you enjoy Blake and Dair's love story.

Rock On!

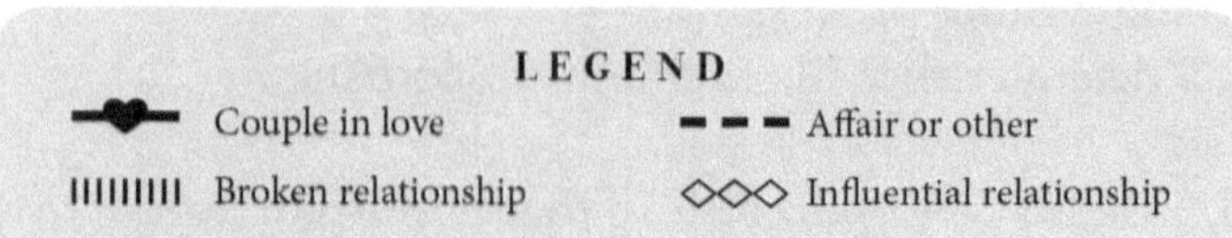

The WORLD of RIVER RAIN

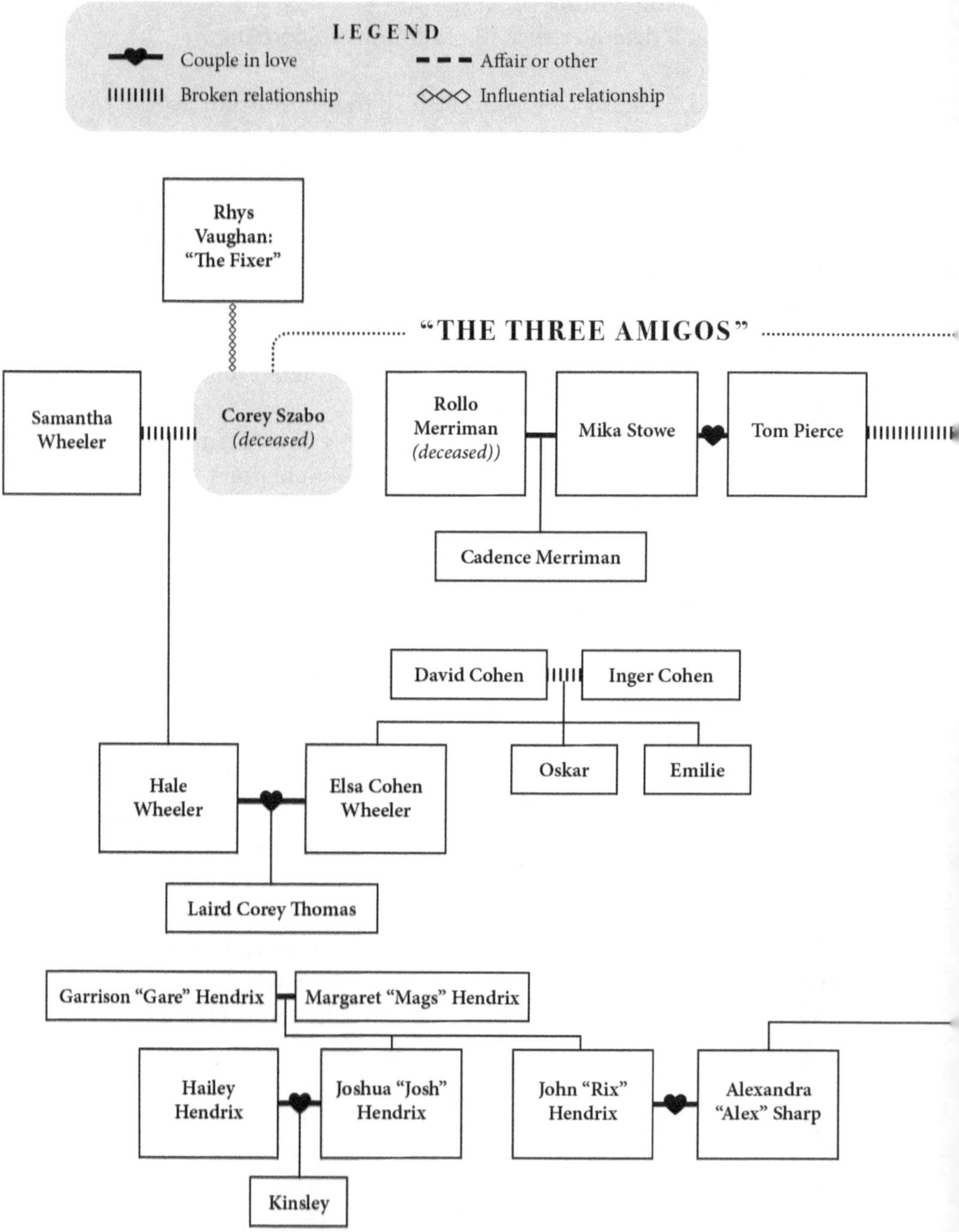

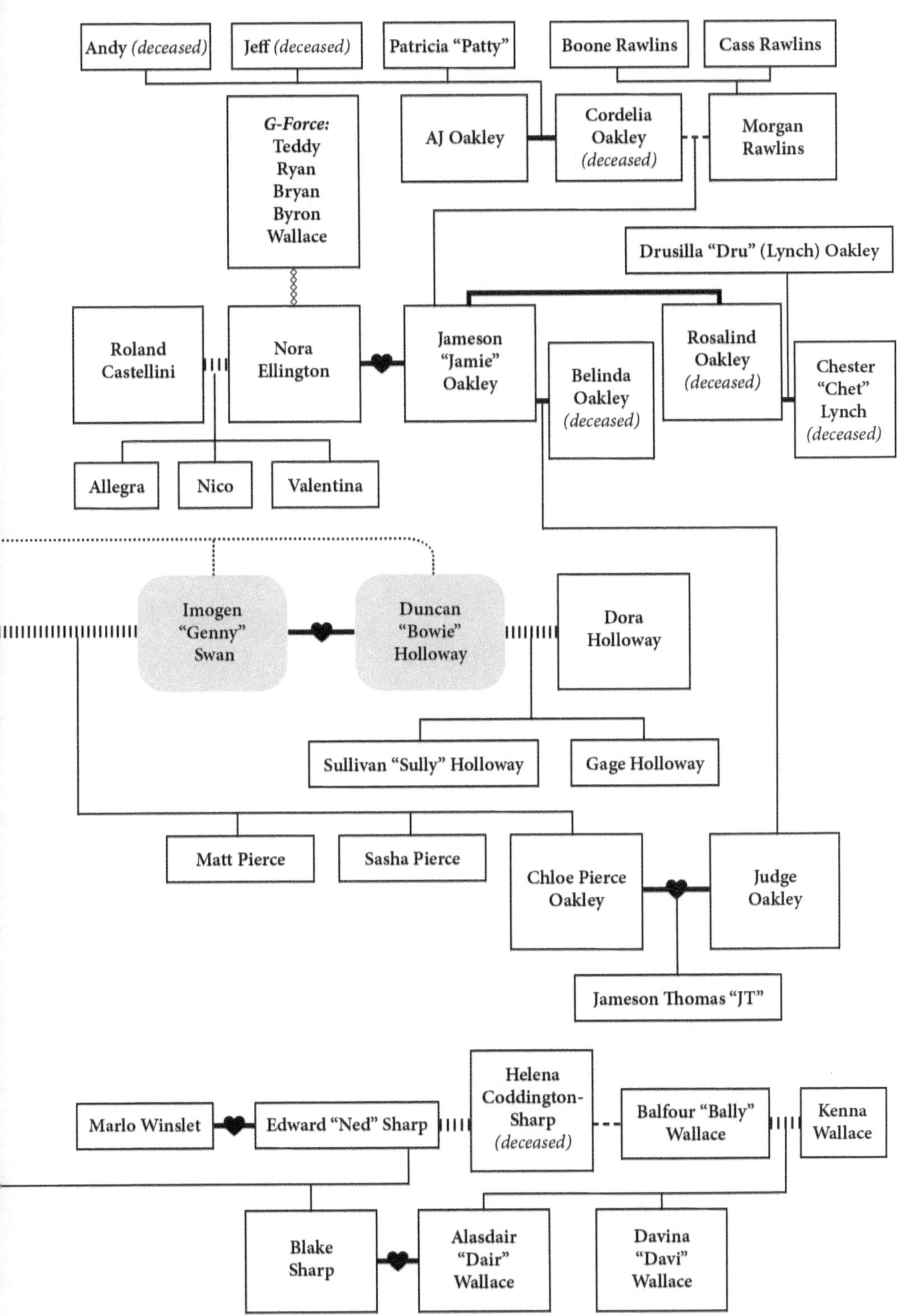

Andy (deceased)
Jeff (deceased)
Patricia "Patty"
Boone Rawlins
Cass Rawlins
G-Force:
Teddy
Ryan
Bryan
Byron
Wallace
AJ Oakley
Cordelia Oakley (deceased)
Morgan Rawlins
Drusilla "Dru" (Lynch) Oakley
Roland Castellini
Nora Ellington
Jameson "Jamie" Oakley
Belinda Oakley (deceased)
Rosalind Oakley (deceased)
Chester "Chet" Lynch (deceased)
Allegra
Nico
Valentina
Imogen "Genny" Swan
Duncan "Bowie" Holloway
Dora Holloway
Sullivan "Sully" Holloway
Gage Holloway
Matt Pierce
Sasha Pierce
Chloe Pierce Oakley
Judge Oakley
Jameson Thomas "JT"
Helena Coddington-Sharp (deceased)
Balfour "Bally" Wallace
Kenna Wallace
Marlo Winslet
Edward "Ned" Sharp
Blake Sharp
Alasdair "Dair" Wallace
Davina "Davi" Wallace

CHAPTER ONE

TALLY SHEET

Blake

"You need to be nicer to Wallace, dear."

I turned at my mother's voice.

"They're an important family," Mum went on when I caught her gaze. "And he's the heir."

This was *so* Mum.

Thus, of course, I rolled my eyes.

"Don't roll your eyes at me, Blake Charlotte Sharp," Mum snapped.

"Alasdair Wallace is a bully," I snapped back and looked across the bar at the man in question.

He was standing with the groom-to-be (tomorrow) Rix and Rix's best friend, Judge.

They looked like a craft beer advertisement.

A very successful one where every man who saw it would want to be them and therefore run right out and buy that beer. Whereupon they'd drink it and think the next day, even after they'd over imbibed, they'd be prepared go on a ten-mile hike that included a bracing swim in a snow-fed lake, get home and still have enough energy to mow the lawn and fuck their woman.

Blech.

Some women might think Dair Wallace was sinfully attractive.

I was not one of those women.

Okay, so he had thick, dark hair and rugged outdoorsman features hewn from centuries of his ancestors being, well…rugged outdoorsmen (along with rebels, warriors and pains in the asses of any English ruler that came along). He was tall and built like a rugby player (because he played rugby).

All my life, when we'd go to England for our visits to Mum, for a week during their summer holidays, the Wallaces would come down from their sprawling estate in Scotland to visit us in her townhome in London, or our family's country seat in Somerset, or worst of this lot, we'd go up north and visit them.

Dair Wallace was the epitome of "oh, he's pulling your hair and teasing you relentlessly because he likes you," when everyone knew that wasn't the case.

No, it was because little boys like that were assholes who weren't taught better.

And Mum was the kind of woman who gave little boys like that as much leeway as possible, because that was the way of her world, but also because his daddy was rich.

And because she was fucking him.

Dair's daddy that was.

As far as I knew, I was the only one who held this knowledge, outside Mum and Balfour Wallace. We'll not get into how I discovered this because I didn't need the resurgence of that particular trauma. We could just say it was not conjecture in the slightest.

We could also say that this affair had lasted forever, and as far as I knew (considering the covert glances they'd been sharing since the Wallace family showed at the party, not to mention, them being at Genny and Duncan's last night), it was still going strong.

Certainly Kenna Wallace, Balfour's wife, didn't know it. Nor did Dair and Davina, their children.

The very fact the Wallace family were here, at this bar, for the rehearsal dinner for my sister Alex's and her fiancé Rix's wedding tomorrow said it all.

They were not family.

Dair nor Davina were in the wedding party.

Rix hadn't even met any of them until yesterday.

This was one thousand percent not some formal celebration where "important" out-of-town guests needed to be catered to.

Alex didn't even have a single *flower* in her wedding décor. Not one. It was all *grass*.

So it was pretty grass. Really pretty. I made sure that was so.

But it was grass, and this was an Arizona mountain bar that was one step up from a honkytonk (all right, I didn't know that for certain, I'd never been to a honkytonk—and I never wanted to go to one—but this place was one step up from what I would suspect a honkytonk would be like).

They were serving a buffet out of *tinfoil trays*, for God's sake. And it was barbeque. Totally messy. (However, also delicious.)

Dad was pissed Mum had invited them. I could tell.

Maybe he knew Mum was sleeping with Balfour, though I doubted, if he did know, he cared. They were so over. They were so very over, they were that before they even began. Something me and Alex lived our whole lives in numerous and vastly unpleasant ways.

Still, even if it was lowkey, laidback and happening in a private area sectioned off in a bar, this was a planned function. One where I finalized the numbers with the owners two weeks ago. And those numbers did not include Balfour, Kenna, Dair and Davina.

That was why Dad was pissed. Because Mum did this kind of crap all the time. And it drove him up the wall.

As it should.

It was rude as hell.

Of course, I inflated the numbers because one of the greatest sins of entertaining was running out of food. That said, I'd allotted for two more people, not four.

And Dair ate like a rugby player too. He'd been to the buffet three times (yes, I counted).

Once, he had nothing on his plate but a massive pile of meat covered in barbeque sauce.

If we ran out of food, I was going to kill Mum.

Though, as usual, it looked like Dair and Davina were fitting right in. Gal and Katie, Alex's best friends, were sizing up Dair like he was a mountain they were determined to climb (and both of them were taken, he was just that sinful to women). And they'd made besties with Davina in what seemed like seconds.

Whereas I'd been regularly coming out to Prescott now for *ages* and it seemed they could barely tolerate me.

Sure, they were nice...*ish*.

But they'd been cackling with Davina for the last hour.

They'd never cackled with me.

So, I didn't cackle. I was too...*me* to cackle.

But that didn't mean I didn't want to be a part of cackling, even if I didn't cackle myself.

"You've barely said two words to him," Mum kept at me.

I refocused on her. "Not true. I said five. They were, 'What are you doing here?'"

Her eyes grew big and horrified.

They then turned to annoyed slits.

"*Blake*," she bit. "Please tell me you *did not*."

I got closer to her and lowered my voice. "Mum, they weren't invited."

"An oversight I'll take *you* to task for since you cast yourself as your sister's wedding planner," Mum retorted.

"I didn't cast myself," I said. "Alex isn't into that kind of thing. She asked me to do it for her. Since I *am* into that kind of thing, and she's my sister, I'm doing it for her."

"She should have hired someone," Mum sniffed.

After saying that, her eyes got mean, so per usual, I braced, something I was very good at since Mum got mean a lot.

Alex learned early to check out.

I wasn't that smart.

All my life (or, until recently), every sting from her hit its mark, releasing the poison.

I'd been infected with it for years.

It was only lately I'd started searching for an antidote.

That search, mind you, hadn't been entirely successful.

But I was getting there (I hoped).

"You couldn't even handle your own wedding preparations," she noted snidely.

I wanted to bite, that bait was so juicy. I really, really did.

But, I told myself firmly, I was not that Blake anymore.

Helena Coddington-Sharp sure made it hard not to take a big bite, though.

With some effort, I changed subjects.

"The rehearsal dinner is for family and members of the wedding party," I hissed. "They're neither."

"They've been family friends for decades," she shot back. "Therefore, practically family."

"Alex hasn't seen any of them for years," I returned.

"That doesn't make them any less family," Mum replied.

"Actually, it does. Newsflash, Mum, like my wedding wasn't your wedding, even if you took it over, Alex's wedding isn't your wedding either."

That made Mum mad, and she didn't hide it. "I did everything as you'd wish it to be."

"How do you know what I wished?" I asked. "You didn't ask. Furthermore, you don't know me. Back then, *I* didn't even know me."

"I know you made the biggest mistake of your life letting Chad Head slip through your fingers."

I blinked, the shock I felt at her statement was so profound.

Then I stared.

"He cheated on me…*a lot*," I reminded her.

"He didn't put his ring on any of those women's fingers," she reminded me.

I knew she was crazy.

But that was *insane*.

"Mum, he cheated on me…even just days before our wedding. At a party celebrating our rapidly upcoming nuptials, he was fucking *a friend of mine* in a broom closet or something."

"This is a woman's lot," she rejoined.

God!

She wasn't to be believed.

"Maybe it was in 1567, when women had no power," I stated. "Now a woman can tell a man who can't keep his dick in his pants to go fuck himself."

Mum opened her mouth, her eyes flicked over my shoulder, she jolted, then her entire countenance changed from infuriated to obsequious.

"Wallace, dear, how are you enjoying the party?" she asked.

Oh hell.

I turned.

And yes, there he was. All six foot four, muscled mass of him wearing a nice, chestnut-colored button down and jeans. If the damned man didn't open his mouth, you'd think he'd been born in the desert mountains we were currently inhabiting.

By the by, Mum had always called him Wallace, and I didn't know why. It felt like some nod to old aristocracy or something, even though her (yes, *my*) family were aristocrats, and the Wallaces were not. They were just filthy rich.

I sensed Dair wasn't a fan of it, but he'd never said anything.

I took him in up close.

He wasn't carrying another plate of food, thank God.

But those perfectly full lips in his tanned, rugged outdoorsman face were twitching like he was fighting a smile.

He'd heard what I'd said about Chad.

And it amused him.

God, I wanted to punch him.

I'd been wanting to punch him since I was six, and he was nine, and he'd taken me to that awful room in that horrible building on his family's estate where they skinned all the deer they'd hunted that day, making me cry and gag and go screaming to my mother, who'd then forced me to eat venison that night.

I had avoided meat as much as I could since then.

I did not count myself as a vegetarian, because that was way too hippie for me (shudder). But I'd never forgotten those beautiful, sad carcasses. And it had been decades.

"Food is great. Rix is a good lad," Dair replied to Mum.

Mum's gaze drifted to where Rix was now standing, talking to his brother, Josh, along with Judge and Judge's dad, Jamie.

And she mumbled, "I suppose."

Dair made a noise like a grunt, and my attention turned to him.

His gray-blue eyes were narrowed on my mother, and he was wearing an expression of distaste easily visible on his features.

"Salt of the earth," he continued, his rich Scottish burr vibrating naturally, but doing it on those words firm to inflexible.

Mum's gaze raced back to Dair, and pure Dair Wallace, he didn't bother to adjust his expression.

"Yes, of course," she said. "Good man. Perfect for my little girl."

Her little girl.

Like she gave that first shit about Alex…or me.

God, she made me want to vomit.

Dair dismissed her completely and turned to me.

I was fighting a smirk at how he so obviously shut Mum out, until he spoke.

"Wicked as fuck how ye publicly humiliated that wankstain."

There it was.

The entire Wallace family had of course been in attendance when I'd left Chad at the altar.

Well, not so much left him there, but instead pulled a huge drama where I exposed him as the cheat he was, something that started a massive brawl in the church. A brawl that Rix and Dad had to rescue me from…physically.

I felt my throat close at the reminder of that particular humiliation, which only Dair would bring up right to my face (well, only Dair and my own mother). Wrestling with the weight of it, I couldn't hold eye contact with him.

"Chad was young, a little wayward," Mum again defended my ex...*wankstain.*

"Ye could be thirteen and courtin' your first lassie and ken not to fuck her about like that," Dair retorted.

"Dear, you *are* in the presence of ladies," Mum admonished him on a valiant forgiving smile. "Perhaps mind your language," she suggested.

"Your own daughter just described that twat as a bloke who can't keep his dick in his pants, and he should go fuck himself." He again turned to me and smiled a blinding bright smile of strong, white teeth in tanned face. "Reckon he only had that choice for a while after ye gutted him. No woman would touch him after ye got through with him."

"I try not to think of Chad in that manner, or *at all,*" I replied.

"Good choice," Dair approved.

Like I needed his approval.

I nearly rolled my eyes again, but I did not.

And anyone would know not to discuss this at a party...or ever.

After it happened, every once in a while, Alex and Dad checked in to make sure I was doing okay.

But now, I was *so* over Chad Head.

Even so, I didn't want to dish about it at my sister's rehearsal dinner.

"Perhaps I'll just leave you two young ones to chat," Mum offered, and before I could stop her (this might be the only time in my life I didn't want her to leave me), she slipped away.

"Not sure that woman kens the definition of young ones," Dair muttered.

He was correct.

I was thirty-four.

He was thirty-seven.

We were hardly young.

"How ye farin'?" he asked.

"Busy," I replied.

For some reason, this made him bark with laughter.

For heaven's sake, his laughter even sounded Scottish. Thick, rich, warm, manly and so very alive.

But I was confused, and I didn't hide it.

"That's funny?" I asked.

"Ye dinnae have a job, lassie," he pointed out. "How're ye busy?"

Nope.

Time and maturity hadn't made Alasdair Finlay Wallace any less insufferable.

"Well," I started snottily, "even though Alex and Rix wanted something small and intimate, Mum horned in, as usual, and Alex caved to keep the peace, so their seventy-five guests turned into two hundred. And even keeping it at that, rather than the three hundred Mum wanted, was a battle. One I waged so Alex didn't have to."

I might have stated this rather pointedly, because I was not going to tell him directly he and his family were not on the first list, but I still just told him he and his family were not on Alex and Rix's list.

Dair didn't miss this and it only made him smile his wide, white smile again.

Totally insufferable.

"And since Alex doesn't like huge gatherings, so she's not a party planner extraordinaire—"

His attractive, heavy, dark brows winged up. "Extraordinaire?"

I ignored him. "—and I am, I took this wedding off her plate. That means searching for venues. Contracting with them. Catering. Floral arrangements. Music arrangements. Invitations. Tracking RSVPs. Cake tasting."

He cut in again. "Dinnae need the whole agenda, Blake."

I ignored him again. "And since one of Dad's PAs got married and moved to Pennsylvania, I took over managing his properties."

Another interruption from Dair. "Reckon so, since ye use them more than he does."

"Actually, I don't," I snapped.

"Oh, right, ye live in your Mum's place in New York."

I didn't need a reminder of that either.

Though, this was Alasdair Wallace to a T.

Total bully.

I should find something I needed to do, make an excuse and walk away from him.

The problem was, I was incredibly good at party planning. Everything had been sorted for the entire weekend weeks ago.

Sure, I had a binder with a dizzying number of checklists. And I had to be up tomorrow at six o'clock to have breakfast and a shower in order to be fueled and ready to go over everything, start making calls to confirm, be certain everyone was where they were supposed to be, everything was in place and all that was taken care of before I got my hair and makeup done so I could walk down the aisle to attend my sister.

But that was just me being over-organized and wanting Alex and Rix to have their day where everything went off without a hitch. My ultimate goal was that all they had to do was show up, say their I do's, then eat, drink, dance and be merry before they were off on their honeymoon.

The fact I didn't have an excuse to pull me away from Dair right then wasn't the reason I didn't walk away.

No, it was because I was done with anyone being a bully to me.

Especially Dair Wallace.

"Your point?" I demanded.

He was studying me closely. "Just teasing ye, lass."

"You don't know me well enough to tease me like that," I noted.

"Known ye since ye were wee."

"What's my favorite color?" I asked.

It was his turn to look confused. "How's that relevant?"

"What's my birthday?"

"Blake—"

I got closer to him and bit, "You've *never* known me well enough to tease me, Dair. Though, that's never stopped you."

His voice lowered, and in doing so, got even more rumbly. "Calm down, Blake."

"I'm perfectly calm," I retorted. "I'm also perfectly sick and tired of allowing people to treat me like shit."

His chin jerked back.

"Enjoy the barbeque," I bid, then stupid me, way too late, I walked away.

I sensed I looked like a fool.

Everyone was in pretty, but casual sundresses (except Chloe, Judge's wife, and one of Alex's bridesmaids, and this wasn't only because Judge was a groomsman, but because Chloe and my sister were tight—but Chloe was also a Pierce, that being the daughter of a famous pro tennis player and even more famous Hollywood actress, so even if she lived in the Arizona mountains with her husband, she still dressed like she was going out to a three hundred dollar dinner in LA).

But I was me.

I didn't own a single casual, pretty sundress.

This was why I was wearing a rose-colored, one shoulder, figure-skimming dress that went to my ankles, had some ruching at the side waist, a billowy bow draped on the shoulder, and a high side slit.

I was wearing this with a pair of Christian Louboutin Sandale du Désert, four-inch, satin ankle wrap sandals.

It was totally over-the-top for this bar.

From what I'd learned, it was totally over-the-top for the entire state of Arizona.

And right then, I felt self-conscious about it, because I felt Dair's eyes heating my back as I walked away.

I should have dressed down.

I just didn't know how.

"This is me. This is me. This is me. It's okay to be me," I whispered to myself as I walked to the bar to get another glass of wine.

It wouldn't be good wine, even though I tried my best with their limited wine menu.

But I was going to drink it.

I'd just got my order in when I heard, "You all right?"

I twisted to see Chloe standing next to me.

"Everything's fine," I lied.

But seriously?

Why did I let Dair get under my skin like that?

I needed to think about why this happened and let go of it.

I didn't like him. I never liked him.

Okay, that was a lie.

When I got old enough to know that boys were more than dirty, irritatingly rambunctious and overall annoying, I had a crush on Dair, because he was almost as good-looking a boy as he was a man.

Then he took every opportunity to remind me how boys were dirty, frustratingly rambunctious and unceasingly annoying, and I got over it (though, truth told, it hurt a little that he didn't like me "like that," as, I told myself, any girl would feel the pain of a boy she had a crush on not liking her back).

Bottom line, he wasn't even my type.

However, I thought my type was Chad, and very tardily realized I was very wrong about that. He was Mum's. I'd gone through the whole fiasco with him just to gain my mother's approval. Humiliating myself and costing Dad thousands and thousands of dollars through the process.

I'd had exactly two dates since I'd dumped Chad on the altar, and they'd both been disasters.

Good Lord, I didn't even know what my type was.

"Blake?" Chloe called.

I got out of my head and into the conversation.

"You sure you're okay?" she asked, not hiding she was scrutinizing me.

"I've just got a checklist on my mind," I lied again.

"If you need any help…" she offered, not for the first time.

"You've been really great with hooking me up with vendors in Prescott already," I told her. "And everything is set. I'm just fretting. It'll all be fine."

"You know you can ask me. Or Mom. Or Nora. Mika. Gal or Katie," she stressed (yes, again).

I nodded. "I know. We'll go over everything at the meeting in the morning, just in case I'm not around to see to something."

She glanced over at Dair then came back to me.

"He's very good looking," she noted.

"He's not my type," I decreed. Then foolishly continued, "As the saying goes, *football is a gentleman's game played by hooligans, and rugby is a hooligan's game played by gentlemen.* But unlike other gentlemen who play that game, Dair doesn't leave the hooligan on the pitch."

Chloe appeared bewildered, and she explained it. "Your mom said you two were an item."

What?

Oh my God!

Why would she say that?

"I worried you guys were fighting," Chloe went on. "You've barely said anything to him."

"That's because he, nor his family, were invited tonight," I informed her. "Davina is okay, though she never had much use for me. But Dair has always been an asshole and that hasn't changed, case in point, our most recent conversation."

"He sure can't take his eyes off you for someone who's just been an asshole to you."

I felt frisson tingle down my spine.

Okay.

What was *that?*

Resolutely, I shook it off.

"We're not an item," I asserted. "I've never understood how Mum's mind worked and now is no exception. Though the Wallaces are obscenely wealthy, and since every available bachelor over the one hundred-million-dollar mark on the east coast won't have anything to do with me after what I did to Chad, and the something I *do* know about Mum is that she wants me to land an heir to some financial throne, she's likely casting a wider net."

Chloe tipped her head to the side. "Maybe, *ma bonne amie*, she's seeing something you don't."

I glanced to where I left Dair, only to see he wasn't there.

He'd changed huddles and was now grinning flirtatiously at Katie.

I turned back to Chloe. "And maybe she's seeing he's a huge flirt and hope is springing eternal."

"Maybe," she murmured, her gaze sliding toward Dair.

The bartender handed me my wine and I thanked her before taking a sip that many would describe as a gulp.

Alex came up to us and put her arm around my waist.

"This is great, Blake," she gushed. "Just perfect."

I studied my younger sister.

Then I spoke.

"You are cordially invited to leave at any time," I replied to my introverted, hates-crowds, hates-parties, hates-lots-of-people-around sister. "Food has been consumed. Toasts have been made. You have officially done your duty to your rehearsal dinner, and no one will think a thing about it if you and Rix take off."

"God," she whispered, her hazel eyes dancing happily, "I love you."

I stilled at the sentiment and how much she sounded like she meant it.

To say we weren't close growing up was an understatement.

Since the Chad thing, I'd been trying, she'd been trying.

But I didn't think she'd ever said anything like that to me.

It felt amazing.

She kissed my cheek, shot a smile at Chloe and made a beeline to Rix.

Chloe moved closer "I cannot tell you how relieved she was when you took over planning the wedding."

"I'm glad," I said distractedly before taking another, much more demure sip of wine.

"I told her I'd do it, but with the pregnancy and the baby coming and running the shops and all..." Chloe let that trail.

"I've loved doing it," I said.

And I had.

If I could put up with bitches like the me I used to be who were having weddings, I'd start my own business doing this kind of thing, I loved it so much.

Since there was no way in hell I'd be able to put up with bitches like the me I used to be, that was out.

Nothing else had come in.

I'd been trying to find myself for four years.

In that time, I realized I liked cooking, thus now, I did it a lot. I realized it felt good to give my father peace of mind about something after spending years giving him no peace of mind at all. And I realized I was radioactive to men after my situation with Chad went viral on social media.

Not a good tally sheet.

But I'd been fucking up for three decades by the time I got my head out of my ass. Four years was nothing.

Right?

"Well, so far, you're killing it," Chloe said.

That meant a lot to me, and as such, I smiled at her.

When I did, I felt that frisson again and turned my head to see Dair scowling at me.

My smile died and I raised my brows at him.

He shook his head, for some reason visibly sighed, like I was annoying him, then he returned his attention to Katie, dazzling her with that rakish grin of his.

Whatever.

Alex and Rix were in the midst of their goodbyes.

This meant I had things to do to wind this party down and shift focus to the next items on the wedding to-do list.

So I put Dair out of my mind and I did them.

CHAPTER TWO

FOR NOW

Blake

Doesn't this just cut it, I thought, sniveling and doing my all not to break down in tears.

I'd forgotten to tuck Kleenex in my bodice.

How could I forget to tuck tissues in my bodice in preparation for this very occasion?

Me blubbering like an idiot and ruining my makeup would just put the icing on the putrid cake that had been my sister's wedding day so far.

It started out okay.

I woke refreshed and ready to roll. I had time to do my under-eye treatment, so my morning puffiness was gone. Topping that with my turmeric, ginger, mango, peach smoothie to assist with any other water retention I may face that day. Some stretches to get limber and a nice long hot shower with a deep condition of my hair.

Then nine thirty rolled around, time for the bridesmaids and women friends of the bride's meeting, and Katie and Gal showed up an hour late.

This was Dair's fault.

Katie, Gal, their men, Judge, Chloe, Josh, Hailey (Josh's wife), Sasha, Matt, Sully, Gage, Dru, Dair and Davina had gone on a pub crawl after the rehearsal dinner. They stayed out late…and got totally smashed.

Well, Chloe and Judge had the good sense not to do that. They'd gone home early, not inebriated, and had a good night's sleep. However, this might have something to do with the fact they were parents, and as such, had a child and needed to get him from the babysitter.

But Gal, Katie and Hailey were crazy hungover.

This necessitated Mika, Nora, Genny, Mags (Rix's mom) and Elsa (a friend of the family, she was Alex and my age, but she wasn't in the wedding party) running around making drinks with IV hydration, and passing around aspirin, Tylenol and ibuprofen like they were Tic Tacs.

Yes, you guessed it. Although Mum was invited to this meeting, she didn't show as one of her many acts of passive aggressiveness sharing she was not at one with this casual, outdoor mountain wedding she had insisted, repeatedly, should be held at our country estate in England (when Rix hadn't even been to that estate in England). And when that was not going to happen, she'd pushed for New York (Alex may have grown up in New York, but even when she lived there, she was about as New York as Dolly Parton).

And Gal let slip the pub crawl was Dair's idea.

Because…

Of course it was.

We got the meeting done in record time so they could keep on top of things just in case I wasn't around to look after them (though, I'd be around, but it didn't hurt to have backup).

This segued into the team of makeup artists being thirty minutes late.

Not a disaster, but not optimal.

Which segued into the florist showing with the wrong grass in the arrangements.

At this point, seeing as I was a bit harried, I had to try really hard not to slide backward into the old me, and say sarcastically that we were not launching a revival of *Oklahoma!*, but instead having a fucking wedding. And therefore, the grass that looked like wheat which was *not* in the arrangements we'd agreed (and I had pictures), not to mention, it was atrociously ugly, had to be pulled. And they had better source the fluffy, feathery grass we'd agreed that Alex just *loved* and do it *toute de suite*.

I managed not to be sarcastic, instead only firm, but I managed it by the skin of my teeth.

They did this, though the new arrangements arrived only fifteen minutes before the guests started to show.

This necessitated me running around in my bridesmaid's gown with my hair all done up and my makeup just perfect, but my feet in flip-flops (the horror!) to help with the setup.

All while stupid, *stupid* Dair, who'd been invited to hang with the men pre-wedding (because…of course he had), stood at a split rail fence in his ridiculously well-tailored suit with the collar of his shirt open, exposing the corded column of his throat. He had one foot up on the bottom rail, both forearms on the top, and all he was missing was the piece of grass in his teeth and the cowboy hat on his head.

And he watched me rush around in flip-flops!

Disaster.

(Even if the flip-flops were Valentino…still!)

He'd done this smiling like a lunatic.

Catastrophe.

He finally approached and said, "Get your arse to Alex. I'll help them finish this shite."

I was too freaked out to argue, not about him helping, not about him calling the carefully crafted arrangements "shite."

Because another part of this debacle of a day was that I had not heard from the cake lady. She was the only person who didn't answer my confirmation call that morning.

And the cake had not arrived.

But in the now, I needed these fucking arrangements arranged and to make sure my sister was okay, the bridesmaids were all good, and I needed five minutes to fan myself so I wasn't red in the face and sweaty during the ceremony (or worse, the pictures).

So I ran to get my binder, opened it to the flower arrangement section, shoved it in his hands and ordered, "Follow that…to the letter."

He stared in open shock at the intricate diagrams I'd made on some software I found, then looked at me, still in open shock.

At this point, I was way too harried to process how he could still be so damned handsome with that expression on his face.

Instead, I jabbed my finger two inches from that handsome face and warned, "To…the…letter, Alasdair. I'll be checking."

With that, even if one side of his lips quirked up in an attractive half-smile when I called him Alasdair, I dashed back to the bridal preparation area.

It was only while we were lining up to do the procession when Nora approached to whisper the cake had finally arrived, something I was happy about, but it made me fidgety because I didn't have time to go see if it was all in order. Not to mention, Dair still had my binder, and I couldn't check it off.

The processional processed (and yes, the arrangements were arranged correctly, thank God), and now here I was, standing in a dress unlike any of the other dresses any of the girls were wearing (Alex insisted that everyone wear what they wanted, it didn't even have to be a bridesmaid dress or formal at all, so we were a mishmash of dresses in shades and prints of green from elegant (Chloe) to boho (Gal) to flirty (Katie) to classy (Hailey) to sophisticated (me)).

And I was holding a bouquet of fluffy grass.

I was also listening to Alex and Rix sharing their heartfelt, handwritten vows, and I was going to lose it.

Good Lord, who knew Rix could be so sentimental? He was a *GUY!* most of the time, in all caps with the exclamation point.

I loved that he loved my sister so much, but he was doing me in!

I took a breath through my nose, and hoping it'd help me get my emotion under control, I let my gaze wander to the congregation.

Which meant it took in Mum, sitting stiffly beside Dad, wearing a massive hat and appearing like she took a way wrong turn on her way to Westminster Abbey.

The guests might be sitting on wooden folded chairs on flagstone among a bevy of beautifully arranged grass, but everyone had dressed nice.

Even so, Mum still found a way to be OTT.

And that was *so* Mum.

I succeeded in not scoffing out loud, and continued to scan the crowd, whereupon my gaze locked on Dair, who was staring at me.

The instant it did, he put his long, attractive forefinger under his chin and pushed it up.

God.

The man had noticed I was fighting tears and was encouraging me to keep my chin up.

Who was he to encourage me to keep my chin up?

No one!

Just a childhood "friend" who was half bully, the other half plain annoying.

I glared at him.

His wide, sexy grin made an appearance.

I glared harder at him.

I couldn't hear it, but with the way his broad shoulders were moving, I could tell he was chuckling.

Gah!

I refocused on Rix who thankfully stopped waxing on about how perfect Alex was for him. And how he would never have fully healed from what had happened to him if it wasn't for her (he'd lost both legs below the knees while fighting a wildfire when he was a firefighter—that part had made Mags sob audibly, and Mags wasn't a sobber, so that in itself shared my struggle). And how he couldn't wait to continue making his life with her and adding making babies.

Through all of this, not one tear dropped from my eye.

Success!

Sadly, the wet came right back after the pastor announced they were husband and wife, and the sheer bliss on Rix's face hit me right in the solar plexus. He then laid the raciest kiss on my sister that I'd ever seen at a wedding or *anywhere*.

This made people hoot, holler and catcall, and I was fighting tears and rolling my eyes at the same time.

But this meant the ceremony was done.

Which meant I had more check marks to put in my binder.

I waited patiently as my sister and her new husband practically floated up the aisle. Gal and Katie, her co-maids of honor, went next, and I hooked arms with Kevin, a friend and co-worker of Rix's, and we walked down the aisle together.

I smiled at Kevin when we were clear then peeled off and went down the side of the wooden chairs to get to Dair's row.

They were waiting for their row to come up so they could file out.

Davina noticed me. I pointed at her brother. She then yanked on Dair's jacket sleeve, and he turned my way.

I did a circling wave to get him to come to me.

He got up and scooched in front of everyone else in the row to get to me.

"Ye did good, Blake."

Whatever.

"Where's my binder?" I asked.

"Sorry?"

"My binder," I repeated. "The one I gave to you to arrange the flowers."

"Dinnae see a single flower in this place."

"The grass then," I amended.

"Who knew grass could be so pretty," he murmured, glancing at one of the arrangements that sat at the end of the row.

I slapped a hand on his chest to get his attention, his head tipped right down to stare at it, then it came back up so he could look at me when I demanded, "The binder, Dair."

"I chucked it."

My insides froze solid.

So it sounded choked when I pushed out, "You...*chucked it?*"

He looked from side to side. "Aye, lass. Day's done."

Was he mad?

Argh!

No, he was just *a man.*

Only a man would think that after the ceremony was finished, a wedding was finished.

Fucking men!

I curled my fingers into the lapel of his jacket and got so close, my breasts were brushing my arm, and I tilted up on the toes of my gold, Giuseppe Zanotti, high-heeled orchid mules.

"The...day...is...not...*even close to done,*" I sniped.

"Heard the man say the husband-and-wife thing, babe."

"We have...we have..." I spluttered and then pulled myself together. "We have photos to get through. Hors d'oeuvres and cocktails. Another *fucking* buffet. Toasts. Dances. Cake cutting. I've written down how much I'm going to tip everyone at the end of the night." I got even closer, so my chest was pressed to his and my voice might have risen two octaves (or three) when I asked, "How am I going to know what to tip everybody?"

"Calm down, darling," he whispered, his brogue sliding over me like velvet, something I didn't have time to feel right then (or ever). "I'll find it. We'll sort it. No worries."

"I've been working on that binder for *a year,*" I informed him.

He put his hand to my waist and gave me a reassuring squeeze. "Blake, we'll find it."

"It has every little thing laid out for the day in fifteen-minute increments."

He stood there staring down at me like he'd never seen me before.

This necessitated me grabbing him by the neck on either side and saying frantically, "Dair, *I need that binder.*"

He kept staring at me, and when I was about to scream, he turned his head, put his teeth to his lip, and let out a shrill whistle.

Everyone turned to look at us.

I slid my hands down to his chest and pushed in, gritting, "Oh my

God, Dair, what on earth are you doing?"

I noticed movement at our sides and turned that way. My hands fell from Dair's chest, but his hand at my waist slid around it as Gage, a friend of, well…everybody, and one of Rix's ushers finished jogging up to us.

"Everything cool?" Gage asked.

"Ye remember that book I had when we were putting out all the grass?" Dair asked.

"Yup," Gage answered.

"Ye see what I did with it?" Dair went on.

"Yup," Gage told him.

"Can ye go and grab it?" Dair finished.

Gage smiled. "Yup." He looked at me. "Lookin' good, Blake."

"You too, Gage," I replied.

He jogged off again.

I turned to Dair. "Thank you."

"Ye ken it's gonna be okay," he said.

"All right," I began to educate him, "you probably never noticed this, but Alex isn't good in this kind of situation."

His brows knit.

"She doesn't like to be the center of attention," I explained. "She's a people person but not this many people. It's practically impossible for me to protect her from being inundated and overwhelmed in this scenario, when it's a wedding, and she's the bride."

"Blake," he said softly, and it was then I realized when I'd turned to him, I was now standing in the circle of his arm.

And I realized this because he tightened it to pull me closer.

Even though his hard body felt really nice, and I hadn't had a man this close in forever, I didn't have time for this.

I tested pushing away, but he only strengthened his hold. Thus, in order not to make another scene after his whistle, I stopped trying to get away.

"I have a plan and in that binder is the plan," I kept on. "It's intricate and I need to follow it so I can keep everyone busy with other stuff and Alex can enjoy her day and walk away from it with nothing but good memories, time with her man and time with the people who matter the most to her."

"Gage'll find that binder."

"Okay, good," I muttered, testing the pulling away thing again.

It didn't work.

"And I'll help ye keep it all sorted," he went on.

My gaze flew to him, and instead of panicking about the idea his "help" might be anything but (the man didn't even know that the end of the ceremony wasn't the end of the wedding!), I assured, "I've got it. Just enjoy yourself."

"I have noticed that about Alex, so I'm in to help ye make your sister's special day as special as it can be."

"Really, I'm good."

He pulled me closer so our bodies were practically flush.

Something else was flushed.

My face.

Okay…

What was going on?

And now he was educating me. "Someone offers to help, ye accept."

"You didn't even know the ceremony wasn't the end of the festivities," I pointed out.

"Been to weddings before, lass. That isn't lost on me. But I dinnae ken what more ye could do now. The food is cooked. The cake is on show. The DJ is set up and soon to be spinning. I didnae know ye had that plan for Alex, and now I'm in to make certain she's covered."

I didn't have time to argue this, so I snapped, "Okay, fine."

His lips curved. "Sweet as ever, I see," he teased.

"I didn't *ask* for your help," I reminded him.

"Well, ye got it regardless," he returned.

I was so done with this conversation.

"Can you let me go now?" I requested.

He turned his head and jerked up his chin, so I turned mine too and saw Gage heading our way with my binder.

Thank you, God.

"Aye, I can let you go," Dair said, and did just that.

I began to hustle toward Gage.

But as I did, I heard him finish, "For now."

CHAPTER THREE

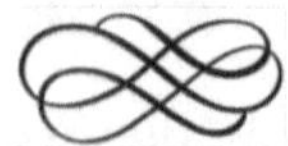

JUST DANCE

Blake

I was tipsy.

And it was Dair's fault.

How?

Every time I turned around (not really, but mostly), he was shoving a full glass of champagne in my hand.

Of course, I didn't have to drink them, but Dair had also been true to his word about helping me keep everything good for my sister.

Surprise of the century: it was safe to say he'd grown more dedicated to the binder than me.

But I hadn't taken into account Alex's wedding would obviously be filled with a ton of people who knew and loved Alex, all of whom would look after her.

Most importantly, Rix.

I didn't need to keep things going at a certain clip, rescuing Alex from floods of Mum's guests who were nice, sure, but they'd overwhelm my sister.

Rix constantly kept his eye on her, going to fetch her when she got besieged, sticking by her side and guiding her away when chats went on too long.

And most importantly, when all eyes were on them, he protected her.

I will never in my life forget how he angled it so, after they'd cut the cake, you could only see a bit of Alex as Rix held her in one arm and they gently fed the cake to each other. And when he hugged her afterward, he slid his cheek down hers and buried his face in her neck so all you could see of my sister was her arms around her new husband and the crown of her head.

It was incredibly sweet.

The same with the couple's dance.

Rix picked the song, and in doing so, he kept surprising me.

He picked "Storybook Love," the theme from *Princess Bride.*

But it wasn't lost on me that the song was very slow, very simple, very pretty and there didn't need to be any fancy dance moves. Just two people in love swaying together in each other's arms while words of love washed over them.

Rix made that dance so it wasn't like they were being watched by two hundred people, but instead, dancing in their living room.

Alex's face had been filled with smiles, her eyes saturated with adoration, and I could tell she was all in that moment with Rix.

In fact, it was so quiet, peaceful and perfect, after it was over, it took a long time for people to clap and cheer. We were all in the moment with them.

Rix gave his wife that.

Rix gave the love of his life that.

Rix gave my sister that.

And I loved him for it.

Now, the photos, the cocktails, the toasts, the buffet, the cake cutting were all done, the dancing was in full swing, and all that was left was having fun, the bouquet toss (the only bouquet that would be actual flowers, and Alex wanted to do it right before she and Rix got in the car and drove away), which was scheduled for just under an hour from now.

We weren't doing the garter. It was Rix who put his foot down about that. Not that I pushed it. But he was having none of it anyway. So that wasn't going to happen.

After the toss, I'd wind things down, hand out tips, and…

Done.

So really, I could relax and sip champagne.

It was good now.

On this thought, Gal collapsed on the chair beside me.

I was taken aback. Gal didn't seek me out very much. Say, *never.* She put up with me when I was in town, and she had to spend time with me because I was spending time with Alex.

Other than that…no.

"Think our girl had a good day," she said, taking a pull from the bottle of beer in her hand (one could say there were no airs and graces with Gal, one could also say I admired it).

"I hope so," I replied.

She tore her eyes off Alex, who was laughing with Nora and Mika, to look at me.

"No, our girl had a good day. All thanks to you."

That was such a shock, I swallowed hard.

"Don't think she missed it," Gal went on.

"I…she didn't miss what?"

"That huge-ass binder," Gal said. "The fact you knocked yourself out so me and Katie could concentrate on Alex. Us showing up for hair and makeup still hungover, which was stupid, but you made that all right too. I don't think she knows about the grass snafu, but she overheard the cake was late being delivered, and she didn't blink an eye because she knew you'd sort it." She held her beer my way. "You're a good kid, Blake."

My belly gave an astonished, happy flutter.

I held my half-empty champagne flute her way and whispered, "Thanks, Gal."

We clinked. We drank. She looked back at the party.

And then she said, "Me and Katie, we've been bitches to you. It wasn't our place, but Alex is our girl. You guys didn't really—"

"I get it," I said swiftly, the belly flutter long gone. Now my chest was feeling tight at the reminder I hadn't been the best big sister for oh, not long. Only thirty years.

They had every right to be wary of me.

Hell, *I* was wary of me one hundred percent of the time. Terrified I'd backslide to that place. That place that was leading me to be a grown woman the same class as Helena Coddington-Sharp.

The scariest place in the world.

She turned back to me. "Maybe you get it. It still wasn't cool." She shook her head. "Girl, the way you went all out to make this day all it could be for Alex?"

She said no more.

She simply twisted to me, pulled me in her arms and gave me a tight, sit-down hug.

I didn't think a girlfriend had ever hugged me, sitting down or otherwise.

Not in my life.

I didn't even know Gal was a girlfriend.

Until right then.

Shit!

I was going to cry again.

I held on, just as tightly, and kept holding on for a bit even after she started to pull away. But I finally let her go.

"Sorry, I'm a little tipsy," I muttered.

"Yeah?" she asked on a grin. "Well, *good.* You deserve it. Before you go back to New York, give us a bell. We'll take you out and get you proper shitfaced."

I let out a startled laugh.

Even though no way I was getting "proper shitfaced," I thought that would be fun.

Just as long as we didn't go to a honkytonk (or maybe I should let my hair down and just go with it—so they might never wear designer at honkytonks, *c'est la vie*).

She glanced sideways and said, "Incoming hot guy."

I turned to where she was looking and saw Dair headed our way.

My heart started beating faster.

Damn it!

Why was stuff like that happening?

"His accent is so thick, I only understand half of what he says," Gal told me as she moved to get up. She stopped so she could shoot me a wink. "But I *feel* all of it."

Another startled laugh erupted from me, but this one sounded more like (good Lord!) *a giggle.*

"Toodle-loo," she bid, giving me a finger wave and strolling away, aiming a big smile at Dair as she passed him.

He handed me a fresh glass of champagne (of course!) before he threw himself down in the chair beside me, not hesitating to stretch one long arm along the back of my seat, slouch down, straighten his long legs and cross them at the ankles.

"So Sasha went to get your money bag and I gave the tip sheet from your binder to Duncan. He's going to deal with the tipping at the end of the night," he announced, before socking back some of his own beer.

I turned on him. "You did what?"

"Dinnae worry. I didnae tear the sheet out of your precious book. I unclipped it. Ye can put it back and keep it for posterity when Duncan is done."

"How did you know where the money bag was?" I asked.

His amused gray-blue eyes caught mine. "Probably shouldn't've written *tip money in leather money bag hidden in bridal quarters at the bottom of my tote.*"

Then he took another sip of his beer, but he was smiling around the mouth of his bottle.

Unbearable man.

"I didn't want to forget where I put it," I huffed, sitting to face forward again.

"Well, that's a good way not to forget. Also a good way to tell anyone who might pick up that binder where thousands of dollars of cash are stashed."

Ugh.

I said nothing. Though I did empty my half-full glass of champagne down my throat so I could start on the fresh one.

"Enlighten me," he said. "That army of men in black suits with earpieces here for Imogen Swan or Hale Wheeler?"

He was talking about the heavy security Dad had ordered because yes, Imogen Swan (known to all of us as Genny) was ridiculously famous, so was her ex-husband, Tom Pierce, and to a lesser extent, her current husband, Duncan Holloway.

But Hale was not only a close friend of the family, he was a particularly close friend of mine.

Also, he was the richest man on the planet.

I couldn't forget to note that Dad, Mum, Alex and me were all objects of media fascination. Dad because he was rich too. Mum because she was titled. Alex because she was their daughter and mixed up with the rest of this famous crew.

And me, mostly because people had filmed my altar scene with Chad, and it had gone viral.

Very viral.

Then again, in my earlier days, when I was walking a dark path, I'd sought the spotlight, and I hadn't done it in ways I was proud of.

But boy, did that defunct wedding mess cure me of *that*.

So those men were not only the security Dad had hired, they'd worked with Hale's and Genny's people to maintain a perimeter so Alex and Rix could enjoy their day.

And I had planned this wedding with the strictest of secrecy.

I'd done this to the point guests were required to check their phones at a staffed phone check station, so no one would even know it was happening until Elsa (Hale's wife, and a celebrity journalist, how's that for ironic?) broke the story.

"Take your pick," I answered Dair's question.

"There a reason why Alex is faking it with sparkling apple cider?" he rumbled.

My head whipped his way again. "How did you know that?"

His lips were curved up when he looked at me. "Saw ye intervene three times when someone handed her one fully-loaded. Ye'd be a shite spy, hen."

I moved closer to him and lowered my voice. "Do you think anyone noticed?"

"Erm…everyone?" he asked.

Oh my God.

"She doesn't want anyone to know until she's passed her first trimester," I hissed. "Only Rix, Gal, Katie, Chloe and me know. And probably Judge, since Rix tells him everything, and if he didn't, Chloe would."

"Secret's out. Now everyone knows she's up the duff," Dair drawled on one of his big grins.

I sat back and stared in a panic in front of me, seeing nothing.

"Oh my God, I gave it away," I whined.

"Be soothed, lass," he said quietly. "I'm fuckin' with ye. Of a sort. The people who care enough to notice are the ones closest to her and they wouldn't say a word until she was ready to share. The others haven't noticed because they're too busy drinking your dad's booze and eating his food."

"I hope so," I mumbled.

He moved his hand so he was lightly stroking my neck from shoulder to the very sensitive spot behind my ear.

It felt *phenomenal.*

Lord.

I should move my head. I should make a statement. I should stop this weirdness that was happening between us.

I didn't even like the man!

However, I didn't do any of that.

It felt too good.

Dair helping me get through the reception felt too good.

God, I was being stupid.

I'd spent years being stupid.

I should stop this.

I didn't.

The opening notes of Ed Sheeran's "Thinking Out Loud" sounded.

Dair got up and set his beer aside. He didn't even ask before he slid the flute from my fingers and placed it beside his beer.

He then took my hand, gently tugged me out of my chair and guided me to the dance floor.

Okay.

This was okay.

It wasn't him stroking my neck, which did not say "childhood friends hanging at a wedding."

You danced with anyone.

This was better than the neck stroking.

Definitely.

On the dance floor, Dair pulled me into his arms.

Close.

My hand in his, he laid them against his chest and started us moving.

I'd danced with a number of men that night. My dad (twice). Jamie. Duncan. Tom. Hale. Judge. Sully. Matt. Gage. Rix.

We did not dance like this.

I tipped my head back and whispered, "Dair."

"Gorgeous in that dress, lassie," he whispered back.

I'd gone dark green. One shoulder. Some gathering and a very short sleeve on that shoulder. An open slit that didn't go too high and had two tailored pleats to make it more interesting. A same-colored waistband that made my waist look tiny.

Simple. Sophisticated. Timeless.

I'd been a size four back in the day. Something else my mother beat into me with emotional manipulation and lowkey verbal abuse.

After Chad, I'd stopped making being ultra-thin my top priority in life and now I was a size ten.

This felt better on me (and I could have a piece of cake more than once a year).

But until that moment, I wasn't sure I wore it well.

"Thanks," I replied.

"Always had class," he said. "Dripping in it. Not like your mum. Snooty and obvious. Always just you."

Oh my God.

I'd never been "just me."

Hell, I'd never been classy (until, I hoped, recently). I'd always been more brash, and acted like my mother, wanting to be the center of attention because I never got any, not even from Dad who'd checked out of the Mum nightmare just like Alex had done. I definitely didn't get any from Mum, or not any that was good.

But Dair said that with total sincerity.

That was how he saw me.

And that made me feel…

A lot.

"Dair—"

I didn't get another word out.

His head dipped close, veered to my right, and he said in my ear, causing a delicious shiver, "Just dance."

Okay, I could do that.

I could just dance.

He held me close, cheek to cheek, as we danced to the song.

My eyes caught on Chloe, who was dancing cheek to cheek with Judge not too far away, and she was smirking gleefully at me.

Damn.

This was totally not childhood friends.

This said something else.

And bottom-line truth?

If I let myself be in this, how it felt right now, I was there for it.

At the same time absolutely terrified of it.

But in that moment, under the fairy lights streaming across the rafters over our heads, this song playing, it was difficult (nay! *impossible*) to pull away from him. Put distance between us. Make a statement about where we were at, or where we probably should be.

Not because I suddenly wasn't sure where that was, but because he smelled good. He felt good. He danced very well.

I felt safe in my skin when I was in his arms.

I felt right in my skin.

I felt right in Dair's arms.

Oh no.

This was bad.

But it felt so good.

I closed my eyes and rested my cheek on his shoulder.

That felt even better.

He gathered me closer and stroked my spine with his hand.

That felt the best.

Oh yes.

This was so, so bad.

I needed to get a handle on it.

I needed to put a stop to it.

I opened my eyes.

And saw his mother off to the side of the dance floor with an expression on her face I'd never seen in my life and wished I still hadn't.

I tensed, lifted my cheek from Dair's shoulder, and twisted my neck to see what she was looking at.

The reception was under a huge pergola (currently decorated by bails and bails of beautiful grass and fairy lights). It was an outdoor event space that had several outbuildings for necessities, like a loo, a massive catering kitchen, and bride's and groom's lounges.

And I caught Mum and Balfour ducking behind the groom's lounge.

I shot straight, moved my attention the other direction, saw Kenna's face setting to pissed and determined, and her body started moving toward the groom's lounge.

Oh no!

"What's up?" Dair asked, and my gaze raced to him, seeing him turn his head to look where I'd been looking.

I caught his jaw and made him face me.

"Nothing," I said fake cheerily.

The fake didn't fool him. I knew this when his brows shot down.

Lord, I needed to distract him so I could rush over there and be sure there wasn't a scene.

Kenna was a nice lady. Pretty (both Dair and Davina got their hair from her, Dair got his eyes from her). Quiet. Not reserved, simply quiet. Stout, in that Scottish get-on-with-it-way.

She'd always been kind to me, even when I wasn't easy to be kind to.

I couldn't imagine she'd instigate a scene, though it was clear she didn't intend to ignore this obvious peccadillo.

Mum, however, would totally cause a scene.

In fact, I didn't know what she was thinking, guiding Balfour back there. Or what Bally was thinking, for God's sake.

Except Mum could turn the attention on her and ruin Alex's day, one she didn't approve of and was not allowed to meddle in (overly much, outside the guest list).

And that would be something Helena Coddington-Sharp would do.

It also seemed like something she was actually doing.

Damn it, I was going to fucking *strangle her.*

I refocused on Dair and spoke quickly. "Can you get me a piece of cake? I haven't had any yet," that last part was a lie.

"In the middle of a dance?" he asked suspiciously.

Still suspicious, he turned his head again.

I repeated my move of grabbing his jaw, but he fought it this time, and I saw it when he saw it.

Shit!

We were mostly just swaying, but he stopped us doing that when he looked down at me, and his expression wasn't sexy or sultry or flirty.

He was ticked.

"Ye ken?" he asked, his voice a lash.

He knew too?

"You know?" I asked back.

He stepped out of my arms. "What were ye gonna do? Cover for her?"

"No," I snapped, not believing he'd think I'd do that. Especially after what he knew Chad did to me. "I was trying to distract you with getting me cake so I could go behind the groom's lounge, talk your parents into doing whatever they're going to do elsewhere, and finding somewhere quiet to commit matricide so Alex won't know I murdered our mother at her wedding. I'll talk to the police about not sharing my crime until she returns from her honeymoon. And I'm happy I wore dark green so the blood stains won't be too obvious on my mugshot."

He glowered at me.

I didn't have time for him to be ticked.

Something had to be done before someone started yelling.

He didn't get over being ticked, or glowering, but he stopped doing that last aimed at me and started prowling across the dance floor.

Tragedy!

I hustled after him as fast as my gold mules would take me.

I did not catch up. His legs were long, and he wasn't wearing high heels. But I didn't stop rushing while trying not to look like I was rushing and smiling a tight smile at anyone who caught my eyes.

Maybe they'd think I was ordering another case of champagne to be opened, um…with urgency.

Yes, I'd totally be a shit spy.

I turned the corner of the groom's lounge and ran right into Dair's broad back.

"We do not need an audience for this," Balfour was saying.

I stepped to the side and got a full view of the very unhappy three-some.

Wait, it was an unhappy twosome: Balfour and Kenna.

Mum was veritably preening.

She was such a fucking piece of work.

"Take Mum back to the hotel," Dair ordered his father.

"Alasdair, this doesn't involve ye," Balfour retorted.

And he looked a fool doing it, with my mother's deep rose lipstick smeared all over his mouth.

It was smeared all over hers too.

Kenna was standing off to the side, looking like her world just ended.

She'd seen them necking.

She maybe knew before, perhaps she was unsure, perhaps living in denial, but she wasn't in any question about it now.

And again, she'd always been kind to me.

Not to mention, I knew exactly how this felt.

But I didn't have forty years of marriage under my belt with Chad.

These thoughts filled my veins with so much fire, I had to let some out.

It came from my mouth, and I directed it at who deserved it.

My mother.

"I never thought much of you, but are you really this woman?" I demanded hotly.

"Blake," Bally said more calmly. "If ye'd take my son—"

"No," I snapped at him. "This is my sister's wedding. I've known what kind of man you are for years, but this is a new low."

Bally flinched.

Dair pulled me to his side and repeated to his father, "Take Mum back to the hotel."

Balfour was repeating too. "This doesn't involve either of ye."

Dair's bark of laughter this time had zero amusement.

"Really?" he sneered. "You using our school holidays to have a fuckfest like the total twat and common tart you two arseholes are, doing this every year since we were wee isn't my business?"

Mum wasn't preening anymore.

It was the "common tart" comment, I knew. She'd hate that, and she did.

"Blake Charlotte, remove Wallace and yourself *this instant*," Mum demanded.

I didn't know what came over me.

Oh wait.

I did.

Years of her being a *total and complete bitch.*

But this…

This took the damned cake.

I broke from Dair's hold, strode forward, and slapped her across the face with everything I had.

It was so violent, she cried out, flew to the side and bent double, her hand going to her cheek.

I wouldn't have done it again, and not only because it made my hand sting hella bad, but it was still good Dair caught my wrist from behind, curled my arm around my belly, yanked me against his body and pulled me back several steps.

I might not have been about to strike twice physically, but he didn't contain my mouth.

"I know this will mean nothing," I ground out between my teeth. "I know nothing penetrates your utter and complete selfishness. But an assignation with your married lover at your daughter's wedding? What is the matter with you?"

"What's going on?"

Fabulous.

Dad was here.

He came up to Dair and my sides and recoiled at the tableau in front of him, his reaction stating plainly he'd translated it without a word of explanation.

In that split instant, several things occurred to me.

One, Dad had it going on. He was older, but he was exceptionally good-looking. He had that Pierce Brosnan thing happening. He'd be hot when he was eighty.

Two, Kenna gave Dair (and Davina) all their good looks.

It wasn't that Bally was a ginger. I'd seen a lot of redheaded men who were gorgeous.

It was that he had a weak chin (and Kenna did not, Dair definitely didn't). She was as tall as her husband (and he was six foot, but Dair was taller, so he got that from his mum too). And Dair and Davina both inherited the olive undertone of their skin from her. It was the kind of skin that took to the sun and just got prettier and prettier the more it soaked it up. Bally, on the other hand, was pale, freckled and ruddy.

Oh, and Bally was totally loaded, but Dad was like, *way* richer.

Since I was being petty, I might as well pull out all the stops, so I'd add that Dad also had a pedigree.

Mum had totally traded down.

"Christ, Helena," Dad bit out. "Here? Now?"

"Your daughter struck me," Mum bleated, hand still cradling her cheek.

Dad looked down at me, eyes wide.

"I'm not proud of it," I said. "But I'd do it again," I added.

"Blake," he murmured, though I didn't miss that now, he was fighting a smile.

"This is not amusing, Ned!" Mum squealed.

Dad's head snapped in her direction, and he hissed, "Keep your voice down."

"Kenna…love," Balfour was saying.

I lost track of them with the Mum stuff, so I looked that way to see Balfour had his fingers wrapped around Kenna's arm.

She pulled vehemently away.

Bally went for her again, but Dair let me go and stepped forward.

"Touch her, I'll ram your fuckin' teeth down your fuckin' throat," he growled.

Bally squared off against Dair, still with lipstick smeared all over his mouth, four inches shorter, having a good thirty pounds (at least) less muscle, a small pot belly, and he couldn't look more of a fool.

"Ye dinnae speak to your father that way," Bally stated.

"You're not my father. You're a common, piece a' shite cheat," Dair retorted.

Bally's eyes narrowed, but even so, I saw how that blow landed, and it did it hard.

"Men," Dad intervened, pushing between them both.

They stood down but didn't lose eye contact.

Dad didn't bother with them further.

He turned to Dair's mother. "Kenna, I'll see to it you're taken safely back to your hotel."

"Obliged, Ned," she said softly, but her eyes strayed to Balfour. "Ye want her so badly, Bally, she's yours."

"Darling—" Balfour started.

"Do not come back to our room. Do not phone me. I'll be gone tomorrow," Kenna warned, and then she assumed another expression I wished I'd never seen. "What we had never really was, not with her around. And now it just plain isn't."

"Kenna," Balfour groaned.

"Excuse me?" Mum asked him.

Balfour looked to her.

Dad stopped from leading Kenna away, and he turned to Mum.

"Get gone from here, Helena, and take him with you." He jerked his head toward Balfour. "If I see you anywhere near the reception, I swear to God, I'll throw you in a car my damned self and tell the driver to take you to the desert, drop you off and leave you there."

Mum put her hand to her chest in open insult.

"Don't test me," Dad stated. "I'm not joking. You aren't the only one who can throw a drama in this family." His gaze raked her up and down. "And I learned from the best." He then looked to me. "You need to distract your sister, sweetheart, so these two can clear the premises." His piercing eyes hit on Balfour. "And you'll be doing that quietly and immediately. Am I understood?"

"I dinnae—" Balfour started.

"I don't care what you don't," Dad cut him off harshly. "Get the fuck away from my daughter's wedding. And if you,"—another head jerk, this one to Mum—"or her, make even the slightest scene, I will stop at nothing until you're ruined. Am I understood now?"

It took a moment for Bally to answer, and when he did, he just jutted his chin.

Proof.

Dad totally had it going on.

He also took this as an affirmative and escorted Kenna away.

"Ye can give me the rental keys, Dair," Bally said to his son.

"Ye can fuck off and walk for all I care," Dair returned.

I got close to him and said, "I can drive you and Davina wherever you want to go."

Or, at least, give me an hour or two to drink loads of water and sober up and then I could do that.

Alternately, I'd put them in one of the cars Dad had ordered to take drunk people home.

A muscle was leaping in his cheek when he looked down at me.

But I saw the pain in his eyes.

God, this was such a mess.

He then dug into his trouser pocket and pulled out a fob.

He tossed it to his father.

He looked down at me again. "Go, darling. Order me a whisky. A big one. I'll see them to their car."

"I…don't want to leave you," I whispered, no clue why, but what I said was the truth.

His eyes flashed, his face got soft (damn, that looked good on him), and he said, "I need a whisky more than ye helping me with this chore."

"Okay."

Oof!

I was still whispering.

And obeying.

He tipped his head toward the pergola.

I nodded and started to move away.

"I will not soon forget you struck me, Blake Charlotte," Mum threatened.

I turned to her. "And I will not forget the lifetime of your neglect punctuated by casual cruelty. Not what you aimed at me. Not what you aimed at Dad. Not what you aimed at Alex, including tonight, pulling this stunt at her wedding. You should be ashamed of yourself, and the worst part, the one that hurts the most, is that you won't be because you don't have even a thread of the moral fiber that would tell you, you should."

Mum just stared daggers at me.

"Go, lass," Dair urged.

I glared at my mother one last time.

She glared right back.

I was not proud of the red welt on her face delivered by my hand.

But I didn't regret it.

I caught Dair's eyes only for an instant before I walked away.

CHAPTER FOUR

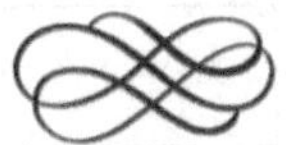

BOUQUET

Blake

I stuck to Alex like glue while keeping a watchful eye on the groom's lounge, before noting Dair stalking behind Mum and Bally on their way to the parking lot.

Things were crazy, my mind in disarray, but even so, it was not lost on me how good Dair looked stalking.

Ugh.

I only relaxed when I saw Dair walking back by himself.

The expanse between disappearing and reappearing seemed to take him a long time.

Rix gave me an intense look before I finally let myself break away and head to the bar.

He would never know about the drama.

I hoped.

I ordered Dair three fingers of whisky and myself an espresso martini, thankful Dad was rich as all hell, so the whisky was damn good Scotch, my martini was made with Belvedere vodka, and those cars were lined up to take us home.

The bartender had the Scotch on the bar and was preparing my martini when Dair came to stand at my side.

He commandeered the glass, tipped it back, downing half of it. He swallowed, then tipped the second half back.

"Whoa," I said.

He put the glass down, tapping it sharply on a bottom edge to demand a refill.

The bartender nodded to him and kept at my martini.

"I take it that was even less pleasant than I thought it would be," I noted carefully.

"Dad dinnae say a word," he told me, hunching into his forearms on the edge of the bar, staring at the barback. "Your mum, though, bitched the whole way about needing ice for her face."

Although I was the cause of that need, and it made me feel yuck (still didn't regret it), I probably should have gotten her some before she took off. It was a good twenty-minute ride back into town. Plenty of time for the swelling to come up.

He tilted his torso my way, not leaving his forearms.

"I texted Mum before I headed back up," he said. "She told me she needs some space but I'll be needing to get back to her so I can check in and be close."

Perhaps that was why it took him so long to return from the parking area.

"Of course," I murmured.

"There didnae seem to be a lot in your binder that still needs done."

Wait.

Was he…?

God, who was this man?

"Dair, you can go whenever you want," I told him. "You could always have done that. But if you're concerned about what's left to do, in about ten minutes, there's going to be a bouquet toss. A driver is then going to take Alex and Rix down to Phoenix, and I made sure they had a car with a partition they could put up because they're going to be banging the entire way. They've got two nights at the Phoenician before they head down to St. Lucia for their honeymoon. Once they're away, the coast will be clear. But for you, it is already."

I felt triumphant that my comment about my sister and new brother-in-law banging wrung a small smile out of his mouth.

But I finished, "So you're good to go. And, uh…thanks for helping me out."

He simply nodded and watched the bartender put my martini in front of me.

I picked it up and took a healthy sip.

He watched that too.

Then he asked, "When did ye ken?"

Ulk.

I didn't want to talk about it.

But I felt I had to, because he obviously did want to have this chat, and we were in the same boat, him and me.

Though, I didn't have a parent's mental and emotional health to consider.

"Feels like all my life," I mumbled into my martini glass. I looked over it to him. "You?"

"Same. How'd ye find out?"

I made a face. "Do I really have to say?"

"I saw them fucking in the stables. I was eleven."

Gross!

The bartender put his whisky in front of him, and fortunately, he didn't down it in two.

He just wrapped his fingers around it and raised his brows at me in question.

"The upstairs hallway," I forced out. "Against the wall. We were all in the country at Treverton, and your mum, Davina and Alex were off tramping around some National Trust property. They thought I'd gone too, but I bowed out at the last minute."

"How old were ye?"

"I don't actually remember. But no more than ten."

Dair turned his attention to his whisky glass. "Not exactly stealth, those two."

"No," I said miserably.

I wanted to ask him if he thought his mother knew, but I didn't want to make this harder on him.

I didn't have to ask, though, because he told me.

"She was their Camilla, your mum."

God, that was so awful.

I sidled closer to him and asked, "So…she knew."

He lifted his glass, took a sip, put it down and nodded to the glass. "She knew. Never told me. But I knew she knew. Put on a brave face. Probably kept hoping he'd end it and come back to her fully." The last he said quieter. "Not sure why she decided tonight to stop pretending."

I wasn't sure either.

"Sometimes, we can't pick our time," I informed him. "Sometimes, we can't stop our emotions from guiding us."

He turned to me and was going to say something, but Davina came up, scorched me with a look that wasn't all that fun, before she directed it at her brother.

"Do ye wanna tell me why Ned was putting Mum in one of the anti-drink driving cars he's got lined up for people who are getting rat-arsed and why ye were escorting Dad and *her* Mum to the car park?" she demanded.

Dair pushed to standing properly and turned to her. "Davi—"

She didn't let him finish.

She looked to me. "Let me guess, they couldn't keep their hands off each other, even at her lass's wedding."

Seemed Davina knew too.

Rix came up then and he only had eyes for me.

Fantastic.

"Can I talk to you for a second?" he requested.

"No need!" I cried breezily. "I'll go get the bouquet so you two can make your getaway."

"I don't give a fuck about the bouquet. I give a fuck about why you and your dad, him," he tipped his head to Dair, "his mom and dad and *your* mom were all creeping around behind a building."

I was okay with Rix being totally in love with my sister.

I was not okay with Rix being so damned observant.

At least, not right now.

"It's nothing," I completely lied.

"Alex doesn't like surprises," he stated.

Oh.

He was worried we had some big scheme planned that Alex would hate.

"It was just kind of…a family meeting," I said.

Davina snorted.

Rix aimed thinned eyes to her, though not long before they came to me.

"You Sharp sisters and your binders," Rix said. "I thought you had it all in hand. She's had a great day. Whatever you have planned—"

"Relax, Rix," Davina said angrily. "She was just back there stopping my dad from humping her mum behind a shed."

Rix's head reared back, and he looked like he might get sick.

My head dropped.

Great.

"Worst kept secret in Coddington/Wallace history," Davina decreed then said to the bartender. "I'll have one of those," and pointed at Dair's Scotch.

"Is she serious?" Rix asked me.

"Don't worry about it," I told him. "I'll go get the bouquet and get your driver in position."

"Is she serious?" Rix repeated.

"It's taken care of, mate," Dair said.

Rix looked at Dair.

I looked at Dair.

He looked pissed. He looked upset.

All in all, he looked wrecked.

My heart squeezed.

"We sorted it," he said to Rix. "Alex doesn't have to know."

Rix turned to me.

"He's right. She never has to know," I reiterated.

Rix didn't take his eyes from me.

This went on so long, I was having trouble not squirming.

Finally, he spoke, "Broke your back makin' this a good day for her. Then you had to put up with that shit?"

"It's over and done, Rix." Well, not for Kenna, sadly. "Put it out of your head. The best part of this whole wedding thing is about five minutes away for you."

At this juncture, my espresso martini splashed all over my hand because, after I quit speaking, Rix's hand darted out and caught me at the back of my head. He pulled me to him and kissed the top of my hair.

"Appreciate you and all your hard work," he said there.

And *seriously*.

Would everyone stop trying to make me cry?

"She does too," he finished.

Gah!

He let me go but looked down at me. "Get the bouquet, babe."

I sniffed hard and nodded.

Rix smiled, but his smile didn't last long before he asked, "You okay with that mess?"

I wasn't going to tell him it wasn't news to me.

"I'm fine," I answered.

"Probably helped that the lassie got a good wallop in on the old tart," Dair muttered into his whisky.

"What?" Davina asked, her voice breathy.

"What?" Rix grunted, his voice stunned.

"Well, uh..." I didn't quite begin.

"Smacked the ever-lovin' piss outta her," Dair shared.

An astonished splutter of mirth emitted from Davina.

Rix stared at me again.

Then he boomed with laughter.

Davina joined him.

Dair smirked, then chuckled.

It was so loud, everyone turned to look.

"God!" I cried then set my drink down and pushed at Rix's shoulder. "Go. Get your wife." I pointed at Dair. "You go find their car. It'll be the longest, fanciest one. No 'just married' or any of that kind of thing. The driver will know his destination and he should be hanging around, waiting. Have him pull up to the exit. I'm going to find the bouquet."

With that, I stormed off, leaving them all still chortling behind me.

On my way, I gave the DJ the high sign to get everyone gathered where they were supposed to be. I also gave a few more signs, specifically to Gal, Katie, Chloe, Dru, Mika, Genny, Nora, Elsa, Hailey and Mags, who were in charge of making sure everyone had the biodegradable confetti, it being biodegradable because the cones it was in were and the actual confetti was freeze-dried rose petals.

I knew exactly where the bouquet was (chilling in the industrial refrigerator in the caterer's kitchen).

I fetched it, thinking I couldn't wait to get my shoes off.

Normally, I could run like Carrie in SatC in heels. But I'd been in these shoes for hours, dashing around like a crazy woman, and I couldn't wait to switch them out to flip-flops.

But I sallied forth, heading back to the pergola to see people forming as they should.

I just had time to get into position, Dru shoved a cone in my hand, while Rix and Alex ran through a hail of rose petals and the DJ played Bad Company's "Feel Like Makin' Love" (another Rix choice, obviously).

I tossed my petals and shoved the bouquet in my sister's hand as she passed me (at her decree, it was white and pale green roses, some little pink flowers, mingled with some succulents you could replant and keep).

And I watched her dash hand in hand with her husband to the door of the limousine that was being held open by the chauffeur.

That's when the tears came.

This time, though, I couldn't keep them at bay.

Alex had picked so perfectly with her dress. It had sheer, fluttery short sleeves, subtle hints of pretty lace and a beautiful back and front vee (the back lower), her shoulder blades covered with that sheer material and lace. The skirt was full but not big, falling gracefully to her feet, a delicate second tier floating around, and a thin belt that tied at a rosette on the side of her waist.

It was feminine. Romantic. Dreamy.

It wasn't her, because Alex wasn't that type of girl. She was no-nonsense.

And it was totally her, because she loved Rix with everything she had, and she wanted him to know it in every way she could.

Especially today.

Marrying him.

While carrying his baby.

She looked so completely happy.

I was so proud of her.

I was so happy for her.

I felt the tears fall as me and all of the other singletons were shoved to the front at Gal and Katie's command.

The chauffeur was rounding the car to get in the front seat.

Rix had hold of the door and was waiting.

Alex turned and looked me dead in the eye.

And she didn't even bother with pretense, subtlety or misdirection of aim.

Overarm, she winged that bouquet right at me.

It hit me with a thud in my chest, petals flying. My hands automatically came up to catch it. Everyone around me laughed and cheered.

As for me, I studiously avoided looking around to find Dair to see his reaction to what had just happened.

Alex blew me a kiss then turned to Dad, who was close and waiting, so she could throw her arms around him for a hug.

More hugs were given out as Gare and Mags (both Rix's parents) were also hanging close.

Everyone shouted good wishes and raunchy advice (that last was Gage, but also Davina).

Rix eventually fell into the car with his arm around Alex's waist, tugging her in with him.

Their legs disappeared.

Her skirt disappeared.

Dad slammed the door and thumped on the hood.

The driver took off.

Some people (the drunker ones) raced after them.
But I stood there, holding my sister's bouquet and weeping.
Until I saw her face in the back window.
She was again looking at me, a massive smile on her pretty face.
She waved.
I returned her blowing of the kiss and waved back.
And I kept doing it until they were out of sight.

CHAPTER FIVE

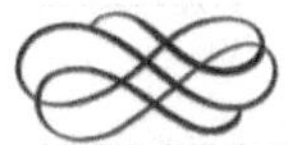

"TWO, RIGHT?"

Dair

air opened his eyes to bright sunlight and confusion as to what was crushing him.

He saw gleaming black hair, some of it eschewed from the pins that had held it up, and creamy skin over a bare shoulder.

And he smiled.

Blake was passed out on top of him.

To say the woman got pissed out of her skull after her sister left was a vast understatement.

One espresso martini turned into four, and it was Dair pouring her (and his sister) in her car after he took the fob off her.

He didn't know where Ned's place was in these mountains. He only knew where Duncan Holloway, the outdoor gear magnate, and Imogen Swan, the award-winning Hollywood star, lived, since that was where they had cocktails and tapas the first night they were in town.

And having his hands on a drunk Blake Sharp was far too advantageous of a circumstance for him to go to Ned, who was still there, quietly sharing a drink with his set, and ask where Dair should take his daughter.

So he took Blake to the posh Victorian hotel off the quaint Old West town square where his family was staying.

Holding it close to her chest like a prized possession, Blake had cooed at and maybe drooled a little over her bouquet the whole ride back.

That was, she did that when she wasn't twisted in her seat, havering with Davina about fuck knew what.

It involved shoes. And shopping in New York.

So he zoned out.

He dragged her and her heavy as all fuck tote to the elevator, Davina following, both of them making too much noise, all of this protestations about going up to their rooms rather than to the hotel bar for another drink.

He deposited his sister at the door to her room, only for her to blow a raspberry at him and throw herself in Blake's arms. They hugged in the hall, blathering rubbish about how neither of them knew how *awesome* the other one was *for years* and how they were *so glad* that was over, and now they could be *best mates forever and ever.*

He let this go on for a while before he peeled Blake out of Davi's arms and guided her listing, slender body in that fucking miraculous dress to his room.

He let them in.

The first thing she did was flip her shoes off.

They went flying. One hit the bed. The other flew over it.

He was setting her tote on the couch, about to laugh at her movements, but she let out a sound that did things to his cock and gushed, "I've been needing to do that for *three full hours.*" She got over that and looked around, asking, "Do you have a minibar?"

"You've had enough," he replied.

She narrowed her violet eyes at him.

Christ, she was stunning.

She'd always been stunning. Even as a little girl.

She looked like her mum.

But there'd been something else to Blake. Something more raw. More real. Warmer.

More vulnerable.

She came to him and poked him in the chest. Three times. Hard.

It probably hurt her finger more than him.

What it did to him was make him want to bust out laughing.

"Who're you to tell me I've had enough?" she demanded.

"The man who's good with ye like this and will not be good rubbing your back while ye boke in his toilet."

She scrunched her nose.

Fuck, he wanted to kiss her.

Regrettably, now was not the time.

"Be good," he warned. "I've have to go check on Mum."

She frowned dramatically.

Still, all she felt for his mum was in it.

And she would know that pain.

So, again, he wanted to kiss her.

He'd been wanting to kiss her since she pulled her shite at her own wedding.

Jesus, she'd decimated that arsehole.

It was magnificent.

But he felt like he was coming out of his skin watching it.

And he didn't understand his reaction.

Dair couldn't say he'd had a thing for Blake Sharp while growing up.

Though he couldn't deny he'd always been strangely fascinated by her.

She was gorgeous, definitely.

But she hated to get dirty. She hated hunting. She complained about the cold and rain. She turned her nose up at the food.

And it was hard as fuck to watch her work her arse off for her mother's approval, when that bitch barely knew either of her daughters existed.

As she got older, Blake became more and more like her mother, except wilder and not in a way it was fun to be around, and Dair had less and less stomach for spending time with her. So he found reasons not to.

That church scene, though.

It looked empowering.

But Dair knew her enough to know he was watching her unravelling.

Aye, he'd sat there powerless and witnessed her publicly unravel the woman her mother had tried to knit her into being.

She was a pool of used yarn on that altar before Rix grabbed her.

Dair had been the one who'd wanted to grab her.

He was surprised by his reaction to it.

He was not surprised she went into hiding after it.

The press and social media had a field day with her.

It was all good, if it wasn't you who was in a wedding gown at an altar sharing how your fiancé fucked everything that moved, filmed it and put it on a website for all his mates to see.

Since then, he'd texted her several times and called twice.

She didn't take either call, but the texts she returned, only to put him off.

He let her be, sensing she needed it.

He shouldn't have.

In the intervening time, she'd become the woman she was meant to be.

Still snooty.

Still uppity.

Still gorgeous.

But the raw warmth wasn't stifled by a need to please, or, at least, the need to please someone who didn't matter.

And Dair wanted all of it.

One thing he got from his father that he didn't mind having, the only thing, was when Alasdair Wallace knew what he wanted, he went balls to the wall to get it.

And from the moment she'd glared at him when he'd walked into Genny and Duncan's bonny house by a lake, he knew he wanted her.

He left Blake frowning, went to his mother's room and knocked.

She didn't answer.

So he pulled out his phone and called her.

She answered that. "Are ye and Davi back?"

"Aye, Mum. I'm outside your door. Can I come in?"

"I need some time, love," she replied. "We'll talk at breakfast. All right?"

"I just want to see ye. Give ye a quick peck. And I'll leave ye alone."

She didn't reply, but the door opened.

She was in her dressing gown. Her thick dark hair with silvery strands was scraped back from her face. Her makeup was gone, her face shiny from her nighttime ritual. But it was swollen, especially her eyes, which were also red.

Taking her in, Dair growled, "I could kill him."

His mum reached up and patted him on the cheek. "Sleep, son. We'll talk with fresh heads tomorrow."

"Blake is with me."

She tipped her head to the side and hid her reaction from him.

She was good at that.

A lifetime with a philandering husband led to it, he supposed.

"She got rat-arsed after Alex and Rix left," he explained. "And I dinnae ken where Ned's staying."

"Does she not have a phone with her father's number in it?"

It was not lost on Dair that Blake was the daughter of the woman who was fucking her husband.

But he had Blake in his room, and that was where she was staying.

"I'm not sure she's capable of operating it."

That made a ghost of a smile coast over his mother's lips.

But it died before she said, "In all Helena did to me, to us, the way she treated her girls…ye ken I dinnae condone violence."

Dair becoming a professional rugby player was not high on his mother's list of career choices.

Dair enjoying his drink like any good Scotsman would, and sometimes brawling in pubs was categorically not something his mother approved of.

"Aye. I ken."

"But I was pleased she was able to share even a little of the pain Helena forced her to endure her entire life."

That was Kenna Wallace.

She'd been gutted that night.

But she had a mind to someone else.

"She put so much force into it, the woman might have a black eye," Dair noted.

Another ghost of a smile drifted over his mother's lips.

"Kiss. Then bed, son," she said words he'd heard thousands of times in his life.

He bent to buss her cheek and lifted away.

"Ye going to be able to sleep?" he asked.

"We'll see," she replied.

There wasn't much more he could do but nod. So that's what he did.

She gazed on him with the love she always gave him as she closed the door.

He returned to his room.

And found Blake sprawled on her stomach in his bed still wearing her bridesmaid dress.

He grinned, took off his jacket, shoes, socks, watch and shirt. He brushed his teeth and spied the bouquet sitting on the nightstand. He took it to the sink in the bathroom, filled the basin, and set it in.

He went back to the bedroom and rearranged her, yanking at the bedclothes so he could get in beside her and pull the covers over them.

She didn't even twitch as he did this.

Which set him to grinning again.

Not long later, he was passed out right beside her.

How she got her body on his without waking him, he didn't have a clue. He'd stopped drinking when she started. Though, Davi hadn't let the glass of whisky he'd had to abandon for the bouquet toss go to waste.

He wasn't a light sleeper; he wasn't a heavy sleeper.

What he was, was a man who would wake up when a beautiful woman draped herself over him in a bed or anywhere.

He stared at her head.

He was dying to take the pins out of her hair.

She had the most extraordinary head of hair. Thick. Raven. Shining with health.

However, every time he'd seen her since he came to Prescott, she had it up.

He wanted it down.

But first, they had to face the day after the scene with their parents.

And then they had to have a chat about what she said to him at the rehearsal dinner about being a bully.

After that, he'd get her on the same page he was on.

Dair wasn't sure with the bully comment if she was.

But she hadn't shrunk away from him touching her neck.

And she'd melted into his arms when they'd danced.

Further, she hadn't wanted to leave him with Helena and his father. And she'd had his whisky waiting for him when he returned.

There wasn't a time in his life that he remembered not knowing Blake Charlotte Sharp.

Though, now was the time he intended to get to *know* Blake Charlotte Sharp.

He was about to touch her to wake her (but also just to touch her), when his phone buzzed on his nightstand.

Blake jolted and groaned, and then Dair watched in complete fascination as she moved her head to rub her face against his chest.

It was something a little girl would do.

It was sweet, cute, and since she was a grown woman, sexy as all fuck, and his morning wood agreed.

He was watching her, so he saw when she suddenly realized what she was about, and her head shot up.

She winced, and he was sure that was her hangover making itself known.

He grinned.

She focused with apparent difficulty on him.

Her eyes got huge.

He grinned bigger.

Then she rolled off him, onto her back, and slapped both her hands on her face, moaning behind them, "Oh my God."

He turned to his side and got up on a forearm. "Guid mornin', me wee bonny Blake."

"Ugh."

"How ye feeling?"

"Stop shouting."

He chuckled.

"Stop shaking the bed."

He chuckled more.

"Bluh."

"Ye need to get moving, love. Ye volunteered for the fire department last night. They'll be expecting ye to pitch up this morning."

"Oh *God*. Shut *up*," she groaned.

She'd held court with Rix's firefighter mates last night. She and Davina had them eating out of their hands. He was actually surprised his sister didn't pull one (and this gave credence to the growing seriousness of the situationship she had going on back at home).

His close presence and Blake hanging on him most of the time was probably the only reason she didn't.

And, aye.

Her drunkenly hanging on Dair was another indication he wasn't in this alone.

Sure, a woman with bad manners could paw on a man when she got drunk, he'd experienced that more than once, and he didn't like it one bit.

But Blake bragging proudly he was her "wedding assistant" and "*so very good at it*" to anyone who would listen and staring at him often like he built the entire wedding venue with his bare hands was not the same as a drunken woman pawing on him.

"Teasing ye, lass," he said through a smile. "Ye need water. And coffee. And something in your belly."

"I need a toothbrush." She plopped her arms down on the bed asking, "Did you bring my—?"

She stopped herself speaking when her eyes fell to his chest.

"What the hell?" she demanded and then gave another mild flinch as her hangover reacted to her words.

"What the hell what?"

Her eyes came to his. "I thought you retired from rugby."

"Aye. I did."

She flung a hand at his chest. "So how are you still that built?"

"I still play, and I'd get the shite knocked out of me if I didnae keep in shape to do it."

She aimed her eyes at the ceiling, releasing a "Gluh."

"And I do rugby commentary for the BBC. I'm often on camera, and I'd look like a twat if I talked rugby from behind a wall of flab."

She tucked her chin in her neck and looked down at herself. "You didn't take off my dress."

He felt his smile change before he replied, "It was tempting." Her gaze cut to him. "Though I didnae think ye'd thank me for it come morning."

She turned her attention to his lower half. "What are you wearing?"

"My trousers."

She squinted at him. "Oh my God. You're a gentleman. That's so annoying."

Even if he knew she needed to get up, move about, hydrate and soak up some of the vodka sloshing in her stomach, and what she didn't need was him shaking the bed, he couldn't stop his laughter.

"You would have preferred me to strip ye down?" he asked.

"Just tell me you grabbed my tote."

"Aye." He tipped his head to the couch.

She looked that way and mumbled, "Thank God." She came back to him. "You need the bathroom?"

"I can go after ye."

She stared at him.

He took her meaning.

"How long will it take you?" he asked.

"Probably longer than you can wait first thing in the morning."

He didn't doubt it.

In fact, she had some sorcery going on because her makeup still looked perfect even if her hair hadn't survived the drunken evening and passing out. That didn't mean it didn't look fucking smashing, long, fat, shining tendrils tangled on the pillow.

His erection had calmed down, but it was threatening to come back, so he spoke.

"I'll go first."

"Good call," she said.

Dair wanted to kiss her, touch her, something.

He didn't.

They weren't there. Not while lying in bed.

So he rolled out and headed to the bathroom.

He did all his business, including brushing his teeth, plucking the bouquet out of the basin and putting it back in when he was done, and he strolled out only for Blake to be lugging her tote in.

"I ordered coffee and croissants to be brought up. Knock on the door when they arrive," she bossed, then closed the door.

He smiled at it, and it didn't fly under the radar that he was smiling a lot around Blake Sharp.

He considered himself a mellow guy. He made a point of doing what he enjoyed as often as he could. He was born to wealth and made his own. In his mid-twenties, he'd had a short-lived, high-profile, unwise marriage to a vain, celebrity-hungry woman whose sole desire was to be a WAG, something she accomplished with him, which ended in a messy divorce, so she accomplished it again with some other poor arsehole (that one ended in divorce too).

But other than that, he had good friends, a loving mother, a close relationship with his sister, and a father he did not respect.

However, outside the man being an inveterate cheat (Dair suspected Helena wasn't the only other woman, though he didn't know this as truth), and too hard on Dair in the "a man's gotta learn how to be a man" department while he was growing up, he wasn't a bad dad.

In fact, in the times Dair could forget all that shite, Balfour was gruffly loving and intensely protective.

To put a fine point on it, Balfour was nothing like Helena.

In short, Dair had a good life. He intended to keep having one. He didn't take it for granted. He recognized it and put the work in to nourish it.

But he still couldn't remember the last time he smiled this often.

He hadn't showered so Blake could have the bathroom. He'd do it after she did whatever she was going to do in there.

But he had to get these suit trousers off.

He switched them out to some track pants and went to his phone.

The text from before was from his mum.

It was to him and Davi.

He read it.

Breakfast in my suite at 9:30. If Blake is still here, bring her as well.

Dair sighed, uncertain about taking Blake to this particular family breakfast. He checked the time (it was twenty before nine) and sat on the side of the bed to answer.

Blake's still here. We'll be there.

He then checked his email, deleted a bunch of them and phoned his sister.

She didn't pick up.

She was probably still passed out.

He'd put on a shirt and go knock on the door later.

But for now, he searched his contacts, wondering if he even had the man's number.

He did. He didn't remember when he got it, but he had it.

So he called it.

Ned Sharp picked up on the second ring.

"How are you this morning, Dair?" he asked in greeting.

"Better than your daughter," he told the man. "Calling to let ye know she's safe and she's with me."

"I saw you all leaving together last night, but I appreciate the call. And thank you for looking after her. She delayed her celebration, but when the time was ripe, she committed to it."

She certainly had.

A hesitation from Ned then, "I hate to bring her up, for reasons I'm sure are obvious, but I must. Do you know if Helena has been in contact with her?"

"I dinnae think Blake looked at her phone all night."

"Again, I hesitate to discuss her, but I'm afraid you're involved in one of her dramas now, and you should know, Helena is not good when she's on her back foot."

Was she good at any time?

"Noted."

"Please find a way to share this information with your mother and sister."

Bloody hell.

"I will," he grunted.

"I'm very sorry, Dair."

"She isn't yours to apologize for."

"I'm still sorry."

Ned Sharp was a good man.

Dair didn't know him all that well, but he'd always liked him.

He'd seemed solid, yet distant in the very rare circumstances when Dair had been around Ned when he was a kid. Christmas holidays, the few times he stiltedly shared them with his wife and daughters when they were in England and Dair's family would come down on Boxing Day. Blake's birthday, which was during the summer holidays, and Ned would fly out.

More when they were older. The girls' graduations from high school. Alex's college graduation. Dair's ill-fated wedding (his mother had insisted on inviting Ned, probably partly because she liked him—mostly, Dair reckoned, because she knew Helena was sleeping with her husband, Helena was invited too, and Ned drove Helena around the bend). Also, Blake's aborted one.

Though, it was only this visit where Dair witnessed true warmth and love shared between the three of them.

Shite happened for a reason.

And he wasn't close enough to know for certain, but it seemed like Blake's wedding fiasco had a profound effect on the emotionally functioning members of that clan.

"Thanks, mate," he replied to Ned.

"When do you leave?"

"I suspect Mum's changing her plans in order to leave today. I may go with her. Though, I'd planned to stay a couple of days. I've never been to Arizona. Judge told me about some trails. We've made tentative plans to hit them."

"This is beautiful country. I hope you have the chance to enjoy it, but I can understand you wishing to see to your mother."

"Aye."

"If you stay, please come to dinner. Blake's very good in the kitchen."

Blake could cook?

This he had to experience.

"If I stay, you can be certain I'll be there."

"Not surprised," Ned said quietly, then in a normal tone, "Until then, Dair, thank you again for looking after my daughter, and I don't envy the day you're going to have today."

"It'll be had, then it'll be done."

"As it always is. Goodbye, Dair."

"See ye efter."

They hung up, Dair pulled on a shirt, nabbed his keycard and walked down the hall.

He knocked on Davi's door.

Nothing.

He banged on Davi's door.

"Shaddup! I'm up! I'm up!" she yelled from inside. "And tell Mum I'll be at breakfast!"

Dair smiled again, walked back to his room and texted his mother with that info.

The coffee and croissants arrived, and once the server got tipped and left, Dair went to the bathroom door.

He knocked and said through it, "Coffee."

He didn't get the chance to step away before the door swung open, and at what hit his eyes, he stood stock-still.

Blake looked like she'd just come from a spa.

Dramatic wedding makeup gone, a fresher, more natural look in its place. She was wearing a sleeveless jumper top in beige that had a mock turtleneck and slits at the sides that came all the way up under her arms. This with matching drawstring pants. Her feet were bare.

And her glorious mane was a mass of lush curls and waves dripping over her shoulders.

What she did not look was hungover.

She looked ready to do a photo shoot.

She glared at him like his simple existence ruined her day, something that tickled the fuck out of him, then she looked beyond him, and her amazing face lit up.

"Coffee!" she cried, skirted him and walked right to it.

Dair peered into his bathroom.

Her tote had exploded in there.

There was a spent towel shoved haphazardly on the rail, her gown was a rumpled pile on the floor, makeup, brushes, perfume, deodorant and other women's face shite was all over the basin.

Now he knew why the fucking thing weighed so much.

But there was something about her mess, God help him, that he liked.

This shook him.

Signe, his ex-wife, was a slob.

They'd had a housekeeper that came in once a week to clean, stock the kitchen, change the sheets and do the laundry.

Signe had wanted one that lived in.

The woman didn't work, and she had no hobbies, outside shopping and trying to one-up her girlfriends (who seemed more like fellow competitors) with how expensive her outfits and handbags could be. Why she couldn't tidy up after both of them between housekeeper visits, he had no idea. Especially when he was in season.

But for fuck's sake.

Blake's mess turned him on.

Jesus, he was in this deep.

He turned to see she was pouring coffee at the same time sucking back one of the two ice waters she'd ordered.

He walked her way as she put the coffeepot and water down to grab her cup.

"That's yours," she said, motioning to the other filled cup with her own.

He reached toward the sugar.

"I did it already, Dair," she said like she was chiding a child. "Two, right?"

Startled, he turned to her. "Ye ken how I take my coffee?"

She did an exaggerated eyeroll, adding a derisive squint. "You made a huge deal about starting to drink it when you were fourteen. To be certain we didn't forget you were all grown up, you kept ordering us all to get you a cup. Of course I know."

"That was over twenty years ago, lass."

She seemed concerned. "Have your preferences changed?"

"No."

Now she seemed annoyed.

"So…?" she let that trail irritably.

He picked up his cup and sipped it through yet another smile.

Blake retaining this knowledge didn't say casual acquaintances.

You didn't remember something that immaterial about someone you didn't give a shite about.

She caught his smile, let out a huff, grabbed a croissant and threw herself into the couch.

"I can take you to a rental place so you all have a car," she offered before she munched.

"We'll do that after breakfast," he replied, getting his own croissant and joining her on the couch.

She looked to her pastry then to him.

"Mum wants us at breakfast in her suite in about five minutes," he explained.

Her eyes widened and now she was openly panicked.

"Including me?" she asked.

"She expressly said, if ye were here, she wanted ye there."

"Why me?"

"Maybe because she's worried about your state of mind?"

"Mine?"

"Ye smacked the shite out of your own mother, hen," he said carefully.

She nibbled her croissant, looking away, and after she swallowed, said, "I did do that."

"You all right?" he asked.

She returned to him. "Yes. Why wouldn't I be?'

"Ye smacked the shite out of your own mother," he pointed out.

She waved her croissant around. "You'd think I'd be conflicted. And I am, just not detrimentally. Do I wish I hadn't done it? Yes. It was unhinged. Not a good look." She sipped her coffee and then, "I guess I had some pent-up shit to get out."

"That was lost on no one."

She pulled a face.

And he was again fucking smiling.

Her tone was different, gentler, when she said, "I think this breakfast should just be for the Wallaces."

He slid against the back of the couch closer to her and said in the same tone, "I ken it's asking a lot, but I think Mum should have what she wants to have right now, Blake."

"Blech. You're right," she said into her cup.

He knew he was.

He was just thrilled she was the kind of woman who knew it too.

Signe was a long time ago, but he'd learned a great deal from her. Lessons hard earned that he never forgot.

In this scenario, she would be gleeful she had something to sell to the gossip rags and dish about with her sister-competitors. His mother's feelings, or his for that matter, wouldn't factor.

Bottom line, a whisky wouldn't have been waiting for him after he got back from the car park.

Instead, Signe would have found a way to rescue her mobile from phone jail and be gabbing to anyone who would listen about what she just learned.

Time to move on.

"I called your dad and told him ye were good and with me."

She choked on her coffee and turned to him. "What?"

"Last time he saw ye, ye were pissed out of your brain and flirting with ten firemen."

"I wasn't flirting."

"All right. They were flirting with ye."

She smirked. "They were doing that."

He was the jealous type. He just was.

But it was hard to get jealous when a woman was hanging on you while ten men flirted with her, and she didn't give that first fuck.

"He invited me to dinner. You're cooking," he told her.

Another choke, this time on croissant.

"So ye ken, I dinnae like celery or squash of any kind," he kept fucking with her.

With that, she chomped down on her croissant while glaring at him.

What she didn't do was say she wasn't cooking for him.

With her in the right frame of mind to buck up against his next, he shared, "He's also worried your mother is going to make this mess messier."

She washed the croissant down with coffee and stated blithely, "Oh, she'll do that. Mum walked away from that scene humiliated. By you. Dad. Even Bally obviously picked the wife he'd been cheating on over Mum right in front of her face. She's totally going to be on the warpath." With that, she shot straight and exclaimed, "Oh shit!"

"What?"

She didn't explain.

She jumped up, put her coffee cup down, and raced to the bathroom.

Through the door, he saw her sweet, heart-shaped ass lovingly molded by the clingy jumper material of her pants because she was bent over, pawing through her tote.

She came out with her phone and scurried back into the room, saying, "I think I have enough charge."

She then poked at it, put it to her ear and started pacing.

Dair knew she connected with voicemail when she said, "Rix, it's Blake. If you haven't thought to do this already, get Alex's phone. Block Mum. She's sure to try to drag her into all this crazy. And if Mum's already texted or phoned, delete them. I'll explain everything to her when you guys get back." She took a breath and finished, "I won't call again. Have lots of fun. Bye."

She stabbed the phone screen, came to the couch and plopped down on it again.

"My mother," she groused.

"And my mother is expecting us about now," he replied.

Her shoulders fell.

"It'll be all right," he assured.

She was visibly unconvinced.

"Can I use your phone charger while we go see your mum?" she requested.

"Be my guest. It's on the nightstand."

She pushed up and went to plug in her phone.

When she came back, he had his keycard and his coffee.

She grabbed her coffee.

He grabbed her hand.

As he led her out of the room and down the hall, she didn't pull away.

And…

Aye.

No matter her cheek, fire and attitude, they were on the same page.

Completely.

CHAPTER SIX

FIND THE ONE

Blake

He'd put my bouquet in a bath of water in the basin.

Alasdair Wallace, the usually filthy, always rambunctious boy who'd turned into the bantering, life-consuming man, thought to put a bunch of pretty flowers in water.

My flowers.

The ones my sister gave to me.

This whole thing with him and me was crazy. Totally.

But I could not get that out of my head.

Because it was so damned sweet.

This, obviously, was my thought when we stopped at a door where the security latch was flipped so the door wouldn't fully close.

But Dair still knocked and waited for his mother's, "Come in," before he pushed it and guided us in.

And there Kenna was.

When I got older, and menopause put an extra twenty pounds on me, I wanted to look like her.

Bright, summery shirtdress with a same-material tie belt and three-quarter sleeves, accompanied by lovely Chloé ballet flats in blush.

Her gorgeous hair was in a side pony. Her makeup was understated.

She'd given up contacts years ago, and now she wore cute, thin-framed, cat's-eye glasses.

Okay, so her eyes were a bit puffy, as they would be.

But she was standing, back straight, totally put together, staring out the window, sipping tea when we arrived.

She turned to us.

And I wondered what the hell was wrong with Bally.

This woman was everything.

"Och, Blake," she greeted me with a small smile, setting aside her teacup in its saucer and holding both hands out to me.

I went to her, set my own cup aside and took her hands.

"Ye did beautifully yesterday, me bonny lass," she said.

Proof.

She'd always been so kind to me.

"Thanks, Kenna," I replied.

Okay.

Now what?

God, this was hard.

"How are you hanging in there?" I decided to ask on a squeeze of hands.

"Och, ye ken," she said, letting me go and turning to her son.

Boy, did I *ken*.

I watched as Dair bent to kiss his mother's cheek and I got pissed at how warm watching it made my belly feel.

So when his eyes came to me after he straightened, his lips twitched, like they always did when he caught me glaring at him. Like he thought it was funny that I thought he was insufferable, even when he wasn't being that at all.

"Help yourselves to food," Kenna invited with a vague wave toward a veritable breakfast smorgasbord laid out on her coffee table. "Who kens when Davina will rouse herself."

"We already had croissants so Blake could soak up the bottle and a half of vodka she consumed last night," Dair said, even as he was refilling both of our coffee cups.

"It wasn't a bottle and a half of vodka," I rejoined. "It was a martini. An *espresso* martini, so it was mostly espresso."

He brought my coffee to me, stopped close, and replied, "I know my way around a cocktail shaker, lass. It's mostly vodka and Kahlua. And you didnae have one, you had four."

"The first one didn't count. Rix spilled half of it."

His gray-blue eyes twinkled as he took a sip of coffee.

Lord, he was intolerable.

Though him saving my bouquet wasn't, but I wasn't going to think about that when he was vexing me.

I decided to cease conversing and drink more coffee.

"Then relax as we wait for Davina," Kenna bid. "But dinnae let the food go cold."

I'd scarfed down two migraine tablets and two Tylenol, cupping water from the bathroom faucet to do so, but one could say my stomach was still queasy, even with the croissant. So I sat on the couch, set my coffee aside and took a plate to fill it.

Dair sat down close to me and did the same, which meant he got in the way of what I was doing.

However, this didn't last long because he started to pile my plate with stuff that he was closer to, like bacon, some fried potatoes and fruit.

Since this seemed like a good system, I piled his with scrambled eggs and a biscuit.

"Jam?" I asked with the spoon hovering over the little pot.

"No marmalade?" he asked back.

"Your choice appears to be strawberry jam or strawberry jam," I informed him.

He shot me another of his unendurable grins. "Then I'll have strawberry jam."

I dolloped a healthy portion on his plate then scraped an even healthier portion of butter there.

"Lassie after my beating heart," he muttered when I shoved the butter knife back in the butter.

I stilled.

He sat back and started slathering butter on his biscuit.

I felt something funny, looked up and saw Kenna watching us.

She had an odd expression on her face, considering the circumstances.

She looked…

Happy.

"Has Dad been in touch?" Dair inquired around a mouthful of biscuit.

The happy vanished.

Oh my God!

What was he thinking?

He should ease into it.

I elbowed him.

He turned to me. "What?"

I lowered my voice and my chin and looked at him under my lashes. "Ease into it, why don't you?"

Kenna sank gracefully into one of the two armchairs across from us. "We're honest with each other in the Wallace family."

I inwardly cringed while she outwardly grimaced.

"Or, the three of us are," she amended.

"I'm so sorry, Kenna," I said, feeling stupid, because that was lame, but it was all I had.

"Dear, ye have nothing to be sorry for," she replied.

The door opened on her words, and Davina strutted in, long, dark hair wild, last night's makeup smeared (she needed a good setting spray), wearing men's boxer shorts and an oversized T-shirt.

I wanted to be the kind of woman who was confident enough to wander the halls of a hotel (even short halls, like the ones at this hotel) in boxer shorts and an oversized tee, but alas, I was not.

I felt weird just being barefoot, even if Dair was too, and now, so was Davina.

"Thank the Lord, coffee and food," she said before she came forward and all but fell on the coffee table.

We all watched as she piled as much food on her plate as both Dair and I had on ours, combined, and sat in the other armchair with the coffee cup tucked between her knees and the plate close to her face.

She looked to me after she noshed on some bacon. "I hate ye. How are ye glamorous after last night?" and she munched more bacon.

"I had a tote bag filled with anything a bride or bridesmaid might need," I explained.

"I could pack for Scotland in the Olympics, and it's all across the hall, and I dinnae look like you."

You didn't wake up next to a hot, ex-professional rugby player, I thought but did not say.

"We're all invited to Ned's tonight for dinner," Dair announced. "Blake is cooking."

One would think he couldn't get more unbearable, but apparently, he could.

"Ye cook?" Davi asked through some potatoes.

"It's a hobby," I said self-consciously.

"What are we having?" Davi questioned while shoving a torn-off piece of biscuit in her mouth.

I trained a pointed look at Dair.

"Ye can't go wrong with steak," he suggested through a playful smile that was playful because he read my pointed look and decided to mistake it.

I turned back to the others. "Whatever it is, it'll be vegetarian."

Davina burst out laughing.

Kenna managed a miniscule, but authentic, smile.

His tone was vastly different when he asked, "You're not going home, Mum?"

She sipped tea then stated, "I took some time to think, and I dinnae see why my holiday in The States should be curtailed due to your father's actions."

"Go, Mum," Davi encouraged.

Kenna checked her slim, gold watch and shared, "And he'll be here in ten minutes."

Davi gagged.

Dair growled, "The fuck he will."

I pressed my lips together and sunk deep into the corner of the couch.

Kenna ignored both her children and said, "I can imagine ye understand why I'll be filing for divorce when I return home."

"Aye, we can understand it," Davi replied. "But, Mum, why is Dad coming here?"

"So he can get his things, of course." Another sweep of her hand and we all looked at the large suitcase sitting neatly by the door. "And I can share with him that he'll need to stay in the flat in Edinburgh and make an appointment with me to come and get his things from the house. Also, so my two children can say what ye wish to say to him."

"I can tell him he can go fuck himself and I'm on your side in a text," Davi declared.

"Darling, he's your father, and you'll eventually get over this," Kenna returned.

"Aye? Ye think?" Davi asked sarcastically, then answered herself. "I dinnae."

"And ye wanted Blake here for this trauma…why?" Dair asked, and his tone made my attention dart to him.

Yes.

He was ticked at his mother if him scowling ferociously at her was any indication.

"Mostly so I could ascertain she was well after all that happened last night," Kenna answered.

"And partly so he'll behave himself, which he wouldn't do if she wasn't around," Dair tacked on.

Kenna's shoulders stiffened in affront. "I'm not using Blake as a shield."

"But ye ken he's gonna show, full of bluster, and act the dick to save face," Dair kept at her. "And with Blake here, he'll temper that, get his shite and go."

"Honestly, Alasdair, I have no idea what your father will do," Kenna said coldly. "I never could quite understand the way he behaved. Sadly, I loved him. No, I adored him. And even knowing it's over, I still do. So, although many things he did were things I did not like, I stayed with him. Not anymore."

I unburied myself from the side of the sofa to wrap my fingers around Dair's muscled knee.

He looked to me.

"Even if I was here as a shield, which I'm not," I said softly, "I wouldn't mind."

"This is your trauma, along with all of ours," he returned. "We dinnae need to add to it."

"This is Kenna's trauma, Dair. I know you feel it. And so does Davina. But what you feel is not the same at all," I replied. "Not even close."

He pulled breath in through his nose, and when he released it, he nodded and seemed less tense.

This, unfortunately, communicated loads to me. That he listened. That he processed what he heard. That he understood. That he wasn't obstinate and had the ability to stand down. Even in an emotionally volatile situation.

Damn, I didn't need to know all of this about Alasdair Wallace.

I took my hand from his knee and returned my attention to the women.

They were both staring at Dair's knee, Davi with an incredulous, elated expression, and Kenna with an incredulous, peaceful one (yes, those didn't seem like they could work together, but they did).

"I can't speak for everyone," I broke their weird fascination with Dair's knee and got their focus. "But whatever you need from me, Kenna."

"She likes steak," Davi said before popping a grape into her mouth.

That made me laugh.

Things seemed less tense after all of that, and we ate and drank coffee (or tea), and waited for the next ordeal to knock on the door.

I didn't have a very good internal clock (probably why I was late too often), but I'd gauge Bally was late too since my estimate was that a good fifteen minutes passed before that knock came.

We were all done eating, thus we were only sipping.

Kenna opened her mouth, but she shut it, her gaze following her son as he unfurled his long body from the couch and prowled to the door.

Prowling, stalking, the man could move.

Lord.

He opened the door.

Bally jolted when he saw him.

"Mum's divorcing you," Dair declared, and I closed my eyes.

Men.

Or rather, protective sons.

I opened them when he kept talking.

"You're to stay in Edinburgh. She'll let ye ken when ye can come and get your shite from the house." He took hold of the suitcase and rolled it into his father's legs. "Now ye can take this and go."

"I'd like to speak to my wife," Bally said through his teeth.

Dair didn't move from barring the door, but he did turn his head to look at his mum.

"Ye interested in anything he has to say?" he queried.

"Actually…no," she replied, like she just had that thought.

"Kenna—" Bally started, trying to push in.

Dair butted chests with him. "Not another step."

Oh boy.

I prepared to stand up and intervene.

Bally attempted to look beyond him and said to Kenna, "I'd like the chance to explain."

I knew Dair was winding up to reply, but Kenna stood and called, "Dair."

He looked at his mother again, hesitated two very long, excruciating beats, and stepped aside, a muscle dancing up his cheek.

Shoving the suitcase out of the way, Bally took two steps in.

Dair closed the door.

"Please, in front of your family,"—Kenna spread her hands before her—"explain."

But Bally spied me, so he requested politely, "Lass, can I have some privacy with my family?"

Even though I wasn't sure I should leave with Dair in his current mood, I moved to stand.

Dair stated, "She's not going anywhere."

I stopped moving.

"No offense, son," Bally said to Dair. "But this is Wallace business."

"And you're a Wallace. And you've been thrusting your cock in her mother for decades. Think she's earned her place on that couch."

Bally's ruddy cheeks got ruddier as he held his son's gaze. "This is private business, and should be private, even from you."

"It wasn't private when I saw you fucking her in our stables," Dair shot back.

Oh shit.

Kenna gasped.

Davi audibly gulped.

"And it wasn't private when Blake saw you going at it with her mother in the hall in Treverton," Dair carried on. He then added, "She was no more than ten."

Bally paled.

Kenna sank back in her chair.

"Ye catch 'em?" Dair asked Davina.

"Not doing the deed, just kissing," Davi said in a small voice.

Her small voice, which was so not Davi, served to enrage Dair.

This led to his tone being hard and tight, and his affect being mildly terrifying (and it was only mildly because his fury was not aimed at me) when he demanded, "So…explain. Tell us why ye put us through this. Why ye broke Mum's heart. Find those words, Dad. We're waiting to hear them."

Bally swallowed and then started, "A man—"

And with that, not that he had that firm of a hold on it, Dair lost it. Entirely.

Spiking toward his father, he shouted, "Fuck that! Bloody fuck that fucking *shite*!"

"Step back, son," Bally said in a shaky voice.

Dair did not step back.

"All my fucking life, you've drilled into me, the last thing ye wanted me to be was a weak man." He reared back only to thump his chest like a caveman. "Real men hunt. Real men dress their own game. Real men play rugby, not football. Real men have a natural seat on a horse. Real men belch after a good meal as a compliment to the chef and can drink their weight in whisky." He got in his dad's face again and continued,

"Real men *provide*. Real men *protect*. Real men gather as much pussy as they can *before* they find the one, but when they do, they cherish her. Did ye cherish Mum while ye were fucking Helena, Dad? Is that what ye were doing?"

"I-I've disappointed you." Bally turned to look at Kenna and Davina. "I've disappointed you all."

"Did ye aye, Dad," Davi sneered.

"I think perhaps, at this time, you might wish to take your leave, Bally," Kenna suggested.

"We'll talk," Bally said quickly. "When we're all home, as a family, once it's not as fresh, we'll talk."

"It isn't fresh, Dad. You've been doing her for decades," Davi said. "We're all just tired of pretending we dinnae think you're an arsehole for doing it."

Bally took that hit and looked wretched.

I didn't feel bad for him.

In fact, I thought every man who broke a woman's heart and shattered a family should have to go through much the same thing.

"Blake—" Bally started, his attention coming to me, and I tensed.

But then Dair was blocking his view of me and growling, "Dinnae even fuckin' look at her."

Good Lord.

My belly warmed again as my gaze pinged from Kenna (who was studying her lovely flats, but her mouth was curved up) to Davina, who was openly grinning as she examined her fingernails.

Okay, okay, okay.

Seriously!

What was happening?

"Bolt," Dair grunted to his father.

"I understand why you're upset with me, Alasdair," Bally said quietly. "It guts me I did that to ye. To all of ye."

"Stop fucking havering," Dair gritted. "And *bolt*."

There were several very tense moments before movement resumed at the door. I couldn't see much with Dair's big body in the way. Though I did see the door open, I heard the wheels on a bag wheeling, and the door shut.

For good measure, but unnecessarily, Dair slapped the security latch closed before he stalked back to the couch and threw himself on it.

I would have bounced, but he was sitting so close to me, he was nigh on sitting *on* me, so he kept me in place.

Whereupon he muttered to himself many words, only a few of which I caught, and they included "bawbag," "arsepiece," and "fuckin' walloper." Although I could put two and two together and understand what those words meant (loosely), it gave me the impression he was curbing his Scottish considerably while talking with me. Seemed they all were, which was kind of sweet.

When he was down to trying to make his coffee cup explode with his eyes, I touched his arm and whispered, "Hey."

He looked to me.

"It's over. And I'll make steaks tonight."

For a second, it seemed like he no longer comprehended English.

That second passed and he smiled his audacious smile.

"Good to hear it, lassie."

Did I just play into his hands?

Well, whatever.

Kenna liked steak too, so did Dad, therefore we were having that with hasselback potatoes, roasted brussels sprouts and bakery rolls. I wasn't going to make the rolls from scratch because I was going to make dessert. My vanilla cake.

All sorted, I snuggled back into my corner of the couch and asked the room, "Now, who all is going to the rental car place with me and Dair?"

"Give me a chance to shower, and I'm in," Davi said.

"I'm going to wander around the square. From what I could see, it looks like there are some lovely shops and Chloe said she had one there," Kenna said.

"I've got to shower too. Half an hour?" Dair asked his sister.

"Ye do ken I have a vagina, dinnae ye?" she asked back.

"You've tried all your life, ye can't make me retch," he returned. "Forty-five?"

She refilled her cup and wandered to the door saying, "I'll be ready when I'm ready."

The door snicked shut behind her.

Dair looked to me. "Keep Mum company."

I smiled. "Of course."

His eyes dropped to my mouth.

My stomach dropped entirely.

"Thanks, hen," he whispered, leaned in, kissed my cheek (my cheek! what was *that*?), angled out of the couch and sauntered away.

"Now, Blake," Kenna said, leaning forward to finally partake of the food, "you've been here often. Which shops shouldn't I miss?"

I shared all the places she could go (definitely Chloe's casual, with some outdoor wear for the stylish set shop was one of them).

And I took her pulse (she didn't hide the sad, but she seemed to be holding up) as we waited for the Wallace kids to shower and get ready.

CHAPTER SEVEN

AWESOME

Dair

Dair's hair was damp, and he was still rolling up the sleeve of his shirt as he walked down the hall to his mother's room.

That morning, once they'd secured their car, Blake had rushed off, saying something about her urgent need to get to the grocery store.

He'd dropped Davi off at the square so she could find their mum, and he'd gone into the hotel and changed clothes, then met Judge for a five-mile hike.

Ned had been correct.

This country was beautiful.

After their hike, he and Judge shared a beer at Judge's house, and Dair again got to spend time with their wee bonny son JT, who Chloe referred to solely as Jimmy, although no one else did.

He'd kicked it home when Blake texted her address (along with three scrolls' worth of directions, something that made him chuckle). After she did, he'd Googled it and realized he didn't have a lot of time to get back, shower, change, collect his mum and sister, and get to Ned and Blake's.

As he walked down that hall, according to Google directions, they'd needed to leave two minutes ago.

And he was keen to get there, for more reasons than just the promise of steak.

His head had been a fucking mess all day. Shitty thoughts of his father, mother and Helena mingling with much better thoughts of Blake. Her hair. Her clothes. Her shite all over his bathroom. Even the way her nails were done, in short almond shapes with a sheer pink over white tips. They were feminine, but not garish. Classy. Stylish.

Blake.

And she could dig in and hold on with those nails.

On this thought and a quirk of his lips, he knocked on his mother's door.

"Come in!" she called.

He came in and immediately flipped back the latch that kept it open. He understood why she did that knowing he was on his way, but if he was otherwise engaged, like away or in the shower, he didn't like it.

His mum was rushing around.

Davina was sitting in an armchair and her attention came right to him.

"I'm almost ready," his mum said as she disappeared into the bathroom.

He lifted his brows to his sister.

She shook her head.

Fuck.

He went to the open door of the bathroom to see his mother bent over the basin, looking in the mirror and putting on lipstick.

"Good day?" he asked.

She popped her lips together twice then turned to him. "This is a lovely town." He got out of her way as she bustled out of the bathroom. "Many fine restaurants. Bonny shops, lovely jewelry, fantastic art. And Chloe's store is fabulous. I waited for Davi to join me, and we had fun there."

She said all of this and didn't look at him once.

She was shoving her lipstick in her purse when he called, "Mum."

She clicked her purse shut. "There. Done. We can go."

"Mum," he repeated.

She finally looked to him.

Jesus.

He went to her and pulled her in his arms.

She began to push away but he only held her closer.

She relaxed into him, circled him with her arms and shoved her face in his shoulder.

"Ye dinnae have to go," he said into the side of her hair.

She tipped her head back and caught his gaze. "I'm fine."

"We can get room service here and spend time together. We dinnae get to do that much," he offered. When she was about to reply, he tacked on, "Blake will understand. Ye ken she will. So will Ned."

Her chin grew stubborn, she pulled firmly out of his hold, and she declared, "I'll not lose another moment of my life pining over my own husband."

Dair glanced at Davina.

She shrugged.

His mother drew him back when she spoke.

"I appreciate ye both looking after me, and I will not lie and say my heart isn't broken. It is. But it has been for years. I've wasted enough time and emotion on your father. If I can, I'll waste no more."

Dair sighed.

"Your choice, Mum," he said.

"So we should go," his mother replied.

He nodded.

His sister got up, grabbed her bag, and they left.

They were in the car and on their way when his mum brought it up.

"What's going on between ye and Blake?"

"Not certain yet," he lied.

Davina made a *pfft* sound in the backseat.

Dair smiled.

"I hope ye ken what you're getting into, son," his mother said.

"And what's that, in your estimation?" he asked curiously.

"She's a beautiful girl, always was. Then again, so is her mother."

Bloody hell.

"But Helena did a number on her two daughters," she continued. "Alex escaped as fast as she could. Even when she was young, Alex was only there physically and only that when she had to be. Blake bore the brunt of it. Perhaps because she was firstborn, and more was expected of her. She got crushed under it and had to act out to assert herself in some manner."

"She's not the woman she used to be, Mum," Davi piped up from the back seat.

"No, I ken. That's clear enough." He felt her eyes on him when she said, "But damage was done."

"Like what Dad did to us?" Davi asked angrily.

He shot his sister a look in the rearview mirror telling her to shut her gob.

Davi returned a mutinous expression and carried on, "Boys and their dads are a thing. Dinnae think ye missed how ragin Dair got with him."

Dair knew his mother was addressing the side window when she said, "It pains me to know ye three all saw them, and how ye did."

Enough of this shite.

"I suggest none of us take on Dad's fuckups," he stated. "It isn't on any of us. Dinnae worry, I dinnae think I'll turn into him because I spent most of my life not respecting the man and understanding I didnae want to be like him."

His mother made a noise, and the sound of it wounded him, but this had to be said.

"Doesn't mean he wasn't a good father. He was tough on me, but I never doubted his love, like Blake had to do with Helena. I'm angry at Dad. We all are. He deserves it. We'll get through it, though. No clue what's on the other side, but we'll get through it. And Mum, you aren't missing anything. There's something between Blake and me. We'll be exploring it. I ken she's been through it. I'll have a mind. But we're both adults. Ye have enough to worry about, dinnae worry about that."

"Ye make a bonny couple, love," his mother said. "And I like the way she is with ye. Seems settled in her skin when she's with ye."

Fuck, he liked that.

"You're like an old married couple already," Davi added. "It's hilarious."

"You have years of history," Mum said quietly. "I like that. It's a good foundation."

Left unsaid, nothing like what he had with Signe, who his mother had detested. She'd seen beyond the hair, makeup and love bombing, whereas Dair had been thinking with his cock, something Signe was very good at sucking.

It ended up being beneficial that Blake sent copious directions even if they had GPS on their phones. He noticed landmarks she mentioned on the winding road way up in the mountains, and because of Blake, he didn't miss the almost hidden turn off to the steep descent of a drive to the house.

But he caught it, and they wound down an attractive lane that had two sides of natural pine and boulders until they hit the house.

And...

Bloody hell.

"Ned Sharp always had good taste," his mum said when the big structure nestled in the woods became visible before them.

She was right.

The modern, flat-roofed home made of stone and glass was all right angles with fantastic lighting. Even with that ultra-contemporary design, it seemed innate in its surroundings, with its landscaping of green grasses and red dirt.

The sun wasn't close to going down, but the house was so deeply ensconced in the shadow of the pines, it was lit within already, adding its lot to the warm glow of the Arizona sunshine.

Dair parked at the bottom of the long, straight row of red, flagstone steps that led to a two-story wall of windows edged in stone.

They were about to get out when they saw Ned at the top of the stairs gesturing to the side.

"Hold," Dair ordered and drove around where they found another path that led up to the house, this one winding, not straight, and wound among more boulders, grass and subtle garden lighting.

At the top of these stairs was Blake.

She'd taken off the jumper outfit and was wearing a black tank dress that had a twist at the midriff, cutout sides and slits at the hem on either side. She wore thongs on her feet with a bow at the toes so big, he could see it from where he sat in their car.

Her hair was a luxurious mass of ebony tumbling over her shoulders.

He felt one side of his lips hitch up as he shut down the vehicle and climbed out.

He escorted his mother up the steps, Davi trailing, and Ned had made it around to their side by the time they cleared the top.

"So glad you came," he greeted, going right to Kenna.

"Och, Ned, this house is extraordinary," his mum replied as she accepted a kiss on her cheek.

"When we understood we'd be out here often, especially when my grandchildren start arriving, I commissioned it from Remy Gastineau," Ned told her, going in to greet Davi.

"Heya, hen," he murmured to Blake, bending to brush his lips along her cheek, and he decided this time to make a wider sweep and ended with them at her ear.

He also had a hand to her waist, so he felt her shiver.

Therefore, he was smiling when he pulled away.

She gave him a murderous look. Or she aimed it at his ear.

His smile grew.

She moved to greet his mother and sister as his mum said, "Remy

Gastineau. Impressive. Wasn't he at the wedding?"

"The Gastineaus are family friends," Ned said. "Now come in, let's get you some drinks."

"No happier words ever spoken," Davi put in.

They trooped inside and it was a tossup if the outside was better than the interior.

High ceilings paneled in wood. Stone walls. Block wood mantelpiece over the fireplace. Inviting furniture in leather or cream. Lots of pillows. A circular coffee table made of a beautifully rendered block of wood. An attractive but sturdy poof even Dair wouldn't hesitate to sit on. Ivory rug under the furniture but over hardwood floors with a taupe design reminiscent of Native American art. Creamy, downy throw blankets to cuddle under. Views everywhere of the understated landscaping made by man leading to the glory of God's personal hand.

It was summer, and hot outside, but cool inside, and they had a fire going which gave a very cozy house an even cozier feel.

He could spend a week here.

No.

He could move here and feel at peace, at home. It had a great atmosphere, welcoming and comfortable, but fantastic to look at.

"Does Gastineau do interior design?" Davi asked as Ned moved to an inlay in the wall that was clearly the bar seeing as it held sparkling glasses, a glass and gold filled ice bucket, window-fronted wine and beverage fridge and more.

"The interior is all Blake," Ned stated proudly.

Stunned, Dair's attention shot to Blake, whose perfect peaches and cream skin now had more than a hint of pink to it as she studied the bows on her shoes.

She lifted her head in a jerky manner.

"Dad, take care of the drinks," she said. "I'll just run and get the hors d'oeuvres."

"I dinnae know what that smell is, love, but I can't wait to taste it," Kenna told her.

Blake shot what looked like a nervous smile his mother's way before she ducked out of the room.

"I'll help her," Dair said.

"I bet you will," Davi mumbled.

He ignored his sister and answered Ned's inquiry of, "What can I make while you do?"

"A cold ale would be good, if you've got it."

Ned nodded.

Dair followed Blake.

The kitchen was as fantastic as the living room. He was a man who liked to cook, and he would be very happy doing it here.

He nearly missed a step when he saw the tall cake with swirls of thick, piped, butter-colored icing on an attractive wooden cake stand on the edge of the kitchen island. He could see the wee, tempting flecks of vanilla beans in the frosting.

"Did ye make that?" he asked and watched her jump up from bending over the oven.

She glanced at the cake then went back to the oven.

"Vanilla cake," was all she said.

"Looks amazing, lass," he told her.

"Thanks," she mumbled, pulling out two trays.

One, crab stuffed mushroom tops. The other, bacon wrapped dates.

When Ned said Blake could cook, he wasn't fucking about.

"Looks great," he told her.

"I'll be out in a minute," she said to the trays as she moved food from them to large, round, wooden plates.

"I'm here to help."

"I've got it."

Like his mother earlier, he realized then, she hadn't looked him in the eye since he got there. Even her murderous look had been directed at his ear.

"All right?" he asked.

"Really, Dair, I've got it," she said, still transferring mushrooms.

He put his hand to the small of her back.

She shot straight and turned to him.

"What's up?" he pushed.

"Nothing," she lied. He could see it in her eyes.

"Blake.'

"Can you ask Dad to make me a martini and kill the vermouth?"

"What's up?" he repeated.

She tried to turn away from him, snapping, "Nothing, Dair."

He put his fingers to her jaw and turned her head his way.

She yanked from his touch.

Oh, aye.

Something was wrong.

"Have I upset you?" he asked.

"No," she bit out. "*You* haven't."

"Then who has?"

"I don't want to talk about it." She finished with the mushrooms and went to the dates.

"Blake, you've obviously worked very hard on dinner. Talk to me so ye can enjoy the night, as ye should."

She transferred dates and said nothing.

He waited.

"If you're not going to leave, there's some fruit in the fridge. Please get it," she requested.

He located the fridge and grabbed the bowls of clean, plump grapes and fat strawberries.

He brought them to her.

She took them and dotted the fruit artistically around the other pieces.

But as she concentrated intensely on her task, he could see her lip trembling, an indication she was holding back emotion.

"Darling," he whispered.

She suddenly threw a strawberry onto the plate.

It bounced off and rolled across the island as she turned to him.

"Mum has evicted me."

"Come again?" he said low and slow.

"She's already in New York and she's hired movers to pack me. She's dumping my stuff at Dad's."

That was when she lost control of her emotions, her exquisite face crumbled, and she burst into tears.

Fucking Helena.

He pulled her into his arms. "Shh, love. It's not like you don't have somewhere to go."

She yanked out of his hold, took two steps back, threw hers to her sides and exploded, "I do! But I don't! It's *Dad's place*. Not mine! *Nothing* is *mine*."

"Baby," he murmured, already knowing something was troubling her, but this was far deeper than he expected.

"I don't have a job. I don't have a house. I don't have *anything*. I'm not *anything*."

Now Dair was angry.

"Dinnae say that shite," he growled.

"Okay, so I have a trust fund, and it's huge. I could buy my own place. But that's money *somebody else* made." She flung up an arm. "Alex has a good job. She's a director at a charity. She does good work. She helps people. She doesn't have to work, but she does it anyway. Dad doesn't have to work either. He never did. He still does and he's good at it. He's made the *piles* of Sharp money into *mountains* of it. Me?" She shook her head. "I'm thirty-four years old and I've accomplished *nothing*."

"You made that cake," he pointed out.

It was the wrong thing to say, he knew, when her eyes turned to slits and she snapped, "Shut up, Dair."

"It's a beautiful cake, lassie," he returned.

"Big deal."

"It will be for us when we eat it. Mum's world crashed around her last night, and tonight, she's eating cake. And that shite." He gestured to the platter. "Which looks great and smells better. But ye working so hard on it will mean everything to her. She'll remember you and your father's, but especially *your* kindness in this time of her life for the rest of it."

She bit her lip and sniffed.

He kept at her.

"If ye did up this house, you're fucking good at it. Ye planned your sister's wedding within every quarter hour, and she had a day that was nothing to her but loving and being loved in return while you were running around arranging grass."

"Dair—"

"Ye dinnae have to make money to be worth anything. My mum hasn't worked a day in her life."

"She raised two children."

"And she's raised millions for charity," he retorted. "She made a home. She made my father look good through entertaining." He aimed a pointed glance at the platter. "There's worth to time spent doing those things."

She licked her lips and stared at the platter like she'd never seen it before.

He got her attention again when he bit out, "Fuck your mother and fuck her flat. Your father adores you. He'll be happy you're home for a spell while ye decide where ye want to land."

"God!" she cried. "Stop doing that!"

Dair was confused. "Doing what?"

"Being all...all..."—another arm fling, this one in front of her indicating him—"*you*."

"Sorry?"

"Why are you so awesome?"

He felt his body jerk in surprise.

Then he smiled again, but this one came very slow.

He took a step to her.

She took a step back.

"What are you doing?' she asked unsteadily.

"Ye think I'm awesome?"

"Oh God," she breathed in a panic.

His smile didn't waver.

He took another step forward.

She took one back.

"Is everything okay?" Ned asked from behind them.

Fucking shite.

"Yes!" Blake chirped fake cheerily, hopping forward to rescue the strawberry. She tucked it on the platter, picked it up and shoved it into his hands. "You take that in." She craned her neck to look beyond him. "Dad, can I have a martini?"

"Already shaken, darling," he said.

"Before those get cold, Dair," she ordered, tipping her head to the platter.

"We're not done talking, lassie."

"I need to open the wine to breathe for dinner. Go."

He didn't move.

"Go!" she snapped. "I didn't toil over wrapping dates with bacon for it to be cold and gross when people ate it."

That got him moving.

But he did it saying, "After dinner, you're coming back to the hotel with me."

She didn't respond.

Even so.

After dinner, she was coming back to the hotel with him.

They were going to talk.

And he didn't intend to bring her home when they were done.

IT HAPPENED AFTER THE THIRD TIME HE REACHED UNDER THE TABLE to take her hand and Blake pulled away.

Ned was at the head.

Blake at the foot.

Kenna was to Ned's right, Dair next to his mother, seated to Blake's left.

Davi was across from them.

By the by, Blake hadn't served them steak.

Oh no.

She served them a perfectly roasted prime rib with crisp, perfectly seasoned hasselback potatoes and the tenderest brussels sprouts he'd ever tasted, the bonus being they were coated with balsamic glaze.

He'd had meals in Michelin Star restaurants he hadn't enjoyed as much.

But his mother noticed everything. It had been the bane of his existence all of his life.

Now it was going to be the bane of Blake's.

That and Kenna's bluntness and honesty.

"I'm sorry," she said shortly. "I heard the raised voices earlier. You're likely to think it's none of my business. However, if it isn't, perhaps ye two should go somewhere and talk out your issue."

"Mum," Davi said low, proving she hadn't missed Blake's actions either, "stay out of it."

"Blake's not mad at me," Dair announced. "She's upset her mother evicted her."

Kenna pulled in a shocked breath.

Angry color came to Ned's face, and he asked, "I'm sorry?"

Fuck.

She hadn't told her father yet.

Something that didn't need to be confirmed was, when Blake slapped his arm and snapped, "*Now*, I'm mad at you."

"Sorry, baby," he muttered.

"She can't do that," Ned stated.

"Well, Dad, she has," Blake said on a sigh. "I was going to tell you tomorrow. I was busy with doing food prep while managing a hangover. I didn't have time to be angry and throw a tantrum. She's having my things moved home." A hesitation and then, "I won't stay long. It's time I found my own place anyway."

"That *is* your place," Ned said.

Blake nodded. "Yes. I know. I've been living there for years and she's hardly ever there. But it's still hers."

"No, darling, that apartment belongs to the Norton estate," Ned explained.

An electric vibe sizzled over the table.

"You are a Coddington," Ned went on. "Heir to the title. She can't keep you out of something you, in essence, own along with her."

Blake said nothing.

Ned angrily tossed his napkin on the table, ground out, "Excuse me for a moment," and stormed out of the room.

"Dad!" Blake called.

Ned didn't stop.

"Excuse me," Blake said, tossing her own napkin to the table, getting up and rushing after her father.

Dair didn't hesitate to move even if his mother and sister exchanged an uncertain glance.

He caught up with her and walked beside her to what was clearly Ned's office.

He had his phone to his ear.

Dair felt his family come up behind them (because, of course curiosity sent them following).

"Yes, it's me," Ned snarled into the phone. "Now, if you don't want yourself embroiled in a massive lawsuit, you will cease packing Blake's things this fucking *instant*. You don't have the privilege of removing her from a family property. And if you fight back on this, the Norton estate will not fund your legal fees, which will be inconvenient for you, considering you ran through the settlement I gave you decades ago."

He paused to listen, but he didn't pause pacing with agitation, though he stopped when he spoke again.

"Oh yes, Helena, I am *very* familiar with the terms of the Norton title, and the entire British peerage system, for this very reason. You are precisely the kind of woman who would use any means necessary to act out against or harm our children to get your way or to strike back. And here you are, doing just that. But I'll not have it. I believe, during our divorce, you learned not to go against me. I suggest you call that lesson up now. If Blake wants to move out, Blake can move out *when* she wishes to do so. What she will *not* do is be *put out* simply because you're pissy that your lover shared his true feelings for you, and those are that you were nothing but an easy lay."

Davi snorted.

Blake choked back a giggle.

Kenna whispered, "Oh my."

Suddenly, Ned's back shot straight.

There was a loaded pause before he said, "Do your worst."

Then he hung up.

"Fuck," he muttered before he dragged his fingers through his hair and turned around.

"You didn't have to do that, Daddy," Blake said.

And Christ, she called him daddy when she was being sweet.

It was cute.

But it was inconvenient.

Dair liked to be daddy.

"Though, that was epic," she continued.

"I've been seeing a woman named Marlo for some time," Ned said on a rush.

Blake's frame froze solid.

Dair went to her and pressed his hand to her back.

"She means a great deal to me. Your mother knows. She also knows I haven't told you girls. And she intends to share it with you. Your phone is probably ringing right now," Ned finished.

"Why didn't you tell us?" Blake asked in a small voice.

"Perhaps we should—" his mother started.

"We were building our family back up again, darling," Ned said softly. "I wanted you girls to have my full attention."

"She means a great deal to you?" Blake asked.

"Yes," Ned pushed out. "A *great* deal."

"And your daughter just got married and you didn't invite her?" Blake's tone was now sharp.

Oh hell.

"Lassie," Dair murmured.

Her head whipped toward him. "Fuck that, Dair." She returned to her father. "How did this Marlo feel about that?"

"It upset her," Ned admitted.

"I'll fucking bet!" Blake near on shouted.

"We'll leave you to—" his mother tried again.

"Don't shout at me, Blake," Ned ordered. "As disappointed as Marlo was, I made the right decision. I put other things before my daughters their whole lives. That had to stop. You're my priorities."

"Well, newsflash, *daddy*,"—ah, Christ, that "daddy" wasn't near as nice—"*you* are *our* priority too." She slammed her hands on her hips and yelled, "Oh my God! You froze out your girlfriend from Alex's wedding. You're never going to come back from that!"

"Marlo understands," Ned asserted.

"How long have you been seeing her?" Blake demanded.

"A while," Ned hedged.

"How long?" Blake pushed.

"Over a year."

Oh fuck.

"*What?*" Blake shrieked.

Dair pressed harder into her back.

"Blake—" Ned began.

"You've been seeing her *over a year?*" Blake asked.

"Yes," Ned confirmed.

"So, is she upset or is she pissed?" Blake demanded.

"Pissed," Ned confessed.

"As she should be. As am I!" Blake was being loud again. "Call her. Ask her to fly out immediately."

"She works, darling," Ned said. "She can't drop everything and fly out here."

"What does she do?"

"She's the Executive Fashion Editor at *Millicent.*"

With what was wafting off Blake, Dair had the urge to step back.

Instead, he positioned behind her and curled his fingers around her hips in case she physically lost it.

"You're telling me you've been keeping your girlfriend, the Executive Fashion Editor of the greatest fashion magazine *ever*, from me?" Blake asked in a deceptively quiet voice. Then she screeched, "*Me?*"

"It had to be the right time to tell you both," Ned defended himself.

"And when would that be? The next millennium?" Blake returned.

Ned's jaw grew hard. "I did what I thought was right."

"Well, Dad, it was *wrong*. Phone her. Tell her I want to meet her. Alex will too. I mean, *seriously?*"

"I'm pleased this is your response," Ned said.

"And what did you think it would—?" Blake cut herself off and then she spoke snidely. "Oh, I know. You thought I'd throw a fit. Blake Sharp, up to her old tricks again."

Dair dug his fingers into her flesh.

"Of course not," Ned bit.

"So? Why? Over a year, Dad? *Why?*" she pushed.

"Because I was enjoying our time!" Ned shouted.

Blake stilled.

"I found the woman meant for me not long after I came to the realization I'd been a shit father and I needed to stand up for my girls!" Ned kept shouting. "You've bloomed into something extraordinary. Rix makes Alex happy. You girls love spending time together. I love spending time with you. But I also love to be with Marlo. What do I do? Which one of you do I disappoint?"

"Daddy, you being happy and spending time with a woman who you care about would never disappoint me or Alex," Blake said softly.

"Marlo is a good woman. Sharp. Clever. Talented. Kind. Beautiful. But we've finally built something priceless, you girls and me. I didn't want anything to disturb it," Ned replied.

"Oh, Daddy!" Blake cried, pulled from Dair's hold, rushed to her father and threw herself in his arms. After they held on for a while, Dair heard her say, "You must phone her. Tell her you told me. Tell her I'm annoyed with you for keeping her from me. And we'll do lunch or something when we get home."

"I'd love that, darling."

Crisis over, Dair moved to leave them to it, and when he did, he saw his mother and sister had already left.

He joined them at the dining room table.

They both stared at him.

He picked up his cutlery and continued eating.

"Are they all right?" Davi asked.

"As rain," Dair answered after swallowing potato that had soaked up au jus.

It was going on cold, but it was still fucking fantastic.

"I must say," his mother started, "it's quite a feat."

"What is?" Davi asked.

"How Blake handpicked all the good parts of her to keep, and held tight, and binned all the parts her mother gave her." Kenna lifted her fork with some beef to her mouth, chewed it, swallowed it and concluded, "She's quite something."

She absolutely was.

Blake and Ned returned and took their seats.

"My apologies for the melodrama," Ned said.

"Och, Ned, you've made my month by calling Helena an easy lay," Kenna said.

Ned's lips curved up.

"We shouldn't have followed," Kenna went on.

"Then you would have missed the good part," Ned drawled. He

drew a line under it when he asked, "Did you save room for Blake's vanilla cake? Or, after we finish here, shall we adjourn to the living room for digestifs and give our stomachs time to settle?"

"I couldn't eat another bite," Davi said even while she popped a piece of roll into her mouth. "But I'm not missing vanilla cake. Or a digestif."

"We'll play Ticket to Ride," Ned said.

"God, Dad, *no*. You smash everyone at that game every time," Blake returned. Then to the table, she declared, "It drives Rix up the wall."

"Ticke to Ride?" Kenna asked.

"It's a board game," Ned told her.

Blake Sharp played board games?

Fuck, the woman just got better and better.

"Which is why we should play it," Ned said to his daughter. "Give you another shot to knock me off my winning streak."

"If it's a game, I'm in," Davi said.

"Me as well," Kenna put in.

"Aye," Dair added.

"Then it's settled," Ned decided.

"You cooked, love," Kenna noted to Blake. "Davi, Dair and I'll do the dishes."

"You relax, Kenna. Dair and I will clean up," Ned stated.

"Works for me," Davi agreed.

"For as long as I can remember, Davina urgently had to use the loo every time there was cleanup to be done," Dair leaned over to tell Blake.

Blake shot him a sweet smile then looked to her father. "Just stack and soak, Dad. I'll clean up tomorrow. You know I like to putz around like that in the morning."

Blake Sharp did dishes.

And she *liked* doing them?

Oh, aye.

Better and better.

"As you wish, darling," Ned murmured.

They finished dinner.

Everyone helped clear the table, but the men put the food away, stacked and soaked.

They had digestifs and Ned annihilated them at the game.

And it didn't seem possible after that dinner, but it was true.

Blake's vanilla cake was the best thing he'd ever tasted.

CHAPTER EIGHT

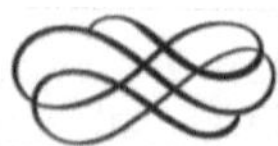

PISTACHIO MUFFINS

Dair

Dair woke to rays of sunshine streaming into a bedroom with walls that were almost entirely windows.

He turned onto his side in a bed that was empty, save him, and commandeered a pillow, holding it to his chest as he looked at the sun streaming through the trees.

And, aye.

He could absolutely live here.

The end of the evening before had not gone as he'd planned.

More drinks were consumed. Blake got competitive and demanded another game of Ticket to Ride (Ned won again). For some reason, this led to the women clustering around Blake's iPad looking at clothes while Ned and Dair shared a whisky. It got late. Ned suggested they stay the night rather than heading home at that hour on winding, dark, mountain roads after many beverages had been consumed.

Conveniently, they had three open guest bedrooms.

His mother accepted for the lot of them.

Therefore, Dair didn't get to take Blake back to his hotel room so they could chat and whatever else he could get up to with her in a hotel room. With the others around, he didn't get to have that chat at all.

He preferred waking up to Blake's warm, soft body covering him, but he'd take that view and knowing she was in the same house…for now.

He threw the covers back and went to the bathroom.

He'd discovered last night that the guestrooms were as spectacular as the rest of the house, and not just the ever-present view.

Blake had done those as well, obviously.

Even though the rooms were large, the décor was darker to give more of a cocoon-like feel, which Dair thought was a stroke of brilliance. His room was on the rustic side. And another Blake touch, the bathrooms were kitted with everything you might need. New toothbrushes, toothpaste, toiletries for men and women.

Dair availed himself of some of that, particularly the dental hygiene. But he saw a bunch of Kiehl's stuff for men and decided to give it a go. The facewash smelled of menthol, which was a nice wakeup call. Paired with the moisture shite after it, he found he liked it.

He'd slept in his boxers, so he tugged on his jeans, shrugged on his shirt and buttoned it up but tucked his socks into his shoes, took them with him down the stairs after he tidied the bed and set them by the door.

His nose, which smelled something stupendous baking, along with the scent of cooked bacon, led him to the kitchen.

He stopped dead while entering it.

This was because Blake, *his* Blake, Blake Sharp, heiress to the Marchioness of Norton title, heiress to the Bernard-Sharp fortune, was standing at the sink wearing a loose-fitting white shirt with wee sleeves, and a pair of white pajama pants with huge red hearts on them.

Huge red *hearts*.

Her hair was up in a messy knot at her crown, long locks floating down her slender neck.

And last, the kitchen was sparkling clean.

Right…

Bloody fucking hell.

He could fall in love with this woman.

"Morning," he called, strolling in.

She jerked then turned his way. "Good morning."

There was a little heart on the left breast of her shirt too.

And she was wearing no makeup, but she was just as stunning as ever.

He couldn't stop his smirk.

He'd made a decision that morning, that decision being, they weren't fucking about with this anymore.

This was why he went right up to her, slid an arm around her waist, and pulled her soft body against his.

Her lips formed an "O," her eyes went lazy in a way he felt in his cock, but she didn't fight his hold.

"Erm, sleep well?" she asked, awkwardly moving her hands to rest them on his chest.

"Slept better with you draped on me." She pressed her lips together. It was only then, after his gaze lifted to her eyes, he saw the dark circles under them. He narrowed his on them and asked, "You?"

"Great."

He bent his head to get close and whispered, "Liar."

She skirted that and queried, "Want coffee?"

"Aye, and I'll get it. After ye tell me why ye had trouble sleeping."

"Dair—"

He gave her a gentle shake. "We're doing this, lassie. So learn now, I dinnae let important shite go. The entire Wallace clan, save the patriarch, talks things out. We're honest. Frank. And we dinnae let shite fester."

"We're doing this?" she asked on a raise of her exquisitely arched dark brows.

"Are we not?" he asked in return.

"What *is* this?" she continued questioning.

"We're going to see," he replied. "But now, you're going to tell me why ye didnae sleep."

She huffed then said, "I got worried about Mum at the apartment. I have things there that mean something to me. I'm concerned she'll do something to them in her snit."

Helena could get up to practically anything in one of her snits.

"Ye have mates there you can call to go in and check on stuff?" he queried. "Or grab the things you're worried about and get them safe?"

Something gorgeous dawned over her face and she said, "Yes, I do," like the idea of her having friends was a shock to her.

He added that to his list to get into later.

But it was low on the list…for now.

"Contact them. I'll make my coffee," he ordered.

She nodded.

He let her go and went to the coffee maker. She went to her phone.

After he added the sugar and took a sip, he looked out the massive window behind the sink that rested at the back of the house and saw her father and his mother sitting on the deck. Ned with one of their substantial rustic mugs, his mother sipping out of a delicate teacup.

He moved back to Blake and rested his hips against the counter close to her just as her phone chirped.

She read the text.

"Oh good, the G-Force is on it," she said to her phone, her thumbs flying over the screen.

He took another sip and asked, "The G-Force?"

She sent her next text, put her phone down and looked up at him. "The G-Force. Kind of like gay superheroes. Though, they only deal in justice within New York's elite social set."

Sounded like men he'd want to meet.

Dair smiled. "Aye, so they'll be all over dispensing justice to your mother."

Her gaze wandered to her phone. "They seem keen about it."

"Feel better?" he asked.

She returned to him. "I should have thought of them before."

That was the perfect lead-in to asking about her seeming surprised that she had friends, but a tone sounded in the room.

Upon which she announced, "The muffins are done."

Muffins?

She moved to the oven and Dair watched as she pulled out a tin filled with what looked like perfectly baked American muffins, browned in bits, but the color was lime.

"What are those?" he asked.

"Pistachio muffins," she answered, resting them on the island.

Holy hell.

They smelled ludicrously good.

But how long had the woman been up?

Clean kitchen. Homemade muffins.

She flicked off the oven mitt and turned to him. "Do you think Davi will be okay if we have breakfast without her? The bacon is done and warming, the eggs are ready to cook. Dad and Kenna have been up for a while. And we should eat these muffins while they're warm. Warm muffins are the best. I can make fresh eggs for her when she gets up."

Dair didn't move.

No.

He *couldn't.*

"Dair?" she called.

Her dad and his mum were outside.

Davina could walk in at any minute.

But after the spread she laid before them last night, she'd made them muffins and was worried about Davi.

Ah well.

Fuck it.

He moved toward her, and she only caught his intent at the very last second.

When he reached her, Dair didn't hesitate to confirm his intent.

He palmed her jaw, his fingers curving behind her ear, and wrapped his other arm around her waist, yanking her up against him.

Again, she didn't tense or pull away. In fact, he didn't even have to tip her head back. She tipped it, and as his head descended, she cupped his cheek and her eyes fluttered closed.

His cock jumped to life.

Fucking hell, she was something.

With her invitation, he tilted his head and kissed her.

Not that first hesitation, Blake kissed him back at the same time she arched into him, like she was as hungry for him as he was for her. Like she'd been wanting to do this since she saw him, just like he had.

As her reward, and his, he slid his tongue along the crease of her lips.

She made a little noise that scored along his cock, her hand gliding over his cheek so she could wrap her arm around his neck. She pressed even closer and opened her mouth to allow him access inside.

Dair felt her and he could smell her subtle scent that was so very Blake. Contradictory. Intoxicating. Surprising.

It was feminine and powdery.

Supremely her, and completely not.

Perfect.

And as he slid his tongue into her mouth, he discovered she tasted of coffee and warmth and woman.

Even better.

A lot better.

So much better, for the first time in his life, his control snapped. He turned her and backed her into the kitchen island, arching her over it.

And it wasn't just him that made the kiss go wild.

Blake matched him, stroke for stroke, nip for nip, suck for suck, crushing her tits to his chest, her soft hips against his cock.

Fuck.

She was amazing.

They'd broken only for the necessity of breath, then he felt Blake's teeth sink into his lower lip as she demanded more of him.

He growled, his cock stiffening, his fingers tensing against her neck. And he went at her.

She matched that too, whimpering, and her hand slid into his hair.

Dair was about to break the kiss only to drag her to his room when…

"Ack! Yuck! I can never unsee that!" Davi protested.

They ended the embrace and Blake self-consciously sidled away from him.

Her hands went to her hair, which was a mess he didn't get the chance to make, but this was nervous self-consciousness he liked from her.

It was fucking adorable.

"Coffee!" Davi cried, making a beeline to it.

"B-breakfast will be in about ten, fifteen minutes," Blake pushed out, visibly having trouble calming her breath.

Oh, aye.

Adorable.

"I focused on those muffins so I wouldn't have more time to internalize the trauma of seeing my brother snogging a friend," Davi replied while pouring coffee. She finished it and looked at them. "Where are Mum and Ned?"

"Outside," Dair told her, silently willing her to vanish from the kitchen and reappear outside so he could have Blake to himself again.

"Right. Then that's where I'll go," Davi declared to Dair's elation, but then she asked Blake, "Unless ye need some help."

"I've got it," Blake assured her. "It won't take long. Do you like scrambled eggs?"

"I like anything I dinnae have to cook myself." Davi waved her mug at them. "As ye were, I'll keep the parental units occupied. But if it starts getting nasty, ye might want to find a room."

With that, his sister headed to the back door.

He turned to Blake.

They heard the door close before she blurted, "That shouldn't have happened."

He did not like her assertion.

As such, his "Why not?" was curt.

"How long are you here?" she asked.

"How long are *you* here?" he countered, making the point that neither of them were home because both of them traveled often.

"Chloe wants my help at the store. I'm here until the weekend."

And of course she'd help Chloe when she needed it.

How could this woman seemingly not know her value?

"We leave two days from now."

"So, the point would be?" she asked.

Now he was getting angry.

He looked to the island and back to her. "Was it ye I was kissing two minutes ago?"

"It was a good kiss," she allowed.

"A *good* one?" he asked disbelievingly.

"Okay, a great one," she said fast. "But Dair, I—" she cut herself off.

"What?" he asked.

She shifted her attention to the muffins.

"Ye what?" he pushed.

She looked to him and his chest felt like it caved in when he saw her face.

"I'm radioactive," she whispered.

"Come again?" he whispered in return.

"You saw what happened with Chad."

"Aye," he agreed. "What does that have to do with you?"

"I picked him."

"Lassie—"

She shook her head and cut him off. "No. I'm not…I don't think I can…I'm no good for anybody."

Oh, *aye*.

Now he was angry.

Being angry, and for other reasons, he didn't temper his movements.

Oh no.

He stalked to her, and she retreated until she had her back to the wall. He caged her in with his body and held her jaw in both hands, dipping his head so his face was right in hers.

"That twat was the cheat," he ground out. "Not you. He wanted you. He was devastated ye scraped him off. How he thought he could treat ye like that and still keep ye, I dinnae ken. I dinnae care. But his shite has not one fucking thing to do with you."

"But I—"

He got so much closer, their noses brushed. "Not one *fucking* thing, Blake. Hear me?"

Even in his hold, she nodded slowly, her violet-blue eyes big and locked to his.

"Your mother is a waste of space," Dair continued. "Not you. She may not have done anything in her life, but you've earned the love and respect of everyone around ye."

"They're only—"

His fingers tensed. "Bloody hell, fucking stop it, woman."

She blinked and grew stiff and angry in his hold.

There was his Blake.

"We're going out tonight. We're talking. We're figuring this out," he decreed. "I live in Scotland. You split your time between here and New York. But we both have the means to get to each other. There's always rugby to call, so I'm not as free as you, but we're both in this. We both want this. So tonight, we're going to talk about it and sort it."

"You're being very dictatorial," she snapped.

And, aye.

That was his Blake.

Feeling she was back to herself, which was a more comfortable place for them both, primarily her, he moved back a smidge. "Do ye disagree with any of that?"

"Only you *telling* me it's happening rather than *asking* me if I want it to happen."

"Ye sucking my tongue practically down your throat and catching my lip because I quit kissing ye for half a second told me ye want it to happen, lass."

He worried she gave herself a brain injury, her eye roll was so dramatic.

Oh fuck yes.

She was adorable.

"You'll be putting on a nice frock tonight, but before that, you'll be telling me what your favorite restaurant is in this town so I can make a booking for us, and we're going out tonight," he informed her.

"Just a note for your future reference, you're supposed to kiss a girl *after* you buy her dinner," she said snootily.

He smiled. "Hen, muffins and bacon and you worried my sister will be upset we started breakfast without her, I had to kiss ye."

"That's a weird reason for wanting to kiss a girl, Dair," she informed him.

"That's because you're so busy self-flagellating, you don't see your worth. It's the perfect reason to kiss a woman, Blake. Your hair like that and you in those cute PJs was just icing."

"All right, fine," she puffed out, though she couldn't quite hide she was pleased with his words. "We'll go on a date tonight."

This time, he grinned. "I know we will."

She squinted her eyes at him. "You can uncage me now."

He looked down at their bodies, moving his hands from her jaw to cage her another way, in his arms. "Like ye where ye are, lass."

She pushed at his chest. "I need to make eggs."

She barely finished that before they heard his mother saying, "Och no. Are we interrupting something?"

Blake pulled from his hold and scuttled out from in front of him.

He turned.

His mother looked better than yesterday.

Her father had a light shining in his eyes as he gazed at them.

So, approval there then.

Good to know.

"No, now's the perfect time," Blake said. "I was about to make eggs, and I could use some help setting the breakfast table."

His mother practically rubbed her hands together with excitement she had something to do. "Tell me what you need."

Blake started giving instructions while pulling out a skillet to make eggs, and the rest of them joined in to help set the round breakfast nook in its nest of even more windows off to the side of the kitchen.

The muffins were exhumed from their tins. The bacon pulled from the warming oven. Bowls of fruit, the butter keeper and sauces were laid out. And they all climbed into the nook around its circular table, with Dair arranging it so he sat beside Blake.

They filled their plates, but before Davi dug in, she announced, "Dair, I reckon you'll be particularly happy to know that Mum and Ned decided we're moving here for the duration of our stay."

Blake made an alarmed sound.

Dair smiled broadly. "Aye, I feel particularly happy about that."

"It's only a couple of days, dear," Kenna said to Blake. "But if you'd prefer us not to be here—"

"No, no," Blake interrupted her. "The hotel is lovely and convenient. But it's far more peaceful here."

"It is that, aye," Kenna said distractedly, looking out the window.

Dair switched his attention to Blake and saw her profile soft with concern as her eyes rested on his mother.

He curled his fingers around her thigh under the table and earned her focus.

"She'll be okay," he mouthed.

Blake nodded, but it wasn't persuasive.

He gave her another squeeze and went after his muffin.

He'd never had a pistachio muffin.

It was outstanding.

"You play golf, Dair?" Ned asked.

"Am I Scottish?" Dair returned on a smile.

"Fancy a round today?"

"Love to," Dair said.

Blake sighed a beleaguered sigh, but when Dair looked at her again, her gaze was still soft, this time resting on her father.

"I'll ring for a tee time after breakfast," Ned declared.

"So we women will be hauling around luggage while you blokes wander around putting tiny balls into tiny holes," Davi groused.

"I'll move us before golf," Dair said.

"I'll arrange the tee time for this afternoon," Ned put in.

Blake tore off a piece of muffin and put it in her mouth, and now she was wearing a peaceful expression.

Christ, she had no idea.

Even sitting in that nook in a kitchen she designed, eating food she cooked, she had no idea.

No idea what she gave, and how important it was.

Dair was really looking forward to helping her find out.

CHAPTER NINE

POINTS

Blake

Oh God, was I going to do this?

Ugh.

I was going to do it.

I knocked on Davi's bedroom door.

"Aye?" I heard from the other side.

I opened the door and walked in, only to have Davi shoot a beaming smile at me while she shrugged on a cardigan.

"I'm leaving Mum and Ned to their whiskies tonight and coming up early to spend hours in that tub," she announced. "I'm rubbish with that kind of thing. I'm thinking of redoing my bathroom at home. Do ye think you'd have time to help?"

Startled, for a second, I didn't know what to say.

"I ken you're probably busy," she went on.

I was never busy.

But, wait.

I was.

I was always busy.

How was I always busy?

And how had I not noticed I was always busy?

"So forget I said anything," Davi finished.

"I'd love to help. I love doing things like that," I told her.

Her face lit up. "Really?"

I nodded.

"That would be pure dead brilliant," Davi gushed.

"And it'd be my pleasure," I replied.

Davi's brows knit. "I thought ye were going out with Dair about now?"

"I am," I told her. "He just knocked on my door and told me he's ready when I was. But, I…could you…" I took in a breath. "Okay, I know I'm going out on a date with your brother, so this might be a strange thing for me to ask, but do you think my outfit is okay?"

I was wearing high-waisted, parchment-white trousers that fit snug at the ass, hips and upper thighs but had a wide leg.

I topped this with a sleeveless, high neck, soft super-faded denim top that was blousy and gathered at the waist and had a bit of a crop, so it showed a hint of skin at the midriff.

High, wedge espadrilles on my feet. Hair down in beachy waves. Makeup two steps up from casual day, three down from nighttime drama. Gold hoops, a bangle, a thick ring with a big white, oblong stone in the center on the middle finger of my left hand. And a camel, Dior saddlebag as my purse.

Davi's eyes grew huge as she stared at me.

"I'm used to going out in New York," I explained.

And not with hot, ex-professional rugby players who kissed like a dream and saw a me I did not see.

"Blake, ye always look great," Davi said. "Tonight, perfect for a mountain-town date with my big brother."

"Sure?" I asked.

Something moved over her face, and she came to me.

Slinging an arm around my shoulders, she led me to the door, saying, "I need a drink, and ye need to let my brother drink ye in wearing that outfit. You look perfect and he's not going to be able to keep his hands off ye."

"We have a lot to talk about before any of that," I noted awkwardly.

She stopped us in the hall. "Ye ken your ex was the wanker to beat all wankers, except for maybe my father."

"Uh, yeah, I ken that," I replied.

She grinned.

But it didn't last long.

"I was at that wedding-not-wedding, Blake. I was proud of you, even if it wasn't my place to be. It gutted me all the same. That said, ye were always snooty, like your mother, but ye could be funny. After that happened, ye found yourself, and I won't give that wanker the credit, but he sure led you to the right path. Dair was once-bitten, a thousand times shy. I haven't seen him this into a woman since Signe. And we all know his dick was more into her, literally and figuratively, than his brain was."

I let out a startled laugh at her brutal honesty.

I also thought about the woman I'd met briefly at their wedding, and had disliked intensely, and I did that immediately. She was crass and obvious. And the way she took so much time to arrange her hair, body and expression anytime a camera was anywhere near her gave me a sinking feeling.

"You found you, be that you," Davi went on. And now I got a saucy grin from her. "Dair obviously likes it."

This was very true.

He obviously did.

I wasn't sure how or why, but he did.

I nodded.

She guided me downstairs in my own house.

And when we hit the living room and Dair turned to me, the look on his face…

Oh yes.

He liked me.

My nerves instantly settled (but other parts of me came alert).

He walked my way, his eyes roaming all over me, but when he took my hand, they rose to mine.

"Ready?" he asked.

Was I?

That kiss said yes.

His speech about my cake said yes.

The way his eyes just roamed all over me also said yes.

My head screamed no.

But my mouth said, "I'm ready."

Dair turned us to the living room where Dad and Kenna were sitting on the sofa, enjoying a cocktail, and Davi was at the bar mixing herself one.

"Don't be out too late, kids," Davi bid.

"Enjoy yourselves," Kenna said.

I looked to Dad. "Dinner is—"

He didn't move an inch, except his mouth. "Darling, I've read your detailed instructions. I can heat up an oven and put a lasagna in it."

"Ooo we're having lasagna?" Davi asked excitedly.

That day, while I helped Chloe at the shop, then came home and cooked, Davi and Kenna spent the day in Jerome, thus she didn't know the evening's menu.

"The garlic bread—" I began.

"Go," Dad urged.

Dair tugged my hand.

Time to go.

I went with him.

He guided me down the steps, opened the car door, helped me in, then closed it.

Okay.

Good kisser.

Add one (a big one, so big, it was more like ten).

Loved my cooking, showed it and thought it worthwhile.

That was two.

Didn't get turned off when I was being snotty, which happened a lot.

And we were at three.

Didn't bolt when I threw a strawberry, or I yelled at my father.

Now four.

Didn't paint me with the same brush as my mother after that crazy scene at the wedding, and the fallout.

Up to five.

Opened my car door for me.

And six.

Boy, he sure was racking up the points.

We were on our way before he broke the silence. "Have a good day?"

"Yes," I said formally. "You?"

"Not sure your father is best pleased with me considering I walloped him at golf."

Oh dear.

"Dad's particularly proud of his golf game."

"I bought the drinks after."

"Well then." I didn't know what else to say.

I knew nothing about golf. I wanted to know nothing about golf. Except Dad liked to play it and he took every opportunity to improve his game.

"Lasagna?" he asked, his tone lightly teasing.

"Dad grills. That's all he does. Someone had to feed your family."

"My mum cooks and there's a town full of restaurants," he pointed out.

"Your mum needs to chill."

"She needs things to do to keep her occupied."

I twisted in my seat to look at him. "Sometimes it's better to think things through, Dair."

"She can think and do at the same time, lass," he returned. "But she's always been a busy person. Even during holidays, she'd find reasons to bustle about. It's her safe space."

"Oh."

"If she wants, let her cook tomorrow for our last night."

Their last night.

Why did that sting?

I sat forward and mumbled, "Of course."

He drove for a while before he asked, "Hear from your superhero friends?"

"Yes. They don't mess around. Mission complete. Apparently, Mum's already gone. But they checked anyway and sent pictures. All is in order."

"That's good, lassie," he murmured.

It was.

Actually, it was a huge relief.

"Do ye ken where your mum went?" he asked.

"No, I don't know. I also don't care. Just as long as she's leaving Alex and Rix alone."

"How long are they gone?"

"They'll be home the Sunday after next."

"Good long honeymoon, then," he muttered.

"Yes," I confirmed.

There was small talk the rest of the way into town, mostly about how we spent our days, and Dair found a precious parking place close to the popular restaurant.

I picked Farm Provisions, and I was surprised he could get a reservation at such short notice, because it was so popular. Maybe it was because it was a weeknight. Maybe it was because of his deep voice and accent, and the person who took the booking was gay or a female.

What it wasn't, was romantic.

Then again, I hadn't had any reason to scout romantic restaurants in Prescott.

But it was delicious food, locally sourced with a busy, bustling vibe that I enjoyed.

And it was bustling, so how Dair scored a table inside was a miracle.

We sat. We ordered drinks. We perused the menu. We ordered food.

As the server was leaving, Dair turned a serious face to me.

Damn.

Here we go.

But he led into it sweet. "We have a lot to talk about, baby."

I cleared my throat and asked, "Like what?"

"We can start with what you said to me at the rehearsal dinner."

So much had happened since then, I didn't remember what I said.

Then it hit me.

Shit.

"You were kind of a jerk to me growing up, Dair," I pointed out.

"You were a prissy wee miss, Blake. As a young lad, it's a moral imperative to be a jerk to a prissy wee miss."

For a second, I sat stunned.

Then I busted out laughing.

I only stopped when Dair rumbled, "Jesus Christ."

He was staring at me like...

Like...

I didn't know.

But it felt great.

So I asked, "What?"

"You're the most beautiful woman I've ever seen. But when you laugh, I see a wee bit of that little girl I knew, except she isn't unhappy like she was always unhappy."

I was utterly shocked he thought I was the most beautiful woman he'd ever seen.

I was not unaware of what I looked like. I knew I was attractive.

But he'd dated models and actresses (and, I'd noted, had one particularly long stint with a pop star).

It was the "always unhappy" thing that freaked me.

"I wasn't always unhappy," I denied.

"Lass, I think we can validate and set aside the fact your mum was a shit mum."

"Yes," I agreed, because...obviously.

"So ye won't be taking any offense when I note she was a horrible mum to you girls."

"She didn't attempt to hide it," I confirmed.

"No. She didnae. If ye were up at our place, Alex would tramp out and do her own thing. But it'd take forever for Mum to get you settled in. Then you'd be in the kitchen with her, making stews or pies. But I think that was the only time ye seemed really happy."

God, I'd forgotten about cooking with Kenna. The last time we'd done that was so long ago.

I didn't do much but peel vegetables or roll out dough.

But I remembered liking those times a whole lot, even if they were rare.

This made me consider the idea this was the reason why I loved cooking so much.

Because Kenna gave it to me.

And Dair was right.

Working in her kitchen with her made me happy.

"Your mum has always been lovely with me."

"My mum has always fretted like fuck over you and Alex."

This was awful, and I wished she hadn't had to do that, but it didn't surprise me.

She was her own woman and had always seemed capable, together and no-nonsense, but when it came to her children, she was *all mum*, openly, even effusively loving and nurturing, but when needed, strict and disciplined.

On this thought, I remarked, "You're very lucky, Dair."

"Aye, I ken. This is why I worry about what marks Helena made on ye."

I shrugged. "I'm not the only kid in the world who had a crappy mother."

"I'm not sitting across from some other grown kid from out in the world, Blake."

Argh.

I didn't want to talk about this. There was nothing to be done about it.

"I thought we were discussing you being a bully when we were kids," I reminded him.

Before he could answer, the server came with our drinks (for your edification, Dair, an ale, me, their Garden Variety Gimlet, though take it from me, it wasn't garden variety at all).

The server left and Dair took us right back to it.

"I was a boy who liked to be outside, and I was too young to realize ye simply didnae. I was told to entertain ye, and the fun shite I knew to do was all outside. You didnae like how cold it was. You complained about the rain. You didnae like horses—"

"I love horses," I stated hotly, because…I did. Even back then.

"You turned your nose up at them."

"I was scared of them. They were *huge*, Dair. You guys bred Clydesdales."

"They're still just horses."

I picked up my drink and mumbled, "Oh my God, I can't believe we're discussing this."

"I think it's pertinent, since I intend to spend vastly more time with you and you told me when we were wee, ye thought I treated you like shit."

Vastly more?

My heart skipped a beat.

"Blake," he growled, taking my mind off my heart.

"Okay, do you want the honesty?" I demanded.

"Always."

"I'd just had a conversation with my mother. Never fun. But it was about the fact your family was not invited to the rehearsal dinner."

"Ah," he said, sitting back in his side of the booth with his beer.

"I'm not being rude," I asserted. "That event isn't for friends of the family. It's for people in the wedding party and close family. Furthermore, Alex left me in charge of the planning, and Mum horning in to do things I knew Alex wouldn't want exasperated me. Something you know, Alex prefers smaller numbers. Add to that, I knew the reason Mum invited you was so she could be around Bally, and that's just gross. So maybe I transferred some of all I was feeling and worrying about on you. For that, I apologize. You're right. When we were kids, we had different interests. You were doing your best. I was uncomfortable because back then I was *always* uncomfortable, but then I knew about your dad and my mum and that made it more uncomfortable. And that's just that."

"That is that, love," he said gently. "And I'm glad we've gone over it."

It just sucked how awesome he was.

Uncomfortable, even difficult conversation, we had it, we said what we had to say, we were honest, and then we were done, and he ended it with his lovely brogue all gentle.

He was impossible.

"Thrilled for you that you're glad," I mumbled and took a sip of my own drink.

He chuckled.

Completely impossible.

I was saved from responding by the server putting the devilled eggs in front of us.

"Thank you," I said to her.

"No problems," she replied and took off.

I went for an egg.

Dair went in after me.

"They source local," I told him as he took a bite. "And just to say, you chose well with the chicken pot pie for your main."

He winked at me.

That was so hot, my heart stuttered to a complete halt.

"Glad you approve," he said through egg while I restarted my heart. He swallowed and pointed at the remaining portion (why they didn't serve four for two people, I didn't know, restaurants had a knack for odd numbers, and it drove me batty—I mean, it made sense to give four portions, two eggs, halved, equaled four, for goodness sake). "And that was bloody magnificent," he finished.

Why did it delight me he liked my favorite restaurant in Prescott?

"You eat the second one," I told him after I consumed mine. "I got the pork tenderloin, which is going to be heavy, and you eat like a linebacker."

"I eat like a tighthead prop," he corrected.

"Whatever," I muttered.

He grinned at me and took the last egg.

I felt something funny and looked across the restaurant.

A man was staring at me.

When he caught my eye, he smiled.

I knew that kind of smile, and fortunately (this time) it wasn't one that told me he'd seen me somewhere on social media in all my glory tearing Chad a new asshole at our wedding or some other hijinks I'd gotten up to.

But unfortunately, it was an even worse kind in this scenario.

For God's sake, he was with a woman, and I was with a man.

I glared at him, shifting my eyes pointedly to the woman he was with and back to him before I turned again to Dair.

But he was looking over his shoulder at the man.

And then he was putting his napkin on the table and sliding out of the booth.

Dear Lord, what was he doing?

"Dair." He couldn't help but hear me (this was a tiny place), but he didn't pause in moving toward the man's table. "Alasdair!" I snapped, trying not to be too loud but needing to stop him.

It didn't work.

I sat helplessly, not knowing what to do, as I watched Dair stand at their table and say things. The man's face was white as a sheet. But as the woman gazed up at Dair and heard what he had to say, her face got red as a beet.

Dair finished and strolled back to our table. But even if he was a big guy who took up a lot of space, I didn't miss the man leaning toward the woman, reaching her way and talking fast. Nor did I miss the woman's straight back, the angry line of her shoulders and the infuriated shakes of her head.

So when Dair slid back into the booth, I leaned forward and bit, "What did you do?"

"I told him to keep his eyes on his woman and off mine. And if he smiles at you again, like he did or in any way, I was going to knock his teeth down his throat."

That was insane!

"You threatened him?"

"Are you sitting across the table from me?"

"Yes."

"Did we share an amazing kiss this morning?"

Gah!

"Yes, Dair," I sighed.

"And is he with a woman who is obviously not his mother or sister and making eyes at mine?"

"You could have just ignored it," I suggested.

"Why?" he asked, sounding genuinely surprised I'd suggest such a thing. "That wasn't for his benefit. It was for hers. She should know."

She should.

Totally.

It stunk that he was right.

"Well, you didn't have to threaten him," I stated.

He took a sip from his beer and said casually, "That was for me."

Lord.

I took a mouthful of my drink.

"Though, I fear this is going to be an issue with how gorgeous you are," he went on. "It's not been lost on me men stare at you all the time."

They did?

Before I could ascertain the veracity of his remark, the server came around and swept away our egg plate.

She had to dodge the woman making an angry exit and the man chasing after her.

Fabulous.

I shot Dair a homicidal look, or what I hoped was a homicidal look.

Dair ignored it and declared, "Now…us."

Outside of his wink and him thinking I was the most beautiful woman he ever saw, so far, this hadn't been all that fun of a date, what with him pointing out I was a bitch to him at the rehearsal dinner and then him ruining some poor woman's night and perhaps her entire relationship.

I didn't get to tell him that.

"I have a match to call this weekend," he started. "Ye probably want to go home to make sure your mother didn't fuck with any of your shit. So the weekend after that, you come to me. Tomorrow, we'll spend the day together, family dinner at the end. We'll sort the next visit when you're out with me."

"I see you have this all planned," I remarked.

"Do ye have plans the weekend after next?"

"No," I admitted

"The whole week after that?"

What was he saying?

"I'm spending a week in Scotland?" I queried.

"We're not going to get to know each other better with ye spending a couple of days with me while you're jetlagged before you fly home."

"That would be an awful lot of time spent together at the start of a relationship," I remarked.

"We're not going to get to know each other better with ye spending a couple of hours with me here and there when we live an ocean away from each other."

He just got worse and worse, mostly because, when we were having words, he was so often right.

I gave in. "I'll have to check my calendar, but I don't think I have anything on."

Though, I'd told Nora I'd help her with an event she was planning, but maybe I could do what I needed to do remotely.

"I'll be getting to ye in New York, lassie, dinnae ye worry," he assured.

Easy for him to say.

I was worrying about everything.

It was like he could read my mind, because he asked, "What's bothering you about this?"

"What if we don't work?" I asked.

"I dinnae ken," he answered. "Though, think we might want to try first before we worry about it not working."

"You're a family friend."

"Your mother was friends with my father, and we know where that's at," he retorted. "This goes sour, we live in different countries, lass. It's not like we're going to be bumping into each other at the market."

This was true.

"Why are ye determined to drive a wedge into this?" he asked.

Why indeed.

"Blake," he pushed.

The server came to set our mains in front of us and Dair—being honest, let-it-all hang-out Dair—expelled a frustrated breath when she did.

She glanced at him and her cheeks went pink, because he was glorious, and he'd just shared he was annoyed she interrupted us.

"We're having a difficult conversation," I explained to her.

"I'm sorry to intrude," she mumbled.

"No intrusion. Maybe feeding the beast will make him more patient," I joked.

The woman smiled at me and ducked away.

"Now that you've made our waitress feel better," Dair said. "How about ye do a wee bit of that for me?"

"Can we just have normal date?" I requested.

"How are we to accomplish that if you're sitting across from me making up shite to keep distant from me?"

I skewered him with another look, because his continued logic in the face of my determined illogic was highly vexing.

"Blake, I think you can see why this is important," he pointed out.

"I like you," I stated sourly.

"And?" he pushed.

"That's it," I said, cutting into my tenderloin and scooping polenta onto the bite before eating it.

So good.

When I refocused on Dair, he was staring at me like I was crazy.

"What?" I asked.

"You don't want us to give this a go because you like me?" he asked like I was what he was looking at me like I was.

Crazy.

I put my cutlery down on my plate and leaned toward him.

"You want honesty, bucko?"

His eyebrows shot up at "bucko," and under them, his eyes lit with mirth, but I ignored both.

"Here it is. I've had two dates in four years since Chad, mostly because everyone *in the world* knows what I did and the heterosexual male component of that wants nothing to do with it."

"Except the one sitting across from ye," he corrected.

"Yes. And you're handsome. And you're tall. And fit. And you like my cooking, you don't put up with my shit, you think I'm worthy, and I know you threw that second game so Dad could retain his winning streak. I saw your cards. You could have made several much better plays, and you didn't. For my dad."

"Blake—"

But I'd picked up cutlery and was angrily sawing at the tender piece of meat that fell apart at the mildest pressure.

And I kept blabbing.

"So…what? You realize I'm a waste of space and you dump me?" I shoved the bite I prepared in my mouth and aimed my eyes at him, chewing irately and swallowing. "Or, for whatever reason, this doesn't work out, but still, you dump me? Where does that put me?"

"What I want to know, love," he said carefully, "is why you're in that place when that place is not this place. That place might not even happen."

I rested my hands on the table beside my plate.

"Dair, listen to me. *I like you.*"

"I like you too, hen," he whispered, watching me closely.

"Clue in."

"To what?"

"You know what."

"Enlighten me."

"When I lost Chad, I didn't pine, and I liked him too. I thought I loved him. It came to me quickly, however, that he was more Mum's choice than mine. I thought he was the key to me finally winning her approval. And maybe he was, and I blew that—"

"Ye didnae blow fuck all," he stated angrily.

"I get that, but—"

"You remember Signe?"

"Of course."

"She was a mess."

I thought it prudent to say nothing.

"Once she had my ring on her finger, she drove me fucking mental. She was a disaster. She married me because I played rugby, made good money and came from even more. She didn't even try to hide it."

Oh God.

That had to feel terrible.

"I'm so sorry, Dair," I said quietly.

"I am too," he replied. "The thing I'm most sorry about is that I didn't see that in her. Everyone around me did. Mum. Davi. My mates. Even Dad wasn't fond of her, and we both know he likes a good-looking woman."

We knew that for certain.

"I felt like a bloody fucking fool," he continued, and now my heart was lurching, because I hated that he felt that. "It didn't occur to me until a lot later that she played me. I saw *none* of that before the wedding. I thought I was the love of her life. I thought she was mine. I was twenty-five and got my hands on a pretty woman who was great in bed, and full truth, my dick was more interested in marrying her than I was. We were all over everything when we were together. Gossip rags. Social media. We were all over everything again when we split. I felt like a fucking moron."

"Well, I think I know a little bit about being played and that happening publicly."

"That's my point," he returned. "That guy played ye, and he had game, but ye won the match. Ye don't take yourself out of play, especially when you're winning."

"It didn't feel like I won."

"Well, you did, baby."

"You haven't been serious with anyone since Signe either," I pointed out.

"Reckon the fates were telling me to hold until I could get back to you."

Whoosh.

All my breath left me.

Because...

Did he just say that to me?

It was like he didn't realize he just rocked my world.

He kept talking.

"My mother and your father like and respect each other, but they're not mates, though I think they could be. My sister is growing more and more fond of ye the more you feed her."

That made me crack a smile.

He continued, "In other words, I know there are things to lose, Blake, especially between you and me. I understand what you're saying. Ye thought ye lost something when ye scraped him off, but ye figured out ye didnae. But you like me, and ye ken already it'll be worse if it dinnae work out. Hen, understand this. I'm feeling the same."

Oh God.

He was feeling the same.

Did that make me feel better, or more scared?

Definitely more scared.

Dair went on, "But I've got the balls to give it a go because it feels damn good and might get better."

"I don't have balls, Dair."

"Thank Christ, but you get me. Are ye going to wimp out on me?"

Oh no he didn't.

"I'm not being a wimp," I snapped. "I'm trying to protect you *and* me."

"From what?"

"Heartbreak?" I asked sarcastically. "Emotional trauma? Another social media onslaught. Have you thought of that? Everything my crew does is plastered all over the place and you'll be along for that ride if you're with me. Trust me, it'll be *way* worse than what happened with Signe."

"Now you're making shite up," he muttered while spooning up chicken pot pie.

"I am not," I stated heatedly. "As I'm sure you know with what you just mentioned about Signe, it's not fun."

"Ye dinnae have any records to sell or movie tickets ye want people to buy. Why do ye give that first shite about what people say about you on social media?"

"Well, *you* have a job in the public eye."

"Baby, I got my trust fund when I was twenty-three and I haven't touched it. I could lose my job and get a job coaching somewhere and be more than comfortable. I was young back then and felt like an eejit. Now, I dinnae give a fuck what millions of people addicted to their screens say about me."

"You have an answer for everything," I sniped, swiping more polenta on pork.

"Because there are answers."

I shoved the food in my mouth and chewed angrily.

"Does it occur to ye, you're being entirely irrational, and I haven't bolted to the door?" he asked before shoving pie in his mouth.

Oh no he didn't.

"I'm not being irrational, Dair," I said low.

He leaned over his pie to me. "This is how I see it. If that kiss is any indication, you're going to be fucking amazing in bed. You're funny. You're full of cheek, and I like it. Ye cook great. You're kind to my mum. My sister thinks the world of ye. You're not boring in the slightest. Ye love hard and show it effortlessly. And you like me. So much, you're terrified of losing me before we've even tried. With all of that, what I know is, this could be everything. It could be wedding, children, our whole futures. And I'm determined to explore that. So worry all ye want, baby. Your arse is still going to be on a plane in a week and a half. And dinnae book a hotel. You're staying with me."

What did you say to that?

I said nothing, just angrily kept eating.

"It's dead already, ye ken," Dair quipped while watching me.

I shoved more pork in my mouth and chewed ferociously.

He busted out laughing.

Was there no distancing this guy?

Bah!

"I'm not terrified of losing you," I groused as I speared a baby carrot.

"Sick with it, love," he said jovially over his pot pie. "Not to worry. I've got the cure."

Oh my God!

He was *unspeakable*.

"Dessert here or go to that ice cream place Mum and Davi were raving about?" he asked.

I was intent to give him the silent treatment for the rest of the date.

But we were talking about ice cream.

"Ice cream," I grumbled.

His tone was vibrating with humor when he said, "Whatever you want, lassie."

I wanted him.

And that was the problem.

Because it scared the shit out of me.

But, what could I do?

I was no wimp.

I was a Sharp. A Bernhard. Even a Coddington (from what I could tell, they were all assholes, but they didn't back down or roll over for anybody).

So we'd give this a go.

He'd see.

I ate more pork and polenta.

Delicious.

CHAPTER TEN

TORTURE

Blake

I sat in the window seat in my bedroom with a cup of coffee and stared out at the pines.

Today was Dair's (and his family's) last day in Prescott.

And I was extremely bummed about it.

The night before last, the rest of Dair and my date was a great deal better than the beginning of it.

He was witty. Clever. Openly into me. Thought I was funny.

And worth a repeat, openly into me.

A man like that, not just his looks, but confidence, his unceasing energy for life, his humor.

I'd never met a man like him.

Indeed, until getting to know him again, I didn't know men like him existed.

On our date, after our dinner, we wandered the streets of Prescott and around the square, his arm around my shoulders, mine around his waist.

And it's safe to say, that felt nice too.

I'd never strolled, connected to a man (or anyone) with no real purpose (except the important mission to get ice cream). No place to go. Just being together, spending time, chatting.

Touching.

We hit the ice cream place. He took his cone, and I took my sundae to a bench on the square. There we sat eating, and while we did, and even after, Dair made up stories about people that passed by that had me bending double from laughing so hard.

It was a toss-up, the walking close together vs. the laughing that hard as to which felt nicer, so in the end, I decided they were a tie.

What wasn't a toss-up was that, regardless of how it began, by far, my date with Dair was the best I'd had in my life. Bar none.

In fact, not a single one even came close.

And I didn't think I'd ever laughed that hard.

Ever.

And this was my decision about the date before we made out on my side in the open door of the car. And although it wasn't as off the hook and all-consuming as when we were going at each other in the kitchen, it was still fabulous.

One could say (and I *so* did), the man could kiss.

More fabulous, I knew he wanted to kiss me, I wanted him to kiss me (badly—enough couldn't be said about our kitchen kiss), and he found a time to give that to the both of us.

But he didn't neck with me in his car outside a house my father and his mother were in, or inside for that matter.

We were grown adults, but I still thought this was him being sweet to me, and respectful of Dad, also his mum.

Again, I liked that.

A whole lot.

Nevertheless, when we got home, we found, even if it wasn't all that late, everyone was in bed, and we headed that way too.

It sucked to say goodbye to him in the hall.

I might have sent a yearning glance his way before I walked through my bedroom door.

Actually, I was sure I did, considering the arrogant smile on his face when he saw it since he was standing outside his door waiting for me to go in mine.

Though, his arrogance was good. It wiped the yearning out of my mind and swept the vexation right in.

After we all went to brunch in town the next morning, Davi and Kenna took the rental car to go explore, Dad took his car to go home, and Dair slid behind the driver's seat in mine because he decided we were spending our day together in Sedona.

I loved Sedona, even if it was more than an hour drive away, so I was all in.

However, as it seemed was us, during our day together, we shared cross words five times.

This started about two minutes after we were underway.

It began with Dair stating, "Ye barely have any petrol, lassie."

"Okay. So let's stop by a gas station."

"Ye should never be this close to empty," he decreed, his tone weighty.

It was the weight in his tone that made me turn to him and ask, "Why?"

"It's dangerous. Ye should always keep it upward of half a tank because ye never know what's going to happen."

"Well, should I ever have the urge to rob a bank whereupon I find myself in a car chase with the police, I'll remember your words when I run out of gas halfway to I-17."

Now his tone was impatient. "What I mean is, there's long stretches in this country with a good deal of nothing. Or ye could get busy and forget. And then you'd be stranded."

"I'm sure it will come as no surprise when I tell you I don't often motor around in desolate rural areas and my car doesn't let me forget, Dair. A warning comes on that tells me precisely how many miles I have left before I have to gas up."

"Ye see what I'm saying, though. Aye?"

"Your accent is thick, but I'm getting used to it, so I *do* understand you. I just don't *agree* with you."

He made a growly noise at that point, which was so scrumptious, it made the entire mildly annoying conversation totally worthwhile.

Our next exchange of words happened about two minutes later, at the gas pump.

When he stopped, he got out.

So did I, with my purse.

He scowled at me like getting out of the car was akin to me threatening world peace.

"I'm pumping," he stated.

I wasn't going to argue that. I hated pumping gas.

"I'm paying."

"No, you're not."

"Yes I am."

"You're not."

"It's my car."

To that, he shoved his credit card into the slot.

"Dair!" I snapped.

"Get in the car, Blake."

"You're impossible."

He grinned and pulled out his card. "You still like me, though."

I hmphed my way into the car.

We then exchanged words about thirty minutes later, when he went off the beaten path.

"Where are you going?" I asked.

"Looked at the routes and this one is supposed to be more scenic."

"It'll also take longer."

"Do we have somewhere to be?"

"Yes, a particularly good jewelry store in Sedona," I retorted.

"I'll get ye there."

"Yes, perhaps *after* someone buys a pair of earrings I would have wanted to own," I shot back.

He sounded in dire need of laughing when he asked, "So you're on my back about the route because of a pair of earrings that may or may not exist?"

I decided to shut up.

We then had words over who was going to pay for lunch (he won).

And last, we had words over when we were going to head back.

I wanted to go a bit early. He wanted to stay.

When I told him I wanted to check on his mum, that discussion, I won.

That said, the day was fun. Even, I had to admit, bickering with Dair was fun.

It felt good to watch Dair marvel at the beauty of Sedona. Not to mention, he was no less witty and charming than ever.

And it felt good to be able to be just me. I could be argumentative and stubborn all I wanted, he didn't mind.

I think he even liked it.

And he bought me a pair of earrings at that store, ones that I liked a great deal, but I was going to pass them up even knowing full well I'd probably obsess about them when I did, which would necessitate me contacting the store and having them shipped to me.

They were dangling square hoops made of round semi-precious stones set in silver.

I'd been attempting to create a Prescott wardrobe, with accessories, that I could leave at the house so I didn't have to pack so much when I went there, and they were the perfect addition, because they'd go with a multitude of outfits.

All of this was awesome, but the best part was it was an incredibly lovely gesture from Dair.

Outside of our squabbling (that I still enjoyed), the day was just… easy.

Conversation flowed. We had history. We knew some of the same people. From afar, we even ran in the same circles. Thus, we had a myriad of connections and connected interests.

Not to mention, Dair was physical, demonstrative, and before him, I didn't think I liked that. And then he did it, and I realized I liked it very much.

To put it plainly, I was proud to be on his arm.

He was so handsome, he got his fair share of looks from the female population, and I felt like preening at his side, because he chose me.

This man chose *me*.

When we arrived home, we discovered that Kenna had indeed commandeered the kitchen. She made a hearty stew that wasn't my idea of summer fare, but it was delicious. And unsurprisingly, considering Dair had known her all his life and he said this would be so, she seemed much more settled after making dinner, having had something to do, and doing it for people she cared about.

We didn't play a game or watch a movie after dinner.

We all sat on the deck, talking and reminiscing and enjoying each other's company.

That was easy too.

It was marvelous.

And scary as all hell.

But now, they were leaving.

And I wasn't conflicted about that.

I was coming to the realization no man I'd ever dated, no man I'd ever been with, was a man *I* picked.

They were men I thought my mother would approve of. And if not her, then Dad.

Some of them were men in my set I didn't even like.

For the first time, I was with a man *I* chose. A man *I* wanted to be with. A man I really, really *liked* being with.

And he was leaving.

On this thought, and a heavy sigh, I got up to head back down to the kitchen to rummage around and see what to make everyone for breakfast. Their plane didn't leave until the evening from Sky Harbor in

Phoenix, but they had to check in two hours early, and it was a two-hour drive, so they had to leave right after lunch.

This brought something else to mind.

I'd always been very late to bed, very late to rise. Hell, in my mean girl heyday, it was rare I was out of bed before noon.

Now, it was the exact opposite.

If I wasn't in bed with a book by nine thirty, I considered it "up late."

But if I wasn't out of bed by six thirty, I thought I'd wasted the day (I was usually up, latest, by six).

It didn't occur to me, until Dair shoved up in my face, how much I'd changed.

But I'd changed.

A lot.

It didn't only make me happy, realizing I had, it made me happy that Dair had held that mirror up to my face and forced me to see the woman who had become me.

The woman he saw me to be.

And she wasn't half bad.

On my journey to the kitchen, I hesitated outside Dair's door, wondering what he'd do if I went in and climbed in bed with him, just to cuddle.

It'd be interesting to see what cuddling with that big, strong body would feel like. Pressing up against it while kissing was sublime. Cuddling, I figured, would be *everything*.

He'd probably want more than cuddling, though, (so did I). And since, during our first kiss, it felt like we were two seconds from banging on the kitchen island with his mum and my dad right outside, I didn't think it was a good idea to tempt fate.

He'd kissed me a lot while we were in Sedona. Small pecks or hard presses here, there and everywhere. Whenever the urge took him, he curled me into him and laid one on me.

We didn't bicker about that.

On no we did not.

I loved it.

Even so, it was a daylong tease.

And again, they were leaving.

It was way too soon (in my estimation) to level up in that manner of our relationship. And it wasn't the time, with Dad and Dair's family around.

But with the way Dair was, all of it, not to mention my very long, very dry spell, I knew I wouldn't want to wait too long to do that levelling up.

Like, when I was in Scotland.

I had a feeling that was something to look forward to.

Very much.

But now he was going to be over three thousand miles away (and yes, I looked it up). And that was when I was in New York. It was a lot further from Prescott.

On this depressing thought, I resumed my journey to the kitchen and found Kenna there making a cup of tea.

"Good morning," I greeted.

"Guid mornin', lass," she replied on a smile.

I studied her closely.

The heavy was still in her bearing. The pain etched into her face. Neither was a surprise.

But the smile was authentic.

"I came down to see what to make for breakfast," I told her. "Any preferences? Or I could run into town and buy some donuts from Bosa."

"Ah, American donuts," she sighed longingly.

That decided it.

"Are there donuts you particularly like? Davi? Dair?" I needed to know them all, but I was especially interested in Dair.

"Both my children have sweet teeth, as do I, so whatever ye decide. I doubt they'll be picky."

I'd get several of each selection so no one would feel like they didn't get what they wanted. I certainly wouldn't mind having leftover donuts around when they were gone (Dad was leaving tomorrow). They might get stale, but nothing ten seconds in the microwave and a quick scarf down my gullet wouldn't cure.

"I'll go get dressed and pop into town," I said, moving to set up a travel mug so I could take some coffee with me.

"I'd wait if I were ye," Kenna advised. "Dair'll want to go with ye."

"To pick his donuts?"

"To be with ye. My son won't be best pleased if he gets up in the half an hour you're gone and you're not here. Especially with us leaving today."

This made me feel all warm inside, because I sensed it was very true.

"Can I talk with you in the meantime?" she asked.

Oh boy.

Was this the mum-with-the-son-I'm-dating talk?

Already?

Or worse, the-mum-with-a-son-who-was-interested-in-a-messed-up-woman talk?

Eek!

"Sure," I said hesitantly, and with no choice, I warmed my coffee, splashing cream in, and met her in the breakfast nook.

She started it. "I asked your father last night. But he's leaving, and he requested I ask ye too, since you'll be around for a while."

Okay, maybe not the mum-with-the-son-I'm-dating talk.

"You asked Dad what?"

"If I can stay here at your house for a wee spell."

"Of course," I said immediately.

The skin around her eyes got soft.

And then my heart broke when her eyes got plain sad.

"I just don't want to go home yet," she murmured behind her teacup before taking a sip.

I could totally understand that.

"I'm certain Dad said the same thing, but as far as I'm concerned, you can stay as long as you like," I offered.

She nodded.

"And Genny and Duncan are in town. They have a posse of friends, not to mention, there's Judge, Chloe and JT. And Alex and Rix will be back in just over a week. If you want company after I leave, you can have it," I continued.

"That's lovely, dear, but I'll be needing some time to get my head on straight."

"Just in case," I said.

"Just in case what?" Dair asked, strolling in wearing faded jeans and a lightweight, light-blue button-down he'd rolled up at his forearms. A shirt, not incidentally, that did amazing things to his eyes.

His dark hair was wet and curling around his ears.

God.

My mouth started watering.

And this man was about to fly thousands of miles away from me.

Torture!

"Get some coffee, love, while Blake puts on some clothes. Ye two are going into town for donuts," Kenna told him.

Dair looked to her then to me, and I skedaddled out of the breakfast nook so I could get dressed.

"Travel mugs are up there, honey," I said to Dair, pointing to a cupboard as I moved. "Pour mine in one, would you?"

I didn't wait for his response.

And I didn't get up the first stair on the staircase.

A strong arm hooked around my belly, I was pulled back into a hard body, then turned in his arm.

I looked up at Dair, "What on—?"

"Honey?" he growled.

I blinked, not understanding his growl or the intense expression on his face.

He called me endearments all the time. Lass, lassie, babe, love and hen were used frequently by Scottish people, but darling and baby, which he liberally sprinkled about when he spoke to me, were not.

Was he upset I said that in front of his mum?

I mean, honey wasn't pookie or love of my life or anything silly or weird and too soon.

Suddenly, his long fingers were fisted in the back of my hair and his face was a breath from mine.

All oxygen left me.

"Dair," I whispered.

"I like that," he grunted.

Oh.

Wow.

Good!

"Okay." I kept whispering.

"Do it more often," he ordered.

I blinked again because…

He couldn't be believed!

"You can't boss me into calling you sweet nothings," I informed him.

"Funny, just did, and you'll be doing it."

"Unbearable!" I declared.

"Still, you like me," he said on a grin, dipped in, brushed his mouth against mine, then turned me, and with a hand *right on my ass*, he scooted me up a couple of stairs. "Hurry, love. Now I have a taste for donuts, and I dinnae want a delay."

I stomped up the stairs, grumbling loud enough for him to hear, "I need to have my head examined when it comes to my taste in men."

To that, he chuckled and made sure it was loud enough for me to hear.

God, that man.

Once in my room, I was faced with an immediate crisis.

What to wear to go get donuts with Dair?

I selected my cream knit set with black stitching on all the edges (armholes, hems of top and pants). The top was sleeveless. The legs were wide and had very wide ribs in them. It was together, but casual and comfy.

Perfect.

I'd done my face regime already, so I rubbed in some tinted moisturizer, some under shadow base on my eyelids, stroked on mascara, spritzed on my perfume and put on some black Chanel T-strap sandals.

And I was ready.

Dad was up by the time I came down and I greeted him while Dair smirked appreciatively at my outfit, his gaze unabashedly aimed at my ass.

Chad told me I was beautiful all the time.

Odd, but I'd never felt beautiful, not even when he said it to me.

Until Dair.

Dair took my keys again, and I didn't fight him. I liked driving, but if he was one of those men who had to be behind the wheel of any moving vehicle, it wasn't worth arguing about it.

We were out of the drive and on the road when Dair asked, "What were you and Mum talking about?"

"She's staying longer to have some peace before she has to go back and deal with things."

"Aye. She told me. She told you too?"

"Since I'll be here another couple of days, she wanted to be sure I was okay with it."

"And you said yes."

"Of course. And I'm glad. You and Davi both live in Edinburgh and she lives out in the country. She shouldn't be alone now. I can keep my finger on her pulse, be there for her to talk to, and report back to you if I have any concerns."

Dair said nothing for several minutes, which I thought was strange, and then he swung into a pull off, which I thought was more than strange.

I turned to him.

"Is everything o—?"

I got no more out.

His seatbelt was back. My seatbelt was back. Then I was in his lap, and he was feasting on my mouth.

Oh my God.

Yes.

We made out, hot and heavy, in my car pulled off Senator Highway, and we did it as I put grave effort into memorizing the feel of his hair, the taste of his mouth, his fresh, spicy, minty scent, and the dominant moves of his tongue.

I knew my hair was no longer in its messy bun when he tore his mouth from mine and shoved his face into the side of my neck.

I struggled to calm my breath, especially when I could feel the warmth and harshness of his against my skin.

It felt like a triumph to make a man like Dair breathe that heavily, but by damn, I'd done it.

"Your sweetness is doing me in, lassie," he murmured there. "Especially considering I'm going to be thousands of miles away from ye come tomorrow and I can't thank ye properly for being all you can be."

Talk about sweet.

I smoothed his hair and called, "Dair."

He pulled his face out of my neck and looked at me.

I could see the heat in his eyes from our kiss.

I could also see the worry for his mother buried under it.

"You're a good son," I said softly. "And she's a strong woman. It's going to take time. But she's going to be okay."

"Fuck, you're killing me, hen."

I pressed my lips together.

"I ken she's going to be okay," he said. "I'm just glad you'll be around for a few days to look after her."

I stroked his freshly shaven jaw. "Of course I will."

"The next week and more is going to be torture."

He thought the same as me.

I couldn't help myself.

I kissed him again.

We necked for a long time, and I enjoyed all that time, before he put me back in my seat (and I didn't enjoy that).

Even so, there were donuts to get because there were mouths to feed.

Dair waited until we were both belted back up.

And I fixed my hair while he drove us to town.

EARLY THAT AFTERNOON, I'D ALREADY SAID GOODBYE TO DAVI, AND she, Kenna and Dad were hanging some ways away, giving me space to say goodbye to Dair.

I didn't want to say goodbye to Dair.

I was in his arms, and I could feel him examining my face while I fiddled with a button on his shirt.

"Look at me, lass."

I lifted my eyes to him.

He grinned audaciously.

"You so very much like me."

I frowned and slapped his chest.

He laughed and took my mouth in a bold, deep kiss, albeit a pitifully short one.

We were *oh so totally* leveling up when I got to Scotland.

"Text me your flight details when ye get them," he ordered when he'd finished kissing me.

I was a little dizzy from said kiss, so I didn't have it in me to give him shit for again bossing me.

"Okay."

"I'll meet ye at the airport."

I nodded.

He gave me a squeeze. "It's not too long, Blake."

"I know."

He touched his nose to mine. Then he touched his lips to mine. After that, he held my jaw and stroked my throat with his thumb.

That felt crazy nice.

God, he was undoing me!

Finally, he let me go.

Totally undoing me.

We held hands back to the rental car.

Davi got in. After another hug with his mum, a shake of the hands with Dad that turned into a man hug complete with pounding of backs, and a tight squeeze and quick kiss for me, he got in.

Dad, Kenna and I stood in the drive and waved as they drove off.

Davi shoved out of her window and waved back.

I had little doubt Dair saw me in the rearview, waving.

Since that probably made me look the forlorn, infatuated woman, I stopped.

Davi popped back into the car.

And then they were gone.

CHAPTER ELEVEN

BREAKING

Dair

Dair stood outside international arrivals at the Edinburg airport, waiting for Blake to come through the doors.

It had been a busy week and a half, and busy normally made time fly, but waiting for her to come to him, it seemed to drag on.

During that time, they texted frequently, and talked every evening (or, his evening).

In the beginning, when she was still in Arizona, he got detailed reports on his mum. When they'd go out for a meal. When they'd cook together. How his mum spent a lot of time alone on the back deck with her tea or a glass of wine, and Blake left her to it to give her space.

She also shared how the sadness wasn't shifting

"But it won't, Dair," she warned. "Not for a while. She's lived with this a lot longer than we probably know, but following through with ending a forty-year marriage is going to be hard."

It settled him Blake was there with his mum, because he knew how deeply she cared for her.

It settled him more she had a sense of what his mother was going through, even if he hated both of them went through it.

However, when she got back to New York, she was a good deal less quick in returning texts, even though she always picked up when he phoned.

This was because she was having lunch with the "G-Force" to fill them in on Alex and Rix's wedding and her mother's shenanigans.

Or she was over at Nora and Jamie's to work with Nora on some event.

Or she was shopping with Cadence, Mika's daughter, for some special occasion.

Or she was busy cooking, because she'd been asked by one of the G-Force to make some dessert of hers that he wanted to use to impress a date.

Or she was at her father's, making sure some repair she'd ordered happened as she expected.

It unnerved him how full her life was in New York. She'd given the impression it was aimless, when it was anything but.

He could live anywhere, but considering the matches he called were mostly European, the commute would be impossible. He'd have to keep his flat in Edinburgh and be there most of the time regardless.

If they got to that place, he'd hoped she'd move to Scotland.

He was wondering about that now.

A long-distance relationship was far from the best-case scenario, but it could work, if you both had a firm sense of where you'd land when that time came.

It'd never work if both parties lived full lives where they were and neither wanted to leave it.

That wasn't a worry for now.

They'd had two dates, multiple phone calls, a myriad of texts, and each had an understanding this was something deep, something special, something they wanted to explore, and that was all Dair needed for the now.

He knew her flight had landed. He'd timed in his head how long it would take to get through Customs and Immigration. And he knew she should be through those doors any minute now.

Five minutes later, she was.

And the instant he saw her, his chest warmed, at the same time he roared with laughter.

She gave him a dour look.

He strode forward, still laughing, and when they met, he swept her in his arms, the massive bouquet of deep red roses he held slammed against their hips, and he heard a variety of things tumble to the ground as he took her mouth.

She tasted of bubblegum and Blake, and it was the sweetest thing ever to touch his tongue.

When he lifted his head, he teased, "Did ye leave any duty-free shopping in the shops, lassie?"

"Shut up, Dair."

He grinned at her, it getting wider as he saw her hair down, the front sweeping back to fall into big fat curls on her shoulders. She was wearing a black cardie over a black turtleneck and a pair of gray trousers with pleats and very wide legs. A thick statement belt was around her waist. And of course she was wearing high-heeled boots.

"Trust ye to look like you're walking off a runway when ye walk off a plane after a seven-hour flight," he remarked.

"I'm famished and I hate airports, so stop being wonderful and get me out of here," she demanded.

Dair continued to smile as he let her go but gave her the flowers, and they were worth every bit of the exorbitant cost of buying them with the way her eyes lit but her expression gentled when she took them.

He then gathered up all her shopping bags and took the handle of her large suitcase.

He rolled it with his arm around her shoulders. She carried her tote, rolled her carry-on and juggled the flowers so she could wrap her arm around his waist.

"Flight go all right?" he asked on the way to the car park.

"It was a flight. It's over," she replied.

"Not a fan of flying?"

"I consider flying downtime. Time I can do things I would think it was a waste to do on a normal day. Like reading fashion magazines or playing games on my iPad. I look at it like a mini-vacation on the way to a vacation."

That was an interesting way to consider it, and smart too.

She carried on, "But people turn into monsters at airports. Their behavior is appalling."

He could not disagree.

"I don't know what it is," she went on. "It's like something is in the air."

"Well, you're here now, hen, safe and sound. I've got plenty of food in. I'll take care of ye."

When he said that, he wasn't imagining that she adjusted so she was closer to him. Now, not only were their hips touching, their outer thighs were brushing too.

He paid for parking and got her and her tote in the front seat of his Range Rover. He tossed the rest in the back, got in and set them on their way.

"A red Range Rover, Dair?" she asked when they he was maneuvering the car park.

"Aye. What of it?"

"It's just so…*you.*"

"As it would be, since I picked it."

She laughed softly.

He listened and enjoyed.

"Heard from Alex?" he asked.

"She's texted some pictures. It looks beautiful there. Seems like they're having a great time. But they don't get back until tomorrow."

It was Saturday.

Blake was leaving the next Sunday.

And he had to figure out how to fit a trip into New York between matches soon after.

Again, that was for later.

She was at his side now.

"Have you been to the Caribbean?" she asked.

"Aye. Turks and Caicos and Bermuda."

"It's beautiful down there."

"It is."

"These roses are beautiful too, Dair. Extraordinary."

He knew she was looking at him when she said that, so he turned to her.

Christ.

Her face was filled with wonder and gratitude.

Fuck, he was glad she was here.

"Glad ye like 'em, love," he murmured, turning back at the road.

Another sideways glance showed him she'd gathered them to her face and was smelling them.

They cost a bundle, but they were just roses.

However, she was acting like they were her sister's bouquet, something he saw she'd painstakingly disassembled and put the flowers in water, and the plants in pots by the time they'd come over for prime rib that first night.

Maybe she just liked flowers.

Then again, she'd been taken aback when he'd bought her earrings, jewelry, not incidentally, she was wearing right now.

She was worth a load. Her mother's estate was worth more. Her father even more.

But she was a woman who sincerely appreciated the small things if there was meaning to them.

"Have you heard from Kenna?" she asked into his thoughts.

"Yesterday," he told her. "She's rearranged her flight to be here mid-week. You'll be seeing her before ye go."

"Wonderful."

She let some time pass before she queried carefully, "Have you heard more from your father?"

"As I've told ye, love, he's been repeatedly attempting contact."

"I know. You said. But he still is?"

"I've texted him that once I told ye about to tell him to back off and wait until I'm ready to speak with him."

"It's good to establish healthy boundaries."

"Aye."

"But even if you're not replying, he's still not recognizing them?"

"No. He keeps trying. I just ignore it. Davi's doing the same thing."

"Your mum?"

It was hard for him to think on that one, because it pissed him off so much.

"Aye."

"He's still badgering your mum?" she asked, her voice pitched higher.

"Aye," he repeated.

"Oh, Dair," she said softly.

"It's okay, baby," he replied.

"It isn't."

"Well, it is what it is."

"Yes. It is that."

They got out of talking about the heavy as he guided them the rest of the way to his terrace flat and he parked in the back.

He wrestled her bags and suitcase up the walk while she rolled her carry-on and hugged her roses to her chest.

He let them into the boot room at the back.

She entered and stopped, taking it in, before he moved them into the kitchen.

She continued gazing around. "God, Dair, this is—"

She ended her words abruptly on a high-pitched squeal.

This was because Sorcha, his Scottish Deerhound, came loping in, and after a cursory sniff and tail wag Dair's way, she went right to Blake.

Blake edged away as Sorcha followed her.

"What is it?" she asked after she butted up against his kitchen worktop, staring at Sorcha like she was being cornered by a diseased rat.

Dair felt his neck muscles tighten, because he didn't like this one bit.

It was a huge problem due to the fact it was a dealbreaker.

You liked him, you liked his dog.

You couldn't love him, unless you loved his dog.

"She's Sorcha, my dog."

Blake's overwrought gaze came to him. "It's a dog?"

"*She* is, aye."

"She's huge."

Sorcha was snuffling Blake's hand.

"She's a deerhound."

"Dogs are supposed to fit in bags so you can take them shopping," she declared.

Bloody hell.

"Are you going to eat me?" she asked Sorcha.

Sorcha panted.

"Even though you're furry, when it gets cold, are you going to let me put a sweater on you?" Blake asked.

Sorcha's body vibrated with excitement.

Bloody fucking hell.

Although Sorcha was taking the opportunity herself, Blake offered her hand for his dog to sniff. She did, before she licked it, then Blake gave her head a rubdown.

Dair relaxed.

"With all that beautiful, shaggy gray-white fur, I'm thinking, cashmere. Black, obviously. How about you?" Blake asked his dog.

Sorcha got even more excited.

"You aren't dressing my dog," Dair asserted.

Now Blake had put down the bouquet and she was rubbing his girl with both hands. "She and I disagree."

"For fuck's sake," he muttered.

She straightened and demanded, "Show me your house."

This he did, with Sorcha trotting along with them.

He ordered Blake to leave her carry-on where it was, they wandered around, and he ended the tour up in his attic bedroom with the slanted roof, so he could deposit her bags there. All of them.

His bedroom had a king bed shoved against the short wall. A skylight over it. Hardwood floor. Gray walls. White baseboards. Gray and white thin-striped sheets. Red and white thick-striped euros. And red desk lamps on both nightstands.

"I'm impressed," Blake told him. "With all of it."

"I had a designer," he told her.

"She's good," she observed.

"Aye. He is," he agreed. "Bathroom through there." He indicated.

She wandered that way.

"Closet next to it," he shared. "I cleared some drawer and hanging space for ye."

She stopped peering into the bathroom and looked to him.

Sorcha sat down and leaned against her.

Absently, she scratched his dog's head.

Oh, aye.

This was going to work.

"We're domesticating very fast, Dair," she purred.

"Ye a woman who lives out of suitcase?"

"Absolutely not."

As he thought.

"So I'm just looking after you."

She moved his way.

Sorcha moved with her.

She put both her hands on his chest, so he put his to her hips, she leaned into him and said, "You seem to do well with that."

His voice was rough when he asked, "Do ye want me to feed you or fuck you, darling? Because if you're hungry, and ye pick fucking, you're going to have quite a wait."

Her eyes flashed, but she said, "I'm actually really hungry."

"Then let's get some food in ye."

With that, he, his woman and his dog headed down the stairs.

THEY WERE ON THE COUCH IN HIS LIVING ROOM.

The bouquet of roses was in a vase on the table between the chairs opposite them.

Sorcha was on the floor beside the couch.

The TV was on low, and Dair was watching a tennis match while Blake—cuddled to his side, her back to the couch, their legs tangled—napped.

He'd made her thick slices of radically buttered toast and Keiller's marmalade, which she'd wolfed down like she hadn't eaten in a year.

The boots came off next.

The cardie after that, exposing her turtleneck was sleeveless, and they'd started talking while drinking coffee on the couch, when he noticed she was fading. So he suggested they stretch out and watch some TV while she had a rest.

She was out like a light within ten minutes.

His phone vibed so he reached to it on the button-top, upholstered, navy ottoman that served double duty as a coffee table.

It was a text from his sister.

She'd sent an image or a video, and the word, *Warning*.

He opened it and felt his mouth get tight when he saw it was a picture of him and Blake snogging at the airport.

She looked phenomenal, and it was an absolute turn on to have visible proof of how into him she was, and he wasn't hiding he felt the same thing for her.

But…fuck.

That didn't take long.

He had one arm around her on the couch, so he had to thumb the phone to hit the image

Another text came in from his sister as he was scowling at a gossip rag's Instagram post, spreading the word that BREAKING: SCOTLAND'S TOP RUGBY HOTTIE AND NEW YORK'S FINEST BACHELORETTE ARE MAKING A STATEMENT.

"Fucking hell," he muttered as he went back to his texts.

I better see her while she's in town, Davi said.

Using his thumb, he replied, *You will.*

He thought he was having a care, but Blake stirred, then stretched, and finally lifted her head off his shoulder.

He tossed his phone on the ottoman and looked down at her.

"All good?" he asked quietly.

"How long was I out?" she asked blearily.

"A couple of hours."

"Yuck," she mumbled.

"Ye mentioned ye dinnae sleep well on planes," he noted, and she had, between massive bites of toast.

"I got some. But I don't want to sleep all day."

"Travel takes it out of ye. This is why I didnae plan anything for today." He stroked her back. "So just relax."

She settled back into him but reached out to pet Sorcha's head.

He didn't know whether or not to tell her about the Instagram post.

"Sorcha needs a walk, and I need fresh air," she stated.

Sorcha was always happy for a walk.

And Dair was happy Blake wanted to take her on one.

"Got shoes without six-inch heels on them?" he asked.

She turned her head his way. "My booties don't have six-inch heels."

He smiled at her. "Five, then."

"I'll have you know, I can probably play basketball in those heels. And they aren't five inches, either."

"Since I'd rather ye not be hobbling around on crutches, I'll take your word for it."

She aimed just her eyeballs at the ceiling.

He bent his head to touch his mouth to hers.

When he pulled away, he said, "Let's take my girl out."

They got off of the couch. She put on her boots and cardie, he put on his trainers, and they headed to the front door where he kept Sorcha's lead on a hook.

But even if his pup sensed what they were about and was winding around them in excitement, before they went out into the world, Dair decided to show her the Instagram post.

"Need ye to see something first, baby," he said.

She turned to him.

He pulled the post up on his phone and showed her.

"Oh my God, it's already starting," she stated irately, glaring at the phone.

"Dinnae worry about it."

Her amazing eyes went from his mobile to him, and he could see plainly she was absolutely worried.

"Aren't you worried about it?" she asked.

"Wasted emotion." He wrapped a hand around the side of her neck. "Remember, this isn't new to me."

"It still stinks."

"Aye." He gave a nod. "It does. But it's out of our control. Though, I ken ye dinnae want to disturb her on her honeymoon, but it's ending, and ye might want to give Alex a heads-up so she doesn't find out via social media you and me are a thing."

Blake nodded. "Good idea."

"And now I have photographic proof of how into me you are."

"Oh my God, you're insufferable," she lied.

This meant Dair was smiling as he reached for the lead.

Sorcha, as was her usual, went mental.

He clipped it on, and they headed out.

They strolled, linked, while Sorcha reacquainted herself with the scents of the neighborhood.

Suddenly, Blake asked, "Did Signe like dogs?"

"Aye," he answered. "We had a prenup. Dad insisted and thank fuck he did. Still would have paid the woman more to be rid of her. I had a beardie when I met her. We adopted a border collie together. Since she didnae have anything to fight about because she signed on to what she'd get if we didnae work, she went after custody of the dogs."

Blake stopped dead, and with wooden movements, turned to look up at him.

"She...*what?*" Before he could respond, she demanded, "Both of them?"

"Aye. But she didnae win, babe," he assured. "It just drug shite out and cost more money than it should." He grinned playfully at her. "Though, in my next prenup, I'll be sure to mention pets and the fact I'll be keeping them."

Blake didn't respond to that. She noticed Sorcha was keen to get moving so she started them walking again.

She did this as she sniped, "What a bitch. I mean, I could see she'd not want to lose the dog you adopted together, or the one she'd grown to love while being with you, but by then I expect they were bonded?"

"They were," he confirmed.

"Ugh," she grunted. "The best way to ascertain you'll be able to see your animals is to not be a total bitch during a breakup."

"Very true."

"Are they...have they passed?" she asked carefully.

"Aye. Nessie, my beardie, died a few years after the divorce. Effie held on a long time. She only died a few years ago."

"I'm sorry, Dair."

He loved that she knew to say that even if years had passed since they'd been gone. He still missed them.

He gave her a squeeze. "Since it's obvious ye like them, why dinnae ye have a pet?"

"I can barely take care of me. How am I going to look after an animal?"

Bloody hell.

Here they were again.

"The correct answer to that, lass, is you're so busy taking care of other people, ye dinnae have time to add a pet to that."

"Well…yes," she mumbled. "I suppose I have gotten to that point. Though, now I'm in Prescott a lot, and I'm of a mind that dragging your pet everywhere you go causes anxiety to that pet. I can see *you* wanting your animal with you wherever you are. But *they* might not feel all that comfortable in a plane or a market or Bergdorf's." She looked up at him. "What do you do with Sorcha when you're not here?"

"Davi takes her. If she's not around, I've got a couple of mates who like having her with them."

"Oh." She turned to face where they were going. "That's nice."

They took a corner and Sorcha stopped to sniff a loo option.

"Do you see her?"

"Davi? Aye. And ye will too. I'm thinking drinks and dinner Tuesday night. We'll give Mum a day to settle in and head out there Thursday. Davi will probably be there too."

"I mean Signe."

Ah.

"No, Blake. Last I heard she moved back to Denmark. Saw her a few times after the divorce. But now it's been years."

She nodded and looked to Sorcha, but since she was doing her business, she looked across the street.

When Sorcha was done, he set them moving again and asked, "What about that twat ye almost married?"

"Chad?"

"Ye almost marry another twat?" he teased.

She pretended to be annoyed at him, but her lips tipped up before she shook her head.

Even shaking her head, she said, "Yes. He tries to contact me once or twice a year. He's married, by the way."

"And he still tries to contact ye?"

"Yes."

"To say he's sorry and let's be friends, or…?" he let that trail.

"The 'or' part," she told him.

"Total twat," he muttered.

"Yes," she repeated.

They fell silent the rest of the walk. It was a bonny end-of-summer day. But the weather was forecast to turn for the rest of the week.

"Hope ye brought warm clothes, lass," he mentioned.

"I did, honey," she replied.

Fuck, he liked that.

He led them back to the house, and after they got in and he took the lead off his dog, Blake turned to him.

"I feel like I smell like airplane. Do you mind if I take a quick shower and unpack?"

"No. But are you hungry? While ye do that, I could put together some snacks."

"That'd be great."

He dropped a kiss on her and bid, "Go."

"Take your time with the snacks," she said as she went. "It's going to take me an hour just to climb up two flights of stairs."

"Cheek."

He heard her soft laugh.

Damn, but he'd already fallen in love with the sound of that.

He'd give it a quarter of an hour then he'd hit the kitchen. He had a taste for bacon and brie sandwiches. And as far as he could tell, Blake had a taste for all food, she wasn't picky, she enjoyed it, didn't hide it, and she didn't haver on about it.

Something else to like about his woman.

Not top of the list, but on it.

It was a long list.

And it was getting longer.

CHAPTER TWELVE

BACON AND BRIE SANDWICHES

Blake

I was fidgety as all hell.

But I was ready.

Or at least that was what I told myself.

I'd had a quick shower, took off my makeup and put on fresh (minimally, for what I had planned it could only be minimal).

I'd found the drawers and open rail Dair had cleared for me in his closet (he'd obviously used a former room to build a walk-in, a decision I wholeheartedly approved, ditto with his bathroom, and my approval). So I quickly unpacked.

Spritz of perfume.

Daring red nightie and matching string bikini panties.

And I was ready.

I hoped.

"God," I moaned to myself as I walked out to the stairwell.

I had no idea in his big (and *tall*) house, if he'd hear me.

What I did know was that you didn't hire an interior designer and say, "Do whatever."

You were involved in the process. You gave your preferences. You guided the project.

And if his house (not to mention his clothes and his choice of car) was anything to go by, Dair had exceptionally good taste.

His living room was a contrast of lights and darks. It was more formal than the lounge. There were patterns and textures in the soft furnishings. Personality to the fireplace wall that looked wallpapered in a dark blue-gray tweed (the fireplace painted black). Inset shelves on either side that told me he read and traveled (the last, I knew, the first I wasn't surprised about). And the modern lighting fixture over the ottoman/table that had dangling globes of gold, milky or smoked glass was a stunner.

His lounge was darker, dressed in deep hues of blue and gray. It had a fireplace too, over which was the TV.

The kitchen that had a view to the miniscule back garden shared he hadn't lied during one of our daily conversations. He cooked.

It was bright and airy with white cupboards, black marble countertops, and a silvery-gray, small-square tile backsplash. In all of that monochrome, he kept some oranges in a black bowl on the windowsill above the corner sink. I expected, for a man, the placement wasn't for aesthetics, but instead to keep it off the countertop, or maybe he was a man who cared about the aesthetics. Either way, it was the perfect pop of color for the room.

His dining room was sparsely furnished and modern, with comfortable chairs around the table, as dining rooms should be. If you were entertaining lots of people and bringing in food, you didn't need to navigate furniture.

He had two guest bedrooms (the lounge was on the second floor).

And his bedroom took up the entire top floor.

It was fabulous. Masculine, without being too masculine. Stylish, without being overly styled and unwelcoming. Comfortable. And spacious.

He only had one parking spot, though. However, Edinburgh had been formed *long* before cars were an idea, so I knew he was lucky to even have that.

But his was a lovely home. Room to move. Room to have space to yourself. Rooms that were cozy so you could enjoy them together.

And we could both be cooking and not bump into each other.

The man liked his clothes, but there was still plenty of closet space.

I could spend time here.

I could be happy here.

Oh so happy.

God, was I running that far ahead so early?

I totally was, standing like an idiot in his stairwell, wearing a racy red nightie.

Because…he bought me roses.

Two dozen (I counted as I stemmed them and put them in a vase) bunched beautifully together red, red, *red* roses.

And he met me at the airport with them.

I thought men like this only existed in books. Men who called you every day. Men who texted you too, so you knew he was thinking about you. Men who weren't about guessing games. Men who were more concerned about what you thought than what their friends thought.

Real men.

Good men.

My man.

"Dair!" I shouted down the steps.

I expected he wouldn't hear me, but I got a quick, "Aye!"

"Can you come up here for a sec?" I requested, that "for a sec" part not at all what I intended, but he'd find that out soon enough.

"Be up in a tick!"

God, how could he make "in a tick" sound hot?

I put it down to the powers of a Scottish accent.

Or maybe it was just Dair.

I scurried back to the bedroom.

It was then I realized I hadn't planned this out far enough. I got to the nightie part and calling him up part and stopped.

I'd never instigated this kind of thing. It was always the guy doing it.

Should I be lounged on the bed invitingly?

Should I sit at the end with legs crossed, arms back, breasts pushed out?

Should I…?

Fuck it.

I sat cross-legged at the end of his bed and fretted.

He hadn't made any moves since I arrived hours ago, except the couch nap/cuddle (and I was correct, cuddling with him was *transcendent*).

Maybe he was worried I was jetlagged (I semi-was, but not enough not to want this).

Maybe he wasn't ready yet.

I'd soon find out.

Yikes.

I heard him coming and instantly changed my mind.

I thought I was ready.

I wasn't.

He appeared in the door.

Too late now.

He took one look at me and didn't freeze or take even a millisecond to contemplate.

After a brief stutter step, he was across the room. His fingers wrapped around my ribs, I was up, and then we were both down, deeper into the bed, me on my back, Dair all over me.

And I meant *all over me.*

All the nerves I was experiencing wobbled when he essentially tackled me.

They vanished completely when his mouth crashed down on mine, and he was kissing me, hard and wet.

He did this while his hands roamed—ribs, waist, hips, the small of my back…down.

Gripping my ass, he pulled me up into his hard hips.

At what I felt there (already!), I whimpered and yanked at his lightweight sweater.

He arched away, tore it off, and I got not near enough time to take in his broad, defined, perfectly furred chest before he tossed the sweater to the side, and he was kissing me again.

However, with all that exposed and available to me, I might not be able to see it, but I embarked on a voyage of discovery with my hands and learned instantly it was the best trip I could take.

Warm, silken skin over steely flesh, plains and dips and jags.

The ridges of his ribs were sensitive, as was the skin just under the waistband of his jeans.

Scrumptious.

He found the sensitive skin behind my ear and manipulated it with lips and tongue until I was squirming under him.

I positioned to flip him in order to make more of him available to me, but as I made a move to do so, his body locked, and his teeth sunk into the fragile tendon of my neck.

This caused a full body quiver.

Oh.

Wow.

My panties flooded at his message of just who was going to dominate the proceedings.

I didn't put up even a minimal fight.

I immediately acquiesced, relaxing under him.

His mouth moved to mine, and he growled his approval against my tongue, and that was so fabulous, I mewed against his.

We kissed and we explored, and finally, Dair's fingers curled into the low neckline of my nightie, and he dragged it across my breast, across my nipple, and it felt so good, I moaned into his mouth.

But that mouth left me to latch on my nipple.

Like he started this, he didn't go slow. He didn't take it easy.

He was demanding and aggressive. He licked, sucked, nipped and scored his teeth across my delicate flesh as I arched and moaned and had no choice but to focus entirely on what he was doing, losing focus on touching him.

No, all I could do was curl my fingers into his hair with both hands and hold him to me.

He switched breasts.

I whimpered my delight.

With his fingers, he played with the wet nipple he left behind, and he didn't do that gently either. Pinches. Tight rolls. There was slight pain amidst the waves of pleasure I was drowning in, and I wanted it, I yearned for it, I was *aching* for it.

This wasn't me.

I knew what to do in bed, but I didn't expect much from it. I'd climaxed rarely with a partner. Usually, they'd have to take care of me after, if they even bothered.

This was…

It was…

It was pure *magic*.

His mouth came to mine just as his hand traveled from my breast to my belly, and as I was learning with Dair, he didn't fuck around.

He went right into my panties, over the tuft of hair there, and with one long finger, he went right into me.

That felt so amazing, I tore my mouth from his and cried out.

His brogue was deeper, rough when he encouraged, "That's it, lassie," as he pumped his finger in and out of my wetness.

My hips moved with agitation to meet his strokes.

"Fucking hell, Blake," he bit out then his finger was gone.

Before I could protest, my nightie was gone too, not to mention my panties. In fact, I thought I felt one of the strings snap as he yanked them off me.

Oh my.

So good.

He pushed my legs apart with unhidden demand, rolled between them, and then he was going down on me.

Holy hell.

My back left the bed as I ground into his mouth.

"Aye, baby," his words vibrated into my sensitive folds as his big hands pressed my legs wider "offer this sweet, pretty, wet pussy to your man."

Oh God.

So good.

He ate me as uncompromisingly and confidently as he'd done everything else to me.

I was in ecstasy, a trembling mess under the demands of his tongue (and sometimes teeth). He stroked and sucked and tongue fucked.

"God!" I cried.

Almost there.

So damned close.

And it was going to be *spectacular.*

He pulled away.

Good Lord, *no.*

I lifted my head to search for him and found him by the side of the bed, shoving down his jeans.

Okay, *yes.*

Jeans off, he straightened, and for the first time, the whole of him accosted my eyes.

Thick thighs. Boxed abs. And a cock that was exciting in length, but thrilling in girth stood proud from a thatch of thick, dark hair.

He reached to the nightstand and came back with a condom.

Watching him work it expertly on that beautiful dick drove me to my knees in the bed.

Watching me watch him drove him to doing something impossible.

Once the condom was on, he caught me tough at the back of my neck, his other hand gripped the back of a thigh, and he swung me through the air.

Naturally, and because I wanted to, when we collided, I curled my other leg around him, he curled the one he had hold of there, and with a luscious grunt from him, and a long, low whimper from me, he was inside.

Standing by the side of his bed, Dair had impaled me on his cock without even guiding it.

That was so fucking amazing, I almost came right then.

I'd be glad I didn't.

He put a knee to the bed, then he was on me, and he was fucking me.

There was nothing gentle to it. Again, no lead up. He still had a grip on the back of my neck, one behind my knee, and he kept both to hold me steady as he pounded into me, his eyes locked to my face, the sound of our flesh slapping together mingling with his grunts of effort and my pants of pleasure filling the room.

Right, *now* I was going to come.

I grasped a hank of his hair, scored my nails down his back, and delighted in his grunted, "*Fuck.*"

And then he was pounding deeper, faster. Banging against my sensitized clit, he yanked my knee up, I pulled the other one high, and suddenly, every stroke inside slammed against something, and let me tell you, it was *extraordinary*.

"Honey," I gasped, holding on tighter to his hair, sinking my nails into his lat, racing toward an orgasm.

"Ye got a beautiful, wet, tight cunt, baby," he rumbled.

Oh God.

Was that the best compliment anyone had ever given me?

Yes.

Yes, as insane as it sounded, it *so totally* was.

I wanted this man to love my cunt.

I wanted this man to love everything about me.

"Dair, honey, yes!" I exclaimed, swinging my calves in and digging in with my heels as I raised my hips to meet his strokes and exploded.

And exploded.

And *exploded.*

I was so far gone, it was just Dair and me and my orgasm, and that was all I wanted it to be.

Forever.

Dair fucked me through it, and he didn't stop fucking even when his grunts turned into a long, hot groan, his hips bucked without rhythm, his hold on me grew dizzyingly, delectably painful, his head snapped back, and I knew he was coming.

I was nuzzling his jaw while he came down because he'd buried his face in the side of my neck.

And I knew it had left him when his grip disappeared, but his hands started skating gently over my skin.

This seemed to take a while, and I hoped that indicated his climax was even minimally as awesome as mine.

Eventually, he took his weight from me by rolling us to our sides.

But he didn't stop trailing his hands all over me.

And he caught my gaze.

"Only thing on this planet I'd be willing to abandon a bacon and brie piece for is a good, solid fuck with my woman in my bed," he declared.

Good God.

He was just so…*Dair*.

"Well, that was flowery and romantic, Sir Galahad," I replied.

He grinned unashamedly at me and palmed a handful of my ass.

Totally so *Dair*.

"What's a piece?" I asked.

"Sandwich," he answered.

Ooo, bacon and brie sandwiches.

"What kind of bread did you use?" I asked.

He started chuckling and took advantage of his clutch on my ass to pull me closer to him. "Love it ye like your food, hen."

"Thrilled, Dair, but you didn't answer my question."

That was when he burst out laughing.

Then he rolled to his back, pulling me on top of him.

And finally answered, "Baguette."

"Are they done?"

"Aye."

"Can I go get them while you deal with the condom?"

His body shook me with his continued mirth. "Aye."

"Can I tell you I haven't had a lover in four years, but I have had several checkups, and I'm clean, so now you can tell me you're clean too, so we don't have to bother with condoms?" I requested.

His eyes got lazy in a way I'd never seen before, and I loved it, as he stroked my jaw with his thumb and murmured, "Poor wee lass, hot as fuck lay like you going without for four years?"

"Considering the fact I've never had anything near as hot, nor as energetic, nor as *assertive*…"

That earned me another unabashed grin.

"And I'll add," I continued, "rarely culminating in anything delightful for me, unless he had it in him to take care of me after, which was even more rare, of course I was hot," I educated him. "And now I'm hungry, but first, I'd like to know your health status, please."

But he was frowning ferociously.

"No one before me took care of ye?"

"Well, no one before *ye* could drag me from the bed and plant me on his dick."

With that, he roared with laughter, rolling us so he was on top again.

When he got control of his humor, he said, "Good you're with me now, then."

Good didn't cover it.

I was in no mood to boost his ego further. I was in the mood to eat, and maybe do what we just did again (multiple times), so I prompted, "Dair."

"I've not had the dry spell ye have, darling," he said gently. "But I always use protection, and I get yearly physicals. I'm clean."

"So, since I have an IUD, we can dispense with the condoms."

His eyes moved over my face as he murmured, "Never knew a woman who was more about that even than me."

I didn't want anything between us.

Again, in an effort not to stroke his ego, I refrained from sharing that, and reminded him, "Sandwiches?"

"Ye can get them, lass. I'll deal with this johnnie."

Since we had a plan, he rolled one way; I rolled the other.

He headed to the bathroom. I located my nightie and pulled it on before I moved to the stairs.

Once in the kitchen (and on the way, I was joined by Sorcha), I saw he had everything all ready, but I wasn't sure how to juggle it all up two flights of stairs.

In the end, I put both sandwiches on one plate, grabbed a bag of chips and carried them in one hand, while I arranged two bottles of sparkling water to carry in the other.

Sorcha accompanying me, I trudged back up the stairs to find Dair in bed, resting against pillows he'd shoved up behind him, and he'd put on a pair of boxers.

Okay, now that I could take in my fill, I could confirm he was perfect everywhere.

Sorcha went to the bed to say hi to her daddy as, on the other side, I entered it on my knees only to freeze when he abandoned his dog and reached a hand to the back of my thigh and trailed it up to cup my bottom.

I stayed frozen at the heat that scorched me from his eyes, not to mention his touch, when he encountered bare skin.

"Ye walked to my kitchen without knickers?" he asked.

"I think you tore them during the festivities," I told him. "But would you have preferred I put them back on?"

He slid his hand over my hip, and it left me so he could help me with the food and drink as he replied, "Darling, feel free to wander my house with that beautiful cunt ready for me whenever you want."

Oh my God.

Now he was being hot *and* annoying at the same time.

Could he get any worse?

I harumphed as I fell to a hip and put the plate on the bed.

Straightaway, I set about eating.

And he said, "Happy you're here, Blake."

"You fuck hard, Dair. I think I got that," I retorted and munched into a delicious sandwich with plenty of bacon and brie in a marvelously fresh baguette.

He shot me another one of his cocky grins before his face turned serious.

"That's not what I mean, lassie," he whispered.

Oh God.

That was so beautiful.

And it meant the world to me.

This man brought flowers to an airport.

Before I got overly gushy (so *not* me), I put my sandwich on the plate, my hand to his cheek and I leaned close to him and whispered back, "I like your house. I like your car. I like your dog. And even though you're vastly irritating, I like you too. To wit, I'm happy to be here too, Alasdair."

With an abrupt *plonk*, the sandwich plate was on the nightstand. A loud crinkle, and there went the chips. Two thuds, and our drinks were set away.

And he caught me with an arm low on my hips and dragged me under him.

"Dair!" I protested. "I'm hungry."

"They're already cold, they can wait a few minutes longer."

I began to offer an alternate scenario, "Or you could wait to—"

That was as far as I got before he was kissing me.

Not long later, he was again fucking me, hard and thoroughly.

And of course, I forgot about the bacon and brie sandwiches.

Completely.

CHAPTER THIRTEEN

IRREVOCABLY

Dair

"And then he ran into the street wearing nothing but his socks, shouting, 'I forgot the ice cream!'" Davi was saying while chortling.

Blake finally allowed her humor to overtake her, tears were in her eyes, she was laughing so hard.

Dair rested back on his and Blake's side of the booth, his arm stretched along the back of the seat behind Blake, smiling at his sister's funny story, but not allowing himself to laugh so he could watch two of his three best girls enjoying each other's company.

It was Tuesday night.

They'd all had dinner together at an Indian restaurant, then went to the pub.

Saturday, Sunday and Monday, he and Blake barely got out of bed. They did so only to get food and tug on clothes to take Sorcha on a walk.

However, he'd been alarmed when he'd seen the bruises he left on her thighs and hips.

These left after he took her hard.

But when he mentioned them, she'd kissed him with an unusual light in her eyes that was both soft and feminine in a cat's-got-her-cream type of way.

And she did this telling him, "I bruise easy, Dair. I always did. And anyway, they don't hurt at all." The soft went out of her gaze and the cat's-got-her-cream took over. "And I like them."

He sensed she told no lies, especially considering her libido matched his, as did her stamina, so he changed his mind and decided he liked his marks on her too.

He'd had some meetings he'd had to be on his computer in his office for that day.

She'd left him alone to have them, taking Sorcha for a walk. During it, she'd texted him five pictures of his dog playing in a park, the last one a selfie of the two of them, Sorcha licking Blake's cheek while Blake's eyes were closed, and she looked to be laughing.

Again, she could be adorable.

And that fucking snap was going in a frame.

Dair was not unaware that he was falling for her.

The distance thing was a concern, but nothing else was.

She was funny. She was bright. She was well-traveled. She could hold her own. She was stylish. She could cook. She could make a mess, but she didn't leave it long before she tidied it up. She was fucking sensational in bed. She liked to cuddle. She could be adorable.

And she liked his dog.

Aye, and she got along great with his sister.

"Obviously, he got arrested. Though, only after the coppers chased him for five blocks with his willie flapping in the breeze," Davi finished, to gales more of Blake's laughter.

It was then Dair saw his mobile, screen down on the table in front of them, light up around the edges. He reached to turn it, seeing he had a call from his mate, Declan.

Dec was a texter, so Dair was surprised at getting a call.

However, Dec and his woman had just had their second child, maybe three weeks ago, and it hadn't been an easy go for Shannon.

Fuck.

"Gotta take this," he said and got both women's attention. "Ye good?" he asked.

Two nods.

He kissed Blake's cheek and slid out of the booth with his phone.

When he got outside, he saw it wasn't raining for once. It had either been raining or misting since Sunday morning. They'd had to walk the dog huddling under an umbrella for three days. The only respite they'd had, Dair didn't get to enjoy, but Blake did when she took Sorcha to the park.

He walked up the narrow close where the pub was, to the Royal Mile. He'd missed the call but rang Dec as he looked up the rain slicked street that had many pedestrians, both locals and obvious tourists, on the pavements, toward Edinburgh Castle, lit up at night.

Dec picked up. "Dair."

"Heya, mate. All right?"

"Aye, Dair. You?"

"All good. Ye called?"

"Aye. And…shit, Dair. Fucks me to tell ye this but think you should know with some urgency. Shannon was on her mobile, scrolling, and she came across some video of a podcast Signe did recently."

Dair felt his neck get tight. "A podcast?"

"Shann did some sleuthing, and apparently you're dating someone?"

"Aye."

"Serious?" Dec asked.

"Aye," Dair answered. "Why?"

"Well, that would explain why Signe is using this to catapult herself back into the consciousness of the masses, mate."

His neck muscles tensing further, Dair shifted to stand next to a building to move out of the way of passersby and asked, "What's she saying?"

"Shann listened to it, and not much, really, except a whole sob story about how ye were the love of her life, and ye married too young, and she expected you'd eventually make it back to each other since ye were meant to be, and shite like that."

Bloody hell.

They'd been divorced eleven years, and his ex was trying to cast Blake in the role of the other woman.

Why the fuck would she do that?

"Thought ye should know," Dec went on.

"I should. And I thank ye. Not sure what's in that woman's head, but whatever it is, she's getting something out of it."

"Maybe they paid her. Shann says your new woman is a big deal."

"A big deal?"

"Some kind of feminist icon or something."

Dair couldn't hold back his laughter.

"She's not?" Declan asked through it.

"It's not going to be hard for ye to learn that Blake went viral a few years back when she gutted her fiancée at the altar of their wedding, exposing he'd slept with most of her bridesmaids. Their men were in the congregation, so things got even more hostile after that. But she's not a feminist icon, at least not intentionally. Though what she did kicked arse."

But it would trigger Signe as well.

Everything about Blake would. That she was classically beautiful. That she came from money. That she had fame for a reason that might be painful to her, but it was worthwhile.

Signe had that blonde hair, pale, blue-eyed prettiness that would never be anything more than pretty, though she was very pretty.

And she used what intelligence she had to connive to get what she wanted, and for no other purpose.

Naturally, because she was who she was, Signe would be feeling competitive.

Fucking hell.

"Got to find that footage, mate," Dec replied.

"Blake doesn't think it's her finest hour, and it isn't, but it's one of them," Dair told him, and got down to the matter at hand, "Could ye get Shannon to text me a link to that podcast? Signe has signed two NDAs. She doesn't have a lot of leeway to talk about us."

This brought up the unwanted realization that his father was the one who took care of that.

Balfour not only didn't like Signe for Dair, he didn't trust her.

But he did love his son and wanted him to have what he wanted, just doing that being protected.

Therefore, he'd not only been on Dair about the prenuptial agreement, and going bullish on it, advice Dair, in the end, thankfully took, he'd pushed an NDA, not only before the wedding, but as a term of the prenuptial, so she didn't get to spew anything after.

In fact, she wasn't allowed to say much publicly but confirm they'd been married and now were not.

"We'll text it, mate. Sorry about this. I thought ye were done with her mess."

"I thought so too," he muttered and heard voices coming up the close. Voices he knew.

His two girls.

He looked around the corner and saw them latched together by their arms, leaning into each other, talking and coming his way.

Blake negotiated the wet cobbles in her heels like she was gliding on ice, going for the gold.

He felt his lips curl up.

Damn, he was totally falling for her.

"It's late. I'll leave ye be. See you next time I'm in town," Dec bid.

Dec, being Irish, lived in Dublin.

"Look forward to that. Say hi to Shannon and kiss those weans for me."

"Will do."

"Bye, Dec,"

"Bye, Dair."

They hung up just as the women made it to him.

"Pub's closing," Davi told him.

He narrowed his eyes. "Who paid?"

He knew exactly who with the smug look on Blake's face even if Davi said, "Secret we're taking to the grave, big brother."

Davi was going to get away with it.

Blake would pay for it…

Later.

"Heading home but I'll be picking Mum up from the airport tomorrow morning," Davina reminded him.

"And we'll be seeing ye both Thursday night at the house for dinner," Dair reminded her.

"Aye," Davi confirmed.

They walked his sister to her car, and she got a hug from Blake and a kiss on the cheek from Dair.

But as his sister drove away, Blake linked arms with him, looked up at him, and said, "It's not raining for once. Do you mind walking for a spell before we go home? Doesn't seem like we've been able to stretch our legs very much since I've been here."

They were challenging their bodies quite a bit, but they were in bed (or in the shower) while they did it.

And he felt a warmth spread low in his belly at her referring to his place as "home."

"Aye, lassie, whatever ye want."

She beamed at him.

He led her up the Royal Mile.

DAIR WAS SEATED ON THE SIDE OF THE BED.

Blake was seated in his lap, bouncing on his cock.

He felt her wet cunt gripping and releasing as she moved up and down at his command with his fingers wrapped around her ribcage, and it felt fucking *phenomenal.*

Making it better was the hungry look in her eyes, the flush across the creamy skin of her cheeks, her nails digging into his flesh where she held him at his shoulders.

For her part in paying for drinks earlier, he smacked her ass, not for the first time that night, and without him saying a word, she went faster, also not for the first time.

Definitely.

He was falling for her.

He moved one hand over her belly, down, in, and thumbed her clit.

Her head fell back, exposing the elegant line of her neck, and she bounced even harder.

Fucking hell, she wasn't something.

She was everything.

It was time to get serious.

He took her with him as he got to his feet, and while he did, he got off on her startled, annoyed, turned-on cry.

He pulled her off his cock, turned her and deposited her in the bed on her hands and knees, that sweet arse facing him.

He took hold of her hip with one hand, his dick with the other, and guided it home.

Her head flew back, and she released a sultry moan.

His balls drew up.

Oh, *aye.*

She was everything.

Standing beside the bed, he rode her rough.

She reared back into him, her excited pants and the sound of flesh meeting flesh egging him on, until he got close.

He reached along her back, tangling his fingers in her hair and giving it a gentle tug.

She mewed and was forced into an arch for him.

Christ, she was gorgeous.

He bent to her, snaking a hand around, and homed in on her clit.

The second he touched her, she went wild for him.

Or wilder.

Riding him hard as he rode her harder, it got to be touch and go who would fly first, and he was relieved when he heard her cry out, felt her cunt clench around his cock, and he knew she'd found it.

So Dair let go and had his own, thrusting brutally and pulling her hair back harder, only for her cunt to clench tighter, and what sounded like a second orgasm took her as his cock jetted inside her and her pussy milked it dry.

As they were coming down, Blake collapsed onto her forearms, her face in his covers, and Dair moved his fingers over her hips and that beautiful ass as he stroked himself inside as long as he could.

When he was losing it, he ordered, "Stay just like that, hen."

She turned her head on the bed in order to watch him walk to the bathroom, but like the good girl she was, she remained in position as he came back out with a wet cloth. He used it to tenderly clean her.

After he bent to kiss the skin at the small of her back, he said there, "Ye can move now, darling."

She shifted, but only to get to her knees, turn his way and grab him by the neck to pull him in for a deep, wet, long kiss.

And…aye.

Her libido matched his.

Absolutely.

When he returned from the bathroom the second time, she was coming out of the closet wearing a silk nightie in a violet the color of her eyes.

He knew there'd be no knickers. He slept nude. He discovered she didn't like to, so he suspected the no knickers thing was about wanting as much of his cock as she could get, including when she woke in the night hungry for him, or he did the same for her, and simply because she'd noted he liked it.

She did that, his Blake.

If he liked something, she noted it.

They both headed to the bed, but Blake did it saying, "Your phone is going again, at this hour, and I hope it isn't something else about Signe."

On their walk, he'd told her about the Signe and the podcast. Dec had texted the link, but Dair hadn't bothered to look at it. He'd do it tomorrow and send it to his solicitor in case Signe needed to be reminded as to the terms of the NDA.

But he went to his phone now, surprised anyone was trying to contact him, seeing it was well past midnight.

His screen told him he had two missed calls from Ned.

This, he didn't like.

They knew Alex and Rix arrived home safe and sound. He'd been lying in bed beside Blake as she had an hour-long conversation with her sister, listening to news about the honeymoon, and telling her not only what had happened with Helena, but that she was in Scotland with Dair.

But Alex was pregnant. She was in her first trimester, where, as he understood it, more things could go wrong.

However, why would Ned be calling him and not his eldest daughter?

And at this hour?

Ned would know the time difference. And unless it was urgent, he'd wait until the morning.

He caught Blake's eyes as he called the man back.

"Well, hell…Dair," Ned said as greeting.

Dair didn't like this either.

Before Dair could reply, Ned asked, "Are you with Blake?"

"Aye, of course."

"Did I wake you?"

"We closed down a pub."

That was over an hour ago, but Ned didn't need to know that.

"Right, okay. Is she right there right now?"

Dair continued to gaze at Blake, and now her head was tipped to the side in curiosity, when he replied, "Aye."

"Can you get somewhere where she isn't?"

Goddammit.

"Aye," he grunted and took the phone from his ear. "I need to take this and I'm going to get us some waters. I'll be back," he said to Blake.

"I can get us waters," she offered.

"Dinnae move," he commanded.

She rolled her eyes, not knowing what Dair knew.

That whatever this call was about with Ned was not good.

He went into the closet to put on some lounge pants then he moved to the stairwell, his good dog Sorcha, who quietly snoozed by the bed while her daddy and his woman were anything but quiet in it, came with him.

He was on the second flight of stairs when he went back to Ned.

"Still there?" he asked.

"Yes, Dair. Are you away from Blake?"

"Aye."

"In a safe spot for you too?"

God *fucking* dammit.

"Just get on with it, Ned. Is Alex okay?"

"Alex?"

"This isn't about Alex?"

"No. It's about Helena."

Dair was on the ground floor, almost to the kitchen, when he stopped dead.

"Helena?"

There was silence before Ned bit off, "Fuck, damn, *fuck*."

"Ned," Dair rumbled.

"I don't know how to do this," Ned told him.

"Just do it, whatever the fuck it is," Dair replied, wondering what that woman was up to now.

"Dair, Helena was killed in a car crash on the M4 this afternoon."

Dair froze solid.

"And I need you to know first, so when I tell Blake, you can be over the initial shock of it and be there for her," Ned went on.

Forcing himself to move, Dair resumed his trek to the kitchen as he grunted, "Right," into the phone.

"As you well know, there's no love lost, but the woman was still her mother," Ned said.

"She was," Dair replied unnecessarily.

"And I know you knew her all your life and especially with what happened recently, you must be having conflicting emotions too, but it's going to be all about Blake and Alex for a while."

"Agreed. Absolutely," Dair told him as he grabbed two bottles of still water from his fridge and moved back to the stairs. "I'm heading back to her. We doing this now?"

"I think we should."

"Agreed on that as well," Dair muttered, and he took the steps two at a time.

"I hate this for her," Ned stated bitterly. "She's happy. I've never seen her this happy. Both of them. Both of my daughters are finally happy, and now this."

Even in this situation, Ned's words weren't lost on him, and they felt good because he knew he played a part in making Blake happy.

But he was still dreading what was about to happen.

Blake was lying in bed, scrolling on her phone, which made Dair uneasy she might run into the news about her mother, but the minute Dair and Sorcha made the room, she set it aside and shot a tentative, still curious smile Dair's way but she reached to Sorcha.

Sorcha went to her side and got a head rub.

Dair went to his side, dumped the waters and got in bed with her.

"I'm back with her," he told Ned. "Ready?"

"As I can be," Ned muttered.

"Speaker?" Dair asked, and he hoped like fuck Ned agreed because he wanted to hear this and monitor how Blake responded it so he knew all he was dealing with.

"Yes, that's perfect, Dair," Ned agreed.

"Here we go then," he murmured and looked to Blake. "It's your dad, love."

Her brows pinched.

This was her expression for mere seconds before a post-midnight call from her father penetrated and panic hit her face.

Quickly, he hit the speaker button on his screen and announced, "You're on speaker, Ned."

"Blake?" Ned called.

"Daddy?" Blake asked tremulously.

Dair wrapped an arm around her waist and yanked her close so her stiff body was fitted to his side.

"Oh, sweetheart," Ned said. "I'm so sorry to interrupt your visit with this news."

"What is it?" she asked, and then she jumped to the same conclusion he did. "Is Alex okay?"

"It's not Alex, darling. It's your mum."

Dair was studying her face, and he watched what was left of the color drain out of it.

"Mum?"

"Blake, sweetheart, there was an accident on the M4 this afternoon. Your mum was on her way from her place in London to her place in Somerset…"

"Oh my God," Blake breathed.

"…seven cars were involved. There were four fatalities. Including your mum and her driver."

"Oh my God," Blake moaned.

"I'm so sorry, darling," Ned said, and even over speakerphone, it was easy to hear he meant it.

"I don't…I can't…" Blake stammered these but said nothing more, so Dair pulled her even closer, and now Sorcha was feeling the atmosphere, so she was snuffling the bedclothes on Blake's side.

"I know it's hard to take in," Ned said.

"Does Alex know?" she asked.

"I told you first. She's my next call."

"My God, I just…" Again, she couldn't finish.

When no one said anything for a while, Ned stated, "I don't know what to say. There's nothing to say. I hate that you're so far away from me. But I'm glad Dair is there with you."

Like she forgot he was there, Blake turned from staring at the phone like it was an object of evil to Dair.

He didn't take offense. He was too busy not allowing his chest to cave in at the expression on her face.

"Love," he whispered.

"Mum's dead," she told him, like this call hadn't come in on his mobile and he wasn't holding it right then.

"I know, baby," he cooed.

"I'm flying out. Tomorrow," Ned told them. "I suspect Alex and Rix will be making arrangements too, once they learn the news."

"Somerset?" Dair asked.

"That's where I'll be heading, yes."

"We'll make plans. Meet you there," Dair informed him.

"Good, Dair. Thank you. I'll keep you apprised of my arrangements. My PA is booking them now."

"Great," Dair forced out.

"Blake?" Ned called.

"I'm here, Daddy," she said in a small voice.

"I know you're not okay," Ned said. "I won't ask if that's the case. I'm just so sorry, sweetheart."

"Me too, Daddy," she replied as if she wasn't certain of her words.

"And I'll see you when we meet in England," Ned said.

"Okay," she replied.

"Now try to get some rest, darling," Ned encouraged. "I know it will be hard, but please try."

"I'll try, Daddy," she mumbled.

"Can I have Dair?" Ned requested.

Blake said nothing. Now, she was just staring at the duvet.

So Dair took the call off speaker and put the phone to his ear.

"Ye got just me."

"Do you have her?" Ned asked, his voice ravaged.

"Of course." Dair tried not to sound insulted due to the circumstances.

"She's going to be conflicted."

"Aye, I ken."

"I'll communicate with you both, and ask Alex to do the same, if you would as well?"

"Absolutely."

"I'm sorry this has upset your visit. Blake was very much looking forward to it."

"Can't be helped, but now we got a job, Ned. Ye hear me, mate?"

"I do, Dair. Glad you're on the team. See you soon."

"You will, Ned. Keep your chin up."

"No choice. Take care, Dair."

"You as well."

They hung up, and he instantly put his phone on the charge pad before he turned back to his woman.

"Up, baby, to the bathroom," he ordered. "Teeth brushed. Your makeup isn't off yet. Let's go."

She nodded, and he pulled her out of bed with him.

They stood at each of their basins, and he watched carefully in the mirror as she brushed her teeth. Then she washed her face.

But while she was putting some gunk on it, she swathed a load of the cream on her cheek, stilled, and suddenly wandered out without rubbing it in.

He followed her.

She sat on her side of the bed.

Sorcha pushed at her hand.

Blake stared at the floor.

Dair made his approach, gently moved his dog out of the way, and crouched in front of her.

"Look at me, love," he urged.

She raised her gaze to his.

He reached to meticulously rub the cream all over her face.

"Thank you," she whispered when he was wiping his fingers on his lounge pants.

That was when the tears started to fall.

He surged up and in, gathering her in his arms and positioning them under the bedclothes. Sorcha whined. Blake burrowed into his body.

"Th-the last time I saw her, I s-s-slapped her," she sobbed into his skin.

"I ken, darling. Dinnae think of that now."

"Oh God," she moaned, pushing closer to him.

"I hate this for you, baby," he whispered.

"M-me too. I hate it too, Dair," she pushed out through weeping.

He held her.

She cried for a long time.

So long, she fell asleep doing it.

He held her longer, and when she didn't move for some time, with extreme caution, he turned out the bedside lamp, called loving words to his dog, listened to his girl settle on the floor beside Blake, and he pulled the covers up further over his woman.

As for himself, he did not want Helena Coddington-Sharp dead, but he wasn't upset she was. She was a shite mother who did harm to both of her girls. She was a shite woman who willfully did harm to a marriage. She was simply a shite woman.

She would be missed by very few, if any.

Dair had no doubt that the best future scenario between Blake and her mother was a détente. They would never build the mother-daughter relationship she might wish they had.

But now, that option wasn't open to her and the last time she saw her mother was not a good memory in the slightest.

And now, Dair was going to have to phone his father and let him know this happened.

As well as tell his mother and his sister.

More, now Blake was the Marchioness of Norton.

She was a peer of the English realm.

She'd just inherited a vast estate, multiple properties, a complicated portfolio, and massive bank accounts.

Her life had just changed irrevocably.

And his life did too.

CHAPTER FOURTEEN

TREVERTON

Dair

Dair turned their rental car through the open wrought iron gates affixed to dual stone plinths topped with urns and onto the sand-colored gravel drive that led to Treverton Manor, Blake's ancestral home.

He'd had a busy morning, booking their flights to Bristol, packing, making uncomfortable calls.

His mother was on a plane.

His sister was not, and she was shocked at the news, but mostly she was worried for Blake.

Since Davi was coming down to Somerset as soon as they had arrangements for the funeral, she was going to take care of Sorcha until then, but Dair needed a backup plan for his dog too. Therefore, he'd set that up as well.

Then he'd called his father, only to discover Balfour already knew, something that wasn't surprising since it was all over the news. Much of it including old photos of Helena and Ned, along with pictures of Alex with Rix, and a different photo of Dair and Blake taken at the airport. This one of them walking and dragging her luggage, connected together and smiling at each other.

To the man's credit, his father didn't push anything else during that call.

He'd asked, "Blake is with ye?"

"Aye. We're headed down shortly."

"How's she faring?"

"Not great."

"Ye need anything, she needs anything, ye ring me," his dad ordered.

Dair didn't reply.

"Obviously, I'll be attending the funeral," his father went on.

Dair continued to say nothing.

"This isn't the time, son. Just see to Blake," Balfour concluded.

"Not something you have to tell me," Dair returned. "I'll see you at the funeral."

And with that, he rang off.

When he was able to turn his phone back on after the flight, he had texts from Davi to say she'd picked up Mum, told her, and they were making plans to come down. They'd be in England by Friday, latest, but they were hoping to be down the next day.

This on top of a variety of group texts from Ned and Alex sharing their plans (Ned was flying commercial and was already on his way— Hale Wheeler was sending one of his planes to Alex and Rix to bring them over).

Blake spoke briefly to her sister on the ride from the airport to Treverton.

His woman had woken up to a call from the police communicating their need to speak to her as well as, since she was in the country, requesting she identify the body.

They were dropping their bags first and then heading to take care of that unhappy chore.

In the interim, they got further news of the crash, and this included a two-year-old had also lost her life.

Blake was wandering around lifeless, but when she heard that news, it visibly crushed her.

In turn, that crushed him, but there was nothing he could do but be at her side and see to anything that needed to get done.

As he drove up the drive, he took in the vivid green lawns and yellow Bath stone of the manor proper.

Wallace money was new money. Balfour—kickstarted by his father's minor but not insignificant success with a small printing company—had built it and diversified it. And when the time came, he constructed a fine home in the country from good red Scottish stone in an old-style that was both roomy and mildly ostentatious.

His mother's hand had kept that at "mildly."

Treverton was old money, which somehow managed never to be ostentatious, even if it was a massive house with an attached, forward angled wing, twenty-five-foot ceilings inside, a dozen bedrooms, and a detached private chapel.

And, not incidentally in this time, a family cemetery behind that chapel.

Dair had always liked Treverton, mostly because the rooms were huge, there was a good deal of land attached to it to explore, and the stables were always full.

Now, he saw it differently.

Because it was Blake's.

She was not fully American legally, since she had dual citizenship.

But she was fully American otherwise.

Nevertheless, Treverton suited her.

A man wearing dark brown trousers, a tan blazer with dark brown edging on the lapel, a white shirt and patterned brown tie came out the front door before Dair came to a stop outside it.

Dair bent forward to eye him suspiciously through Blake's window and realized his estimate of the bloke being "a man" was generous.

"That's Jeff. Mum's butler," Blair told him tonelessly.

Butler, his arse.

The bloke couldn't be over thirty. He was blond, tall, tanned, fit, and obviously a boy toy.

Jesus Christ.

The tentacles of Helena's bullshite were so strong, they reached even beyond her death.

They got out and he moved around the car to take Blake's hand as they walked to the front door.

On their journey, Jeff was eyeing him too. He did it with surprise, and he was far from happy to see Dair approaching at all, much less holding Blake's hand.

"Hey, Jeff," Blake greeted when they arrived.

"Blake," the man replied.

"Lady Sharp," Dair corrected, and got both their attention.

"We don't—" Blake started.

He looked down at her.

"You're Lady Sharp now, darling," he said gently.

For the first time since they woke up, light hit her eyes as she considered him.

But for once, she decided not to quarrel.

Instead, she turned to Jeff and introduced him.

"Jeff, this is Alasdair Wallace."

"Yes, I know. Big fan," Jeff lied stonily.

"Always great to meet fans," Dair replied on his own lie, or it was in this instance, then went right into, "Ye can get the bags and take them to Blake's room. We'll be sharing it." With that, he handed the man the car fob but warned, "We'll be needing to leave soon, so I'd like that back promptly."

There was angry red in the man's face as he stiffly nodded, and Dair considered this evidence he was rarely asked to do any menial tasks around the house, if he ever was.

No. His tasks were not menial in the slightest.

Dair guided Blake into the house.

She took him to one of the less formal rooms, though it was all formal, so this one was incrementally less formal.

There, she turned on him and he was relieved as fuck she had a spark of fire in her.

"Was it necessary for you to piss all over your patch with Jeff?"

He didn't respond to that.

He asked, "What's the staffing situation here?"

"Sorry?"

"Jeff's the butler. I assume that's full time."

"I…think so," she said hesitantly.

"And does he live here?"

She nodded. "As far as I know."

She hadn't put two and two together.

Then again, she wouldn't. No one wanted to think of their mother boning a man half her age.

"Who else works here?"

"There are some maids," she told him. "At least one I know works full time, but Mum, or Christine probably, hires extras when Mum's around. At least one more to get the house entirely in order and keep it in order when Mum's here. If there's a house party, they hire extras."

"Christine?"

"She's the cook and housekeeper. She's definitely full time. Been here for years."

"Wouldn't it be the butler's job to hire on any needed staff?"

That flummoxed her.

She had a huge learning curve ahead of her, his poor wee lass.

"Any others?" he pressed.

"Gardeners. I think there's a whole team of those."

He nodded and made a decision.

Chat with Christine, who was probably as thrilled with Jeff being there as Dair was. Then a conversation with Jeff. One that would either end with him packing his bags or properly doing his job.

She cut into his thoughts. "Why are you asking me this?"

He sidestepped that by saying, "We're going to have a full house soon, love."

Her gaze grew far away, and she mumbled, "Oh, right."

"Not your worry. I'll have a word with Christine. Do ye want to freshen up before we go?"

She focused on him again and nodded.

"Where would I find Christine?" he queried.

"A guess, in her office off the kitchen. Do you remember where that is?"

He nodded and guided her out of the room to the staircase.

He touched his mouth to hers at the base and said, "Take your time, but just to say, let's get this next chore done so ye can settle in and relax a little."

A shadow moved across her features as what they had to do next came to mind before she gave him another nod and started up the stairs.

She was halfway up, and he was watching her go, when she stopped and turned.

"Thanks for taking care of…well, everything so far, honey."

"Dinnae think a second about it," he replied then jerked his chin to the stairs. "Up. We'll be on our way when you're ready."

She walked up the wide flight of thick pile, red-carpeted stairs like she was going to the gallows.

Once he lost sight of her, he made his way to the kitchen.

Christine was bustling out of her office. She didn't look elderly, even though she obviously wasn't young.

She looked competent.

And harried.

When he saw her, he remembered her, though he couldn't remember the last time he was at Treverton. Maybe when he was fifteen? Perhaps sixteen.

So, indeed, she'd been around awhile.

She was there but unobtrusive and he'd had no direct dealings with her.

He was going to now.

"Christine?" he called, startling her.

She put her hand to her chest and breathed, "Oh my," then went on to say, "Well, young Master Wallace. I haven't seen you in ages."

"Yes, it's been quite a while," he agreed.

"Is Lady Blake here?"

"She is. Upstairs, freshening up."

This made Christine scowl, probably because Jeff hadn't informed her of their arrival. He'd been busy greeting them and seeing to their bags, but the bloke had to have a phone so he could text her.

"We have some…official business to see to which we shouldn't delay," Dair finished.

She understood him, and Dair couldn't quite read her new expression. It wasn't grief, per se. It wasn't elation either.

Apparently, anyone Helena knew had conflicting emotions about her passing.

Nevertheless, he said quietly, "I'm sorry for the loss of Lady Norton."

"Yes," she replied vaguely.

"Just so ye understand, Blake and I are—"

That brightened her up. "Yes. I saw the picture. Delighted for you both."

"Thank you, Christine," he said. "I assume ye ken Mr. Sharp, Alex and her husband, Rix, and very likely others will be arriving soon."

She gave him a quick nod. "Mr. Sharp's assistant has shared the details. I've everything in order. Just need you to tell me when you'd like your meal tonight. It's my understanding Mr. Sharp will arrive around five."

Blake had barely eaten anything all day, excusing this by saying she wasn't hungry.

"If ye can manage something substantial," he requested. "Blake hasn't been eating properly today."

"Poor little miss," Christine murmured.

They heard someone approach.

Christine looked beyond him and did not hide he was correct in his assumptions.

When he turned, he knew it was Jeff coming and he knew that Christine had no respect for him and possibly liked him even less.

Jeff came to Dair and said, "Your fob, *Mr.* Wallace."

Decision made.

The man had to go.

"Your bags are upstairs," Jeff finished.

"Thank you," Dair replied.

Jeff jutted his chin mock-diffidently, shot an inscrutable look to Christine, then turned and walked away.

When Dair went back to Christine, he caught her mid-eyeroll.

"Not fond of Helena's butler?" he inquired.

She blanched and said quickly, "No, sir. It's just—"

"I ken who he is, or rather, *what* he is, Christine." He paused before he added, "We'll talk later."

Her eyes widened, but her surprise swiftly turned to relief which then segued to, if he wasn't wrong, glee.

For certain, Jeff was an issue that had to be dealt with.

Christine's emotional journey ended on worry.

"Does Lady Blake know that—?"

Dair shook his head. "I dinnae think she's put it together yet."

"For the best," Christine mumbled.

"We'll be on our way just now." He looked at his watch. "Dinner at six thirty work for you?"

"Yes, Mr. Wallace—"

"Dair," he corrected her.

Her mouth twitched.

She heard the *Mr.*

"Dair," she said. "I've all her favorites in, Lady Blake's. We'll get something in her stomach. Keep her energy up, if not her spirits."

"Thank you, Christine. Terrible circumstances, but lovely to see ye again."

"Yes, erm…Dair."

After giving her a smile, he walked away and headed toward the stairs, using his memory of where Blake's room was when they were young.

That was where he found her.

So he collected her, took her to the car, programmed the SatNav and drove them to the morgue.

***

EARLY THAT EVENING, THEY WERE BACK IN THE INCREMENTALLY LESS formal lounge having a drink.

Blake was sitting on the sofa, barely sipping, mostly staring morosely out a window.

Dair was next to her, definitely drinking, and watching her face.

He was hoping he never again in his life had to identify another body.

Helena had looked peaceful, but the blanket had been pulled up under her jaw.

She hadn't been wearing her seatbelt. She'd sustained massive internal injuries during the crash and was eventually crushed. She'd also broken her neck.

Her driver was wearing his seatbelt, but he'd also been crushed.

According to witnesses, a boy racer was zigzagging between lanes while speeding, lost control of his car, and on the busy motorway, he took seven other cars with him. Though, the police told him they were lucky he didn't involve more.

The boy racer was the last on the list who'd lost his life.

Even so, several others were still in hospital, including the dead little girl's mum.

While viewing her mother, Blake had not wept. She kept the stiff-upper lip her mother's side of the family gave her, signed the paperwork, spoke briefly to the police, and then Dair hurried her back to the car and home.

"Anything specific on your mind, lass?" he asked.

"I just…" She shot straight then her head whipped to him. "Daddy!"

She put her drink down and raced from the room.

Much slower, Dair followed suit.

By the time he made the front door, Blake was crying, "Nora!"

Dair stood on the front step as Blake ran to give a quick buss to Nora, then she went direct to her father and threw her arms around him.

And aye, there was Nora Ellington, a family friend of Blake's, looking classy and elegant and not at all like she'd boarded a plane at the crack of dawn her time.

Dair moved into the gravel drive to go to Nora.

He touched his cheek to hers, stepped back and said, "Glad you're here."

Nora had eyes only for Blake. "How is she?"

"She's had half a banana today and my girl likes her food."

"Hmm," Nora hummed, then turned, and he saw her brows immediately arch up. Not long later, he saw a supercilious expression come over her face. "Helena, not exactly full of surprises, but still she manages to surprise," she said under her breath.

Dair didn't have to turn, but he did, to see Jeff standing at the front door.

Blake was coming to say a proper hello to Nora as Ned moved his way, his focus on Jeff, his face carved from granite.

Nothing escaped the man, it seemed.

He wiped his expression clean when he offered Dair his hand. "Dair."

"Ned, good you're here."

Ned sent a sideways glance to his daughter who was chatting with Nora.

When he returned his attention to Dair, Dair shook his head once, doing so communicating a number of things including, no, she was not okay, and no, she didn't know what Jeff was.

Ned let out a sigh.

"God, that would be awesome. I'm *so* glad you're here and that will help *so* much," Blake was saying to Nora.

"What will help?" Dair asked as Blake clamped down on her father.

Dair offered his arm to Nora who took it.

"Nora is going to help with the funeral arrangements. I've no idea where even to begin," Blake said over her shoulder to him.

Then thank fuck she was there, because he didn't either.

They stopped awkwardly at Jeff while Blake made introductions.

"You'll be needing to see to their bags as well, and telling Christine we have an extra so we need another room made up and another plate for dinner," Dair tacked on when she was done.

"Of course, *Mr.* Wallace," Jeff all but snapped.

Ned gave Jeff a narrow look.

Nora raised her brows again.

Blake remained blithely unaware.

Jeff marched to the car.

They returned to the room they left and Dair went right to the bar. "What can I get ye?"

"Man after my own heart," Nora replied, then said, "Alcohol."

Ned chuckled and replied, "Scotch would be good."

"Nora likes martinis and cosmos and palomas and gimlets and negronis and, well…" Blake trailed off.

"Whatever Blake is drinking, dearest," Nora said.

He made Nora's cosmo first, then he poured Ned's Scotch.

As he resumed his seat and reclaimed his drink, Nora said, "Jamie will be here at the weekend. He's got some meetings he can't miss."

"He doesn't have to come. I know it's a headache," Blake said. "And neither did you."

"Pish-posh," Nora replied, and spoke no more.

He barely knew the woman. He met her at the wedding.

Even so, he liked her a great deal.

"Alex and Rix will be here in the morning," Ned stated. "I've got a car meeting them at the airport. They should be to the house by ten."

"Excellent," Dair said.

Small talk was had until the drinks were drunk and then Nora asked if she could be shown to her room to freshen up before dinner.

Blake popped up to do so.

The women left, the men watched them, and when their voices couldn't be heard anymore, Ned turned right to Dair.

"Is she fucking joking with that 'butler?'" he clipped.

"I'm not certain how to answer that," Dair replied, getting up and taking both their glasses back to the bar cart to recharge.

"It doesn't seem like Blake has put it together," Ned remarked.

"She hasn't and hopefully will continue not to do so until I can get rid of his arse," Dair said, pouring both of them more Scotch. "The good news, I dinnae believe Christine will state his case for him."

"I wonder how many more nasty surprises Helena has in store for my girls," Ned muttered.

This was what Dair was wondering.

Dair brought back the drinks, gave Ned his, and again sat down.

He did this before he asked, "Is there anything particularly nasty she could do?"

"Helena had a knack for 'particularly nasty,'" Ned said into his drink.

"I mean, regarding the estate or the inheritance."

Ned looked to him. "Say, bequeathing it to her young stud?"

Dair nodded.

Ned shook his head.

"No. She could name him in her will. Give him a monetary bequest, or a personal gift, but it would be minor and appropriate to a servant, especially since most of Helena's assets were owned by the estate. There's no circumventing the terms of the passing of assets or title in a hereditary peerage. It's my understanding, to do something like that, she'd need direct permission from the king, and unsurprisingly, he wasn't very fond of Helena."

"What about providing for him? Any terms that would make it difficult to sack him?"

For the first time since he arrived, Ned smiled. "Absolutely not."

"Good," Dair murmured. He cleared his throat and said, "Now's not the time, but she's going to have a lot shoved her way she'll have to get her head around."

"Helena didn't manage this house, Dair," Ned explained. "The housekeeper, Christine does. I very seriously doubt Jeff has taken on any of those duties. And she has financial advisers who act as trustees for the estate," Ned shared. "Yes, Blake will have to familiarize herself with all of this, but thanks to Christine and the trustees, I believe the estate runs very well without the need for her to be overly involved, unless she wishes to be."

"Good," Dair repeated and took another drink.

"I've made arrangements to stay a while," Ned informed him.

It might have come late, but he was a good father.

"I won't get underfoot, and if you need me to give you privacy—" Ned continued.

"It's a big house, Ned," Dair murmured, not wishing to get into the awkwardness of why they would need privacy.

Ned swiftly set that aside. "But I intend to be here not only to support my daughter, but to look over everything and go over it with her so she understands what she's taken on."

"That's good too," Dair replied.

"She looks pale, haunted," Ned got to the important shite.

"She's barely eaten today. Christine said she's making Blake's favorites. She needs food. She needs rest. She slept like the dead and woke like she hadn't slept in a year. You're here. That helps. Nora helping with the funeral will be appreciated. And when Alex is here, I think she'll feel even better."

"And you're not saying?" Ned prompted.

"The last time she saw her mother, she struck her violently."

"I was worried her mind would turn to that," Ned sighed.

"It can't but," Dair replied. "Regardless that Helena deserved it for a variety of reasons."

"We'll watch over her," Ned decreed.

Aye.

They certainly would.

IT WAS THE FIRST DAY SINCE THEY'D STARTED HAVING SEX THAT THEY didn't have sex.

Dair was completely fine with that.

What he wasn't fine with was watching his woman wander around listless.

The edification of Ned and Nora showing wore off after dinner and Dair was heading straight to alarmed at how little energy and life Blake had while going through the motions of getting ready for bed.

But now they were snuggled in bed. It was dark. Quiet. No city sounds could be heard as white noise.

Just them in this big room in this massive house.

"Ate well at dinner, hen," he noted.

"I forgot what a great cook Christine was. Her garlic roasted chicken and Boursin mash is the best. And I can't believe she pulled out the Eaton Mess. That's my favorite."

It had been a stick-to-your-ribs dinner, that was undeniable.

And fortunately, Blake had her fair share.

"I'm a bit worried about ye," he admitted.

She lifted her head from his shoulder to look at him through the dark.

"I don't want you to be worried, honey," she said softly.

"Of course ye dinnae," he replied. "I still am."

"My mum just died."

"I ken."

"I haven't really…" she trailed off, Dair said nothing, she picked up the thread, "I don't know what I'm feeling."

"Do ye need to define it?"

"I…well, I guess not."

"It feels shite. It's going to feel shite for a while. Ye dinnae have to make it harder on yourself by untwisting all you've got to have twisted in your head right now. Ye have time. Get through the funeral. Get a handle on the changes this has made to your life. Then ye can get a handle on what losing Helena makes ye feel."

"The changes this has made on my life?" she asked.

Well…

Christ.

Had she not put it together?

"You've inherited a rather important title, lass," he said carefully.

He heard a snort, and only Blake could make a snort sound ladylike.

"All my life I've wanted to be Marchioness of Norton," she decreed. "I mean, how kickass is that?"

He felt a smile forming. "It's pretty kickass."

She pressed closer. "And anyway, I was gearing up to be in the UK a fuckuva lot more. Right?"

His tone was guttural when he replied, "Right."

"So that's not a thing," she said.

"Good to know."

More apt: *great* to know.

"I know it's going to sound crazy to say this," she began, "but it's true. I just wish I had a mum who, when she died, suddenly and without warning, I was devastated."

Fuck, his poor wee lass.

He turned into her and gathered her tight against him. "I wish that too."

"As macabre as this is, and warning, it's very macabre, I think she'd like that she went out the same way the most famous princess in the world did. She hated her. Said she was the death of the true monarchy. But she was obsessed with her. Even after she was gone, Mum watched every documentary and read books about her. Is it weird that I feel some solace in that?"

"Nothing is weird, lassie."

She tucked her face in his throat.

He stroked her back.

"I'm going to be okay," she assured. "I just need Alex here. With Dad here, Nora helping with the necessities, Alex here and you here, I'll be okay. So don't worry. All right?"

He'd worry until he knew *she* was all right.

But he said, "All right."

"So go to sleep," she ordered.

"That's my line."

If he wasn't mistaken, he felt her smile against his throat.

And he was surprised when, not long later, she drifted to sleep.

Since she did, he followed her.

CHAPTER FIFTEEN

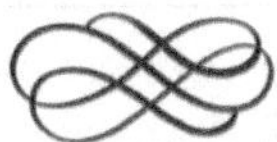

FELLOW CAPTIVES

Blake

"Babe, c'mere," Dair called from the bedroom.

I stopped brushing on eye shadow and left the bathroom to see Dair in nothing but dark blue, drawstring pajama bottoms lounged in my bed.

I'd always loved my room at Treverton. The muted, light green walls. The ivory bedclothes with contrasting light green elements mingled with a subtle floral in ivory, green and pink. That floral also covering the padded headboard and draped as curtains that framed the head of the bed around a panel of ruched green silk. The glossy, dark wood bureaus and nightstands with brass accents.

It was very pretty.

And very English.

But Dair lazing in that big bed, one long leg straight, the other bent, his back to the flowered headboard, his broad, furred chest on display, his hair tousled with sleep.

He was hot.

He was handsome.

He was beautiful.

He was mine.

I was emotional, obviously, considering the circumstances, but the wave of emotion that overwhelmed me at seeing this man in my bed in this house didn't have anything to do with that.

I knew I was falling for him before we heard the news about Mum.

But how many men—when they've just started something with a woman, her visit turns into a fuck-a-thon, but this gets interrupted by some of the worst news you'll ever receive in your life—drops everything to be there for her?

I heard him on the phone yesterday telling the network he wasn't going to be able to call an upcoming match. And I was a mess, and he took pains to be subtle about it, but I still didn't miss how busy he was sending texts and emails, probably bowing out of meetings and rescheduling things. Though, I said "probably" because he didn't mention a word to me about having to do any of that.

He took care of the plane tickets, the rental car, Sorcha.

I'd helped with my stuff in a kind of automaton way, but for the most part, he'd packed us both.

And now he was lazed in my bed on my iPad.

He was not on the phone blatantly dealing with work, giving the subtle hint of how much he was sacrificing for me and that I should appreciate it. He took care of all of that yesterday, subtly, without that first indication he was making a production of it so I didn't miss it, thus I would be appropriately grateful when the time came for him to use the brownie points he'd racked up.

So…yes.

I'd already been falling for him.

I was falling faster now.

I moved to the bed, asking, "What?"

"Take a look at these," he bid.

I entered the bed to rest on my stomach, and he turned the iPad my way.

I stared at what I saw.

"Which one ye like?" he asked. "I'll order it and have it expressed."

"I…you…" I stammered then tore my gaze from the screen to look up at him. "What on earth are you doing?"

"Buying you riding clothes."

"I can see that, Dair, but—"

"Christine says your mum has two horses in the stables. They need exercise."

"I can ride a horse in jeans, regular boots and a sweater." I flipped a hand at the iPad screen. "I don't need a formal riding habit."

His huge grin made an appearance, and he teased, "Lady Norton doesn't wear jeans riding, lassie."

I screwed my eyes up at him. "Is this some kind of kink?"

That grin turned roguish, and he answered, "Wasn't, until I thought of your ass in these jodhpurs."

I slapped him on the stomach. He grunted, but I sensed it was just for show.

I then pushed off the bed and headed back to the bathroom with Dair calling behind me, "I packed ye and ye don't have any jeans."

"I have riding clothes here," I called back, picking up my makeup brush again. "I ride when I'm at Treverton, Dair, because, as I've said before, I love horses, and I'll add, I love riding."

"We'll ride this afternoon then," he said.

Riding with Dair on my mother's estate.

Strike that.

My estate.

Yesterday sucked.

I would never in my life forget seeing Mum in that awful room I could tell they tried to make soothing, but they were doomed to fail. Seeing her lying under a blanket without her signature rosy-pink lipstick on.

Eyes closed.

Lifeless.

No spite.

No snide words forming from her mouth.

No disappointment, emotional manipulation or passive aggressiveness.

Just…

Peace.

To my shock, I didn't like it.

And I would never in my life forget knowing the day she died— having lived her life the way she had, the last thing one daughter felt compelled to share with her was a vicious slap (and I still winced thinking about that), while the last thing the other daughter experienced from her was the need to be protected from her shenanigans—that a two-year-old little girl had died not even getting a chance to make a life.

No, I would never forget any of that.

But today was…better.

Not great. I wouldn't be settled until I saw Alex.

But it was better.

And riding with Dair later would make it even more so.

So I wasn't bouncing with joy with the thought of taking on the day.

But I was no longer a zombie either.

Progress.

I'd take it.

Dair, Dad and Nora following, I flew out the door straight to Alex.

I didn't have to navigate the gravel in heels on the run for long, she raced to me.

We collided in the middle, wrapped our arms around each other and held on.

I'd seen I had more surprises upon her arrival. Rix wasn't the only one who came with Alex.

Hale and Elsa were there, and obviously, they'd brought their baby boy, Laird.

Chloe, with JT, and Mika were with them.

I had good friends, and I was overwhelmed by their kindness.

But I could only hold on to my little sister.

"This sucks," she said in my ear.

"Yes," I agreed.

"You okay?"

"No. Are you?"

"No."

We kept holding on.

Eventually, I pulled my head away to look at her.

She looked tan and healthy…

And sad.

Which made me mad.

She was just married. Just home from her honeymoon. Pregnant with the love of her life's baby.

And now…

This.

It wasn't Mum's fault, but no matter how irrational it was, I still blamed her.

"I'm glad you're here," I said.

She gave me small smile. "I'm glad I am too. I feel better, seeing you."

It meant everything she felt the same.

"Me too," I replied.

"And I brought reinforcements," she noted.

I took my cue and let her go, saying, "I see."

Rix gave me a super tight hug that I couldn't breathe through, but it felt crazy good.

I got much the same from Chloe, Mika and Elsa, they just weren't as strong as Rix so I could breathe.

Hale's hug lingered, as did his gaze. We were close. But he was a very busy man.

And he was here for me.

"Means the world you're here," I said quietly.

"Where else would I be?" he asked casually.

A million other places.

I didn't share that because it might make me cry.

Instead, I pulled Laird out of Elsa's hold, kissed his beautiful head, and then invited, "Come see the house."

When I turned, I caught Dair's attention on me, and I nearly tripped at the expression on his face.

He was taking me with Laird in, and I didn't know if he wanted to wrest the child from me and hand it off before he carried me to our bedroom or if he wanted to shove me and Laird in a car so we could kidnap him.

He visibly jerked himself out of whatever thoughts he was having and winked cheekily at me.

I wasn't fooled by that wink.

We hadn't gotten anywhere near talking about kids, but now I knew that conversation would be perfunctory.

I wanted them (two, hopefully both girls).

And I knew he wanted them as well (hopefully also two, but likely he wanted boys).

I bounced Laird on my hip and sashayed into the house, talking gibberish to him.

And again, the weight of Mum dying hadn't lifted.

But I was feeling even better.

ALEX HAD THE WARDROBE OPEN AND WAS TOUCHING THE CLOTHES.

I was sitting at the vanity and touching the bottles of perfume.

"I know it's soon, but just saying, when we get there, we can auction these off for charity," Alex said gently.

We were in Mum's room.

"Yes," I agreed, picking up one of the bottles, taking off the stopper and smelling it.

Bad idea.

It obviously smelled of her. And because it did, memories crashed and clashed, unbidden, through my brain.

Not one of them good.

I stoppered the perfume and put it down.

"Five things."

I twisted on the vanity stool to look at my sister, who was now sitting on the side of Mum's bed.

"Five things?" I asked.

"We need to find five good memories of Mum. Memories with nothing bad attached."

She might as well ask me to go with her to Mars to plant a garden.

"Alex—"

"We don't have to do it now, just…can we make a date, before I leave, to have some sister time and compare notes?"

I could do that, seeing as she was staying a week and a half, and it'd probably take us that long to find five good memories of Mum, so I nodded.

"I wasn't…" I couldn't find the word, so I decided, "*right* until you were here," I confessed. "It's not like I'm right now, I just feel better that you're here."

She tipped her head to the side and whispered, "Same."

I shook my head and continued my confession, "I was such a shit sis—"

Alex corrected her head with a snap. "Stop it, Blake."

She got up and walked to me, then sank cross-legged on the floor in front of me.

There was something so Alex about that, but I was not this Blake at the vanity table, not anymore.

Thus, I got up, pushed the chair aside and sank down on the floor with her so our knees were brushing.

Her gaze warmed at my actions, and she reached for my hands.

We both took hold.

"We were like…fellow captives," she said.

Oh God.

That was the perfect way to describe it.

We *so* were.

"You did what you could to survive," she went on. "And so did I."

"I wish I'd snapped out of it a lot sooner," I remarked.

She shook our hands. "Who cares when you did? You did. And I carry guilt because I left you to it."

That stunned me. "You left me to what?"

She lifted a shoulder, but her half-shrug was ill at ease. "You were the next in line. She focused on you. It was like she was grooming you to be like her. Blake, I knew she was doing that, even when I was young and I didn't understand what it was called. I knew it wasn't fun for you. And I escaped. I left you to it."

"It was hardly your job to protect me from her."

"We should have been a team."

"We were," I asserted, and her head twitched. "Okay, maybe not a very functioning one."

She started to laugh.

I tightened my hold on her. "But we made it through."

"Thank you for all you did for the wedding."

"I loved doing it."

"It was the perfect day."

"I'm glad."

"And thank you for taking the hit of Mum's...*scene* so I didn't have to think about that while Rix and I were in St. Lucia."

I managed not to flinch at thinking about Mum's "scene."

More progress.

"Not a problem."

"You're a good sister, Blake." She leaned toward me and added, "The best."

The tears stung so bad, I had to release them.

Though she was watery, I saw the same happen to her.

Listing forward, we hugged.

We heard a throat cleared at the door, let each other go and looked that way.

Dad was standing in the door, a gentle, settled look on his handsome face as he took us in.

"I'll not interrupt except to say I love you both very deeply," he stated.

And then he was gone.

Alex's hiccoughing sob broke the air.

Mine followed it.

And we were in each other's arms again.

Fellow captives.

A team.

Sisters.

I WAS MOVING DOWN THE BACK HALL TOWARD THE KITCHEN, LOOKING for Dair, because Mika told me she'd seen him heading back there.

It wasn't lost on me that bumping into friends and family anywhere I went in Treverton was a balm to my frayed emotions. I couldn't remember the last time Treverton had so many people in it, making the house come alive.

And there was never a time when there were so many people there that I loved, and they all hadn't even arrived yet.

It was like we were making happy memories in the midst of a tragedy, and there was something beautiful about that.

This was a weird bi-product of Mum dying, but I'd be eternally grateful for it.

Just like I was grateful that Dair and I had a date to ride. Doing something we both enjoyed, and doing it together, would be another happy memory to add to that prized pot. Not to mention, I hadn't been riding since the last time I was in England, and that was another reason I was looking forward to it.

I was in my jeans, those tucked into riding boots, and a sweater, ready to roll.

"It's a problem," I heard Christine saying as I closed in on the corner that would round into the kitchen. "He says he's in mourning, which means he's not budging."

"I dinnae give a shite how he feels, he has to move," Dair replied angrily.

So angrily, I stopped.

Why was he angry at Christine?

"I'm not one to tell tales," Christine declared.

"You'll be telling this one," Dair demanded. "I have to know what I'm dealing with."

There was a moment of silence before Christine spoke again.

"Because not as much staff was needed as in olden times, and he was having trouble retaining people who would live in, the old lord, Lady Helena's father, had the staff quarters on the top floor converted to apartments in an effort to entice hires. They're very nice. Sitting room. Bedroom. Little kitchen. A nice bathroom," Christine explained.

"You're telling me this…?" Dair prompted.

"He should be there. In the staff quarters."

"Aye, he should be."

"He's not."

"Aye, I ken. This is what we're talking about. Genny and Duncan and my family are arriving tomorrow. Tom, Judge and Jamie will be here at the weekend. Dru, Cadence, Sully, Gage, Sasha and Matt are looking at coming. Blake will want her people close, not in some inn somewhere. We need the room. Dru and Cadence, Sully and Gage are going to have to bunk together as it is."

"I'm looking forward to having a full house again," Christine verbally rejoiced.

"I'm pleased for ye," Dair replied impatiently. "But Dru, Cadence, Sully and Gage aren't going to be sandwiched between the butler's room."

The butler's room?

"He thinks that's where he belongs because Lady Helena put him there, and frankly, he doesn't know any better," Christine said.

All right.

Enough.

I turned the corner and asked, "What's going on?"

Christine jumped like she was guilty of something.

Dair looked to the ceiling, his wide chest expanded, making it impossibly wider, and then he let out a deep sigh.

He turned to me. "Nothing, love." His eyes traveled up and down my frame before he suggested, "Meet at the stables?"

I came to a stop at them and demanded again, "What's going on?"

"Erm, I'll leave you both to it," Christine said.

"No, I'd rather you stay and explain what's happening." I looked between them, continuing, "I thought we had plenty of room for everyone."

Dair's jaw tightened before he stated, "Ye would. If Jeff wasn't in one of those rooms."

"Jeff?" I asked.

"Jeff," Dair replied.

He didn't speak further.

I was confused. "Wait, are you saying Jeff stays in the main house?"

Christine was looking anywhere but me.

Dair was looking like he wanted to shout very loudly.

He didn't.

He requested, "I'd like your permission to have a word with him."

"Why would you need my permission?"

"Because you're lady of the manor, love."

I turned to Christine. "Actually, don't you—?"

Christine cut me off. "Staffing, apartment allotments, most everything is ultimately overseen by a butler."

"So Jeff knows we need that room," I pointed out.

"He lives there, Blake," Dair said. "In that room."

"And he has for three years," Christine mumbled.

"Okay, I'm obviously not catching—" I stopped speaking abruptly as it hit me.

And then I couldn't continue speaking because I wasn't sure, if I opened my mouth, vomit wouldn't come out.

After I swallowed the bile, I forced out, "Mum and Jeff...?"

Christine was studying the wall beyond me.

Dair jerked up his chin uncomfortably.

"Oh my God," I whispered. It was much louder when I exclaimed, "Gross!"

"Let me deal with this, darling," Dair offered.

Hell no.

I looked to Christine. "Does he do anything a butler would do?"

Christine didn't appear much more comfortable than Dair when she said, "Probably in order not to get the sack, he's putting on a show right now, but no. When your mum wasn't here, mostly he had his mates over to drink her liquor, eat her food, ride her horses, play footie in the back garden and mess up the lounge with pizza boxes and cans of lager."

"But he didn't work," I said to confirm.

"Not as..." her eyes slashed to Dair before she finished, "such."

Ulk!

"And now...what?" I pressed. "He's refusing to move out of his room which is now *my* room?"

"Blake—" That was Dair.

"Yes." That was Christine.

Again.

Hell no.

I turned on my very attractive riding boot and stomped down the corridor, Dair coming after me, calling, "Lass."

I went faster.

Drat his long legs, Dair caught up with me.

But he didn't stop me.

"Maybe let me deal with this," he suggested again as I was jogging up the steps.

I stopped on the half landing. "Why?"

"Because ye have enough on your mind."

God, he was such a good guy.

"Stop protecting me, Dair."

"Ye ask the impossible, Blake."

Man, I needed to suck his dick.

He was a mouthful, but he had a very delicious dick.

I'd do that later.

For the now, I resumed jogging up the stairs.

I heard Dair heave another sigh before I heard him follow me, and when I made the first floor, I went on instinct, and yes (yuck!), you guessed it.

There was a television sounding from the room that had an adjoining door to Mum's.

I'd learned ages ago this was because, back in the day, it wasn't done for couples to sleep together. So the woman got the bedroom (the only boon she got back then), and the man was relegated to sleep in his dressing room and only attend her when they had business to see to.

Oh, and this likely gave him ample opportunity not to get caught coming and going on his bent to gamble away the fortune or meet one of his mistresses.

The television noises were coming from that room.

Everyone else was downstairs, chatting, or in Nora's case, on the phone bossing people around (kindly) while making funeral arrangements.

I knocked hard on the door and didn't wait for a call to come in.

I opened it and took two steps in.

I felt Dair come in behind me.

And we both watched Jeff scramble off the bed wearing nothing but a pair of long shorts.

"Enjoying a break?" I asked.

"Um..." he didn't answer.

"As you know, we've had several people join us today," I pointed out. "We have four more arriving tomorrow. Three at the weekend. With possibly six more coming. A funeral is being organized. I'm aware that Christine has hired another maid she trusts from the village, but there's work to be done. Can you explain why you're in your room, watching TV?"

"Well—"

"Did my mother pay you?" I asked.

His gaze pinged back and forth between Dair and me before it settled on me. "Yes."

"Are you up to date with your pay packet?" I went on.

A flush crept up his neck and he pushed out, "Yes."

"So, I'll repeat, can you explain why you're watching TV when there are things to be done?"

He moved to a chair, and it was then I noted he did, indeed, live here.

The place was a mess of clothes, athletic shoes, spent cans of beer, dirty plates that needed to be taken to the kitchen (some of them needed that two weeks ago), and various personal items, like trophies and electronics.

Oh, and it smelled like *boy*.

He pulled on a T-shirt and turned to me.

"With Helena, I had a—" he started.

"Please, don't," I interrupted him. "I think I know what you had with my mother. And now I know she's dead, the duties you performed for your pay are eternally suspended, and you are occupying a room that's needed for guests."

His face set. "She said this is my space."

"She's dead, Jeff," I snapped. "Now, please remove your personal belongings from this room…with haste…and open the windows so we can hopefully air out this scent before someone needs this room."

Jeff got pissy. "Your mother is not even in her—"

Oh no.

One thousand percent *no*.

"Do not *fucking* pretend you give a shit about her, Jeff," I bit at him. "If you did, you wouldn't treat this like a crash pad you could impress your mates with when she wasn't around. If you did, you'd be upset right now, beside yourself with it, and you are not. If you meant something to her, she'd have taken you with her when she wasn't here. If you meant something to her, she'd bring you into the light, not pretend you were her butler. If she meant something to you, you'd respect her property when she was around. Let's call a spade a spade, shall we? She was your sugar momma, and that's all she was."

He sniffed. "You don't know what we had."

Seriously?

Gross!

"Jeff, she was old enough to be your late-in-life-birth mother. You're younger than Alex. You seem to have no duties here, at least, not anymore, and you get a salary. If you haven't clued in to what *exactly* you are, I suggest you do it now. Because with her death, your duties have ended. And if you don't get your shit together, your employment will too."

He swallowed.

"Now," I kept at him, "over the coming days there will be bags to lug around, cars to park, cars to retrieve, horses to saddle. We're already inundated with flowers, so also deliveries to deal with. I don't know how Christine has it sorted, but undoubtedly, she'll be needing someone to run to the market more than once. I'm afraid I'm going to have to tell you you're demoted. You'll take your orders from Christine from here on out. But I'm the ultimate boss, and the first thing I expect you to do, again, *with haste*, is move out of this room to an apartment in the employee quarters and open the windows while you do. Then put on some clothes and report to Christine to see what's next."

"This isn't what I signed on for," he sneered.

"Too bad. It's what's happening. Your other choice is to pack and leave. Make it. Now," I demanded.

"Now?" he asked.

"Right now," I stated.

He glowered at me. He then glowered at Dair. It faltered when he looked at Dair, and that didn't surprise me. Dair could be scary.

He returned his attention to me when I spoke again.

"To aid in your decision, I'll also be looking over the estate's accounts," I told him, or I would ask Dad to do so and explain them to me considering I'd probably not be able to make hide nor hair of them. "And considering your demotion, your pay will likely be altered and not in a positive way."

"I don't have anywhere to go," he forced out this admission.

"Well then," I swung an arm in front of me, "you best get cracking."

Jeff hesitated before he started gathering his stuff.

Dair put a hand to my back.

I twisted my neck to look up at him.

"Go, love. I'll oversee this."

I was annoyed our ride was going to be delayed, but I didn't want to stand in that room another second.

It was the smell, of course.

It was also the knowledge that my mother had me here in this house with her and her much younger lover, passing him off as a butler.

Women should do what they wanted, when they wanted, how they wanted, with who they wanted. I strongly believed that. If you were of a certain age and got off on fucking young studs, and you had one in your bed, more power to you.

Although I found it sad, and perhaps skeevy, that she had a man like Jeff, it was her life, her body, and not my decision.

But she hid it.

She pretended he was her butler, when he was her gigolo.

She didn't protect me—her daughter—from that.

And that was just…

Foul.

I nodded to Dair and moved to leave the room, but he caught me with an arm across my belly.

I didn't look up at him because he bent to put his mouth to my ear.

"That was hot as fuck, lassie," he rumbled there.

For the first time in two days, I felt a smile curve my mouth.

"Ye up for a different kind of ride this afternoon?" he whispered.

I turned to catch his eyes. "Absolutely."

This time, it was his mouth that curved, and at the look in his eyes, I did a full-body shiver.

I gave him a peck on the lips.

I started to leave but he called, "Blake?"

I looked back at him to see his smile had turned into a sexy smirk.

"Those jeans, baby…" His pause was perfectly timed. "They work perfectly."

Ugh, he was the worst.

And I was totally falling fast.

I shot him a look, but strutted down the hall, feeling his gaze on me.

Then I skipped down the steps to search for Nora in order to get the lowdown on what was happening with Mum's funeral and to see if I needed to do anything.

Because Helena Coddington-Sharp needed to be laid to rest.

In a number of ways.

CHAPTER SIXTEEN

"JERUSALEM"

Dair

"*I* know this is in bad taste, but it must be said," Gage began. "When I die, do up my gig right in this place. It is the absolute shit."

"You're correct," Sully told him. "That was in bad taste."

"He's also correct that this place is the absolute bomb," Cadence added.

They were in Wells Cathedral, because the passing of the latest Coddington merited a fucking cathedral.

It also merited the study at Treverton eventually being turned into a kind of war room with everyone pitching in considering there were hundreds of "mourners" showing, a good number of them people of importance.

This not only necessitated organizing eulogies, floral arrangements, choir selections and choices of hymns, but also coordination of security details, collaboration with the police, and plans to contain the media.

It was like a fucking timed tactical mission.

And Nora Ellington was, as far as Dair could tell, the general.

He was standing in the vestibule of the cathedral with Sully, Gage, Dru, Cadence, Rix and Hale.

Though Dair reckoned it was only he and Hale who had their eyes glued to Blake (he'd noted she was especially close with the multibillionaire) as she stood wearing a classy, though demure (however, it was skintight, and she was Blake, so not that demure) black dress and very un-demure, high-heeled, shiny black pumps. Ned and Alex were with her.

Rix likely had his attention locked on his wife.

The G-Force, all of them (as well as a couple of Blake's girlfriends) were surprise arrivals.

They were taking this opportunity to have a holiday in England, and as such, were staying in London as their first stop. They'd texted a couple of days ago to share they'd be coming. They'd taken the train that morning in order to attend the service, but mostly, to attend Blake.

However, taking time out of their lives to fly across an ocean to be there for Blake had shaken his woman—in a good way.

And Dair had been right. He'd met Ryan, Bryan, Byron, Wallace, Teddy and Faunus, and he liked them immediately.

He liked them more now as they circled Blake and her family like sharks, ready to take a bite out of anyone who caused the slightest unease. So, aye, it was safe to say he liked them very much.

Regardless of how the two sisters felt about her, even if Nora was at the helm, Blake and Alex had painstakingly crafted this event as something Helena would approve of. The flowers, music choices, and for some reason it was important that they were both wearing hats.

Alex's was no-nonsense black, 20s style what Blake referred to as a "cloche."

Blake's was more daring and dramatic, had some see-through elements, a bow at the back and was worn tipped high on one side and slanted over the other eye.

They were perfect for each woman.

Those hats had been a scramble, one of many Nora had bested. Then again, Dair had noticed that there wasn't much Nora couldn't best. She was a stern but loyal general and a miracle worker rolled into a tall, attractive, loving package.

"You know, the 'butler' is a problem," Rix said, keeping his voice low, and gaining Dair's attention.

"Blake gave him hell a few days ago," Dair replied. "He should toe the line for a while. Or at least until she figures out how to get rid of him."

"Days ago?" Rix asked in a tone that made Dair stop watching his woman and look to Rix.

"She did it the day you and Alex arrived," he said.

Rix shook his head. "Man, I hate to tell you this, but that asshole has been seeping attitude everywhere he goes."

Hale grunted his agreement.

Dair started to get pissed off.

"Chloe needed something for JT," Rix went on, "and he told her to keep her pants on, using those words. Then he never showed with it. Chloe isn't at home. She doesn't know where shit is. Eventually she flagged down one of the maids who got it for her."

Dair clenched his teeth.

"Chloe is not one to cross," Hale put in. "The only reason she's keeping quiet about it is because she doesn't want to upset Blake, Alex or Ned."

"His deal is, he's being cool whenever those three are around, and you," Rix added. "Outside of that, he's being a total fuckwad."

"Hmm, I heard the word 'fuckwad' said in a church. Are we talking about *Jeff*?" Chloe asked as she joined them.

"Baby," Judge, who was with her, murmured his warning.

"Apparently, Blake had words with him," Rix filled her in. "Just not enough of them."

"Yes, like he needs to behave all the time, not just when a Sharp is around." She turned her attention to Dair. "Or someone *very* Sharp adjacent."

She meant him.

"I'll have a word with her, or more likely him, when we get back," Dair told them.

"Are you fucking…" Rix started.

"Joking?" Hale finished on a growl.

Dair turned back to where they were looking, or more to the point, scowling at the Sharp family greeting funeral guests in the vestibule, something they decided to do that flew in the face of tradition because most of the attendees were acquaintances.

Helena, unsurprisingly, had very few true friends. Those true friends were invited to the burial ceremony followed by tea at Treverton after the service.

But Blake and Alex had decided, especially due to the clamoring of paparazzi outside, they wanted to get out of there and get home as soon as they could when the service was over.

However, at what he saw when he turned their way, he felt fire ignite in his veins.

"Excuse me," he grunted.

"I should think so," Chloe snapped.

As he prowled to his woman, he took in Ned's angry shock, Alex's stunned surprise and Blake staring at her ex-fiancé in complete astonishment.

And distress.

Aye.

Chad fucking Head was there.

The man who cheated on her. The man who humiliated her. The man who broke her heart.

A man who should know better than to show up, unannounced, and as far as Dair could see with the reactions of all three of the Sharps, uninvited at her mother's funeral.

And he was now a man who was reaching for Blake's hand and staring at her earnestly.

Oh…

Fuck no.

The G-Force was preparing to pounce, he could tell, but they backed off as Dair got right up close to him. So close, Chad jerked and turned to look at him.

"Can I help you?" he asked, shrinking back.

"A word," Dair clipped.

"I don't know you," Chad stated.

"Then ye dinnae pay attention to social media, or ye would," Dair retorted, seeing as, with Helena's death, they were all fucking over it.

There were photographers at the end of the lane at Treverton, 24/7, for fuck's sake. Hale had to have his assistant switch out all their rental vehicles for ones with tinted windows so, if they needed to go somewhere, they didn't do it and half an hour later, have a picture of them racing over the Internet.

And right then, outside, there was a pack of media behind steel cordons, taking photos of the people who arrived.

"Then again, I could see why ye wouldn't ever get on social media," Dair continued.

The man seemed to be getting angry.

Dair ignored that and said, "Now, I'd like to have *a word*."

"I'd have a word with him if I were you," Alex suggested.

Chad looked to Blake. "I just wanted to be here for you today—"

Dair pushed between Chad and Blake, planted a hand in his chest and carefully pressed him back. When he did, he heard several members of the G-Force make noises of approval.

"Excuse me," Chad ignored the G-Force and snapped at him.

"I'm her man," Dair told him quietly. "And we'll be having a fucking *word*."

"You are…you…" His gaze went to Blake, to Dair, up and down Dair, back to Blake, then again to Dair before he turned and walked away.

Dair followed him.

Chad stopped well to the side of the doors to the sanctuary.

"Is this necessary?" he asked irately. "I realize you know who I—"

Dair cut him off. "Aye, I ken who ye are which begs the question why you're here."

Chad looked dumbfounded by the demand. "We were once very close."

"And now you very much are not."

Chad squared his shoulders.

He was still three inches shorter than Dair.

"Helena has been a family friend for years," he stated.

Dair looked around then back at Chad. "So, where's your family?" He narrowed his eyes. "And where's your wife?"

Chad stretched his neck out to the side, suddenly appearing uncomfortable.

Bloody hell.

"I see," Dair said quietly. "It didnae work out."

"I can't imagine why you would think that's your business," Chad returned.

"It's my business because you thought to use her mother's funeral to get back in with my woman. I believe ye can see why, considering the 'my woman' part, I'd think it'd be my business."

Chad opened his mouth, but Dair didn't give him the chance to speak.

"I dinnae know ye, but what I know about ye, I shouldn't be surprised you'd pull something like this. It's out of line. Completely. You treated her like rubbish. You're not an old friend. You're the man who betrayed her. Her mother just died. So I must ask, what the hell's the matter with you?"

Again, Chad was winding up to say something, but he couldn't because Ned was there.

"The service is starting shortly," Ned announced, looking at Dair.

His attention shifted to Chad and he didn't hide his expression of distaste.

"Since you made the effort to be here, you may attend, but you'll be sitting at the back and keeping your head down. Do not attempt to speak to Blake again. Leave, and crawl back to wherever it is you came from when this is over." He returned to Dair. "My daughter needs you to escort her."

Dair nodded. "Aye."

He wasted a glance Chad's way to see him pouting but that was all he took in before he smelled Blake's perfume and felt her hand slide through his elbow.

He looked down at her.

"Let's go," she whispered.

Taking her in, Dair completely forgot Chad Head, and for Blake's part, she didn't even look at him. It was like the man wasn't even there.

She'd been doing well these past few days. Not entirely herself, but the day she woke up at Treverton, and once Alex showed, she was no longer the walking dead.

Now, she seemed hazy, unsettled.

He pulled her closer to his side and moved to where Ned, Rix and Alex were standing, waiting for them to walk into the sanctuary.

Their other friends had entered the cathedral proper.

After they arrived at her family, they stood there as Nora approached.

"The choir will begin singing 'Jerusalem' once I sit down," she told them. "Just walk down slowly and take your seats. And the service will begin."

She squeezed Alex's hand, Blake's arm and hurried down the aisle of the very full church to where Jamie sat with Judge and Chloe, Hale and Elsa, and JT and Laird.

"Ye all right, lass?" Dair whispered.

She was gazing at her father, but at his words, she looked up at him.

Then she got on her toes and said in his ear, "Marlo should be here for him."

The week Blake was in New York, Marlo had been traveling for work, and because of that, a meeting couldn't be arranged.

Now, Dair studied Ned, and he saw for the first time how Helena's death had impacted him. His bearing was straight, his jaw strong, but there was a haunted feel to him.

"Take your sister and go to him," Dair urged as the opening notes to the hymn began.

"But you—"

"Get Alex and go. Rix and I will follow."

"You'll meet me in the front pew?"

This was the decision. Even if he didn't think they were there yet in their relationship for him to have that place of honor during these proceedings, Blake had insisted on it.

And if she needed him there, he was there.

"Aye, lass, I'll meet ye. Ned's about to enter the sanctuary. Go."

She released his arm and scurried to Ned, tagging Alex's hand and dragging her sister along with her.

Alex read the situation instantly and they both took one of Ned's arms, to the man's open surprise. Ned glanced back at Rix and Dair as they formed together behind the trio.

Dair nodded to Blake's father.

The choir started singing and Ned led his girls into the cathedral.

Dair and Rix followed.

He felt a muscle jump up his cheek when he came abreast of the row his mum and sister were in, both stiff-backed and staring straight ahead.

This was because his father was sitting in the row with them.

He hadn't seen the man arrive, and undoubtedly, he'd maneuvered that so he could be right where he was sitting. Next to his daughter, who was next to the wife he'd cheated on with the woman in the casket at the front of the church.

Christ.

Per Nora's instructions, their row was supposed to be Ned, Blake, Dair, Alex, Rix, in that order.

But Blake arranged them so Ned was between his daughters, Rix at the head of the row next to Alex, Dair at the other end by Blake.

They sat, and the rousing hymn that had been used by the English for practically any purpose, from weddings to funerals to anything in between that had anything to do with England or Englishmen and women ended.

The casket gleamed under a spray of monochromatic roses and orchids in a deep rosy-pink color. A spray that was so enormous, it almost entirely covered it.

The reverend made his approach.

And the memorial began.

During the service, the congregation sang "All Things Bright and Beautiful." The choir sang "Lord of All Hopefulness." Kind words were found for a woman who hadn't done a kind thing, that Dair knew, in her life.

It was a beautiful ceremony.

And then, thank fuck, it was done.

THE SHORT, PRIVATE CEREMONY FOR HELENA'S FEW GOOD FRIENDS was had at the cemetery behind the chapel in Treverton.

They left so the casket could be laid to rest, the spray of flowers draped over the loose soil on top.

High tea was served in the main house by Christine, the three maids, and a bumbling, frowning Jeff.

Now, the guests were gone, and they were all in the lounge having changed out of their funeral black.

His father hadn't dared to attend the private ceremony or the tea. Then again, at the ceremony, neither his mum nor Davi came (though, they didn't miss the tea).

However, he had two texts from the man since the service, Dair just hadn't read them.

They were chatting and having pre-dinner cocktails.

Though, Blake and Alex were fussing over their father.

"You must stop. I'm all right," Ned said in an undertone as Blake pinched off a fleck of non-existent lint from the poor man's jumper.

"Can Marlo fly out?" Blake asked in the same tone.

"I don't think you girls are ready for that yet," Ned murmured.

"I think we were ready a year ago, Daddy," Blake retorted.

"All right then, darling, then I'll say now is not the right time," Ned said.

"For her, you or us? Because I can share, for us, we want you to have the support you should have," Blake returned.

Dair didn't know Alex knew about Marlo yet, but apparently, she did.

Ned sent him a beleaguered expression.

Dair read the "for God's sake, save me" look and he wasn't surprised about it. Blake and Alex had been tag teaming Ned since the memorial.

He was about to make a move to do so when he heard Rix announce, "All right, people, we're doing this."

He looked that way to see Rix standing, and he had Alex in his hold.

"Oh my God," Blake breathed with excitement, clutching her

father's hand in one of hers, and reaching out for Dair with her other.

"It's time for some good news," Rix said when he had everyone's attention. "And that good news is, I knocked up my wife."

Trust Rix to put it that way.

Dair laughed while others did the same, while clapping or crying out, and everyone got up to rush them with hugs and kisses and good wishes.

If Ned was troubled before, there was nothing left of it. He was beaming, proud and happy, as he gave his youngest a long hug and turned to his son-in-law to do the same.

"How far along are you?" Genny asked when they settled back down.

"About ten weeks," Alex told her. "It's a little early to share, but we thought everyone could use some good news."

"Och aye, and that's the best news ever," his mum called out.

"This deserves champagne," Blake decreed, pushing out of her seat. "I'll go talk to Christine."

And off she went to do that.

This left Dair sitting on a sofa with Ned.

He scooted into the spot Blake left and said, "I ken ye didnae miss it, but she's worried about ye. And she's keen to meet Marlo."

"No, I haven't missed it. She hasn't made a secret of it either," Ned said on a sigh.

"You're correct, now isn't the right time. But I think she'll settle having met the woman."

"This isn't Helena's place anymore, it's Blake's," Ned replied. "And Helena is put to rest. Marlo is in Paris. I'll see if she wants to swing a trip to the UK before heading home."

"I think that'll be good for all of you."

Ned nodded.

Blake came back.

Champagne was served.

Ned's attention was taken with something Elsa was saying.

"Everybody is going to start leaving tomorrow, and that sucks," Blake complained in between sips of champagne.

"We can stay as long as ye like."

"But you have matches to call," she reminded him.

"Aye, and I can journey to them from here just as easily as I can do it from Edinburgh."

That statement was as profound for her to hear as it was for him to say, and she didn't hide it. She just added a kiss to the hinge of his jaw to punctuate how it made her feel.

When she sat back, Chloe was there with JT.

"Can you take him?" she asked Dair.

"Absolutely," Dair replied instantly, setting his glass aside and laying claim to the precious wean.

He vaguely noticed Chloe smirking knowingly at Blake, but he was mostly busy bopping the baby's nose so he'd giggle.

"I want two," Blake announced.

Knowing what she was referring to, a tidal of warm goodness washed through him as he looked to her. "Aye?"

"You?" she pushed.

"Two is good."

She reached in and stroked JT's cheek.

He giggled at that too.

"You don't sound convinced," she noted.

He looked to her. "That I want weans?"

"That you want two of them."

"Prefer three."

Her brows drifted up.

"But I won't be carrying them around in my body," he carried on. "So if my woman wants only two, I'll settle for two."

Her expression turned triumphant.

He bent to her and kissed her curved lips.

JT landed a baby smack on his jaw while he did, and that meant they were both smiling when they broke.

"I'm visiting a voodoo practitioner to make sure they're girls," she warned.

He burst out laughing, and that made JT giggle too.

"Do you want boys?" she asked through it.

"I want healthy weans and a healthy woman when it's all said and done. Dinnae give a shite what they come out as."

She frowned. "Don't say the s-word in front of a baby."

"Lass, his vocabulary consists of gurgles and whatever sound comes from drooling."

Her gaze moved to the baby. "Who knows what they soak in at this juncture?"

"Safe to say, with as much research as there's been put into it, a lot of people ken that at this age, they dinnae understand a thing." He lifted the baby to bounce him. "If JT starts speaking with a Scottish brogue, we'll know they're all wrong."

"Whatever," she muttered, then stole the baby from him.

In the last days, it hadn't been lost on him she enjoyed children. He had to admit, it was a bit of a surprise. She didn't seem like the hang-with-kids type. Though she talked gibberish to them, and took every chance she could to hold and play with them, she wasn't the gushing, ooing and ahhing type. It was more she just enjoyed their company.

And he enjoyed that one fuck of a lot.

"Is it freaking you out how easy things are with us?" she asked JT a question aimed at Dair, the gravity in her voice communicating itself to the baby, who in turn assumed an expression like he was trying to understand her.

It was bloody adorable.

"No. Why would it?" he answered.

She turned to him. "It's a little freaky."

"It's not."

She went back to JT, bounced him, and in a baby voice said, "It is. It so is, my sweet little JT. Things don't usually come this easy to Auntie Blake."

"Darling," he called.

She looked again at him.

"We're older. We ken what we want. We also ken what we dinnae want. We ken what we like, and dinnae. We ken what's important. So we can identify all of that when we find it."

She cuddled JT to her chest in a manner that should have been a warning to him, but he was so struck by how beautiful she looked cuddling a baby, he missed it.

"What I'm trying to say is…I appreciate how amazing you've been since Mum died, Dair. The latest being you rescuing me from Chad. And I'll add, I appreciate how hot that was too."

He grinned.

She kept talking.

"I don't know if I would have been able to handle it if you hadn't been there for me."

He stole the baby back but slid into her on the couch so they could share him before he replied, "Ye would have handled it, love. You just didnae have to. Ah, ah, ah…" he warned when she was about to say something. "Not done speaking. I'll finish by saying you're welcome, but it was my pleasure. That sounds strange in these circumstances, but it's true."

He knew how profound that was to her when she aimed the kiss this time to his mouth.

And her aim, as ever, in many ways, was true.

His woman could suck a cock.

And this was what she was doing, curled on the floor between his spread legs beside the bed where he was sitting.

Dair was back on his forearms, but with his head up, watching her bob up and down on his slick, aching shaft.

She circled the head with her tongue then her eyes came to him, heated and aroused, the violet looking like velvet, and she kept his gaze as she trailed the tip of her tongue down the pulsing vein on his dick.

She trailed it up and gobbled him whole.

Good Christ.

He heard the small gagging noise she made, but when she added the suction, it felt so bloody fantastic, his head fell back.

She worked him, and then he felt her cup his tight balls and give them a squeeze.

He lifted his head again and growled, "Aye, lass. That. Harder."

Her eyes flared, she squeezed harder, sucked harder, going faster, and added her other hand to keep the pressure going, trailing it after the movements of her mouth.

Fuck, her skills at sucking cock were stellar.

None better.

Not a one.

His head fell back again, and he lost her mouth along with both her hands stilling.

This made him raise his head, and he caught a wholly different expression on her face.

She explained it right away.

"I can't even handle it, you're so fucking beautiful."

All right.

That did it.

He surged up, catching her under her arms, pulling her up his body, then tossing her to her back at his side.

He then mounted her, straddling her belly and taking his cock in hand.

"Dair," she whispered, eyes wide and so hot, he felt the burn.

He jacked himself as she watched, her hands coming to his thighs, her nails digging in, her tongue trailing along her lower lip, her eyes sharing precisely how much she liked to watch.

Which meant, not long later, when he jetted on her chest, it seemed the long ropes of cum wouldn't stop coming.

But naturally, they did.

And the second he could, he knelt between her legs, wrapping one around his waist. Both of them in position, it was his turn to watch.

He did as he finger fucked her and played with her clit while she squirmed. He listened to her mews, felt her clench around his fingers, and finally, with an arch and a cry, her hand flying back to fist in the bedclothes, she coated his fingers with her juices as she came.

Given the invitation, Dair dropped chest to bed and ate her clean which meant he ate her to another orgasm.

And by the time he was done, he was ready for her again, so he dragged her on top of his dick and made her ride him, his cum still drying on her creamy skin, until they both found it one last time.

Of course, this meant she collapsed to his side, limp, but this was no matter. Dair frequently got out of bed to clean her up, and this time was no exception.

When he returned after doing that, he brought her nightie with him.

"You're going to have to put it on," she informed him. "I'm fucked out. I can't move. I probably won't be able to move tomorrow. Or the next day either. You need to stop working out. You need to slow down. You're gonna kill me."

Chuckling, he pulled the nightie over her head, and she lifted her arms to push her hands through the straps. Then he tugged it down her body before arranging both of them under the covers and turning out the lights.

Only then did he say, "I'm not going to kill ye. Who'd I fuck if you're dead?"

"Reanimate me, please. I don't want you fucking anyone else."

That would not be a problem.

A woman who could come four times and keep up with him—because it hadn't ended on him doing the work, but her, and she put that work in deliriously.

That woman being Blake Sharp, who could pull off the hat she wore that day like she was the next queen in succession then hours later coo to a baby she was bouncing in her lap.

No.

No problem at all.

"Ye need to add some cardio to those exercises ye do," he told her.

And, aye.

He'd walked in on her wearing sweet yoga clothes, lying on her back on the floor, doing repeated bridges with a resistance band around her thighs.

That explained a lot when it came to the power of her hips.

"I do plenty of cardio when I'm in New York. Also, here, when I'm not planning a funeral and playing host to all my friends and family, I like to take walks."

They'd managed to squeeze a ride in, but the weather had not been cooperative for much more than that.

Even so, he was shocked.

"Ye walk the English countryside?"

"I'm a lady peer," she stated. "Of course I put on warm clothes and walk around in the drizzle and fog like the ghost of Cathy searching for Heathcliff."

He busted out laughing.

He saw her smiling at him when he was done.

She rolled into him and stroked his jaw, mock frowning. "My Heathcliff isn't very broody."

"His Cathy sits on the floor like a disciple to his cock and tugs on his balls as any good girl should, there's no reason to brood."

Her eyes widened and she stopped stroking his jaw so she could slap his arm.

He grinned at her.

"You're impossible," she declared.

He put his mouth to hers, still smiling, and said, "But ye like me anyway."

"Bluh," she said against his lips.

She liked him.

He kissed her.

Not long later, they settled into bed.

And with Helena at rest not far from where they lay…

They fell asleep.

CHAPTER SEVENTEEN

LADY NORTON HAD SPOKEN

Dair

"Yo, bruv," Davi greeted as she strolled into the stables where Dair was saddling one of the horses to take it out for a ride.

It was Wednesday.

Nearly everyone was gone, but his mum, his sister, Alex, Rix and Ned.

His sister was working remotely, but she had to get back. She had plans for the weekend. His mum was going with her, and they were leaving on a flight out that evening. Dair was taking them to the airport.

At that moment, Ned, Blake and Alex were going over the estate's accounts with Christine in the study.

Rix was supposed to meet him at the stables for a ride.

Dair had a match to call at Twickenham on Saturday, and he and Blake had made plans.

The next day, not only Blake, but all of them were going to come to London with him and catch the game. They'd return to Treverton on Sunday, after they took Ned, Alex and Rix to Heathrow because they were flying out that day.

There had been no talk of Blake going back to The States.

But there had been talk of her returning to Edinburgh with him.

He wasn't mentioning her going home to New York.

As far as he was concerned, she was now home.

At Treverton.

Which was a far sight closer to his home than New York.

This was all good.

Blake, Alex and Ned seemed to be getting on all right since experiencing the closure of the funeral.

So that was all good too.

The only issues to be had were Dair's.

Primarily his father continuing to try to get in touch with him, his mum and his sister.

With Helena laid to rest, Dair needed to stop procrastinating with that. Hear what his father had to say, not that there was anything he could say, but he owed the man at least that respect.

And then he could make a decision about how he felt about it.

He'd look at doing that when they returned to Edinburgh.

He'd also finally taken the time to listen to Signe's podcast.

He was no solicitor, so he couldn't say for certain, but it didn't seem like she'd broken the non-disclosure agreement. It was well known they were together, same with their divorce. The woman harping on about how much they loved each other could also be construed as common knowledge.

He sent it to his attorney regardless.

In the meantime, probably due to more photos of he and Blake making the rounds, mostly arriving at and leaving Helena's memorial, Signe had done another podcast.

This one was more popular, had more followers, and as such, meant Dair had received numerous communications from mates who had heard it or of it.

He hadn't had the chance to listen to that one.

But from what he heard in the first, Signe was definitely playing the star-crossed lover, trying to paint him as the other half of that, and as such, erase Blake out of the picture altogether.

He'd shared none of this with Blake. There was nothing she could do about it. And she had more important things to concern herself with. Primarily wrapping her head around the running of an estate, all her new assets, finalizing the inheritance and hopefully considering a permanent move to the UK.

But now, he had his sister, who was wearing an expression he did not like.

"All right?" he asked.

"No."

He already knew that, but he waited for her to share.

She stopped at the horse he'd just finished saddling and started stroking his neck.

"Rix is meeting me, Davi, so…" he prompted when she didn't seem inclined to speak.

She let out a harassed breath and launched in.

"I've debated mentioning it at all, but since you all are leaving tomorrow, and leaving him here, well, there's no way to ease into this. I should be telling Blake, or maybe Ned, but I dinnae want to disturb them. They seem to be doing okay, but—"

"Tell them what?" he interrupted to ask, since his sister had descended into awkward havering.

She made a face and said, "Our illustrious butler, Jeff, made a pass at both Dru and Cadence while they were here."

Dair didn't move.

"Doesn't take a genius to work out he's looking for his next meal ticket, no insult to them. They're both gorgeous, and this time, age appropriate, but I reckon he'd have a go at all the single ladies, including Mum, if given a shot."

"What do ye mean, made a pass?" Dair asked, and his sister focused more fully on him.

"I mean he said a few things to Dru, which weren't hard for her to translate since she might not speak the King's English, but she speaks English. She rebuffed him, repeatedly. It didnae take, and Sully got wind of it, so he had a word with him. It ended for Dru after that. Cadence is younger, and he cornered her in a hall—"

At these words, abruptly, Dair left the horse tethered and saddled as he stalked by his sister toward the doors to the stable.

"Dair!" she called, and he could hear her running after him.

He didn't slow.

But he did speak.

"He try it on with you?"

"He's been giving me looks, but I can take care of myself," she told his back, still chasing him.

And she continued to do it until they hit the study inside the house.

The three Sharps and Christine, all bent over an open book on the desk, looked right to him when he did.

As her gaze caught him, Christine recoiled.

Ned straightened from the ledger they were poring over.

Alex's chin went into her neck.

Blake's brows pinched and she was the only one who spoke. "Are you okay?"

He addressed Christine. "Kindly find Jeff and bring him here."

Understanding dawned, though he doubted it was specific, before Christine proved his doubts true and asked, "What's the lad done now?"

"Can ye just bring him here?"

She nodded before she scuttled away, passing Rix as she did.

"Saw you headed in here," Rix remarked. "I thought we were meeting at the stables."

"Aye, we were," Dair agreed. "Something must be done first."

"What's that something?" Blake gained his attention with her question.

He looked to her. "Sully had to intervene for Dru, seeing as Jeff was making a play for her."

Alex's body went visibly tight, as was her voice when she asked, "He was what?"

"Once Sully did that, he cornered Cadence in the hall." Dair looked to his sister to finish sharing the dire news.

However, the room had already electrified.

"It was physical," Davi shared cautiously, considering the atmosphere was zapping with intensity, and Dair felt his blood pressure spike at this addition. "She pushed him off. Gage heard about it. And then Gage had a word. No other events were reported after that."

"Why didn't anyone tell me?" Blake demanded.

"Because you're mourning the sudden loss of your mum" Davi pointed out.

"I'm a woman and a former mean girl," Blake bit off. "I can multitask, mourn Mum and tear someone a new asshole, both at the same time."

Dair nearly smiled.

That was his girl.

"How about you let me handle this, darling?" Ned requested.

"Um…no fucking way, Dad," Blake shot back just as Jeff strolled in like he owned the place, Christine bustling after him.

Christ, this bloke was a twat.

"You summoned?" Jeff drawled.

"Might wanna rein it in a notch, bud," Rix warned, his voice rough with anger.

"I might?" Jeff asked like the suggestion was ludicrous. Then, as they all stood there, staring at him, he threw himself into a chair that was probably a priceless antique. He did this crosswise, his legs over an arm, completely at home. "Why might I want to do that?"

"I know you used the estate's cars when Mum wasn't here, and when she was, and therefore do not own your own vehicle," Blake began, her voice not rough at all, but smooth as pulled silk. "So I suggest you phone a friend to come collect you before Dair and Rix escort you to your rooms so you can pack."

Jeff raised a lazy brow. "Am I going somewhere?"

"As I'm firing you from a job you never really had"—she indicated the ledger with her hand—"even though Mum paid you like you were a butler so the estate would cover your..." she paused for drama before she emphasized, "*fees*...make no mistake, I am indeed firing you. In case you're curious, I'm doing so for gross misconduct."

Jeff smiled a slimy smile. "Your mother had no complaints about my conduct."

Alex made a disgusted noise.

"Seriously suggest you get smart fast," Rix warned, and his tone had deteriorated.

Jeff righted himself in his seat, put his elbows to his knees, but tipped his head back so he could keep his attention focused on Blake.

Even though she'd proved she could hold her own, both Dair and Ned closed in on her back.

"This is the way I see it," Jeff began. "None of you are going to want the reputation of Helena Coddington-Sharp, Lady Norton, an esteemed Marchioness, to be besmirched by news leaked that she was fucking a twenty-eight-year-old and she'd been doing it since he was twenty-four."

Bloody hell.

"So,"—Jeff sat back—"the way I see it, I'll be staying as long as it takes me to find another position I enjoy, a place where I want to live, and I won't be doing it at my current salary. Instead, you'll give me an increase, that of twenty-five percent, with no duties, free access of the Defender, room and board provided...all I can eat, by the way...oh, and, let's say, a million pounds deposited into my account."

No one spoke or moved, and Dair suspected he wasn't the only one keeping himself in check so he didn't punch this arsehole in his larynx. Rix was likely doing the same. And perhaps Ned too.

"Is that all?" Jeff asked when the silence lingered.

"If you could leave us for a moment so we can talk," Blake requested.

Jeff crossed his legs and smiled. "I think I'll stay right here. If you want privacy, *you* can go somewhere else."

"Christ, I'm finding it hard not to thump the fuck out of this asshole," Rix said.

Aye.

He was correct.

Rix was feeling it too.

"If you touch me, that'll be leaked as well, unless I get another half a mil," Jeff replied.

"Actually," Blake began nonchalantly, "we don't need you to leave to discuss this." She looked to her sister. "Do you give a shit about Mum's reputation?"

Jeff twitched.

And at first, Alex seemed startled, then her lips quirked.

"Not really," she responded.

"Dad?" Blake asked.

"Not at all," Ned replied, sitting back down at the desk and relaxing in the chair.

Blake hefted an arse cheek on it and returned to Jeff, who was suddenly not looking so certain of himself.

Dair nearly barked with laughter.

"So, I suppose, be our guest to whatever you can get out of some gossip magazine to print the story about you servicing an older woman," she invited. "Actually, in this current atmosphere…you know, the whole resurgence of the feminist movement, I think there will be many who applaud Mum taking care of her needs in that manner. I mean, why not, if some guy is willing? It's hardly scandalous. Men do it all the time. And you did well on your end. Arrangements like yours have been going on for years, though the majority of the time with a gender swap, but still."

Blake seemed to be pondering something before she went on.

"Though, you might have trouble getting laid again. I don't mean finding another client. I'm sure they'll be lining up. But, say, you were attracted to someone like"—her eyes changed, they turned poisonous, and Dair hoped like fuck he never earned that from her, it not even being aimed his way gave him a wee shiver—"Dru or Cadence, you know, someone your age, you'll be fucked. And not literally."

This time, Jeff didn't move or speak.

"Rethinking that, if you tell your tales, you might find clients hard to come by too," Blake carried on. "No one likes their filthy little secrets shared."

Jeff's face flushed.

"Now, I think I made myself clear," Blake continued. "But just to reiterate, I want you out of my home. You have two hours to vacate the premises, or I'll be phoning the police."

"Okay, I'll keep quiet for half a million," Jeff scrambled to negotiate.

"It seems you've not been following," Blake retorted coolly. "To make myself perfectly clear, you are not getting another fucking pound out of the Norton estate."

"A hundred thousand," Jeff said desperately.

Blake drew in breath and crossed her arms on her chest. "I get it. You have nowhere to go, and let me guess, you blew all the money she gave you."

Jeff didn't reply, but his face said it all.

Stupid eejit.

"I hope you understand that is not my problem," Blake went on.

Jeff opened his mouth.

And Dair was done.

Because Lady Norton had spoken.

"It's over, mate. Get up." He jabbed a finger toward the door. "Let's go."

"Helena would never do this to me," Jeff groused as he pushed out of the chair.

"I keep telling you, my mother is gone," Blake retorted. Then she huffed, "Kids these days. Never planning for the future."

"Let's go, bud," Rix urged.

Jeff didn't move.

"Right, I'll tell you the easy," Rix said. "You go pack your shit and get the fuck out. That's the easy. The hard, Dair and I put you out right now, we pack your shit and throw it by the road when we're done. Which way is this gonna go?"

"Fuck you," Jeff spat at Rix.

"Thanks, no," Rix muttered.

"Fuck you all!" Jeff shouted with a swing of his arm.

"Ye done?" Dair asked.

"Fuck you too," Jeff snapped unnecessarily, but then he stormed out of the room.

"Can you see to the wee horse, lass?" Dair asked his sister.

"No worries," she replied.

As Dair followed Rix, who had followed Jeff, he didn't miss Christine grinning madly.

So he wasn't the only one thinking that was superb.

Unfortunately for Jeff, he had a lot of stuff.

Also unfortunately for Jeff, he didn't have many mates who were okay to come get him and all of his shite, dragging it to their place and letting him crash there.

In the end, his mum came and got him.

Which, as they discussed it over dinner that night, they all found hilarious.

STANDING IN THE DOORWAY TO THEIR BATHROOM THE NEXT MORNING, Dair asked his woman, "You're doing what?"

"You don't have to go," she replied, releasing a lock of her hair from a curling iron.

"Maybe ye need to think more on this, love."

She turned from the mirror to look at him. "Why?"

Dair moved into the room, rested a hip against the basin and a hand on her waist.

"This will be a lot for ye."

"I know."

"Ye dinnae have to put yourself through it."

"I know that too." She turned back to the mirror and lifted the iron. "Blake."

She put the iron on the counter and again turned to him.

"Alex and I agree. We have to go."

"You never met the wee lass," he said gently.

Some bloody way, Blake had learned that the funeral of the two-year-old girl was that day, and she was getting ready right then to haul her arse into a car with her sister and go to it.

"You know, I'm glad Mum had Jeff," she announced. "He was a dick, and he didn't care about her, just her money, but she was Mum. She didn't care about anyone. She probably knew that, and it didn't matter in the slightest to her. She was a woman who wanted what she wanted and got it however she needed to get it. Including him."

"All right," he said when she stopped speaking.

"I've been through all the paperwork with Dad. She had a massive allowance. That was probably why she had a ton of designer clothes in her closet. Expensive perfume on her vanity. And a jewelry box that would make most women weep."

"Aye," he said on another prompt when she said no more.

"I'm sure when we get there, we'll find the same in the London house. She vacationed in Cannes and Capri. She skied in Switzerland. She had two lovers, that we know of. She delighted in making her daughters' lives living hell, and she enjoyed that pastime copiously."

"Darling—"

"She lived her life, Dair," she said, her tone suddenly harsh.

No, *grating*.

And it grated right over Dair's heart.

"Baby," he whispered.

"And that little girl didn't get the chance to," she went on.

Her eyes were getting bright with tears, so he used his hand on her, engaged the other one, and pulled her to his body.

"I'm not over it. I'm not okay with it. Mom dying," she announced, her voice having turned husky. "It feels weird to laugh and enjoy time with family and friends when the flowers on my mother's grave are still fresh."

"Aye, it would," he soothed, rubbing a hand up and down her back.

The tears were threatening to spill. "I don't feel sad. I don't *not* feel sad. I don't know how I feel. Except, I struck her the last time I was in her presence. I can't think about it without cringing. Physically."

"I wish I could help you with that," he told her. "But just to say, words would never reach her, if you tried to explain what she did to you. But that made its mark, and you deserve that, Blake." He wrapped his arms around her and pulled her tighter to him. "Even if it didnae penetrate, all ye had pent up that you needed to say to her, you deserved to have that moment where ye let it be known."

"That's certainly a way to pretty it up, Dair."

"Makes it no less true, right?"

She looked to his shoulder and took a shaky breath into her nose.

When she came back to him, she said, "I just need to be with that family. I don't know why. I'm not going to make a big deal about it. I'm not going to introduce myself or intrude on their grief. I just have to…*be there*. And when I talked to Alex about it, she said she was feeling the same thing. I think it'll give us closure Mum's funeral couldn't. To be around the love that little girl had. To be around love…and loss that isn't conflicted. Loss that's just loss. Am I making sense?"

Aye, she was, and he felt for her at how confusing Helena's passing was emotionally.

Therefore, he gave in.

"All right, lassie, then we'll go."

Her eyes lit with hope, but her mouth repeated, "You don't have to."

"Aye. I ken. But I'll not be letting ye go on your own."

"Alex will be with me. Which means Rix will too."

"And I will too."

Both her hands came up to hold his cheeks.

She stared into his eyes.

He stared into hers.

Fucking hell.

It hit him like a bullet.

He already loved her.

And, Christ.

She felt the same.

"Thank you," she whispered, saying that instead of the words he read in her eyes.

"Never thank me for looking after ye, lassie," he whispered back.

She got up on her toes at the same time she pulled him down to her so she could press her forehead hard against his while closing her eyes tight.

He gave her that moment to pull it together.

She took it, and as Blake had a tendency to do, bested it and rolled down to her feet, let him go and turned back to her curling iron, saying, "We have to leave soon, honey."

He took his cue.

Fortunately, as it happened, Nora had arranged for a selection of hats for the Sharp women.

They both went understated, Alex in a black and white tweed blazer, black trousers, a black blouse and a simple black hat with a downturned brim.

Blake redefined funereal elegance in a slim black pantsuit, black turtleneck, black heels and a little black hat that came down further over her head and had a little veil.

They sat at the back, but even so, caused a mild sensation to those who caught sight of them.

They didn't bother the grieving father and mother, the latter of whom was in a wheelchair with her arm in a sling, a cast on her foot and torment etched in her face.

Regardless of the occasion, and the privacy it should have earned, someone snapped shots of them.

They were all over social media within hours.

So going to that wee lass's funeral hadn't been the least bit fun, but it gave his woman some peace.

Even so, because of those photos, it would become a problem.

"Ye were faking it?"

That evening, Dair and Rix were in some room clearly designed for men to smoke cigars, drink port and scratch their balls. It was so masculine, even Dair felt overpowered by it.

They were there alone because, at first, Blake and Alex had some sister date they'd arranged that was just for the two of them. Not too long ago, though, they'd come and collected Ned to be a part of this date.

Leaving Dair and Rix.

"At first," Rix replied to his question. "That's how Alex and me began. And heads up, Chloe is a matchmaker. Judge told me, after our wedding, she'd shifted into ultrasonic gear, conniving with Nora and Mika on ways to get you two together. She said it was going to be her ultimate challenge, considering you both live in different countries. She was bummed when she found out you were already together before she could meddle."

Dair chuckled.

"So, naturally, she's shifted focus," Rix continued. "That's why she's been shoving JT and Laird in your or Blake's arms every chance she got."

Dair chuckled at that as well, though this time, he spoke through it.

"Didnae miss that."

"Yeah," Rix said on a smile. "So back then, Chloe got wind that Alex told Blake that she and I were together, and I'd be coming as her plus one to her wedding because—"

Abruptly, he stopped speaking.

"Because?" Dair prompted.

Rix cleared his throat and shifted his lounging position in the battered leather armchair that was such high quality when it was made, the battered part only made it more comfortable, the leather was like butter, and it smelled vaguely of cigar smoke, though Dair thought that added to its charm.

But Dair was confused.

"Rix?"

"You've known Blake all her life, right?"

Dair nodded.

"So you know she wasn't…who she is today?"

Dair relaxed. "Aye, I ken."

"She was a total bitch to Alex."

Dair tensed again.

That, he didn't know.

"That mean girl comment yesterday?" Rix asked.

Dair jerked up his chin, indicating he remembered.

"Well, Blake took the cake when it came to mean girls," Rix told him. "Alex lied about me coming to the wedding as her plus one just so Blake would have one less thing to be shitty to her about."

Dair felt an unnerving sensation scratching at the back of his throat.

"There's more," Rix kept talking. "Alex didn't even know she was in the wedding until a few weeks before. She wasn't invited to the shower or the bachelorette party. She was expected to lay out a bunch of cash for her dress and shit, all at the last minute. Not like my woman isn't loaded, but she doesn't spend her money on crap like that."

Dair turned his attention to his tumbler of whisky, fighting that feeling that hadn't left his throat.

"Saw her throw a tantrum myself, and it wasn't pretty," Rix muttered and took a sip of his own whisky. "Night and day, who she is now and who she was then."

Dair said nothing.

"Anyway," Rix carried on, "Chloe got wind of Alex sharing that with Blake, and in the end, my woman was going to make excuses for me not attending, but Chloe stepped in and suddenly, I was Alex's fake fiancé."

"Right," Dair forced out.

"Safe to say, I was into her, I just didn't know it. Not sure even for a friend I'd do something like that. We got deep. I got lost. I almost lost her. I figured my shit out and"—he lifted his glass—"here we are."

"Here ye are, married with a wife who's up the duff," Dair said quietly.

Rix smiled big. "Yup."

Dair smiled back, but it wasn't big, before he swirled his scotch and took a drink.

He knew the situation with Chad had sparked change in Blake.

But fucking hell, not telling her sister she was in the wedding party, and if he read between the lines, a sister giving her sister shite for not having a man?

He also knew Blake had been careening down the path of becoming Helena, before she stopped herself.

But that shite had Helena written all over it.

It was ugly.

And even cruel.

"Not sure Chloe has to work hard on the whole get-married-have-babies thing she had going on with you two," Rix remarked. "Seems you guys are tight. And seems you're good for her. Never seen her this chill since I've known her."

Dair didn't have a response to that, though he didn't like it. He was all in to look after his woman. He was not all in for her to lean on him to be her moral compass, or worse, her acting like she didn't have one.

So he grunted.

"Here you are," he heard Blake say from behind him.

He twisted to see she and Alex were entering the room.

Night and day, those two. Blake classically beautiful, slim, chic and outgoing, Alex with her abundance of red-brown curls, curves, no-nonsense attitude and quiet demeanor.

Alex was the perfect woman for Rix, as he was the perfect man for her.

Until just minutes ago, he would have felt sure in saying the same thing about he and Blake.

"God, you can still smell the smoke even if neither of them smoking," Alex said.

Blake sat on the arm of his chair and smiled down at him. "I need to buy you some cigars."

"Have some at home, lassie," he told her.

That made her smile bigger.

"How was your date?" he asked.

But it was Alex who answered. "It took us a while, and we had a goal of five, and could only come up with four memories of Mum that were good without any bad attached."

"We had to call Dad in to figure out number four," Blake added. "But even with him there, we could only add that one."

Four unblemished memories in a lifetime of mother and daughters?

Not good.

But Blake seemed lighter, so whatever worked.

"And heads up," Alex announced. "Marlo is flying to London

tomorrow. We're meeting her for dinner."

Dair studied Blake's face.

No anxiety, she just looked excited.

The men finished their whiskies as they all chatted.

They then all went to bed.

The fuck he shared with Blake before they turned the lights out and settled in was no less intense and satisfying.

But even as his woman drifted right to sleep draped down his side, Dair stayed awake staring at the dark ceiling.

He'd read Signe wrong. The woman he fell in love with was nothing like the woman he found himself married to.

But if given a choice of only those two, he would take being married to a fame-hungry, gold-digging woman to being tied to another version of Helena Coddington-Sharp.

He'd make that choice every time.

He wanted nothing to do with a mean girl.

God damn.

Fuck.

CHAPTER EIGHTEEN

QUESTIONING

Dair

"All right, we're done," Blake said to Rix, who was sitting next to Dair in the first-class carriage of the train taking them to London.

She didn't say "please" or "do you mind switching seats again?"

She just said "all right, we're done" with a girl-who-gets-whatever-she-wants smile on her face, and Rix moved from where he was sitting beside Dair to resume his seat across the aisle beside his wife.

Blake plopped down next to him and grabbed her tote so she could tuck the letters inside that she'd brought with her and just spent forty-five minutes going over with Alex.

"What're those?" he asked.

"Patron requests."

"Sorry?"

She set her tote aside and looked at him. "Patron requests. Apparently, members of the aristocracy patronize various charities. They want money, of course, but they're also looking for someone to help them raise more of it, as well as awareness. Unsurprisingly, Mum didn't patronize any charities, but Christine goes through the mail sent to Treverton. She gave me those letters, and when she did, she told me Grandfather was a patron to several." She looked beyond him and out the window when she finished, "I suspect I'll be getting more requests. It's early days. But Alex works in charity, and I wanted her to help me narrow them down so I can eventually make some decisions."

"You're going to be a patron to charities?"

Even if Dair was still troubled by what he'd learned about Blake the evening before, and he hadn't had a chance to talk to her about it, he hadn't meant to sound that disbelieving.

And his tone earned him a sharp, wounded look.

"Is it so unbelievable?" she asked.

He moved swiftly to cover.

"Ye need to be in the UK to do them any good, hen."

Mercifully, that settled her.

So much so, she twisted, wrapped both her arms around his and leaned into him, tipping her head way back.

This was his Blake, with that impish light in her eyes.

Impish, mingled with love.

As much as he liked that look, Dair adjusted himself restlessly in his seat without losing her hold, because, fuck him, he was questioning it.

"Do I need to make it official?" she asked quietly.

Setting aside his contradictory thoughts, and settling in with this Blake, *his* Blake, he felt his lips curve up. "Dinnae reckon ye do."

The impish light switched to a soft, loving one.

Aye.

He was with his Blake.

"I thought we'd head back up to Edinburgh soon," she suggested. "Get Sorcha out of doggie prison."

He laughed. "She isn't in doggie prison. She's with Auntie Davi now. She loves her Auntie Davi."

"I bet she loves her daddy better."

She'd win that bet.

"So, we'll get my family to Heathrow on Sunday," Blake planned. "You can go home for Sorcha. I'll stay here for a while. It will save you from the mess I'll be making while I go through Mum's stuff at the London house. Also, I've got to go over things with Sarah, the housekeeper there. I'll head back to Treverton. Do the going over things with Christine. Pack up and grab a train to Edinburgh."

"How long do ye think all that will take you?"

She shrugged. "I can aim to be with you on the weekend, but I'll have to head down again. Alex is going to come back out, and soon, before she gets too far along in the pregnancy. We have to make decisions about Mum's things. We're going to auction a lot of it, and I should know who I'm going to be a patron for before we do. We can auction it off for one or several of the charities I select."

"You're going to give that money away to charity?"

Again, he sounded more skeptical than he intended to, but this time, her eyes narrowed, she let him go and sat back in her seat.

"I hardly need the money, Dair. Norton is loaded, and I am too," she said haughtily.

"I didnae mean it like that, lass."

"How did you mean it?"

How did he mean it?

Why was he even surprised by it?

She'd given him no indication she was not who she seemed to be, when, looking back at it, if he hadn't been so blinded by all he was feeling for Signe, she did. And those close to him saw right through her, whereas those close to him loved the idea of him being with Blake.

He was still surprised by it.

And questioning them.

He couldn't get into what Rix told him right now and how it was fucking up his head. Alex and Rix were sitting across the aisle from them and Ned was at a table section behind them, working on his laptop. They'd overhear.

"It's just a lot of work for ye," he hedged.

"What else am I going to do?" she asked. "I don't have a job. I have plenty of time to do just about anything. Alex doesn't even have to come out, except I don't want to accidentally give away something she might want. Dad's already been through Mum's things. There was nothing he'd want, they've been over for decades, but he checked anyway, and he didn't find anything. He's good. But Alex is different. However, by the time she comes out, I want it organized for her so she doesn't have to sift through a lot of stuff. And, Dair, Mum had a lot of stuff. But Alex has a job that matters. She can't be spending weeks sorting through Chanel she's not interested in in the slightest."

"So you'll head up to Edinburgh but have to go back down to Treverton to finish seeing to that?"

"Will that be a problem?"

It wouldn't.

They'd known each other their whole lives, but what they had now started fast, and it continued even faster. It had barely been a month before they became an us.

A break, or several, would be good.

Time to take a breath. Time to assess. Time to see if it was just history, dramatic events and great fucking instead of what it seemed to be, the rest of their lives.

Maybe Blake was right.

Maybe how easy this had been should freak him.

Maybe they both needed time apart to understand what it really meant to them that they were together.

"No problem, lass," he said. "If that official bit ye were mentioning earlier means you're going to be in the UK a lot more, then I'll take ye an hour-and-a-half plane ride away a good deal easier than that ride being seven and requiring getting through Immigration."

"Yes," she said slowly, watching him carefully, "the official bit meant I was going to be in the UK more now."

However, how she said that made him think that wasn't what it meant.

But she tugged her tote to her and busied herself rummaging in it, and Dair took her hint.

He looked out the window at the English countryside rushing past.

They had Marlo tonight.

She was going to be confronted with more of her mother when they hit Helena's London residence.

He had a match to call tomorrow.

Whatever had gone on before, she was close to her family now, and they were leaving, so she had to deal with that.

And he had to go home, get his dog, and she had to deal with more of the flotsam and jetsam left in the wake of Helena's passing.

They could have a break from each other, and he could talk to her about what Rix said when she got back to Edinburgh.

On his decision, he reached to take her hand, and he didn't like it when she hesitated before her fingers curled around his.

But they curled around his.

So all was good.

For now.

BLAKE WAS IN THE BATHROOM, FUSSING WITH HER HAIR, WHEN YET another text came in from his father.

Dair read it. *I have to speak to you. Urgently.*

He knew his mum was home, figuring out her own shite.

Davi had his dog and a date the next night with the man she was having her situationship with who Dair hadn't yet met, but he could tell with the way Davi was talking, she liked him better than most.

And if anything happened to either of them, he'd get a call before his father would.

He glanced at Blake through the bathroom door.

She'd had her hair down the last time he looked at her, now it was half up and half down.

They had to leave in fifteen minutes. Ned had ordered a car to come and get them.

But apparently, whatever she was doing was going to take a while.

And Dair needed to stop fucking around with this issue with his father.

He moved the door to the bathroom.

"Babe?" he called.

She turned to him and pointed to her head. "How does this look?"

"Gorgeous."

"Better or worse than all down?"

He grinned. "Baby, dinnae ask me that. The answer will always be 'all down' because I'm thinking of my fist in it or it all over my lap when you're sucking me off."

She made a face at him, but he didn't miss the fire in her eyes.

Then she bossed, "There are two outfits on the bed. Pick a meet-your-dad's-girlfriend-who-means-a-great-deal-to-him one and put the other one back in the wardrobe, please."

At least she tacked a please on that.

"On it," he told her. "I'll do that and then I have to make a call."

"Right," she said to the mirror, so preoccupied with her hair, she didn't ask him what call he had to make.

He registered that thought but set it aside and moved to the bed.

And he heard her say from the loo, "And don't pick the sexy one you want to fuck me in."

That made him chuckle.

He didn't even really look at the two outfits. They were both gorgeous. Both classy. And she'd look fantastic in either of them.

But he picked the ivory satin set with the sleeveless top that had a very high neck with a twist at the side that created some gathers across her chest, and it turned in at a bottom that was high so it'd expose some skin at her middle. This had matching trousers with deep pleats and a thin rope belt that cinched a paper bag-looking waistband.

Right, so he picked that because it would cling to her, it was sexier, and the gold heels she had on the floor under where she'd set it out were fuck-me shoes.

But it was still stylish and more her than the conservative dress laid out beside it.

He put the dress away and took his phone with him as he moved toward the door of the bedroom, saying to Blake, "All sorted."

She had her hair down again but was bunching it up when he passed. "Thanks, honey."

The hair thing made him halt.

"Stop fretting," he ordered. "She's going to like ye."

She turned to him and the anxiety was no longer hidden.

Bloody hell.

His sweet girl.

He went to her, kissed her nose, her forehead, then her mouth before he pulled back a wee bit and reiterated, "She's going to like ye."

"Okay," she whispered.

He winked at her and walked out.

He jogged down the steps of Helena's—no, Blake's—Belgravia townhome.

This place seemed more Blake than the stodgy, lived-in, but still attractive Treverton. It was all feminine, pale colors, mixed with creams and ivories, and it was more modern, elegant and sophisticated.

He moved into the lounge on the first floor (she couldn't hand him shite about his townhouse now, seeing as the bedrooms in this one were on the second floor too), which was just all creams and ivories. Once there, he went to the French doors that led out to a narrow balcony.

He made his call and looked out the windows at the park across the street.

His father answered after one ring.

"Dair."

"Dad."

"Where are ye?"

"London. I've a match to call tomorrow."

"When are ye back in Edinburgh?"

He didn't want to tell the man this, but to move things along, he said it anyway. "Sunday."

"We'll arrange to meet for lunch Monday. My office."

Dair took in a deep breath and let it out before he said, "I'm not ready for that yet."

"Dair—"

"Still pissed at you that ye had the gall to force yourself on Mum and Davina at the funeral."

"Son—"

"The funeral of your dead lover," he went on.

"Listen to me—"

"So you're going to have to give me time."

"I need—"

"And I'll be asking ye to leave it with Mum and Davi too. When they're ready, they'll tell you."

"This isn't about Helena or what's happening with your mum and me. This is about Signe."

His head jerked. "Signe?"

"She's causing some problems."

"What problems?"

"The podcasts—"

"I know about those and she's not saying anything she's not allowed to say."

"She has a TikTok channel with not a small amount of followers and a lot to say."

Fucking hell.

"What's she saying?"

"She does makeup and style stuff and tells people what to eat. But lately, quite a number of her videos have been waxing poetic about the two of you and sharing pictures of you and her in your beginning."

Dair was not a dick pic kind of man, and didn't like men who were.

He was also tactile, not visual.

He could appreciate a sexy nightie, and he appreciated all of Blake's, but he'd rather be touching her, kissing her and fucking her than admiring her nightie.

Though, he'd enjoy the build up tonight, watching her in that outfit.

So he didn't have any pictures or videos that Signe could share that would be an issue.

Of course, their more intimate moments, private times that were just the two of them and were none of anyone's business.

But there wouldn't be anything embarrassing in those.

"I'd have to reread the NDA, but I'm not certain that breaks it," he noted.

"Och, aye, it does, son."

Fuck.

"I read it after it was drafted," his father continued. "I helped finalize it. And I've recently reread it. She needs a cease-and-desist letter sent to her."

"Let her haver, Dad. Nothing is going to come of it."

"What she's sharing is none of anyone's business."

"Agreed, but I could have my solicitors send that letter, she could put that out there too. Give people the impression I have something to hide. Give them the impression I give a shite about what she's up to, when I dinnae."

"Would ye allow me to talk to the firm and see what we can do that will be discreet?"

"It's a waste of time."

"They're on retainer. I pay them for the privilege of wasting their time."

Dair had not forgotten his father was private and protective. He was both of these in good ways. Dair had always appreciated it, especially when he started to get attention when he'd begun his career as a professional athlete. Balfour Wallace had been supportive, always had time for his son (furthermore, rarely ever missed a match) and was thoughtful in sharing his wisdom which, back then, Dair had always accepted gratefully.

This had meant that, outside the situation with Signe, Dair hadn't made a misstep in his career, and partly because of that, he had one after he retired.

It seemed both he and Blake were dealing with conflicting emotions when it came to a parent.

It was just that Dair's was alive and breathing.

"If ye want to do that, do it. But I dinnae want Signe approached unless I sign off on it," Dair warned.

"Done. Now about lunch Monday…"

Fuck it.

He had to deal with this, he might as well just deal with it.

"Make it Wednesday. I'll have things I need to see to after being away."

"That's a better idea. We'll have had time to see where we are with Signe and we can discuss it. My office. Where we can talk privately."

"Fine."

He sensed he wasn't alone, turned and saw Rix and Alex walking in.

Alex had makeup on, just not much. She was also wearing a matching black and cream striped skirt and top made of jumper material with boots, which was lovely but easy. Her curly, auburn hair was unbound.

And there was color to her cheeks and a lazy look in her eyes that told him she hadn't spent the last hour fussing over her hair and what she was going to wear, but instead, getting into certain activities with her husband.

He knew this because Rix had that same lazy look in his eyes.

Ned had left several hours ago to pick up Marlo from the airport and have some time with her.

"I've got to go, Dad. We have dinner plans," Dair said into the phone.

"Right, son. I'll see you. Noon. Wednesday."

Shite.

"See you then."

His father's voice was thick when he said, "Miss you, son."

He didn't want to be an arse, but, fuck that in this situation.

"Bye, Dad."

With that, he rang off.

"Blake's not here?" Alex asked when Dair tucked the phone in the inside pocket of his blazer.

"She's redone her hair three times so far," Dair told her.

Alex smiled fondly.

Rix walked out of the room and could be heard shouting in the hall, "Blake! Get your ass down here! The car your dad sent was here five minutes ago!"

"It wasn't, we just got the text right before we came down," Alex confessed to Dair.

He smiled at her.

"Coming, coming!" they heard Blake call and then she was in the room, fiddling with a lightweight gold trench coat that looked like it was made from silk, and wearing the outfit Dair had selected for her.

The side of the top where the twist was meant that it exposed all of one shoulder and part of her collarbone, and the hint of skin at her middle was sexy as all fuck.

He'd chosen well.

Most of her hair was in curls tumbling over her shoulders, but the top was in a messy bunch at the back.

She'd chosen well too.

He approached her and took her coat. He shook it out for her, and she gave him a grateful smile before she turned her back to him, and he helped her put it on.

"Ready?" Rix asked.

"Ready," Dair said.

They walked down to the car.

THIS DINNER WAS NOT GOING WELL.

Marlo Winslet was an exceptionally attractive woman who looked maybe five years older than Blake. Then again, Ned looked fifteen years younger than he actually was.

But Marlo's casual confidence, and the fact she was obviously well-read, well-traveled, well-educated, enjoyed life, was driven and had an edgy, sexy style that reminded him of Blake, but Marlo wore it like a second skin, shared she was likely quite a bit older.

She had a heavy fringe that teased her eyes and long hair that was light brown with loads of blond streaks in.

And she clearly thought the world of Ned.

If there were fireworks due to her not being invited to Alex's wedding, they were over now. It was unmistakable they knew each other well, very much enjoyed each other's company…

And were very much in love.

Dair was pleased as fuck for Ned. She seemed the perfect woman for him.

But they were through cocktails, starters and on their mains, and conversation was stilted, when it was there to be had, and this mostly came from Ned, Rix, Dair and Marlo.

Alex was naturally quiet.

Dair had no idea what the fuck was up with Blake.

Visions of Signe's competitiveness with her "friends" stormed through his head, what with Marlo being a woman Blake might feel in competition with. And just by virtue of the fact her maturity led her to be more comfortable in her skin, she might win it. Therefore, Blake would be pissed off about it.

And he was not liking that at all.

He was about to do something, nudge her foot, squeeze her thigh, when Rix spoke up.

"Right, Alex isn't the talkative type, so don't take any offense to her not gabbing it up," he announced. "She's hell on wheels with listening. And Blake's nervous. Dair said she did her hair at least three times before we left the house. She's been dying to meet you and gave Ned hell we didn't do it at our wedding. Now we see you, and you're all class and shit, and this is obviously more serious than we thought, when we knew it was serious. So both Ned's girls are freaking out. Silently. Don't hold it against them. They'll snap out of it soon enough."

Dair couldn't help but like the guy, and his brutal honesty and ability to communicate it without being an arsehole was part of why he did.

After he spoke, everyone started laughing, including Marlo, who seemed visibly relieved by this explanation.

Aye.

The dinner had gone that way, and it was not a good way.

"Is that an Alaïa blouse?" Blake asked Marlo.

"Good eye," Marlo replied.

"It's scrumptious," Blake oozed.

"Thank you," Marlo replied, and even though she likely knew it was a great top, Blake's comment openly pleased her. "Your outfit is stunning."

"Dair picked it out."

Marlo tipped her wineglass his way. "Your man has a good eye too."

"Don't listen, Dad," Blake commanded.

Ned looked to the ceiling.

Blake leaned into the table toward Marlo and stage-whispered, "It was sexier than the other one."

Marlo did the lean thing and whispered back, "I bet."

"I'm not really into designers," Alex admitted after they sat back.

"You could have fooled me. That's the perfect outfit for you," Marlo told her.

Alex colored with pleasure.

Rix tossed an arm around the back of her chair and beamed.

"And congratulations to you both. I hope you don't mind…"

Marlo placed her hand on Ned's, who turned it immediately so they could link fingers.

Oh, aye.

Dair was happy for the man.

"Ned told me your happy news," Marlo finished.

"It's out there," Rix said.

"He's been wanting to hire a sky writer since I showed him the stick," Alex shared.

Marlo laughed. "I can see why. It's news worthy of skywriting." She subtly drew her shoulders back before she said, "But I'm very sorry you two lost your mom."

"I'm sure Dad's told you about her as well," Blake replied, digging into her mushroom wellington.

"We've spoken about Helena," Ned remarked.

"So I guess you know it's all been not only sudden, but confusing," Alex said.

"I'm sorry about that for you girls," Marlo murmured.

"How about this not be about Mum?" Blake suggested. "May she rest in peace." She lifted her glass of wine. "But here's to happy futures for those of us who remain."

Any concern about the awkwardness of the dinner drained away from Marlo and her smile was fantastic.

Ned's smile could light an auditorium.

They all lifted their glasses, clinked, there were some "hear hears" and "to the futures" before they drank.

"Now, we have to lay ground rules," Blake declared after she put her wineglass down and went after her meal again. "For me, it's that you can only be visibly annoyed the third time I ask you for tickets to a fashion show and you're put on the spot to have to refuse me."

More laughter from Marlo while Ned gazed at his daughter with open pride and adoration.

"I think I can probably get my hands on some tickets for you for whatever show you want," Marlo said. "I know we've agreed not to mention Helena, but you *are* the new Lady Norton, and I can imagine the designers will be happy to court you."

Blake swallowed the bite she took and replied, "Oh, I intend to throw my new title around profusely to get my way. Just you wait."

And more laughter from the table.

Now everyone was relaxed.

Including Dair.

He draped his arm around his woman's chair as well.

"My ground rules are," Alex piped up, "you can't be upset that I don't ask for tickets to fashion shows."

Marlo turned a smile on her, but Blake said, "Oh my God. Think of Chloe. She'll kill you if she knew you said that."

"Chloe can get her own tickets. She's got some connections," Alex retorted.

"So true," Blake said and placed more puff pastry, mushrooms and tarragon sauce in her mouth.

"Are you coming with us to the match?" Alex asked Marlo.

Marlo glanced at Dair. "I'd love to, if you don't mind."

"I can get another ticket," Dair told her. "Rugby fan?"

"Ned stop listening," Marlo ordered.

"It is not lost on me you enjoy watching fit men tackling each other any way you can find them," Ned teased.

"Okay then, yes," Marlo said to Dair. "I'm a rugby fan. Sports on the whole. My favorite is tennis, because, you know, those male tennis players' legs."

More laughter erupted from their table.

"But rugby is a close second," Marlo finished. "But only partly because of their legs."

And still more laughter.

"Perfect for you, Dad," Blake noted, then told Marlo something she probably already knew. "He'll watch anything that keeps score."

"Yes," Ned said quietly, sharing a private look publicly with Marlo. "Perfect."

This led to Blake and Alex sharing a private look publicly, and it might not be the same.

But it was just as happy.

<hr>

"OH MY GOD!" BLAKE SAID ON A TWIRL WHEN THEY HIT THE BEDROOM that night. "She's perfect." She came up to Dair and slapped her hands on his chest, shining a bright happy smile up at him. "Absolutely perfect for Dad."

"She is, aye, lass," he agreed, grinning down at her.

"He seems happy. Do you think he seems happy?"

"More than happy, darling."

And he loved that she was more than happy for her father too.

She twirled away, saying, "I'm so glad she's coming to the match tomorrow."

"Same," he replied, shrugging off his blazer.

She sat on the side of the bed and reached down to take off her shoe.

He tossed his jacket aside, moved to her and snapped his fingers.

She looked up at him before that look he adored came into her eyes and she lifted her foot to put it in his waiting hand.

"I thought I was going to blow it in the beginning," Blake

remarked. "I just couldn't think of what to say. She's so... *together*."

"You're together too, love."

She smiled. "Thank you for thinking that."

"Need to get your eyes and ears examined if ye dinnae agree."

He tossed her shoe to the floor, offered his hand again, and she changed feet.

"You need to get those shoes off fast, honey," she demanded. "So I can jump your bones and not sprain an ankle."

Dair burst out laughing.

But in doing so, he didn't delay in taking off her shoe.

CHAPTER NINETEEN

WARY

Dair

The next morning, water from the shower was jetting down on his back as he held Blake by the cheeks of her fine arse against the wall and thrust inside.

She had the fingers of one hand fisted in his hair, the nails of the other digging into his lower spine, and her pussy was clutching and releasing on his rhythm.

Aye, and her tongue was darting in and out of his mouth the same.

He felt his balls draw tighter, tore his mouth from her tongue tease and grunted, "Your cunt is goddamned magic."

"You say…" she paused through a thrust, "the sweetest," another thrust, "*things,*" she finished on a moan, her fingers tightening, her nails digging deeper, her legs wrapped around his ass holding on as her pussy clenched his and didn't let go because she was orgasming.

He pulled her from the wall and turned to hold her under the water while she shoved her face in his neck, held on and helped him with some wee bounces as he pumped into her under the spray until he found it.

As usual, it was big, it lasted long, and he had to throw out an arm to plant a hand on the tile to steady himself through it.

When he came down, Blake had all four of her limbs wrapped tight around him and was pressing little kisses up the side of his neck, along his jaw and to his mouth.

And the water continued to rain down on them.

"How am I going to survive a week without you?" she whispered against his mouth, smoothing a hand along his slick hairline at the back of his neck.

His sweet lass.

Dair took his hand from the wall to put it back to her arse and used both to give her a squeeze.

"Phone sex?" he suggested.

She laughed softly and kissed him again.

But she didn't say no.

He kissed her back, then lifted her off his dick, and they finished their shower.

THEY WERE STANDING IN KING'S CROSS STATION, SNOGGING.

The day before, Dair had to go in to work early, and Blake had spent the entire day with her family.

By the time he met them for dinner, something Blake, Alex and Marlo cooked together in the kitchen at the townhouse, it wasn't as if those women had only met the evening before. It was like they'd known each other for years.

Along with the rugby match, which Blake told him was "a revelation," and "who knew dirty, sweaty, bloody men could be so sexy?" (and obviously, that made him laugh and do it for a long time), the women had squeezed in some shopping. But Blake told him "it didn't count" because they'd been looking at baby things.

It was abundantly clear Ned was living his best life, not only having his daughters accept the woman he loved with open arms but also seeing his girls with a more mature woman with whom they connected and enjoyed spending time.

Marlo was more Blake's speed, but between her and Blake, they managed to make Alex comfortable in their trio.

"She's the absolute shit, brother," Rix had said to him in a moment it was just the two of them. "It's like, they lost Helena, and it was no loss, then they turn around and get Marlo, and they hit the motherlode."

All through an evening filled with chatter and laughter, it seemed what Rix said was exactly the case.

Ned put his foot down about Blake and Dair not wasting any time seeing them to the airport. Therefore, they'd all had brunch then they'd lingered over goodbyes on the pavement before the rest headed to Heathrow.

He could see his woman was borderline devastated to say goodbye to them, but plans had been made for Alex's return, and Marlo said she'd try to come with, considering the things they would be sifting through were her forte. Although Blake had experience with high fashion, Marlo was an expert in it.

And this meant, if Marlo came, Ned would as well.

So their separation wouldn't last long.

They'd had just enough time for him to get back and pack, and for both of them to take a car to King's Cross.

And that brought him to now.

He was aware people were staring at them, and no doubt some taking photos, and he didn't give a shite.

What he gave a shite about was that his train was leaving in five minutes, and he needed to get his arse on it.

And in doing that, he had to do something he really didn't want to do.

Leave Blake behind.

He understood logically that a separation would be good, even healthy.

That didn't mean he wanted one.

With no choice, he ended the kiss.

Her lips turned down and her fingers stroked behind his ear.

In this instance, he didn't like the first, but the last always felt nice.

"You have to go," she whispered.

"Aye, love. Unfortunately."

"You'll call when you get home?"

"Aye."

"You'll give Sorcha a snuggle for me?"

He smiled at her.

Christ, he loved that she loved his dog.

"I'll give her two."

"Call me on your way home from lunch with your dad."

She'd eventually asked about the phone call he made, so he'd told her about his dad and Signe.

"I will."

Her gaze wandered to the turnstiles that took you to the platforms and she said wistfully. "It's not an ocean away, I suppose."

Safe to say, he also loved it that she didn't want to separate either.

He gave her a squeeze and regained her attention. "You'll be up on Saturday, and we'll talk in between. Just like when you were in New York. When you come back to me, I'll meet ye at the station. And you'll feel better having things as ye want them for when Alex and Marlo return."

She nodded. "Right."

"Quick kiss then we need to let go."

Her hold on him tightened.

Ah, his bonny lass.

"I…"

Whatever she was going to say, she trailed off and that lingered so long he had to give her a shake.

"Ye what?" he prompted.

She painted on a bright smile. "I'll see you Saturday and talk to you in a few hours."

"Aye, you will." He bent, touched his mouth to hers and said there, "I'll miss ye, hen."

"I'll miss you too, Dair."

He kissed the side of her hair, let her go, bent and hefted the strap of his duffel on his shoulder, also taking hold of the garment bag which he threw over the same shoulder.

He shot her a grin as he walked toward the turnstiles.

She put her fingers to her lips and blew him a kiss.

And, aye.

His woman could be totally adorable.

Once through the turnstiles, when he looked back, she was still there.

So he stopped and stabbed a finger toward the doors behind her.

She rolled her eyes, but she got her arse moving.

Oh, aye.

Totally adorable.

Dair texted her when the train was underway and called when he got home. He also sent her a picture of Sorcha after he retrieved her. The snap of his dog looked like she was smiling.

Her reply to his picture of Sorcha was so many double pink hearts, he had to scroll down twice.

Absolutely, he loved that she loved his dog.

And he loved that she was falling in love with him.

He took that opportunity to make the picture of her and Sorcha at the park his lock screen photo.

He called her the next evening, and they drank a glass of wine together long distance while she did most of the prattling. This chiefly consisted of her shock at the abundance of her mother's clothes and "I don't think in forty years she's given that first thing away. This is like a museum to St. Laurent, Gucci, McQueen, and I could go on."

Blake had, however, also asked about Davi and his mum, and gently probed into how he felt about speaking to his dad and the shite Signe was pulling. He was not gentle in his replies that he wasn't fond of either.

He called her the next morning, and made her come with his voice, and listening to her climax, she made him come with the assistance of his hand.

They spoke again, briefly, in the evening because, "You'd think this would not be a complaint ever in my entire life, but I'm covered in Prada and Givenchy, honey. I will never consider myself a clotheshorse again after sorting through this tangle. We're about to lick it here, so I can take the train to Treverton tomorrow. But I want to fill a couple more boxes before I give up for the night."

As such, he'd let her go so she could crack on with it.

In the meantime, Dair had decided to set aside what Rix had told him.

He was not unaware that Blake had worked hard to change her ways. How she'd treated her sister was not good nor was it right. But it was done.

This Blake, *his* Blake, was a different woman.

It was in everything she said, everything she did, and how everyone around her treated her.

She hadn't been at his house with him for long, but they'd either been with each other or within a walk from one room to another for some time.

The short while they'd been separated, Dair already felt the keen sense of missing having her near, and he knew that was in a way this feeling was communicating something deeper.

He wanted her with him.

All the time.

The morning after that, she texted him, telling him she'd be on the afternoon train back to Treverton, wishing him luck with his lunch with his father and reminding him to call her as soon as he could on his return home.

He didn't miss she was worried about him because she didn't hide it.

He didn't want her to worry, but even so, he loved that too.

He replied with a red heart.

And two hours later, he got in his car to go have lunch with his dad.

THE DOOR TO THE OFFICE WAS CLOSED, AND ANY ADDITIONAL CHAIRS that normally sat around the circular conference table in the corner by one of the windows had been taken away.

The table was covered in food.

It was on the tip of his tongue to tell the man he couldn't repair what he'd done to Dair's heart and their entire family with hefty sandwich triangles, chicken skewers, samosas, smoked salmon on toast and miniature hazelnut dacquoise and éclairs, but he didn't want to spend any more time there than he had to.

So he didn't tell him that.

He just sat, took a plate and filled it.

"I see we're not bothering with the pleasantries," his father mumbled as he sat opposite Dair.

"Not feeling pleasant, Dad," Dair replied. "And I've had the opportunity to reread the NDA. You're right. Signe's prohibited from sharing private photos. I also looked at her TikTok. She seems determined to paint us as star-crossed lovers with Blake keeping us apart. And it's pissing me off."

"I'm glad ye think so." Balfour was also filling his plate. "Because the solicitors believe she needs something stronger than a cease and desist."

"That would be?" Dair asked before he shoved a roast beef sandwich triangle with horseradish sauce in his mouth.

"An all-expense paid trip to Edinburgh for a meeting whereupon we'll share things will become very uncomfortable if she doesn't stop fucking ye about."

"That seems overkill," Dair remarked.

"Then I'll fly to Denmark and threaten her personally."

At this offer, Dair froze with a samosa halfway to his mouth.

"No one fucks with my son," Balfour declared.

He felt something tighten in his chest even as he said, "That's unnecessary, Dad."

"We disagree on that, and when you have children, you'll see why."

Dair sat back in his chair. "Ye dinnae have to go this extra mile because of what ye did to mum and how that affected our family."

Bally leveled his eyes on his son. "This isn't about an extra mile. This is about someone fucking with my son. Something I fully intend to put a stop to. But just to say, ye can advise me on how to make amends for doing something weak and stupid, causing pain to the ones ye love most in your life if you should ever do anything as utterly weak and stupid as I've done." He took a breath into his nose. "I dinnae ken what I was thinking. I look back at it, the years of it, and question my sanity. Though, I'll say, as long as it went on, I questioned the state of my mental health through the entirety of it."

Dair had no response.

"These are words for your mother, if she'll ever speak to me again," Bally continued. "But you should hear them too."

"Allow her to guide that and leave me and Davi out of it," Dair stated.

"Ye ken I almost married Helena."

At this surprising declaration, Dair sat stunned and still, staring at his dad.

"We were both very young, but that didnae mean we didnae know our hearts. But I wasn't good enough for her, according to her father," he went on.

"Bloody hell," Dair muttered.

"I loved her," Bally announced. "Deeply. Besotted with it. This meant I was pissed off she tossed me aside because I was hurt when she did it. I was then pissed off when she married Ned. I obsessed about it." He shook his head. "I ken this seems nonsensical with what I just said and the timing of it, but make no mistake, I fell in love with your mother. She was no consolation prize. She was everything Helena wasn't, everything I truly needed, everything I actually wanted. She made me very happy. So ye can see, knowing all of that, how I questioned my mental health."

Oh, aye.

Dair could see that.

Bally continued talking.

"It didnae make it any better, when I realized what kind of woman Helena was, that I did it, and I continued to do it. But these last weeks, you'll find it no surprise, I've spent a great deal of time reflecting on my actions, and I realized I did it mostly as a fuck you to her father, who eventually was no longer even breathing. It does not paint me as a decent man, but I'm speaking in truths here. I not only made Helena my whore, I got off on it."

Dair remained silent.

"And the worst of it was, it made me feel the big man. Beautiful, loving wife at home, beautiful, stylish mistress on the side. Maybe I had something to prove with that, to her father, to myself. Though, as difficult as it is to admit this, really, it was just a fault in my personality to fall into the trap of the stereotype of being that kind of man."

Although Dair was shocked his father had this deep of an insight into himself, and could speak the words out loud, Dair had no response.

"Say something, Alasdair," Bally ordered harshly.

"Were there others?"

Bally shook his head.

Dair watched closely but his father never broke eye contact.

So it was just Helena.

He was shocked by that too.

"Ye loved her? I mean, before Mum?"

"Very much so," Balfour admitted. "And to this day, as much as Helena could feel this emotion, I think she loved me too, in the way she could. This isn't an excuse, though I would tell myself it was as I continued doing what I was doing, but I convinced myself she needed me. I was the only happiness she had. But the truth is, I think I was."

Fuck.

Dair examined his father's face and saw he sincerely thought that, so he didn't want to say what he had to say.

But they were speaking in truths here.

"Then I hate to tell ye this, and I truly do, but she has so many clothes, even Blake thinks they're too much, and she had a twenty-something boy toy she kept at Treverton. He's been there for years. Blake had to confront him and deal with a blackmail threat to get him gone." As Bally sat, openly staggered, Dair finished, "Dad, what I'm saying is, Helena enjoyed her life to the fullest, with or without you."

Balfour stared at him for long moments before his attention drifted to the window.

Christ.

He'd had to say it, he couldn't not.

However...

"I'm sorry, Dad."

"It was a paltry excuse anyway," Bally said to the window.

Shit happened in relationships.

Dair had heard stories from his mates—women who were stressed by having careers and still being expected to do everything at home, or being cast as a mom when they have children, their partners losing hold on the fact they're still women, and on the flipside men whose partners lost interest in their sex lives and weren't willing to work on regaining their intimacy, or the partner got so lost in the family life, they forgot they had a relationship to nurture—where he couldn't condone, but he could understand why they strayed in search of the kind of connection they weren't getting at home.

However, carrying on a decades-long affair was an entirely different thing.

Dair ate the samosa to give his father some time.

Balfour was still talking to the window when he said, "I dinnae think your mother will ever forgive me."

"And I hate to say this as well, a bit less, but I still do. I think you're right," Dair told him.

Bally looked back at his son. "I'll let her call the shots. I'll text Davi to let her know I'm there whenever she's ready to talk, but I'll leave her alone in the meantime. And I'll finish this in the way I didnae conduct myself the entirety of it. With some decency."

"That would be appreciated."

Balfour put some salmon in his mouth in a manner he was doing it by rote, not with any appetite, and when he swallowed, he said, "Now we need to talk about Blake."

That ominous sensation came back to his throat at his father's tone, and he asked, "Blake?"

"In dealing with Signe, some things have come to light about Blake I feel ye should know."

It was hesitant when Dair asked, "What things?"

Balfour pulled his phone out, engaged it, found something on it, and turned it to Dair.

It was a photo of Blake at a party, one Dair remembered because he attended. It was the rooftop cocktail party Ned had thrown for her prior to her wedding to Chad.

She was wearing a daring dress, and he could very much see how daring it was not because he remembered seeing her in it, but because her breast was exposed all the way to the nipple. She seemed to be meaning to give that show with how far forward she was leaning. But the photograph appeared to be a candid, because it had done the impossible with a woman as beautiful as his. It wasn't very complimentary to Blake, considering how far open her mouth was.

Dair's first instinct was to be pissed as all hell a photo of his woman exposed like that was a photo his father could get his hands on, which probably meant anyone could.

Dair's next instinct would be vastly different.

"She sold that photo of herself to some gossip thing," his father shared.

Dair's throat closed, so he had to force through it, "What?"

Balfour tucked his phone back in his jacket. "It's my understanding that was something she did. She had a go-between, but she frequently sold pictures of herself in order to remain a feature in that shite."

"You investigated Blake?"

Bally shook his head. "Not in the way ye mean, no. It came to the fore as a matter of digging into Signe. Trying to assess what she might plan for the future. Which meant assessing where ye might be vulnerable, and since you're with Blake, we had to assess her too. We had to look into what Signe may be able to discover in order to harm ye." He waved his hand in front of him. "No worries. Money has exchanged hands and documents have been signed. No one will know Blake did that."

Although Dair distractedly noted his father, yet again, made moves to protect Dair, this time doing it also protecting Blake.

But he didn't have it in him in that moment to have a mind to it.

"Why would she do that?" he asked a question his dad couldn't possibly answer.

However, he did.

"Why, for the same reasons Helena did it."

Now Dair was finding it difficult to breathe.

Balfour kept talking. "To remain relevant. To fix her place in society. To make herself seem important. To compete with the women in her circle." His father fixed him with a stare. "I ken ye two are hot and heavy right now, Dair. She's a beautiful girl. I always thought she was a little lost, and Helena was no help guiding her in being found. Seems from what I've witnessed recently, she figured that out for herself. Even so, I'll just suggest…be wary of her. Although it appears she's made her own way, I see a good deal of Helena in that girl, and I always did."

"Helena sold photos of herself too?"

Balfour gave a sharp nod. "Aye, all the time."

After his father said that, if asked an hour, two or even ten days later, Dair could not say what else happened at that lunch.

It vaguely penetrated that his dad was giving him concerned looks by the time he left, and he texted him twice after Dair was gone, but in the days to come, outside that, his dad left him alone.

But the only thing Dair could think was how Blake had eviscerated Jeff (twice) without blinking. The lad had deserved it, but she hadn't hesitated in doing it.

And he thought about how she'd blanked Chad. When she'd claimed Dair in front of him, it was like the man wasn't even there. Again, he deserved it, but he wasn't even a blip for Blake.

Not to mention, the things Rix said.

And the fact she'd sold pictures of herself, including one that exposed her own body, *globally*, in order to…

He didn't know.

Chase fame?

And that was not good.

Chase notoriety?

That was worse.

To compete with her mates?

Also not good.

None of it was good.

There was no excuse for it.

And he had experience with this kind of shite.

He'd been very wrong.

He needed to talk to her about all of this.

He could not get into another mess like the one he made with Signe, one that he was still dealing with over a decade down the road.

He certainly couldn't marry her and bring children into it. His father and mother's marriage was over, and even with Dair and Davina fully grown and living their own lives, it was devastating their family.

His head was so full of this shite, he didn't phone Blake on his way home from lunch with his dad.

He avoided her frequent texts and her call that evening.

As he did the ones the next day. Though, he did text to say he was busy, reiterating he'd collect her at the station on Saturday, two days away.

He did that because this chat needed to be had, face to face.

He got no communication after his text.

But he was at the station to pick her up.

And this was the first step he didn't know he was taking in making the biggest mistake of his life.

CHAPTER TWENTY

MISTAKE

Dair

The hug they shared at the station when Blake arrived in Edinburgh was awkward.

The anxious, rattled looks she was giving him were torture.

The silent ride to his house was wildly uncomfortable.

The only thing that happened between them that was sweet and relaxed was, after she took off her coat and he wheeled her bag to the boot room, when they entered his kitchen, Sorcha showed how excited she was to see her and Blake returned that with a full-body rubdown of his pup and lots of puppy cooing.

"Would ye like something to drink?" he asked.

She straightened from his dog, looked right at him, and she didn't lead into it easy.

"Actually, I'd like to know what's going on with you."

No, this wasn't easy.

But it was good.

They could get into it so they both could get beyond it.

"Aye." He nodded. "We do have something to discuss."

"I think I got that with the ambiguous ghosting I've been getting from you since your lunch with your dad." Her eyes narrowed and she tipped her head to the side. "Did he upset you?"

"It wasn't any easy talk," was the only way Dair could put it.

He could tell she was getting angry on his behalf when she demanded, "What did he say to you?"

They weren't going to do this standing in the kitchen.

"Let's go in and sit down."

She gave a single, irate nod and stomped out of his kitchen.

Sorcha followed her.

He never wanted Blake to be upset (though, what was about to happen was bound to be upsetting, until they got past it).

But he couldn't deny it felt good she was so angry, and she was that for him.

She went to Dair's sitting room, right to the couch, pulled off her heels and sat cross-legged in it. His dog sat beside her and Blake's hand automatically went to Sorcha's head so she could scratch behind her ears.

Blake looked comfortable, mildly cute, and completely classy wearing her posh black trousers and jumper and petting his dog.

He loved seeing her like that in his space.

And he hated that they had to have this conversation.

But he had to know.

He couldn't make the same mistake twice.

He sat down beside her, crossed his legs in front of him, but rested an arm along the back of the couch and turned her way.

"Ye sure ye dinnae need a drink?" he asked.

And, damn.

He was procrastinating.

"Just spill, Dair," she commanded. "So I can get on with controlling my urge to find your father and throttle him. I've been worried sick about you for days, and it seems I had cause to be."

Worried sick about you for days.

Again, even if he didn't want her to have that emotion, it felt great she did.

Jesus, this was going to be rough.

"This isn't about Dad."

That threw her. "What's it about?"

"I told ye about Signe—"

She cut him off by tossing both her hands up irritably and letting them plop on her legs. "So this is about her? God! Now what's she up to?"

"I need to explain something to ye first, lass."

Either she finally caught the feel of him, or she realized this was something deeper, because she changed.

She became hyper-alert and hyper-still.

He should have taken that for the warning it was.

Sadly, he did not.

"In the beginning with her, it was perfect," he began.

Blake said nothing.

Dair did.

"They didnae call it this then, though maybe they did, and I never heard it, but she was all about love bombing. I could do no wrong. She could do no wrong. She read me and ascertained what was important to me, and she became that. Precisely that. If I did something she didnae like or that annoyed her, I had no idea I did, because she gave me no indication I did. She had all the time in the world for me. She'd bend over backwards to give me what I needed. Be the person I wanted her to be. And she made me believe I was the man of her dreams. I'm not a romantic man, but it felt like a fairy tale."

Blake didn't speak.

"After we were married, that changed. Wholly. I didnae ken the woman I was married to. And life was far from a fairy tale."

He'd told her all of this, mostly.

But she didn't remind him of that.

She didn't say anything.

Dair found this troubling, but he'd begun, and it was important, so he had no choice but to continue.

"Now, I dinnae want to throw Rix under the bus," he started cautiously. "He thought I knew when he shared how ye treated Alex before your wedding to Chad."

After he said that, she didn't move. Not a muscle. Not a nuance of her facial expression changed.

She just kept those alert, violet eyes locked on him, and that was it.

Dair didn't find this troubling.

He found it alarming.

He kept going anyway, because he had no choice.

"Did ye ken they faked their engagement at first so ye wouldn't be unkind to her because she didnae have a man?" he asked.

Finally, she broke her silence.

"Alex has shared this story with me," she said stiffly.

"All right. So ye didnae invite her to your shower, or hen party, and ye waited until the last minute to demand she buy an expensive dress?"

She made no response to that, and Dair reckoned that meant yes.

This wasn't good, but it wasn't the end of the world. Mostly because it was clear Alex was over it because they were obviously close now.

And as he had no choice but to forge ahead, he did.

He pulled his phone out of his pocket, went to the photo he had at the ready, and turned it to her.

"Did ye sell this to some gossip rag?" he asked.

She looked to his phone.

But outside that, again, nothing from Blake.

"Blake, listen, ye wanted so badly to go to that little girl's funeral, and you'd never even met her, and we hit socials with that—"

Instantly, she uncurled her legs and reached to her shoes, Sorcha popping up to get out of her way.

"Blake?" he called.

He watched as she put on her heels.

"Blake," he repeated.

She got up and walked from the room.

Sorcha was undecided for a moment, and then she followed Blake.

"Fuck," he bit off and followed them both.

He found them in the kitchen with Blake's head bent to her phone.

"I'd like an answer, love," he informed her.

She shoved her phone in her back pocket and looked to him. "I have a car coming. I'll wait for it outside."

Wait one moment.

What?

She went to the boot room and collected her jacket.

He moved so he could see her through the doorway.

"We're not done talking," he pointed out.

"Oh, we're done," she said to the floor as she flicked her hair out from under the collar of her coat.

She commandeered the handle of her luggage that he'd left there and rolled it into the kitchen.

"Stop it, Blake. We're in the middle of a discussion," he clipped.

She grabbed her tote and moved to walk by him.

He caught her with an arm around her belly.

She looked up at him.

"Ye can't get out of a difficult conversation by throwing a drama," he warned.

And then it happened.

The mask she'd soldered onto her face cracked, Blake came through, and instantly, Dair realized his mistake.

"Let me go, Dair," she whispered.

"Darling, we need to—"

She started nodding, fast, and it seemed she couldn't stop because she kept doing it even as she spoke.

"I get it. I didn't know it until a few years ago, but Mum did the same thing to Dad that Signe did to you."

Fucking hell.

That was news.

Not a surprise if you thought about it, but news.

"It affected him so badly, he checked out," she continued. "Checked out of our family, out of his daughter's lives. It took an Act of Chad for him to check back in. I know he had lovers, but I never met even one of them. And, as you know, it took him over twenty years to find Marlo."

"Blake—"

"So, I can understand you'd have issues with trust. I get it."

"Good, then take your jacket off, come back with me to the sitting room, and we'll talk about it."

"I'm leaving."

"No, you're not."

"Let me go, Dair."

"Lass, I get I might not have handled that—"

She wrested from his hold and walked fast from the room.

Fortunately, he had longer legs, so he caught up to her, he passed her, and he stopped in front of her in the hall in order to bar her from moving closer to the front door.

"We have an issue, we talk it through," he rumbled when she came to a stop in front of him. "Ye do not have a tantrum and walk out."

"Don't speak to me like I'm a child."

"Dinnae behave like one."

She shook her head violently, like she was clearing water from her ears, and demanded, "Please, move out of my way. My ride share will be here shortly."

God fucking dammit.

He lost it.

"For fuck's sake, Blake, stop blowing this out of proportion!" he shouted. "Ye said ye fucking understood what I was feeling."

"I do."

"So stop this shite, take your fucking coat off and we'll talk through it."

"You made me believe."

"What?"

"You made me believe."

"In what?"

It felt like a building collapsed on Dair as he watched the tear fall from her eye and she whispered, "In me."

God.

Fucking.

Damn it.

The word was guttural when he said, "Baby—"

"I thought I wasn't that woman, and *you* were the one who showed me that."

"Listen—

"But you don't believe in me."

He sure as fuck hadn't.

He reached for her.

She scuttled back, running into Sorcha, who definitely felt the atmosphere, because she started whining.

"Please, get out of my way, Dair," Blake requested huskily.

"Love, get your phone, cancel the ride and please, fucking *please* come into the sitting room with me."

"I'm not her, but I am. I can't escape it."

"What are you saying to me now, darling?"

"Mum. I'm not her, but I am. I always will be. And I see that's a problem."

Christ, he'd fucked this.

Huge.

"Fucking *please* come into the sitting room."

Another shake of her head, this one not violent, but instead, sad, and it wrecked him. "Like I said, I can't escape it, and you can't either. What happened between her and your dad. Who she made me."

"She didnae make ye anything."

"She made me who I am."

"Blake—"

"God!" she cried, lifting both hands in fists crossed at the wrists to her chest, the tears falling freely from her eyes now. "Please! Get out of my way!"

"Where ye thinking of going?"

"Not here."

"I can't let you leave like this. I can't let you leave at all."

She'd been hanging on by a thread, he knew.

But this was when she lost it.

"Dair, *it's done!*" she shouted, leaning toward him. "It's over. We can't be. Don't you see?"

Oh, aye.

He totally fucked this.

"No, I do not see," he gritted.

"I'm not going to be that woman for you. I'll never be your Marlo."

"No, because you're my Blake."

"I'm not your anything."

"Damn it, Blake—"

"Yes," she hissed, spiking toward him. "To answer your question, *yes*, I treated my sister like shit. Actually, what Rix didn't tell you was that I didn't even tell her I was getting married until a few weeks before the wedding and I only did that because Dad made me. Same with making her my maid of honor. Though, I didn't have a hen night, because they're vulgar. But I did have a shower before I even told her I was having a wedding. My own sister."

Her voice hitched, and hearing it, Dair's chest caved in.

"I also gave her shit about her weight," she kept at it. "And definitely about her not having a man. And yes," she hissed again. "I sold that picture and many more to anyone who might buy them. I did a lot of other shitty things too, Dair. That's me."

"It's not."

"Would you like to know what else I did that's me?"

"Love—"

"I'd act up. Just to be a bitch. To Mum. To Dad. But also to Alex, who would get in trouble right along with me if I did something horrible, even if she had nothing to do with it, which she never did. And that's one of the reasons why I did it. I honest to God do not know how she can even stand to look at me."

"This really—"

Blake spoke over him. "There are still stores I'm banned from in Manhattan because I acted like *such* an entitled asshole. Then there was that time I crashed Grant's family's boathouse and got sued."

Crashed a boathouse?

She kept going. "And the many times I had parties at Dad's house where thousands, maybe even tens of thousands of dollars' worth of damage was done. Dad spent years cleaning up my messes, which, you should know, included me getting arrested. Twice. Suffice it to say, even my own grandmother couldn't stomach me."

"I dinnae need to know all of this, lassie," he said gently.

Her neck turned abruptly like she was looking behind her, then she came back to him.

"My phone is vibrating. My car is here."

"You're not leaving."

She came at him and didn't stop, like she could push through him, so he caught her by the arms to communicate she could not.

She kept pushing forward against a man who could manage himself ably in a scrum.

"Settle down, lass," he murmured. "I'll go talk to the driver and give him a few quid."

All of a sudden, she stopped pushing against him and looked him right in the eye.

Hers were still full of tears.

"If you care about me at all, you're not going to put me through this. Put me through eventually being a disappointment to you. Put me through being the one you teethe on for practice before you find the one for you."

"That's not what's happening."

"No? So the next time you find out some shitty thing I've done, we're not going to sit down on your couch to have a chat so I can explain myself to you?"

He was realizing he hadn't simply made a mistake with that.

He hadn't fucked this.

He'd delivered an injury, perhaps a mortal one.

And it had wounded her.

It was also wounding him.

And if he didn't fix it, it was going to kill *them*.

"No, what's happening is, I'm falling in love with you."

He thought that would work.

It didn't.

He knew it when she returned, "You don't even know me."

"I know ye, Blake."

"Really?" she asked and pointed toward the sitting room.

Fuck, he'd fucked up.

Before he could say more, with a vicious wrench, she pulled free.

He got tangled up in his dog, who again didn't know who to be with, so Blake was out the door before he could catch her.

As gently as he could in his state, he pressed his dog back and sprinted after her, out the door, down the walk, seeing her giving her bag over to the driver who had the trunk open.

She hustled to the side door of the car and was standing in it, head aimed down, when he caught her with both hands.

"Dinnae do this, darling," he begged.

She lifted her head and gutted him with her expression.

No.

He hadn't wounded her.

He'd destroyed her.

"Thank you," she said so softly, he almost didn't hear her.

Then she lifted a hand to his cheek, and he closed his eyes momentarily at the feel of it.

He opened them when she spoke again.

"Thank you for letting me pretend I was someone I'm not, even for a little while."

Christ almighty.

He'd entirely *fucked this.*

"Please dinnae do this, baby. I fucked up. Let's work through it."

She sniffed, swallowed, and swept her thumb over his lips, a miniscule, wretched smile on hers before she whispered, "It was beautiful."

The force of that blow was so substantial, he was still recovering from it as Blake slipped from his hold, folded into the car and pulled the door to with such force, he (and Sorcha, who'd followed him) had to jump out of the way.

He heard her lock it.

His woman had just literally slipped through his fingers.

And he'd not only allowed it, he was the one who made her do it.

The driver shot him a look filled with blame he had no idea Dair richly deserved as he walked to the driver's side door.

And Dair stood there, powerless, as the man got behind the wheel, Blake stared steadfastly forward, and they drove away.

CHAPTER TWENTY-ONE

CATHY AND HEATHCLIFF

Blake

Since I was lying in the dark in my bed at The Edinburgh Grand, I saw the light coming out from under my phone where it sat screen down on the nightstand.

In order to further torture myself, like I'd done all the other times this happened, I reached out, took hold of it, turned it to me and stared at the notification that shared Dair was calling.

I did this until it went away.

I continued to stare at my phone until the notification came up that I had a voicemail.

That was voicemail three.

I had six texts from him too.

None of them I'd listened to.

None of them I'd read.

I needed to book train passage down to England.

Or a flight.

I didn't.

I put the phone back to my nightstand, face down, turned my back to it, curled my knees to my chest, held them there with my arms and stared into the dark.

Feeling nothing.

TWO DAYS LATER, I SAT BEHIND THE BARONIAL DESK IN THE STUDY OF Treverton, the one where possibly thirteen Marquesses of Norton sat before me, and I watched Christine bustle in.

I'd texted her I wanted to chat.

She had a smile pinned to her face and worry in her eyes as she came to me.

"You good, love?" she asked.

"Peachy," I lied.

She knew I was lying but sat across from me without saying anything.

"Should I get us some tea?" she offered.

"I need to talk to Alex about this, but I'm thinking about selling the London house," I announced.

"Oh," she mumbled.

"It's my understanding that isn't a part of the Norton estate I can't touch."

"I wouldn't know anything about that, luvvie."

"Dad explained it to me," I shared. "Great-grandfather bought the townhouse with some personal earnings and didn't entail it to the estate."

"Right," Christine replied.

"So I can sell it. Give the money to Alex's charity."

"That'd be nice, but where would you stay when you're in London?"

I held her gaze steady, but my tone was soft when I said, "Once I deal with Mum's personal belongings, I won't be back to England for some time."

"I was afraid of that," she whispered.

"Will you be okay here, on your own, with the help of a maid, seeing to things?" I asked.

"Prefer company, Blake. Yours, to be precise."

That felt lovely.

Even so, I nodded and said, "I'm sorry."

Her face got hard. "I am too, and I've got the urge to hunt down a notable Scotsman and give him a word or two."

"We'd only been together a few weeks, Christine."

"Your eyes are haunted. You've got dark circles under them, so I know you're not sleeping. You aren't eating properly. You keep yourself busy adding your mother's clothes to that rolling rail we bought and texting your sister pictures—"

"It's not necessary for her to fly halfway across the world to look at some clothes and jewels."

"I see you're having a mind to your sister's state, but, if you don't mind me saying, luv, this isn't about your sister being pregnant and having an important job. It's about you hiding in this big house away from whatever happened to you up in Scotland."

It really was not her place to speak to me like that.

I didn't inform her of that fact.

"You need to talk to someone about it," she carried on. "I know I'm not that person to you, but I could be if you're willing to share with me."

"I'm not a nice person and Dair found out I wasn't," I told her.

She looked stunned. "How are you not a nice person?"

Honestly?

It just hit me that I was at my happiest when I was in this house.

I felt at home.

I could ride horses.

I liked taking walks.

I could hide in a million (slight exaggeration) different rooms, doing my own thing without Mum bearing down on me.

I'd behaved here.

So she didn't know the real me.

I wasn't about to enlighten her.

"Just…trust me."

"I—" she started.

I spoke quickly. "Since no one will be around to exercise them, the horses need to be sold. Unless you or Erin ride."

The hardest would be the townhouse. I loved that house. Even before Dair and I made memories in it.

But the horses would be hard too.

Because the estate had always had them.

More, because Dair and I had ridden them.

Not to mention, they were beautiful. Mum had excellent taste in horseflesh.

Then again, from what I could remember, that was a Coddington trait.

"You shouldn't make important decisions when your heart is hurting," Christine advised. Her voice lowered. "You need to trust me on that, luv."

"I need to have all of this done and be away from here."

Christine nodded. "Yes, I reckon you do. But give it some time, some distance, before you do something you can't undo."

This was smart advice.

I was a mess. So numb, it was beginning to frighten me.

I knew I didn't have my head on straight.

I needed to take a breath and give it some time.

Sure, I'd been falling in love with Alasdair Wallace.

No.

The truth: I already knew I was in love with him. I just worried it was too soon, and this was why I almost told him I was when we were at King's Cross, but I didn't.

Boy, was I glad I didn't now.

And okay, he'd said he was doing the same with me.

But I told no lies to Christine moments ago.

This ending shouldn't be that sad, because we'd hardly even begun.

It felt that way.

It felt like everything.

It felt like forever.

It just wasn't.

"Sarah is having the things we boxed up at the London house sent out here so it can all be in one place. Alex has asked me to set all the jewelry aside, and some other things, for her to have a look at when she has the time to come back out. We can put them in storage until she does. She might not want anything, but she's starting a family, and her children might. Or at least they could sell it and put themselves through college with it or something."

"Yes," Christine agreed.

"I'll find an auction house for the stuff we know is going. I'm making some calls this afternoon."

Christine nodded.

"And outside that, I won't make any other decisions until…later."

"I think this is wise, Blake."

"Okay," I said. "Good talk."

She smiled at me and this one wasn't fake.

I smiled back and mine was.

"Is that all?" Christine asked.

"For now, yes. Thanks for coming up here, Christine."

"My pleasure, luv. Are you sure you don't want to come down for a spot of tea? I made a Victoria sponge for your dinner. It's one of your favorites."

She was always so kind to me.

Always.

"We can cut into it a little early," she suggested.

"I'll wait for dinner. But how about you eat with me? Erin too."

I could tell she wasn't entirely comfortable with that.

"We can do it down in the kitchen," I said. "It's cozier there."

She got up and put her hand on the desk. "What I think is that you need to ring your little sister, or someone, and pour your heart out. That's what I think." She pushed away from the desk. "But in the meantime, I'll set up supper in the kitchen for six thirty."

"Thank you, Christine."

She gave me a long, lingering look, pushed out a concerned breath and left the room.

I was not calling Alex, that I knew.

She would be lovely. Supportive. Everything I didn't deserve her to be.

And I didn't need that.

Especially not now, when the memories were so fresh of what an absolute bitch I'd been to her.

Dad was now so overprotective, he might get mad at Dair, when Dair was just protecting himself.

So Dad was out.

I was close with all of the G-Force, particularly a couple of members.

But they'd now met Dair too, and I could tell, they liked him very much, especially for me. They'd probably lean my way, but all of them knew the mean girl I used to be, so they'd get where he was coming from, and I didn't need that either.

There was also Hale, who was always there for me, but ditto on the overprotective thing.

The bottom line was, I didn't have anyone to blame for this but myself.

Maybe someday, I'd find another Chad, and put up with his cheating and neglect, but perhaps I'd be able to raise our children so they didn't turn out to be assholes.

Like me.

Or maybe someday I'd be like Mum. Foot loose and fancy free, fucking young studs and living it up in St. Tropez.

I made a face at that.

Because I'd earned it, I continued my prolonged and sustained torture and reached to my phone.

It was face down on the desk.

I turned it over.

No texts from Dair since I last checked.

I opened the phone.

The voicemails were up to seven, all unheard. I'd lost count of the texts.

I should block him, but he might know somehow, and I thought that would be insulting, and I didn't want to insult him.

I just wanted him to stop wasting energy on me.

I thought about texting him to tell him that.

But I didn't.

There wasn't much more of Mum's stuff to go through, but that was the only thing keeping me here.

I had to get it done so I could get out of there.

And far away from Dair.

Thus, I got up and walked out of the room in order to see about doing that.

THE PHONE CALLS STARTED THE NEXT DAY.

The first was from Alex.

"Hey," I greeted. "You're up super early."

"I'm always up early. So…what's up with you and Dair?"

God, how did she know something was up with me and Dair being all the way in Arizona and never getting on social media (that I knew)?

Not that anything had been reported about us. The last thing that made the rounds was us going at it at King's Cross.

I should save some of those photos.

You know, more torture.

"Blake?" Alex called.

"We broke up."

I could almost feel her shock. "Seriously?"

"We were…we had a big fight. One you can't come back from."

"About what?"

About me.

Me being…*me*.

"I don't want to be a bitch when I say I don't want to talk about it."

There was a massive amount of hesitance in her, "Okay."

"How did you find out anyway?"

"Davi phoned me."

Oh God.

I hadn't even thought about her.

I was losing Davi. And Kenna too.

The weight of that was so heavy, I sunk into the nearest chair and dropped my head.

"Blake, you're worrying me," she said.

"Why?" I asked, trying to sound like everything was okay.

"I don't know. I just…you don't sound good."

There you go.

I failed at sounding like everything was okay.

"I liked him. He was the first guy I liked since Chad," I admitted. "It sucks but it didn't work out. I'm…upset." Ding! Ding! Ding! Understatement of the Year! "I'll eventually get over it." And that was a lie.

Alasdair Wallace was a man you didn't get over.

"I thought you two…"

She didn't finish that.

I thought "us two" too.

"I'll be okay," I lied.

Never.

I'd never been okay.

And losing Dair, who I'd stupidly cast as my redeemer, I never would be.

I was just me.

And that wouldn't change.

So I had no choice.

I had to get on with it.

"Anyway, if you want to talk, you know how to get me," she offered.

"I do, Alex. Thanks. And I'll be coming home soon."

"I think that's probably good. Why don't you come out here? Rix and I are fighting about nursery stuff. He's buying band posters *for a nursery*. I need you on my side."

I almost smiled at that, and fortunately, that sentiment could be heard in my voice when I said, "I'll get out as soon as I can."

"I love Rage Against the Machine, but I don't need their poster over my kid's crib."

I forced out a laugh and it didn't sound entirely fake.

"I love you, Blake," she said.

God, she was always a better person than me.

"I love you too, little sister." I quickly changed subjects. "Everything going okay with Rix and the baby?"

"Outside the nursery issue, Rix and I are great. My morning sickness lasts until the afternoon, which is unfun. I'm keeping my fingers crossed I'll be one of those pregnant women who move out of that when I move into my second trimester."

"I'm keeping my fingers crossed for you. And we'll need to start talking about your shower, which I, of course, will be hosting."

I was pleased to hear the humor was back in her tone when she replied, "Of course."

"If Gal and Katie want in on that action, we can co-host. I'll text them."

"Awesome."

"All right, I'll let you go," I said.

"Okay, honey. I'm so sorry about you and Dair. Take care of yourself and call me if you need me."

"Will do."

"Later."

"Alex?" I stopped her.

"Right here," she said.

I closed my eyes.

I opened them again and said, "I don't know if I ever apologized for being such a bitch to you pretty much our whole lives."

There was a moment of silence before she said, "I thought we got over this that day in Mum's bedroom."

"We did, kind of," I replied. "I just think the words need to be said."

"What brings this up?" she asked suspiciously.

"I just…it's important you know I understand how awful I was to you."

There was another moment of silence before she said, "Fellow captives, remember?"

"I remember but…no excuse."

"Blake, we've been over this, *we were kids*," she said staunchly. "I removed myself from the dysfunction, mentally, and whenever I could, physically. Which meant the brunt of it was focused on you. It should be me who's apologizing."

God, my sister was so awesome.

"Hardly," I replied.

"The point I'm making is, yeah, you were a mean girl. No, it didn't feel good. *But I understand why you were,*" she stressed. "And the minute I reached out a hand with any real intent to fix what was broken with us, you took hold." I could hear the humor in her tone when she finished, "And you did it with some serious panache."

One could say I definitely did that.

"Does this have something to do with what happened with you and Dair?" she queried.

Yes!

"I've just been thinking on things." And that wasn't a lie.

"Well, stop thinking on that. I love you. I love talking to you. I love spending time with you. I love eating your food."

A surprised laugh erupted from me.

"I just love you, Blake," she said. "It may have taken us a while, but I'm going to say this again, and this time I hope it gets through. You're the best big sister a girl could have. I just hope I'm the same in the little sister department."

I was choked up when I replied, "You are. You absolutely are."

"Good."

Enough of this.

I'd done her dirty my whole life (almost), I didn't need to put her in the position of making me feel better about it.

That said, she'd made me feel better about it.

And I guessed that was what sisters did.

They were there for each other and made each other feel better about things.

And only then did I realize, this was how it was done, if you were doing it right.

Another way of doing it right was understanding it wasn't all about you. She had a life and a job to get to, and I was on a mission, so it was time to wrap this up.

"I've got about ten thousand more items of clothing, jewelry, shoes and accessories to go through so I can get home. I better get on it."

"Okay," Alex replied. "Are you good?"

No, I was one thousand percent not.

I didn't lie to her about that.

I said, "I will be."

"Okay, I'll reiterate, I'm just a phone call away."

Totally loved my little sister.

"Thanks, Alex."

"Anytime, Blake. Love you. And later."

"Love you too. Bye."

I went away from that one relatively unscathed.

The next one came the next morning.

Dad.

"You and Alasdair have split up?" he asked without greeting after I answered the phone.

"Dad—"

"What's the matter with him?"

"Nothing. We just…it didn't work out."

"With the way you two seemed, I thought I'd be paying for another wedding. One, like your sister's, I was happy to write checks for. Though, I didn't mind paying for your first, since it ended so splendidly."

God, I loved my dad.

"Yes, well, I don't know what to say. We just, like I said, didn't work."

Dad was silent.

I thought he was contemplating the fact his first-born child was going to die alone, and before she was lowered into her grave behind the family chapel, her boy toy was going to make off with the family heirlooms.

But at the sound of his voice when he asked, "Did he hurt you?" I knew he was instead contemplating the fact he might have to commit a murder.

Did Dair hurt me?

Suggesting I attended a little girl's funeral for the photo op?

Fuck yes.

But frankly?

Dair's question was no less than I deserved.

"There's a lot of history with this. Between him and me. Not to mention Mum and Bally. It was insane to start with. I think we'll both eventually come to terms with that."

And what I said was only a hint of a lie.

"*Eventually?*" Dad asked.

"I can't—"

"Darling. Come home. Catch the first flight tomorrow. I'll buy your ticket."

"I'm almost done here. When I am, I'll be home. A couple more days."

"I don't like this," he groused.

I didn't either.

"I'm okay, Dad. Promise."

I was *such* a liar.

"A couple more days, Blake, then I want you home. With me. Not your mother's place. Here. With me and Marlo."

Was there news?

"You and Marlo?" I snooped.

"She's moving in, not moved in, but moving in," he announced.

Yes, there was news.

And finally, it was good news.

Seemed like Dad was very much done putting the brakes on him and Marlo and now was full steam ahead.

I was all for it.

"That's great," I said.

"I'm glad you think so. But the fact you texted her more after we left London than you did me, I already guessed that. I will add, however, that she's concerned too, since those texts stopped, and we now know why."

"I'll be home. Soon. And you can see for yourself I'm fine."

This meant I had to start eating (bluh). I was losing weight.

And I had to figure out how to start sleeping (yikes!), since I'd probably averaged around three hours a night since it happened.

On the bright side, I was a dab hand with concealer.

"Text with your flight details," Dad ordered. "I'll send a car."

That meant he'd be in the car.

I made a mental note to put the concealer in my carry-on.

"Okay, Dad."

"I love you, Blake. Very much. You understand that, don't you?"

Who knew it was harder to be loved than to be a total waste of space and do all sorts of crap *not* to be loved because you'd learned that the person who was supposed to love you the most—namely, your mother—didn't love all that great. So you did everything in your power to keep everyone who might hurt you far, far away.

And it sucked to say much the same about Dad, but until the Act of Chad, he'd left me to it.

So there was that.

God, I needed therapy.

Inpatient.

For about five years.

"I understand it, Dad. And I love you too."

"I'm proud of you as well. You're a good kid."

Unexpectedly, the tears hit.

"Don't make me cry," I said throatily.

"Crying is good. Feel your emotions, darling. This family doesn't bury them anymore. Now, I love you, I'm proud of you, and I'll let you go."

He suddenly sounded distracted.

"Okay, Daddy. Again, love you too. Bye."

"Goodbye, my darling."

I'd learn why he was distracted when I barely let the tears begin to fall, deciding feeling numb was a whole lot better than feeling *this*, and my phone was ringing again.

This time, Marlo.

I did the time zone calculations in my head, and surmised they were having breakfast or something before they took off for their days.

I sniffed hard to pull myself together and took the call.

I forced my tone to chipper. "Hey, Marlo."

"Your father isn't in hearing distance. I was listening in while you two were talking. I told him I wanted to speak to you so that's why he ended the call so abruptly. And we're still getting used to this together thing so it didn't occur to him he could just hand me his phone."

That was funny, and cute, so I let out a little laugh before I said, "Okay."

"I know we don't know each other very well, but I also know we both have the same equipment, and the same sexual preferences, so I'll share now, until I met your father, I'd been through my fair share of assholes. Including a marriage that was not a barrel of laughs."

That was particularly forthcoming.

"Um…okay."

"In other words, if you need a sounding board, or a shoulder to cry on, or advice from someone who's been there, this is me extending the official invitation."

Oh shit.

With that, there was no way to hold them back.

I burst into tears.

"Oh, honey," Marlo said through them.

Which only made me cry harder.

So much harder, I bent double and shoved my face between my knees.

"Get it out," she cooed.

I shot back in my chair and declared, "I hate my mother."

God.

Why did that feel so good to say?

"Honey," she whispered in my ear.

"Why couldn't Dad meet you thirty-five years ago?"

"Well, beautiful girl, I was only thirteen so that might have been a bit problematic."

I barked out a laugh, the second one in our conversation that was surprisingly genuine.

"Talk to me now," she urged.

"I…can't. It's too fresh. But…" I hesitated, then went for it. "Can we have a girls' date when I get home?"

She did not hesitate.

"Of course. And if I have to chain Ned in the dungeon of this mausoleum to keep him from fawning all over you because he's worried about you, I will."

I was laughing again about her calling Dad's house a mausoleum.

It was beautiful.

But it was sterile.

I hoped she did something about that. Finally made Dad's house a home.

"I mean," she continued, "I don't know if there is a dungeon. But I'll find it if I have to."

"I would…" I cleared my throat. "That would be awesome. Not the dungeon part. Just the girls' time part."

"It's a date. So, are you going to be okay until then?"

No.

"Yes."

"Pretty liar," she murmured. "I'm a phone call away, okay?"

"Okay. And Marlo, lie to Dad and tell him I'm fine. Please? Tell him he doesn't have to worry. Hearts mend, right?"

"They do, my sweet. It takes time, but I promise, they do."

It took Dad decades.

But he did it.

"I'm glad he has you, and I swear that isn't selfish, because I'm glad I have you too," I said.

"That isn't selfish. A woman falls in love with a man who has children, she falls in love with a family. And I knew when you walked into the restaurant wearing that *fabulous* outfit, I'd fallen for you."

Damn.

I was crying again.

Because she was amazing.

Because I was so, so happy Dad had found her.

And because Dair picked that outfit.

"I'm not helping," she remarked.

"Oh, you are," I sniffled.

"Good. Chin up, Blake. You've got this until you get home," she bid. "And then we'll have you."

We'll have you.

She was just *the best*.

"Thank you, Marlo, and I mean that. *Thank you.*"

"My pleasure, honey."

We rang off, and I sat there sniveling and weeping in the pretty morning room that was one of the few totally feminine common rooms in the house, a room I wasn't sure Dair had ever stepped into (which was why I was in it).

I was pulling myself together, my thoughts on finding some tissue, when my phone went again.

I looked down at it.

It was a number not programmed into my phone.

But since I'd contacted three auction houses two days before, and I was expecting callbacks, I took it.

I wiped my eyes, sniffled again, and answered.

"Hello?"

"Blake. Balfour," Bally grunted.

I blinked at the priceless antique carpet in front of me.

"Bally?"

"Davi's been buzzing in my ear," he stated.

Uh-oh.

"Bally, I think—"

"I have apologies to make to you for my behavior with Helena but now is not the time. Now is the time to admit I inadvertently shared some information with my son that it seems took your relationship on a wrong turn."

So Bally was the one who told Dair about the photo.

I'd been wondering about that (or, to be honest about it, almost obsessed by it along with my heartbreak).

"Please take no offense"—or, please *do*—"when I say I'm not talking to you about this."

"Aye, we are, lass, considering my daughter tells me my son is a wreck."

I sat very still.

"You must understand that Signe—" he began.

That pulled me out of my stupor.

"Trust me, I very much understand about Signe," I snapped.

"I was looking out for him when I told him what I told him about you."

"And you did your fatherly duty well," I returned. "You saved him from being tied to another crap individual."

"Sorry?"

Oh no.

He didn't get that.

"What I'm saying is, this is for the best, Bally. For Dair. For all of us. What you did with Mum. Who I am. Dair will come to that realization eventually."

My son is a wreck.

My son is a wreck.

A wreck.

How could a broken heart beat so fast?

"Who you are?" he asked.

"I explained myself to Dair," I retorted. "I'm sorry, but I don't feel I need to explain myself to you. It says a good deal you're trying to look out for him like this, but please, lose my number."

"Blake—"

I hung up on him, and although I didn't block Dair, I had no problem blocking his father.

My son is a wreck.

A wreck.

I looked to my phone and even checked it.

I hadn't had a call or text from Dair since last night.

He was coming to the realization he'd dodged a bullet.

Good for him.

God!

"I'm not going to fucking cry again," I bit out as I pushed up from the chair.

I stomped to my room where I changed from my slippers to my Jimmy Choo, knit, pearly, lace up sneakers.

I then stomped down to the kitchen to tell Christine I was going for a walk.

She lit up. "Breath of fresh air, even in this mist, will do you a world of good, me darlin'."

And yes.

I'd been holed up in the house since I got back to it.

Therefore, I resumed my stomping, this time to the mudroom where I tugged on Mum's Max Mara poncho style raincoat (which was sublime, and totally not going on the auction block).

And I headed outside, through the gardens, to the fields beyond, in my state, not oblivious to the dense fog, but instead, welcoming it.

Cathy and Heathcliff never got together.

And now I understood perfectly why he brooded on those moors.

CHAPTER TWENTY-TWO

WET LEAVES

Blake

Shit.

"Am I fucking lost?" I asked the misty fog that was hiding the huge-ass house I should be able to see from here. Surely.

I was giving myself one hell of a moisture facial out in this weather.

But for goodness sake, I'd turned back at least half an hour ago, and by now I should be seeing the house forming through the fog.

This just cut it.

Lose my shot at love and life and children with a man who unbuckled my shoes and took them off for me, then die of exposure maybe a hundred yards from my ancestral home.

"I hope Rix doesn't mind being daddy to the next Marquess of Norton," I muttered into the mist. "Or Marchioness."

I kept tromping, pretty sure my cute Jimmy Choos were a loss to the mud and wet, also realizing I chose poorly with footwear, considering the cold and wet was oozing through the knit.

And as I walked, I saw a figure forming in the mist coming toward me.

Oh God.

How embarrassing was this?

Christine got worried about me and came out to fetch me.

Some English aristocrat I was. I couldn't even take a walk on my own estate without needing a rescue.

But…

Wait.

That wasn't Christine.

The figure was too tall.

The shoulders too broad.

It was a man.

No, it was *the* man.

I stopped dead.

Holy hell.

It was Dair.

What was he doing there?

Panicked, I stared at him.

He kept prowling toward me.

Even more panicked, I looked left then right.

All I saw was fog, drizzle and the bleary outline of some faraway trees.

Totally panicked, and not thinking, I turned on my Jimmy Choo and started running.

"*Blake!*" Dair bellowed.

I kept running.

In my dash, I tripped over a rock (or something), flew forward while careening, nearly went down, jarred my back with the effort not to (and it hurt like crazy), but I righted myself and kept going.

"Oh my God, how do people *do this*?" I wheezed as the trees started to take shape through the mist.

"Blake!"

That sounded closer.

A lot closer.

I kept running.

I heard him bounding after me.

Trust me to get in a foot chase with a professional athlete.

Someone shoot me.

I hit the woods and zigged and zagged through the trees.

"Bloody hell, stop!" Dair shouted from what sounded like right behind me.

I zigged again.

Then it felt like a cinderblock, or twelve, hit me square in the back, and I went down on my stomach in the wet leaves, a heavy weight landing on top of me, and I did this with an "*Oof!*"

I hadn't even begun to get my breath back when he wrenched me lower under his body, turned me then dumped all his weight on me.

"*Oof!*" again!

"What the fuck are ye doing?" he growled in my face.

"Running," I panted.

"Through thick fog where ye can't see a goddamned thing? Ye nearly broke an ankle back there."

He was still growling.

What he was not doing was panting or even breathing heavily.

Ugh!

He was *the worst*.

"Get off me," I demanded.

"No fucking way. Ye might run again."

I was never running again *in my life*.

"You tackled me," I accused.

"Aye, because you were running from me."

"Take a hint, hotshot, a woman runs from you—"

His big hand covered my mouth, and that pissed me off so badly, I felt my eyes nearly pop out of my head.

"You've said your words, lassie, and now I'm going to say mine."

I glared at him, even knowing I looked like a moron lying in damp leaves, my hair a wet, tangled mess. I hadn't put makeup on that day (which turned into a boon because in this weather, it'd be all over my face). And I was doing this under a mountain of muscle with his hand wrapped over my mouth.

But what else could I do?

"Are ye going to keep quiet so I can talk?" he asked.

"Fuck no," I said behind his hand, which came out as "Fug nah."

He understood it anyway, which was why he said, "Fine. We'll do it like this."

I tried to heave him off.

I didn't so much as budge him.

God!

I kept glaring.

"I'm in love with ye."

I stopped moving entirely.

I even stopped breathing.

"I dinnae give a shite if ye were a bitch to your sister," he carried on. "Or ye were arrested. I want to know the houseboat story, but I dinnae give a shite if ye come off bad in that one too. That isn't the woman I fell in love with." He pressed everything into me, his body and his hand over my mouth. "*This* is."

I remained frozen beneath him.

"And dinnae take that as me giving a shite about any of that at all, lass. It's you. It's what made you. It was the path you took that led you to me. And since it was, I'll take all of it and be glad to have it when it comes to you."

Oh my *God!*

He'd just winded me again (without landing on me).

And he wasn't done.

"Ye are not Helena," he asserted. "You're not one thing like Helena."

Oh God.

I started squirming.

"Stay still," he grunted.

I bucked.

He didn't shift an inch.

God!

I gave up.

He kept at me.

"You were a girl who was lost. You found yourself, Blake. Dinnae lose yourself again because I was piss poor in communicating my shite to you."

I went back to glaring.

"I got in my head. You mentioned we should be freaked at how good it was between us, then Rix told me about Alex, and I got stuck in my head. I did that because it started the same with Signe. Nothing but good."

With that, I began struggling in earnest.

He took his hand from my mouth to grab both my wrists and pull them over my head.

"Get off me, Dair!" I shouted.

He transferred both wrists to one hand, held them easily (he was totally *the worst!*), and put the other over my mouth again.

GAH!

His face came so close, he had to be speaking against his hand. "You are not Signe either. My concerns were relevant. I got burned. I fell in love with a woman who didnae exist. That boiled up and it made me fuck up. I should have explained that to ye better. I should have explained where my head was at. But I treated you like a child. And I said shite to you that should never have come out of my mouth."

"Yes, you did," I said into his hand. But it came out "Hes, hu deh."

His beautiful gray-blue eyes melted, and he whispered, "Baby, I'm so fucking sorry."

Oh no.

That got to me.

I turned my head away and his hand came with it.

So he rested his forehead against my temple and spoke in my ear.

That got to me too.

"I ken who ye were, and I ken how ye changed. When I told Mum what I did to you—"

Shocked he spoke to his mother about us, I righted my head with a snap, which wrenched my back, and damn.

I had a feeling I might have actually hurt myself.

"She tore me a new one, hen," he said quietly after he caught my eyes. "It was only me promising to come down and sort it with ye why she's not down here herself, blackening my name and disowning me."

I just stared at him.

"You two girls were alone. Ned was lost in the fuckup of picking Helena. But Mum told me that you were the focus for Helena. You bore the brunt of it. Maybe she was jealous of ye. Maybe she thought she was doing what she was supposed to. I dinnae fucking know, and I dinnae fucking care. She didnae mark you. She scarred you. And I didnae take that into account when I spoke to you. I didnae take into account ye just lost her and you were trying to understand how you felt about it. I didnae look after my woman, and if I lose ye because of it, I'll regret it 'til my dying day."

Damn.

That got to me too.

Because, how could it not?

He took his hands from my mouth and wrists so he could frame my face with both of them.

"It's miraculous what ye made of yourself, darling," he said tenderly. "You were given no foothold at all, but ye found a way to climb out of the pit she tossed you in anyway. And that's amazing."

"You don't have to do this, Dair," I said shakily. "I'll call Kenna in a few days and tell her it's all good. It's for the best. You need someone who knows how to love. I don't know how to do that."

Now Dair was staring at me.

This went on a while.

So long, I requested, "Um, if I ask nice, will you get off me?"

"No."

I glared again.

"Ye dinnae ken how to love?" he asked.

"Well,"—I flipped out a freed hand—"obviously."

"Obviously?"

"Are you going to repeat everything I say?" I demanded.

"Until you start making sense, aye."

"Dair—"

"Ye took care of everything for your sister's wedding."

"You should know, I had a wedding planner for mine, and I treated her like shit too."

Dair ignored me. "You made Marlo feel welcome in your family, for her, but mostly for your dad because you adore him."

"That wasn't hard. She's—"

"Nora dropped everything to come out and plan your mother's funeral. All your friends dropped everything to be there for you."

"They were there for Alex."

"The G-Force wasn't there for her."

This was true.

Hmm.

Dair wasn't finished lecturing.

"And Alex isn't the new Marchioness of Norton. Alex didnae have important people she had to impress with hymn choices and floral arrangements. Aye, they were there for Alex, and they were there *for you.*"

I decided to stop speaking.

"Ye looked after my mum in Arizona after all that happened with Dad. You were pissed on my behalf when ye thought Dad or Signe upset me." He paused, considered me, then asked, "Am I getting through to you at all?"

"You're crushing me."

In one lithe movement (bloody athletes), he rolled off and to his feet, and he offered me his hand.

I ignored it and tried to get up myself.

My back spasmed, and the pain was so bad, I fell to my ass in the wet leaves, which made the pain worse.

"Babe, take my hand," he ordered.

I tried to get up on my own again and winced.

He instantly crouched down beside me.

"Are ye hurt?"

"Why, yes, Dair," I snapped. "A huge man chased me through a forest and tackled me to the leaves."

He grinned.

Stupid Dair.

"Know my tackle didnae hurt ye, lassie. I ken my tackles."

"Well, on top of jarring my back when I tripped, it—"

I said no more because he frowned, then, before I could blink, I was up in his arms.

Good Lord.

This was worse!

"Put me down!" I shouted, wriggling in his hold as he started walking through the woods.

"Stop moving or you'll hurt yourself more."

"Dair, put me down this instant," I demanded.

"Hot bath. Some ibuprofen. And a stiff whisky will do ye," he decreed.

What he didn't do was put me down.

I went limp in his arms and asked the tree canopy. "Why? Why did you forsake me?"

"Ye need to give up those heels, lassie. They're fucking up your back."

That earned him the glare to end all glares.

"I am *never* giving up my heels. I'll be a hundred and five and toddling around on my heels."

"Then we best stock up on ibuprofen." He paused. "And whisky."

"Or, say, you don't chase me across the English countryside and tackle me to the forest floor," I suggested sarcastically.

His arms gave me a slight squeeze and he muttered, "Aye. That probably didnae help."

"You think?"

"Hear this, love," he said, still walking, "ye can try to run around the world to get away from me. I let you slip through my fingers once. That's not going to happen again. I'll grab hold any way I can." His eyes came down to me. "So dinnae run next time."

"You're the *worst*," I declared.

"Aye," he said softly. "But you love me."

I looked away.

"She loves me," he whispered.

He was *intolerable*.

Not long later, the house started to come into view, and if I had my bearings correct, I'd been all of maybe twenty feet from seeing it.

Ugh.

"You wearing a poncho?" Dair asked like he'd just noticed it.

"It's a Max Mara raincoat with poncho-like detailing," I corrected.

His grin returned. "My Blake in a poncho."

"It *isn't* a *poncho*. It's a Max Mara raincoat with *poncho detailing*," I repeated.

"It's a poncho, love."

Argh!

Treverton fully formed, and with it came the sight of Christine outside, wearing a thin puffer coat and, for some housekeeper reason, wringing a dishtowel.

When she caught sight of us, she rushed forward.

"Oh my goodness, is she hurt?"

There went my English aristocrat street cred.

"She took a tumble," Dair told her.

"That's a nice way of saying, he tackled me," I added.

Christine's eyes grew wide.

Dair chimed in again. "She needs a hot bath, with salts if ye got them, a generous tumbler of whisky and a bottle of ibuprofen," Dair said.

"I'll start with the bath," she said and scurried away.

"Now you've worried Christine," I accused.

"It wasn't me who took off running."

"No, it was you who chased me."

He sighed and we were inside.

The warmth against my chill skin felt prickly.

I did need a hot bath.

Seriously.

Carefully, he crouched while tilting me, and let my legs go, but when I was on my feet, he held me steady with his arm around me.

"I can stand, Dair."

He let me go only to slip the raincoat over my head (which would make one assume it was a poncho, when it *was not*).

Raising my arms hurt my back again.

Even so…

"I can take off my own stupid coat, Dair," I snapped.

Before I could even begin to back away, he picked me up again.

It twinged my back.

Not good.

But again…

Even so.

"Dair, put me down," I demanded.

He stopped in the hall and looked at me.

"Do you love me?"

Oh no.

A direct question.

I looked over his shoulder.

"Blake,"—he gave me a squeeze—"are ye in love with me?"

I turned on him as best I could in my position. "I don't know how, since you're insufferable, but I am."

Oh my God.

Did I just dip down two inches because his shoulders sagged in relief?

I didn't have time to assess if I was correct.

He bent his head and kissed me.

He smelled like leaves and rain and Dair, and tasted like heaven, so I kissed him back.

Who could blame me?

When he broke it, he said, "Ye can share what ye want. Ye can hold what ye like. I ken who my Blake is. I love her, she loves me. From here on, that's all that matters."

Oh God.

I was *not* going to cry.

Regrettably, my eyes did not take direction.

So I shoved my face in Dair's neck and wept all the way to the bathroom.

I WAS LYING ON MY BACK ON A HEATING PAD ON MY BED.

Dair was lying beside me, on his side, up on a forearm, his thumbs moving over his phone screen.

I'd had my bath, my whisky, my pain pills, and yes, Dair had undressed me and set me in the tub himself. He'd then gone to get the other stuff from Christine, along with my book, and made me stay in there for a full hour, coming in occasionally to add more hot water so it would never go cool.

And yes.

The man hadn't even let me reach to the faucets of a bathtub to warm up my own bath.

Therefore, by the time he decided I was done, my back was feeling a whole lot better.

Even though I insisted this was the case, he toweled me down and brought me panties and pajamas, helped me into both, and then he took me to the heating pad.

As in, carried me.

Where I was now.

I heard the whoosh of him sending the text, he twisted, put his phone on the nightstand, and came back to me.

"Talked Mum down from disowning me, though to do it, I had to promise we'd be at her dinner table for Sunday supper."

My brows went up. "Sunday supper?"

"Aye. We'll fly up Saturday night from Dublin."

Um…

"Dublin?"

"I'm calling a match there Saturday. You're coming with me."

My eyes narrowed. "I am?"

"Ye are, lass," he stated blithely. "We'll fly out Friday from Bristol. Fly to Edinburgh Saturday night. Have dinner with Mum and Davi Sunday. And if ye need to be here, we'll load up Sorcha and drive down Monday."

"Have it all planned, do you?" I asked.

"Well…aye," he answered like my question indicated I had a screw loose. "In the meantime, you're resting that back."

"It's just a tweak, Dair. I'm fine," I dismissed it.

In answer, his hand came to my face.

And I lay very still under his touch as he tenderly swept a thumb under my eye, only for his hand to move to my side where he glided his knuckles gently over my ribs.

"My woman's not sleeping," he said softly, and my breath hitched. "Only days since she left me, I can see she's lost weight. She runs from me, I tackle her after she wrenched her back. And I made her run from me. Twice. Not doing such a good job at looking after you, my love."

My love.

Now totally finding it hard to breathe.

"Dair," I whispered.

"What I said earlier, about making a promise to Mum I'd sort this, that wasn't what drove me back to you. I told myself I was giving you time. But I hurt ye and I didnae ken how to fix it. I was going to come to ye as soon as I figured out how to fix it."

He was going to come back to me.

I started to turn to him, and he scowled.

"Stay still," he rumbled.

"Honestly, I feel better," I assured.

"You need to rest it and you'll be resting it," he commanded.

Whatever.

I settled back and started, "Dair—"

He interrupted me.

"Though, feel it necessary to note, I might have had a clue in how to fix it if you'd answered one of my texts or phone calls."

Oh dear.

"I only say that because it needs to be said," he went on. "This shite is not going to happen to us again. I take full responsibility for fucking that up, and I earned your response. I'll never fuck up that huge again, but I can't promise never to fuck up, and you can't either. But if we get into it, I need you not to shut me out so we can work it out."

This was needed advice for us to have a healthy relationship, so I nodded.

He again didn't hide his relief from me.

God, I knew honesty and candor was hard on some occasions, but even if it was, it worked a whole lot better than the other way around.

"When we were on the train, and you asked me if you needed to make it official, ye didnae mean spending more time in the UK. You meant being with me."

How he'd misinterpreted that at the time hurt in a way I didn't want to remember it, because I'd already sensed he was pulling away, but since he brought it up, I couldn't stop myself from sucking in both my lips.

Not that he would, considering he was only maybe twelve inches away, but Dair didn't miss it.

"Christ, I fucked this," he muttered.

"We're working it out," I reminded him.

"Aye, but just to say, we're flying to Dublin, then to Edinburgh, and then collecting my dog and coming back here if ye need to be here. Because I dinnae mistake ye now, lassie. And we're making it official."

"I think, before I agree, I should know precisely what that means," I said carefully.

"What you meant it to mean at the time. We're doing this. I'm with you, you're with me. Always."

Oh boy.

"Do you think we're going too fast?"

"Did you drive away from me with tears in your eyes and hurt I put in your heart and spend five days not sleeping or eating?"

I did.

"I ate." That wasn't a lie. I just didn't eat very much.

"Babe," he growled.

"No one saw me," I blurted.

His head ticked. "Sorry?"

"No one saw me. That's why I sold the pictures. All my life, I felt like I'd gone unseen."

"Baby." Now he was whispering.

I sucked it up and carried on.

"After I narrowly missed living a wretched life with a man like Chad, the man my mother wanted for me, I took a long, hard look at myself. How I behaved. How I treated people. What I'd done. Who I was becoming. And I realized that was why I did it. I didn't care if the attention was negative. I just wanted people to see me."

"Ye dinnae have to explain this to me."

"I know. But sharing it with you is like explaining it to myself. And I do need to do that."

He nodded, and his hand was still at my ribs, so his thumb started stroking.

And at his nod, his touch, it struck me, he was listening.

Really listening.

And he saw me.

Before our blip last weekend, he was the first one in my life who really *saw me*.

And that strike was like a bolt of lightning, because I felt safe here with Dair, telling him these things, unlike how I felt my whole life, including when he laid me out in his living room.

But I was safe now.

With him.

And now that we were beyond that blip, with all he said while I was lying on those wet leaves, I knew I'd always be safe.

With Dair.

So I kept going.

"That's why I acted out too. But it was more. It was a way to hold people back. If I was a bitch, if I was difficult, if I wasn't so much fun to be around, I could insulate myself."

"Insulate yourself from what, darling?" he asked.

"From love," I answered. "Because what I knew of it, love hurt a lot, and what I didn't realize, but how I was acting, was that I didn't want any part of it."

He closed his eyes, dropping into me, growling unintelligibly, and his forehead came to rest on mine.

Good Lord, this man, this glorious, *glorious* man really, *really* loved me.

"And then came you," I told him.

That caused him to groan and shift his head so he was kissing me.

It was unlike any kiss Dair had ever given me.

It was wet and it was deep, but it was also soft and sweet.

When he ended it, his hand came to my neck and his thumb stroked my throat.

Oh yes.

We'd had our blip.

And now I was totally safe with this man.

"Can we put the last few days behind us, learn from it, and move on from here?" I requested.

"Aye, lass, with an emphasis on learning from it, that learning being me looking after you a whole lot better."

I wasn't liking his commitment to punishing himself about this.

"Dair, you have to let it go. It happened. Did you handle it well? Maybe not. Was it going to happen one way or another as we got to know each other? Probably. So we did it. It hurt. It didn't go great. It's done. I'm going to Dublin with you and then having dinner with your mum, and if you'll let me move, I can have everything sorted here so we can stay up in Edinburgh for a while."

"If you're in that place, I'm there with you, Blake."

I patted his cheek.

He grinned at me.

That damned grin.

I worshipped it.

But now…onward.

"Tell me about your lunch with your father."

His grin died, I hated seeing it go, but we had to talk about this, he knew that, so he sighed.

Then he shared the news that his father and my mother were an item before Bally met Kenna. That my grandfather had forbidden the match (that was *so* Grandfather, I had no memories of that man being anything but a colossal, privileged dick). And it all went on from there.

But…seriously.

Mum totally was their Camilla.

Dair also shared what Signe was up to and that she was breaking her NDA.

"Dad said he was going to fly to Denmark to threaten her personally, but I've been preoccupied since then with something important, so I haven't followed up on that yet," he concluded.

Something important.

Nice.

But busy Scottish industrial magnate, Balfour Wallace, dropping everything to fly to Denmark to protect his son?

Hmm.

"Have you looked at her TikTok?" I asked.

"Not keen to see what she might put up there," he answered.

I'd left my phone in the raincoat so I ordered, "Get your phone."

Another sigh from Dair before he turned to reach a long arm out to get his phone, then he came back to me. He engaged it, did some touching of his screen, studied it for a while and handed it to me.

"She's not stopping," he said and tapped the screen for the TikTok to play.

Lewis Capaldi was singing "Someone You Love" over a collage of videos and photos of a younger Dair and the very pretty, sexy, girl-next-door-wearing-way-too-much-makeup-à-la-Pamela-Anderson-from-back-in-the-day Signe.

Them laughing in each other's faces with their arms around each other on some beach, her in a bikini, Dair in board shorts, sand on their bodies and wind in their hair. Signe filming Dair as he walked beside her, giving her *my* grin. Dair, dirty and sweaty and hugging her wearing his rugby kit after a match.

A selfie of them with their heads together on a pillow in bed.

I gasped.

"How dare she!" I snapped. "She picked a fabulous Scottish singer. She doesn't get to use a fabulous Scottish singer to serenade her unhinged fantasies."

"Blake—"

I sat up.

My back protested just a little bit, but it was so much better.

I totally ignored it and went to his contacts.

Dair pushed up too.

"Lie back down," he ordered.

"No," I retorted, found the number I needed, and hit go.

"Who are ye calling?" Dair asked.

"Dair?" Bally answered.

"Bally. It's not Dair. It's me," I replied. Dair grunted in surprise, but I sallied forth. "Do you have people who can leak things to the press?"

"Blake," Dair clipped.

"Is my son with ye?" Bally asked.

"Yes, we worked things out. This is why I'm calling on his phone," I pointed out like he was a dim bulb. "Now I have a plan to deal with Signe. You haven't flown to Denmark to threaten her yet, I take it."

"Not yet."

"Good. I'm going to contact Davi and Kenna, and I'll do some ferreting around here at Treverton. We'll get you some pictures of when we were all kids. Particularly Dair and me. Your people need to disseminate them widely. We'll just see who was meant to be after the world gets a load of the fact Dair and I have essentially been leading up to being together since we were *fucking born*."

"Baby," Dair said quietly, but his tone was heavy with wonder and pride, so I looked to him.

"I guess being a media whore in my younger days has served a purpose," I said to him.

My grin returned to his face.

Man, he *so* loved me.

God, it made me feel positively *squishy*.

"Are you okay with releasing those kinds of pictures?" I asked him belatedly.

"Absolutely," he replied.

"This is the perfect strategy," Bally said in my ear. "Beat her at her own game. Get me the photos, and I'll handle it."

"It might be tomorrow. I can barely move after Dair tackled me," I lied.

"For fuck's sake," Dair pushed out.

"He tackled ye?" Bally asked, but I no longer had the phone.

Dair slipped it from my hand and put it to his ear.

"She wrenched it running, Dad. Long story. But you can see to this?" He paused. "Good. Appreciated." Another pause and then a, "Aye, Dad. Thanks."

With that, he hung up.

"Another learning moment, you control the narrative," I educated him.

"We were meant to be together since we were born?" he asked.

"I believe I said 'leading up to,' but that works as well. Though, I should mention I had a huge crush on you when I was a kid."

His brows shot up. "You did?"

I nodded.

"How much better is your back?" he asked.

Mm.

I knew that look in his eye.

I loved that look in his eye.

"Could ye handle me going down on you?" he pressed when I didn't respond.

I could handle him going down on me if I was dangling from a building by my fingernails.

"I think I could struggle through it."

He kissed me.

Then he went down on me.

He refused my offer to reciprocate and instead went to find Christine to tell her we were eating dinner in bed.

And that was what we did, watching telly and cuddling.

I fell asleep during *Mad Max: Fury Road* (one could say that movie was not for me, though Tom Hardy wasn't hard on the eyes).

And when I slept, tucked close in Dair's arms, I slept like a baby.

CHAPTER TWENTY-THREE

DOOR NUMBER TWO

Blake

A knock on the door (kind of) woke me.

Dair slipping away from my body made me open my eyes.

Still bleary and half-asleep, I watched him walk in his pajama pants to the door (he usually slept nude, but he put them on so we could be comfy watching telly and his junk wasn't right there, taunting me because he wouldn't let me have it).

He opened the door, and I saw Christine was outside.

"I'm sorry to disturb," she said. "But Hale Wheeler is here."

I blinked and pushed up to a hand.

"Hale?" I asked.

"Aye," Dair said to Christine like he was expecting this visit from Hale. "I'll talk to him."

Christine nodded to Dair, cast a glance at me still in bed, her face got all happy, and she bopped away.

Dair went to his duffel, pawed through it and came out with a T-shirt.

"Did you know Hale was coming?" I asked.

"How's your back?" he asked in return through the shirt he was pulling on.

I did a bitty twist to check it, and no pain.

"All good," I told him.

"Stay resting anyway," he ordered. "It can seem better, and then ye stress it, and you're back to where ye started or worse."

He said this while walking to the door.

"Dair," I called. "Dair!" I said sharply when he didn't stop.

He turned at the door.

"This is being loved the right way, lassie," he said mysteriously, then he was out the door.

Therefore, I was out of bed.

Okay.

Ow.

I froze, but it was just a little twinge, and then it was gone. Really not bad, but he was right. I should take it easy.

But I could still walk, and I did so to walk out of the room, down the hall and the stairs. I just did it slowly.

I made a guess, and headed in that direction, and I knew my guess was correct when I heard men's voices coming from the lounge.

"I'll be seeing her," Hale was saying.

"Aye. I'll let her know you're coming up and then ye can go up," Dair replied as I hit the room. "But she hurt her back so she'll be resting."

They were standing in the center of the room, and I could almost see Hale, but most of what I saw was Dair's back.

"And I'll be speaking to her alone so I can ascertain her state," Hale declared in a hard voice.

"My state?" I asked.

Dair turned and both men's attention came to me.

I smiled and moved forward. "Hey, Hale."

I made it to him and gave him a hug, but when we broke, I moved to Dair who slid his arm around my shoulders as I did the same around his waist.

Hale watched all of this with rapt attention and a weird hint of animosity.

"Are you good?" he asked me.

"Fabulous," I replied. "More so with this surprise visit. What are you doing here?"

He stared at me, then looked to Dair, and back to me, he said, "I was attending some meetings in Cardiff."

"You should have said. It's just over the bridge. I could have come to you."

Hale again stared at me, then Dair, then again to me. "I think I missed something."

"What?" I asked.

Dair gave me a squeeze so I looked up at him. "What *you* are missing is that the richest man in the world got wind I'd hurt ye, so he dropped everything and hauled arse here to see to you."

"I…"

Oh my God.

Seriously?

I turned to Hale. "Is that what's happening?"

"More that Alex, who was worried about some conversation you two had, shared that with Chloe. Chloe called me and told me to get my ass over here to look in on you since I was the closest of us all," Hale replied. "But even if Chloe wasn't being her usual bossy, once I heard you two had split, I'd have come anyway."

It felt like my heart had grown so big, my chest would explode.

And bizarrely, that wasn't a bad feeling.

"So, aye, lass," Dair piped up. "Tell me again how ye dinnae ken how to love."

"Excuse me?" Hale asked.

God, Dair was *impossible*.

I waved my hand in front of me. "Nothing. Just some stuff I'm sorting through."

"Helena did a number on her," Dair piped up again, this time to Hale. "Blake didnae think she knew how to love. She thought you all were here for the funeral for Alex."

Hale looked incredulous and a little hurt.

"Even me?" he asked.

His reaction made me pull from Dair's arm before I smacked it.

"You don't have to be all honest all the time," I complained.

"I'm trying to prove a point," he retorted.

"Well…*duh*," I shot back.

Dair burst out laughing.

I screwed my face up in a poisonous look aimed at him which only made him laugh harder.

I gave up on Dair and turned to Hale.

"Not you. I knew you were here for me," I assured.

The animosity fled, and Hale's lips twitched. "I take it you two made up."

Two could play the honesty game.

"He tackled me in the woods and hurt my back."

"Aye, I did," Dair copped to it right away, and if my ears weren't deceiving me, he did it proudly. "She was running through thick fog. She'd already tripped once and wrenched her back. Any second, she was going to run into a tree."

"I was hardly going to run into a tree," I disputed.

"Did ye have that first clue where you were heading?" he asked.

"Away from you," I answered.

"And undoubtedly eventually into a tree. Or a heart attack. Ye were breathing so hard when I tackled you, ye were wheezing."

I was one thousand percent wheezing.

I settled into silence and a glare.

"Well," Hale broke into our bickering, "since everything seems all right, and I'm here, you want to go out and get some lunch?"

Lunch?

"What time is it?" I asked.

"Ten thirty," both men answered me.

Ten thirty!

I hadn't slept that late in years.

"It'll take her an hour and a half to get ready," Dair told Hale.

"That's why I suggested lunch and not brunch," Hale told Dair.

"If ye can hang for fifteen, I can take a quick shower and we can catch up while Blake does her hair and picks an outfit," Dair said.

"Works for me," Hale replied.

"I *am* standing right here, you know," I pointed out.

"Go on up." Dair jerked his chin upward. "Start the onerous selection process for your outfit. But go slow and take it easy. I'll bring some ibuprofen and coffee up."

"It was just a twinge this morning," I informed him.

"You're getting ready to go to lunch. Then going to lunch. And coming right back to the heating pad," Dair bossed me.

"I—"

"As entertaining as this is," Hale cut in and looked at me, "it does take you an age to get ready. And that's no judge. Elsa's the same way. The results are always worth it. From both of you. But if you don't get started, we won't have lunch until three thirty."

Suddenly, I realized I was starved.

"I'll go on up," I said and headed that way.

"Lass," Dair called.

I turned to him.

He pointed a long finger to his gorgeous lips.

I released a harassed breath and stomped to him, got up on my toes, and kissed those gorgeous lips that were now smiling.

I then headed back out saying, "I won't be long."

"Right," both men replied in dual tones of disbelieving.

Whatever.

I walked up the stairs trying to decide on what sweater I'd wear.

But forcing its way into that decision-making process, the knowledge hit me that Hale was, indeed, the richest man in the world.

And maybe the busiest.

And he was here.

Because he heard I was hurting.

And because he loved me.

He also heard that from Chloe, who heard stuff from Alex, and they were both worried about me.

Because they loved me.

I had two choices on how to react to this tardily dawning apprehension.

Bawl my eyes out.

Or smile and get on with it.

I chose door number two.

And not incidentally, a few minutes later, I chose the perfect sweater.

In the end, it took me two hours to get ready, because, in order to stop everyone I loved who loved me in return from worrying about me, I did a group text to tell them Dair and I made up.

This meant doing hair and makeup while fielding a variety of calls.

But considering my excuse, neither man I loved (who loved me in return) minded.

———————

"AYE, LASS," DAIR ENCOURAGED GRUFFLY.

He was on his knees, his head bent, his hands to the headboard, his legs spread, and at his command, I was reaching through his glorious thighs and stroking his cock.

Yes, at his command.

Like I was his good girl.

Though, I totally was.

I mean, just the command put me there, but how he was right now? *Yum.*

"Fuck, that little twist ye do," he grunted, beginning to pump into my hand.

I'd done the twist while stroking his cock by accident close to our beginning, but I added it to the festivities when I heard the noise he made when I did it.

I was thoroughly enjoying this, so much that…

Dang it.

I needed him to fuck me.

"Dair," I breathed.

He heard it, I knew it, when I lost hold because he turned, tossed me onto my belly, kneed my legs apart, settled between them, and slammed inside me.

My head flew back, that felt so damned good.

"Honey," I panted as he thrust into me, fucking me into the bed.

His arm snaked under me, and he drove his thick dick home before he got up to his knees, taking me with him, and kept hold of me with an arm around my hips as his finger on his other hand went to my clit. He started working me there too as he resumed driving inside.

"Oh God," I moaned, powerless to do anything but feel all the good he was giving me and fist my hands in the sheets, this being one part of many why this was so good. "Dair!" I cried out as my orgasm scoured through me.

His thrusts went faster and harder as I climaxed around his cock, whimpering into the bedclothes and trembling in his hold.

And even as I drifted down, my body jerking as I kept taking his cock, I got off on it. The sound of his grunts. Our flesh slapping together. His dick filling me, stretching me.

He went even faster before he slowed, groaned, and through his glides, he came inside me.

I got off on that too.

It was Friday.

We were in Dublin.

He had a match to call tomorrow.

And suffice it to say, considering Dair made me take frequent breaks with the heating pad, my back was all better.

He pulled me off him, rolled me to my back, and, starting just above the hair between my legs, he licked, sucked, nipped and kissed a line up my body, my throat, over my chin to my mouth where he kissed me deeply.

I so fucking loved this man.

And I was so fucking his good girl.

When he broke our kiss, he brushed our noses, then used his to slide along my jaw, before he asked in my ear, "Ye all right?"

"Do you mean my back?"

He lifted his head.

Before he could answer, I said, "Because you can't mean me after you got me off while holding me up from the bed with only one arm and fucking me stupid. Because I'm totally okay with that."

He smiled, there was only a little smugness, mostly it was just happy, and that made *me* happy, then he said, "Aye. I mean your back."

"Hunky dory," I told him.

"My Blake, wearing ponchos and saying shite like hunky dory."

I pulled a face.

He smiled again.

I pulled a bigger face.

He started chuckling.

Ugh.

"Get off me, you big lug," I demanded. "I need to go clean up."

He didn't get off me.

He kissed me again.

Only after he'd done a thorough job of that did he roll off and order, "Go clean up. If your back is okay, it's time for round two."

Really?

Nice.

With that promise, I didn't waste time getting out of bed and going to the bathroom to clean up.

And then I didn't waste time heading back for round two.

"We're hashtag Blair."

"What?" I asked, turning from the magazine I was reading on the plane from Dublin to Edinburgh to see Dair holding his phone my way.

"They gave us one of those mashup names. We're hashtag team Blair."

I took his phone from him and saw he was on TikTok.

It was silent, but on the screen was a talking head, and behind her was a picture of me on a horse, Dair standing next to it, holding the bridle.

I didn't remember for certain, but I thought I was eight in that picture, which meant he was eleven.

We were at Treverton.

And we were smiling at the camera, probably because Kenna took that picture. And when we'd gone over the photos we were okay to release, I'd given Dair all kinds of shit at the proof he knew full well I liked horses, so he was just being a bratty boy when he was giving me shit about their Clydesdales.

But on his phone, this picture segued to a snap of us outside a café on one of the few sunny days we'd had lately. That café was in Clevedon, by the beach, and Hale was with us. We were all laughing, but Dair and I were sitting close. Making us closer, I was leaning into him, and he was taking my weight.

It was snapped by someone during our lunch.

And in the caption #TeamBlair could be seen.

I positioned myself in the seat so that Dair could see the phone. I then touched the hashtag which brought us to a grid of a number of videos, some of which you could see the childhood pictures that had been released, others were pictures of us at Edinburgh Airport, King's Cross station, the lunch with Hale, in cars going to and from Treverton, me, Alex and Marlo sitting at the rugby match Dair was calling and Mum's funeral. The most recent video on the grid being a picture of us touching lips before I'd folded into the car at the stadium not but hours ago. Dair was holding the back door of the car open for me.

Boy, Bally didn't mess around.

"Go to Signe's page," Dair ordered.

I went to search, typed her name in, and tapped one of the videos that clearly had Dair in it.

"Comments, lassie," Dair directed.

I hit the dialogue bubble at the side and the comments came up.

The first one said, *OMG. It's been years. Let it go.*

That one had thousands of likes and seventy-four replies. I tapped the reply line, and the first one under it said, *Right? Just…GROSS!*

The one after that, *Blake is so many levels up from her, Signe can't even see her. She knows it and it's driving her crazy. But I'm happy for them. #teamblairforever!*

A tiny giggle escaped me.

I closed that thread, and the next comment down on the video said, *This is getting sad. Let the man be happy, FFS.*

And the next, *Get over it. The ship has sailed for Wallace to be your meal ticket.*

Harsh.

But true.

The next one, *Should this be reported? It's getting into the zone of stalking. At least it feels that way.*

The next, *Can you spell pathetic? It starts with an S and ends with an i-g-n-e.*

Again, harsh.

But, by my estimation, true.

There wasn't anything better after that. In fact, for Signe, they just got worse. Even in two scrolls, there wasn't a single positive comment.

Dair closed the screen and took the phone from me.

"Think she'll give up on the whole star-crossed lover shite after that," he said.

Oh, she was one thousand percent going to give it up. No woman could take that much abuse, even if she was addicted to attention.

Trust me, I knew.

I settled happily in my seat and was about to return to my magazine when Dair spoke.

"Life is fucking weird," he said. "But it can't be denied, it gives us the skills we need to survive."

No, indeed.

That couldn't be denied.

And I absolutely adored that he twisted the way I struggled through those years in order to put a positive spin on it.

Regardless, even with that spin, what he said was true, and that was best of all.

I smiled at him.

He kissed my smile.

Then he put his ear buds in and went to some sports thing on his phone.

I pulled my iPad out of my tote and handed it to him so he'd have a bigger screen.

"Thanks, love," he murmured and sorted himself out.

I went back to my magazine.

CHAPTER TWENTY-FOUR

FRIENDLY FAMILY

Blake

Dair opened the door to his family home that was situated in the countryside about an hour north of Edinburgh, and Sorcha nearly bowled us over as she dashed inside.

I'd always thought their house was a mite bit strange.

It looked like a castle, and that part was pretty, but it had an attached garage, and that looked weird.

That said, I thought the interior was anything but strange, probably because that was all Kenna. It was an attractive, inviting mix of sturdy, warm, leather, plaid, soft toss pillows, comfy throw blankets, multiple seating options, books, crossed swords, antlers, dog statues, great lighting, wide hearths, timbered ceilings and SCOTLAND!

I'd always felt at home there too. Like I didn't have to take off my shoes. Like I could curl up and read a while.

Like I was welcome.

Like I was safe.

Wow.

Our whole lives *were* totally leading up to Dair and I being together.

Dair had shut the door and was taking my jacket when we heard Davi coo, "Who's my wee bonny lass? You're my wee bonny lass."

Evidently, Sorcha found Auntie Davi.

I waited until he'd shrugged his own coat off and tossed it on the coat stand then took my hand and guided me into their sitting room.

We barely got over the threshold when Davi called, "Warning, bruv, Dad's coming to dinner."

"Davina!" Kenna snapped, bustling in with a dishtowel slung over her shoulder

"He needs as much opportunity to prepare as he can get," Davi defended herself.

Kenna made it to us.

"Son," she said to Dair and accepted his kiss on her cheek while patting his face. She then turned to me and offered both hands. "Our bonny Blake."

"Hey, Kenna," I said, taking her hands, and we held on while we touched cheek to cheek to cheek.

She didn't let me go when that was over.

She said, "I'm so glad you two could work things out."

"Aye. And I'm so glad to learn the great Alasdair Wallace can be a tosser," Davi put in. "It came in the nick of time. I was getting an inferiority complex."

Kenna let me go and whirled on her daughter. "Do I need to uninvite ye?"

"Relax, Mum," Dair drawled. "She's messing with ye. Davi hasn't had an inferior thought in her life."

Davi fake preened. "This is true. 'Tis the result of being born rich, gorgeous, smart as hell and funnier than Billy Connolly."

"I see you've learned how to control your ego," Kenna remarked.

"Oh, I forgot that on the list of things that are awesome about me," Davi replied. "I'm humble."

I burst out laughing.

When I was finished, I didn't feel like laughing, more like skipping, after I caught the expression on Dair's face as he'd watched me do it.

"Get your woman and yourself a drink," Kenna ordered Dair. "And get your sister to shut her mouth. Ye just won her back, we dinnae need Blake taking a runner again."

With that, she swept off toward the kitchen.

"Do you need help?" I called.

"I've got it!" she called back.

"Dad's coming?" Dair asked Davi.

"Apparently, they had a very civilized dinner at The Dome after Dad told her Blake's plan to stop Signe from further embarrassing herself, and Mum realized Dad was stepping up for ye," Davi replied. "They've hashed everything out. They're getting a divorce. But we're all still going to be one big friendly family.”

I watched with concern as Dair's head slowly turned toward where his mother disappeared.

Distracted, he looked down at me. “Wine or a cocktail, darling?”

“Whatever's easiest,” I said.

He nodded, glanced at his sister's glass because he was a gentleman, and gentlemen ascertained the need for drink refills before they left a room, then he followed his mother.

I moved and sat in the armchair next to Davi's.

“Are you okay with this friendly family stuff?” I asked.

“Not even a little,” she told me. “I think Dad should squirm for as many years as he made Mum put up with his cheating.” She shrugged. “But it can't be denied he went all out to help Dair deal with Signe. So I guess he's still a dad.”

He did go all out.

And he'd always be a dad.

Last, the thing with Signe was good and over.

I'd had a peek, and when I saw she'd taken all the videos down on all her platforms that had anything to do with Dair, I'd shown him we'd won.

This victory was sweet.

I let my questions about Bally coming to dinner go, and Davi and I made small talk for a few minutes before Dair came back.

After handing me a glass of white wine, with his Scotch, he sat on the sofa cattycorner to Davi and my armchairs, both that faced the lit hearth.

The two sofas that flanked the fireplace were smaller than couches, bigger than loveseats, and presently, Dair was glancing at the space beside him, that glance came to me, then he pointed a finger at the space beside him.

With a long-suffering sigh, I got up and sat next to Dair.

He draped an arm around my shoulders and tucked me to his side.

Okay, so it was worth putting up with his bossy.

“Bloody hell, he's such *a man*,” Davi grumbled, but her eyes were bright and happy as she watched us.

“Mum says she told Dad to be here half an hour after we got here so we can adjust to the fact he's going to be here,” Dair announced.

“Are you okay with that?” I asked him.

After Hale left, and I'd unearthed some pictures of us when we were kids someone (not Mum, for certain) had put in a scrapbook, and arranged for them to be overnighted to his dad, while I was on enforced rest on a heating pad, he'd told me his thoughts had grown even more confused about how he felt regarding his father.

I could see why it would be difficult to wrap your head around loving a man who was as protective and supportive of you as ever, the same man who had done what Bally had done.

"This is who we are now, I reckon," Dair answered me.

I wasn't fond of his answer.

Kenna came in carrying her own wineglass, the dishtowel was gone, and she arranged herself elegantly in the sofa across the plaid upholstered coffee table from us (yes, it was an upholstered coffee table with a bench area around the coffee table part, it was huge, and it was fantastic).

"Everyone have what they need?" she inquired.

"Outside of an explanation of why we have to put up with that man, sure," Davi replied.

Kenna sent her daughter a soft look and said, "Love, if ye feel I'm forcing this too soon, then I'll meet your father at the door and tell him we'll have to do this some other time."

She took a sip of her wine and then addressed the whole room.

"But ye must know, I've come to terms with the fact I've been mourning my marriage perhaps since it began. What was upsetting me was that I allowed it to go on as long as I did. I should have ended us long ago. When I was younger."

Davi shifted agitatedly in her chair, and I sensed this was because, if Kenna had done that, their family would not have had what it had all this time. A father and mother who did indeed love each other—it was just messed up by my mother being, well…Helena, along with Bally's flaws—that mother and father loving their children.

I couldn't imagine all Davi was feeling. Guilt, for being happy her mum didn't do that so they could have their family. This mingled with regret for the time Kenna lost. And obviously anger, for her dad fucking all of it up.

"It took time to realize I *didnae* regret it," Kenna went on. "I loved your father. He loved me. We made happy memories. We shared the pleasure of raising you two and watching ye grow into smart, capable, responsible, talented, lovely people."

She took another sip before she carried on.

"I'm actually excited to start a new phase of my life. Your father has agreed to give me the house and my solicitors say the settlement he's offered will see me very comfortably. Though, I've secured a part-time job doing some fundraising for the local SPCA. I start tomorrow."

Wow, Kenna had been busy.

And by the by, the SPCA was the Society for the Prevention of Cruelty to Animals, one of the charities I was considering patronizing.

"It goes without saying," she continued, "ye need to have whatever feelings you have. Those are yours and not mine to dictate. So if this is too soon, when he arrives, I'll ask him to go away. But the shock of it is over. The decisions made. And I'm looking forward to my future. Though, I will say, I hope that future includes this family adjusting to become something loving and functional again, if different."

"And how is Dad with your decisions?" Dair asked.

Kenna looked to the fire, her expression a warring mixture of sadness, triumph and contentment, and I understood that.

It was over, and she was smart enough to allow herself to feel sad about it.

But she was now calling the shots, and it was Bally who had to put up with her decisions, that was no small victory, and it was one that was well-deserved.

Last, she'd worked through it and was in a better place, and that brought peace.

"He wishes to attempt a reconciliation." She turned back to her children. "That will not be happening."

"So he's all right with this friendly family thing?" Davi asked.

"He says he'll take ye both, and me, remaining in his life after what he's done any way he can have us," Kenna shared.

I really didn't want to like Bally.

But he was behaving in a manner it was hard to hold onto that.

Perhaps feeling his discomfiture, Sorcha moved from resting her head on Davi's leg for pets, to her daddy, where she rested on his leg for pets.

Dair didn't scrimp in giving them.

The doorbell rang.

And the room descended into a profound quiet that confused me at first, before it hit me.

That was Bally, and he had to ring the doorbell to their home, and that was strange, weird, wrong, right, and sad all at once.

I looked to Dair to see his jaw bulge.

So I put my mouth to his ear and whispered, "You're unbearable.'

He started and turned to me.

"Love ye too, lass," he said softly.

My smile was just as soft before I looked to the room and started to get up, saying, "I'll get the door."

"No," Dair said, setting his drink aside. "I'll get it."

He pushed up.

Sorcha shifted to me.

Davi brooded at the fire.

Kenna calmly sipped her wine.

Dair and Bally came in.

I got up. Kenna got up.

Davi remained seated, brooding at the fire.

Kenna and Bally touched cheeks, and I wanted to give a cheer at how Kenna did it. She was entirely comfortable. It was only awkward on Bally's part.

His attention came to me, and I set my glass down and approached.

"Hey, Bally," I greeted.

I tipped my head for him, and he seemed startled before he touched his cheek to mine.

I pulled away and Dair claimed me.

"Our Blake," Balfour murmured, his gaze shifting between Dair and me. "So glad you two worked things out. You're a bonny couple."

"Thanks," I mumbled.

"Drink?" Dair asked.

Bally glanced at Kenna.

She did a barely-there lift of her chin.

"I can get it," Bally said.

Davi grunted unhappily, still ruminating toward the fire, but now she'd lifted her feet to rest them on the upholstered coffee table.

Bally shot a devastated glance at his daughter and left the room.

No one said anything as we returned to our seats, but Kenna switched hers so she was sitting next to Davi, and Bally would not be doing so.

Bally returned with his drink, sat on the sofa, and as it seemed was the way with the Wallaces, he didn't fuck around.

"Davina, my darling, if ye and I could go somewhere to—"

"Save it, Dad," Davi sniped to the fire. "I'm all in to do this friendly family thing, but you're going to have to give me more time to be"—she slowly turned her head his way—"insanely pissed off at you."

"I can give ye that time," Bally said quickly.

"Good," she spat.

Bally looked to Dair. "Son?"

"You made me a promise in your office and you're keeping it," Dair proclaimed. "Mum has the house, as she should. You're providing for her financially, as ye should. You assisted with the Signe problem, and I appreciate it. You shared honestly what prompted this mess with Helena, and I appreciate that too."

Davi made an unintelligible grumble, and just a quick note that, since our reunion, Dair had shared that he'd told Davi everything.

"But I still hold anger," Dair continued. "That said, I want this friendly family thing too. For Mum, for Davi and me, and so Blake doesn't have to put up with our shite. She's had enough family shite for two lifetimes."

Aw.

He was so sweet!

Dair reclaimed his glass, sucked back some Scotch, and finished.

"So, we're giving this a go, and I'll do my bit to make it successful."

Bally's shoulders slumped in relief.

"Ugh, I'm going to have to get over it," Davi announced. "I can't have Dair being more adjusted than me."

There was laughter, and even Bally risked a small smile.

Dair relaxed back into the sofa, tucking me to his side again. "What's for dinner, Mum?"

"Fish pie," Kenna said.

"Of course, your favorite." Davi aimed this remark to Dair.

"Starting with Cullen skink with crusty bread." Kenna aimed this at Davi.

"Your favorite," Dair drawled toward Davi.

"I hope ye dinnae mind doubling up on the seafood, Blake," Kenna said to me. "I was in a fish mood."

She was in the mood to spoil her children.

So obviously, I replied, "I don't mind. I love fish."

Dair gave me a squeeze.

And then he broke the ice.

"Did ye see Signe has taken down all the videos about me?" he asked his dad.

Bally sat back in the sofa. "Didnae see, but I was told she was getting hit with some backlash."

"Aye," Dair confirmed. "Though 'some' is an understatement."

"I'm disappointed she took them down," Davi said. "It was my new favorite pastime to see all the people on social media telling her to go stuff herself."

I laughed.

Kenna sipped her wine through a smile.

And then Davi did her bit.

"I'm obsessed with the TV show *Ludwig*. Anyone seen it?"

Conversation flowed from there, through dinner and dessert (Kenna hadn't mentioned the raspberry cranachan, which was the perfect addition), with the only continuation of the early awkwardness happening when Bally was the first to leave.

As for me, I waited until after Dair, Sorcha and I were home, Dair had given me an orgasm, so, more importantly, I could give him one too, and we were under the skylight in his dark bedroom, cuddling before sleep.

"That went okay," I said quietly.

"Aye," he agreed.

I gave him a squeeze. "Are *you* okay?"

He was silent a moment.

Then he released such a huge breath, even I felt the relief of it.

"Aye, my love," he said. "This isn't a perfect world, as much as we want it to be. That's as good as it's going to get, so I'll take it."

"Your mum is amazing."

"Aye," he agreed more readily to that.

"I love you, Alasdair Wallace."

He knew it, of course.

But it was the first time I said it out loud.

He was again silent, and this moment lasted longer.

I was disappointed.

Until he turned into me shoving my legs open so his hips could fall between them when he got me on my back.

"Dair, I'm still so full of your mum's amazing cooking, you were lucky to wring one orgasm from me," I lied.

"We'll get ye into shape," he said against my lips. "In the meantime, I'll do all the work."

And then…

He did.

EPILOGUE

A HUNDRED MILLION WORDS

Blake

I was in my new Le Chameau Chasseur boots, Sorcha was wearing her normal fur, and we were tramping through the first frost that was covering the turned-over-for-the-winter beds of the back garden behind Treverton when Sorcha loped away from me.

I looked to where she was heading and saw Dair shrugging on a navy down jacket with horizontal stitching.

He was heading my way.

Man and dog made it to me but only the man part of that was smirking at my boots.

He'd given me so much shit since I'd bought them, I should be over shoveling it back.

But I was me, Dair was Dair, and we were us.

I had a feeling I'd never get over shoveling it back.

"I'm an English aristocrat," I pointed out not for the first time, and not only on this topic. "I need a good pair of wellies."

"Hunters wear those boots," he pointed out, also not for the first time.

I wrinkled my nose at him before I sniffed, "I need them when I'm mucking about in the stables or tramping around my vast estate. You know, all the healthy, outdoorsy pursuits of the good English aristocrat I am."

"Your version of 'mucking about in the stables' is entering it to mount a horse and then exiting it after you get off that horse."

"A marchioness doesn't saddle her own horse, Dair," I educated him.

"I ken, since I saddle it for her."

"Yes, that's your job. To be handsome. Give me many orgasms. And saddle my horse."

He busted out laughing.

I couldn't hold the haughty watching him do it, so I was smiling at him before he stopped.

"Are we going on a wander?" I asked after him coming out.

"Aye, but first, I've got some news."

I wasn't certain about the new expression on his face.

"What?" I asked, not hiding the uncertainty.

"Jeff must have found himself in a bind and needed some fast cash. He sold his story about what he was to your Mum to a rag."

Well…

Damn.

"Dad called with the news just now," Dair went on.

"I suppose we should have known he'd do that," I remarked.

"Dad's people are monitoring the reaction, and Jeff isn't coming off so well."

That was interesting.

"What's the response?"

"A lot of 'good for Helena,' and 'if you got it, use it,' and some unflattering, but accurate, epithets for Jeff."

Now it was me smirking.

Dair added his grin to my smirk.

"Ready to wander?" he asked.

I nodded.

Before we took off, Christine shouted from the back door. "A ploughman's for lunch?"

"Aye!" Dair shouted back. "Sounds good."

"Thank you, Christine!" I was also shouting.

"Enjoy the air!" And yes, she was shouting too.

So, okay, I was probably the first English aristocrat that had shouted conversations with my housekeeper like she was my favorite auntie and not on the payroll.

But…

Well…

Fuck it.

That was me.

Dair slung his arm around my shoulders, whistled for his dog who came dancing to us, and we took off across the crunchy turf during a bright, sunshiny, bitterly cold day.

And like we had all the time in the world, which we did, we wandered my ancestral estate.

———

AS THE FLORISTS LEFT, HAVING COMPLETED THEIR TASKS A FULL HOUR after they should have, with buried annoyance I studied my binder and made ticks next to FLOWERS DELIVERED, FLOWERS ARRANGED, FLORIST DEPARTURE.

Alex, only minorly showing a baby bump, bustled up to me.

"Dad texted. They're on their way," she told me.

I looked to my binder and checked off, DAD'S TEXT. I was close to checking off SHARP FAMILY TIME, but since that was about to happen, and it hadn't yet, I didn't.

But before I was solid on that decision, the binder was whisked out of my hands by Mika, who passed it off to Cadence, before she said, "Go."

She'd obviously received a text too.

The ceremony had been private, and neither Alex nor I argued that.

In this instance, it was whatever Dad wanted, we were happy to give to him.

The only ones in attendance at the justice of the peace ceremony were the bride and groom, Jamie, Dad's best man (who obviously brought his woman, Nora), and Capucine, Marlo's best friend and maid of honor (who, I'd recently discovered, was nearly as amazing as Marlo was).

Alex took my hand as we both searched the Rotunda at The Pierre where the small, intimate reception was to be held.

We found them, unsurprisingly, at the bar.

My sister and I headed that way, collected our men, and then we all made our way to the bridal suite.

Rix opened the champagne.

Dair passed him the glasses while he poured.

Alex and I made sure we all had the ivory rose petals.

So when the door opened, Dad and Marlo entered to a shower of downy beauty.

Dad was beaming.

Marlo was radiating.

She was also wearing a simple, but supremely elegant, long-sleeved ivory gown that had a boat neck and a three-foot train.

I started weeping.

Ugh!

When did I become a weeper?

Jamie shut the door, closing us in on Sharp Family Time.

Dad pulled me in his arms, then he reached to Alex to add her to his huddle, and once my sister was there, he immediately drew Marlo to us too.

I felt better when I saw Marlo crying as well.

"I love all my girls," Dad said hoarsely. His gaze went to Marlo. "Never been happier."

I hiccoughed a sob.

Alex whimpered beside me.

We all held on.

And then I said to Marlo, "Oh no! You're ruining your makeup."

This comment broke our huddle with Marlo dabbing carefully at her eyes, saying, "Worth it."

"I'll get some tissue." Alex ran off.

Rix handed a glass of champagne to Dad. Dair did the same with Marlo. Alex came back with the tissue. And our men gave us our champagne.

Once I was fortified with an alcoholic beverage in my hand, I assured Marlo, "I have a kit fitted out with everything. I'll fix your face before you go down."

"Thank you, my sweet," she replied.

"Can we toast now? Or do you women want to carry on for another hour?" Rix asked.

Alex batted his arm.

Dad raised his glass.

We all followed suit.

"You could talk until you're blue in the face," Dad began, "and say a hundred million words, and you would never convince me I'm not the luckiest man on the planet."

Oh God.

He turned to me.

Oh God!

Dad kept going.

"I have a beautiful, loving firstborn who has such strength of character, it takes my breath away. She doesn't let anyone walk all over her. And she'll do anything for someone she loves."

I managed to hold it together, sniffed and aimed an air kiss Dad's way.

Dair slid his arm around me.

Dad turned to Alex.

"And I have a beautiful, loving second born who knows her own mind, is wholly herself, spends her time doing good things for people who unfortunately need her to do that work, and will do anything for someone she loves."

Alex sent Dad a wobbly smile.

Rix already had his arm around her.

Dad turned to Marlo with such a besotted, happy expression on his handsome face, I nearly lost it again.

Dair somehow felt it and pulled me closer.

For my part, I braced for what was to come.

"And now I have a beautiful, loving wife who fills me with such happiness, I cannot wait to start each day by her side, and end it in the same manner. Marlo, my darling, you've enriched my life so completely I could use a hundred million words and add a hundred million more and still not express how much you mean to me. I love you. And I'm so damned happy you let me make you my wife."

Marlo lost it and Dad took her in his arms.

So, of course, Alex and I lost it again too.

Thus, Rix held his wife.

And Dair turned me into his embrace.

A half an hour later, after time spent together (and me fixing Marlo's makeup, not to mention, Alex's and my own), Dair and me, Alex and Rix hustled back to the Rotunda so the newlyweds could make their grand entrance through the flower festooned double doors.

I went right to Cadence so I could check off what just happened.

When I returned to Dair, he muttered, "I'll be glad when ye can retire that fucking binder."

"I still have the one for Alex's baby shower," I warned him, *and the one I've just started for my revamp of the NYC flat and the other one for Davi's bathroom reno*, I did not say.

"Aye, and I'll be glad when that one's gone too."

He said that, but his gaze had wandered.

I followed it to where Davi was sitting with her recently-promoted from-casual-fuck-buddy-to-boyfriend, Ewan, and Kenna was sitting with her new beau, Craig.

I returned to my man.

"You all right?" I asked.

And my all-honest-all-the-time Dair said, "She's happy. He thinks the world of her and treats her like it. It's just…I'm not used to it, lass."

Davi wasn't used to it either, but she was ecstatic.

Bally knew about it, and he was devastated.

Dair wasn't used to it, but he'd get used it because of what I was about to say next.

"She's happy."

He cast his eyes down to me. "Aye, my love. She's happy."

I smiled at him.

"Ms. Sharp?"

I turned to the staff member who was hovering.

"They're approaching," she told me.

I nodded. "Thank you." Then louder, I announced, "They're approaching."

Excitement swept through the room, and everyone gathered around the double doors.

"I cannot *wait* to see what she's wearing," Chloe said as she came to stand by me.

"You won't be disappointed," I assured her.

She wasn't, as the happy couple, wreathed in smiles, strode through their arch of flowers.

A cheer went up.

More glasses of champagne were pressed into their hands.

And a hundred million words couldn't tell you how thrilled I was for my father, my pregnant sister…

And me.

It hadn't been the easiest journey.

But we made it.

Boy, did we.

Brilliantly.

Dair

"AND THEN, *KABOOM!* WE SLAMMED INTO THE SLIP ABOUT FIVE FEET left of where we should have, and that's…it," Blake finished.

Dair roared with laughter.

"I'm glad you find it funny," she said snottily. "I was lucky Dad had attorneys on retainer. He still had to pay for the houseboat repairs and the damage I did to the slip."

"Remember, lass, your dad mentioned this story last night, and he was laughing about it nearly as much as me."

Ned hadn't shared the details, they were all just reminiscing about a variety of things, and he'd brought it up.

But Ned hadn't hidden, even if it might have pissed him off at the time, he gave no indication it did, and now he found it hilarious.

At this reminder, Blake just pouted.

"You weren't even drunk?" he asked.

"No."

"Not even tipsy?"

"No," she snapped. "And I know how to handle a boat. It's just, apparently, I don't know how to handle a houseboat."

He laughed again.

She cast her gaze to the side in annoyance.

In was after the wedding and they were in her bedroom at her father's house. Rix and Alex were down the hall in Alex's room. His mum was in the guest suite, aye, with Craig (and Dair was making absolutely certain not to think about that). Davi was in another room down the hall with her man.

Rix's family had chosen to stay at a hotel that was closer to things they wanted to see in the city.

Last, Blake was lazing on him, naked, after coming back from cleaning up post-sex.

"She did it," Blake said.

He let his laughter die and asked, "Who did what?"

"She redecorated my room and Alex's. It's subtle, like she just enhanced what was here so we wouldn't feel like she'd edged us out. But she did it. And she hasn't done much to the house, but what she's done, it's entirely different."

"Sorry, lass, dinnae ken what you're talking about."

"Marlo. Look."

She pointed across the room.

On the dresser, there was a picture of her and her father dancing at Alex and Rix's wedding. This was eight by ten, pride of place, but in front of it, positioned so you could see the photo at the back, was a framed snapshot of Blake, when she was maybe ten, blowing out birthday candles with Alex standing beside her, smiling at her.

There were some pretty candles dotted around the photos.

"And those." She pointed to each nightstand and then the coffee table in front of the couch in the sitting area across the room.

On these, there were some fake flower arrangements that he'd had to touch, because the flowers looked so real.

There were also more candles and massive books, all on art or fashion.

Not to mention, on one of the nightstands, there was a framed picture of Rix and Alex sitting together at Alex's wedding reception right before their first dance.

"Alex showed me her room and it's the same," Blake continued. "Pictures of her and Dad, her and me, her and Rix. Coffee table books about outdoors stuff. Alex's room used to look like Dad was selling the house, it was so bleak. The whole house did. It almost looks like we live in these rooms now." Her gaze went far away as she concluded, "Who knew family photos and some candles and items that share you have interests and personality could make a house a home?"

He'd obviously never been to Ned's house, but he found it warm and welcoming, the art and architecture stunning, and he had no idea the copious photos of Ned, Blake and Alex on display all over the space hadn't always been there.

"I love her for him *so much*."

When she said that, his woman's voice was thick.

This necessitated Dair rolling her to her back, with him on top, and cradling her head in his hand while he ran his thumb along her jaw, rubbed circles in the apple of her cheek, and just waited while she felt what she had to feel.

When she seemed to have a handle on it, he noted, "You gave them a beautiful day."

"It was fun organizing it with Marlo."

She hadn't hidden that, even if the engagement came fast, and the wedding faster.

Ned clearly was done fucking about.

"Everyone is happy," she whispered.

"Aye," he whispered back.

"Being me, when it comes to Mum, I redefined the stages of grief and cut out everything but anger and added confusion."

"Mm," he hummed.

She ran her hands up his back then locked her arms around him.

"Now I'm circling back to sad," she told him. "Sad, because Dad is such a great guy, and she missed out on all he could have given her. Sad because Alex is awesome, and they didn't have a lot in common, but she could have seen what she had a hand in creating with Alex, and she never did. And sad because she and I *did* have a lot in common, and she didn't share that with me. She died having everything a woman could possibly want in her life and having lost it."

Christ, he loved that she knew exactly what that "everything" was that a woman could possibly want in her life.

But she was correct.

It was a tragedy Helena never recognized it.

"That is sad, my love," he murmured.

"And now she's just gone, and nobody misses her and that's sad too."

"It is," he agreed and asked, "You think you'll make it to acceptance?"

"I already have," she told him. "Though it's a sad acceptance. And I think I have to further accept it always will be. But I hit that zone when Dad and Marlo walked into the bridal suite tonight looking so amazingly happy. I have you. Alex has Rix and a baby coming." She tightened her arms around him. "How could I not accept being happy?"

I have you.

"Aye, it's impossible for you not to be happy, hen, since you scored a catch like me," he teased.

Her eyes got wide, and she tried to buck him off.

He chuckled and kissed her.

She stopped trying to buck him off.

But some time later, she did some bucking.

And as was her way, it got both of them off.

SORCHA WAS STANDING AT THE TOP OF THE STAIRS WHILE DAIR climbed them.

He gave her pets when he hit the landing, but didn't call out, because he could hear Blake talking on the phone over what sounded like water running.

"If that's the tub you want, that's the tub we'll order," she was saying as he and Sorcha hit the bedroom. "But I want you to look at the specs again. It isn't very wide. It'll fit your ass, but if you want Ewan in it with you—"

Dair had stopped in the bedroom to look around, hearing her voice coming from the bathroom.

He'd had a meeting that day with the Scottish Rugby Union. They'd been trying to recruit him for a couple of years.

After a conversation with Blake, they agreed it was time for him to get serious about considering it. His contract would be up soon with the BBC, and with Blake in his life, and a future to build, he needed something that didn't require him flying all over Europe and most of the world every week.

Blake was worried he was giving up something he loved when she told him she adored travel, so she could come with him, or she could take the opportunity when he was gone to go to Treverton or New York if he had a longer haul than normal.

But they wanted bairns, and he didn't want to be that dad who was gone all the time, or that man who made his woman deal with everything because he was.

Fortunately, he had choices.

With what was on offer, particularly working with kids, that day, he got serious about it.

However, he'd left after Blake that morning. She was meeting his mum and Davi to look at some stuff for Davi's new bathroom.

And when he was about to leave, their clothes from the night before were on the floor, the bed was not made, and the bathroom was a disaster from Blake getting ready.

He'd thrown the clothes in the hamper, but didn't have time to do more than toss the bedsheets up so they were less of a mess. And he left her shoes where they were, because she was careful with them and had a specific place for each pair in the closet, and he didn't have time to figure out where they went. Then he took off.

Now the bed was made, the shoes were put away, and when he moved to the bathroom, he saw it was tidy, except for the towel she had laid out where she was resting the makeup brushes she was cleaning.

He heard her laugh.

"Okay good," she said into the phone "I'm glad you're reconsidering. I think you'll be glad too." Her eyes came to him standing in the doorway, and she gave him a big smile.

Fuck, she was beautiful.

"Dair's home, and he doesn't know it yet, but he's making me his bangers and mash because I might be more in love with his mash than him," she said to who he knew was his sister.

Now Dair was smiling.

"Right, I'll tell him. Speak soon and love to Ewan," she said, then wiped her hands on a towel and took the phone from where it was tucked between her shoulder and her ear.

"You could have put her on speaker," Dair noted.

"Hello to you too," she replied.

He moved in, took hold of her hips, then took what he wanted from her mouth.

She looked dazed when he lifted his head and said, "Hullo."

This smile she gave him was a little hazy, but he liked it too.

She recovered and explained, "The faucet was on. It was easier to hear and be heard that way."

"Right," he replied.

"Davi sends her love."

"Right," he repeated.

"How was the meeting?" she asked.

"They're working up an offer."

Her brows lifted. "Are you happy about it?"

"Aye. Very."

Her smile returned.

"I'm making bangers and mash?" he asked.

"Please," she replied.

"How's Davi's bathroom coming on?"

"I think we licked it for all the important bits. We just have to find a contractor to fit them."

"Not the easiest part."

"No, but we'll lick that too."

He had no doubt.

She had renovations in full swing at the New York apartment because, "I've always wanted to do that to make it more me, but Mum always pushed back," and she was nowhere near that flat.

Then again, she insisted on still looking after her father's properties being nowhere near them either.

All this meant more binders but fuck it.

She was like his mum. She liked to be busy. And she loved to do things for people she loved.

"I'll get started on dinner," he said.

"Great, but just a note we popped into St. James Quarter, and I grabbed you that Kiehl's stuff you like. It's in your top drawer by your sink."

Dair blinked slowly before asking, "Sorry?"

"You used it at Dad's place in Prescott?" she asked for confirmation.

"The face stuff?" he asked the same.

She nodded.

"You noticed that?"

"I could smell it after you used it." She appeared bemused. "Did I get it wrong? Don't you like it?"

"Aye, lass, I just didn't think about it after we left."

She turned back to the sink, saying, "That's what you have me for. To think about those things for you."

Fuck.

Fuck.

She was something.

She was lathering up a brush.

He decided to leave her to it and exited the bathroom to go make dinner.

As if sensing food might soon be spilled on the ground, as it was her job to clean that up, Sorcha came with him.

But Dair stopped in the bedroom again.

He'd always liked his bedroom. It was simple, uncluttered, and therefore, restful.

But now, on his side of the bed, there was that photo, framed, of Blake and Sorcha on their day in the park.

He'd put that there.

And on her side of the bed, there was a picture of her and him, Ned and Marlo, Alex and Rix, all in a line with their arms around each other under the arch of flowers around the doorway that led into Marlo and Ned's reception. This sat along with a white pot with a white orchid coming out of it.

It was not much, but it made a house a home.

As such, Dair was humming as he and his dog jogged down the stairs to the kitchen so he could make his woman dinner.

———

SEVERAL DAYS LATER, DAIR WALKED BY HIS OFFICE IN THEIR townhouse and saw Blake in there, pacing, her phone to one ear, his dog doing the pacing with her, another bloody binder open and cradled in her arm in front of her.

"No, poinsettias are too…on the nose. Holly as well. Though we should stick with the berries and Amaryllis," she was saying.

She'd decided which charities she was to be patron for, and unsurprisingly, one was the SPCA.

So now, along with all the other stuff she was neck deep in, she was neck deep in some function she and his mother were planning.

The writing was on the wall that he was going to share his life with a bevy of binders.

And he couldn't say he was upset about it.

He went to the lounge, stretched out on the couch, flicked on the telly, found a golf tournament to watch, and his dog abandoned her mum to stretch out on the floor beside her dad.

Sorcha wasn't fond of the binders either.

He was idly stroking her fur when Blake came in, plopped her book down on the ottoman and then did the same with her body on Dair.

He grunted with no small amount of exaggeration and wrapped his arms around her.

"Talk Mum down from poinsettias?" he asked, not giving that first shite about her answer, but she did, so he'd listen.

"No. She says they're traditional. And I suppose she's right."

"Aye, lass, she is."

She puffed out a breath to get some hair out of her eyes.

Adorable.

"Done with the binders for the day?" he asked.

"Yes."

"Want to go out and get a curry?"

"Yes."

"Want to marry me?"

She went solid on top of him.

He pushed into the pocket of his jeans, came out with the ring, took her hand, and slid the large emerald cut diamond surrounded by a band of diamonds on her left ring finger.

"You're not allowed to start another binder until after our curry." He paused and added, "And after our celebratory fuck."

She turned shining, wondrous violet eyes from the ring to him.

And then she kissed him.

He took over and they ended their kiss with her on her back and him on top.

"I'll take that as aye," he said.

Her irises rolled up. "You're excruciating."
He grinned.
She caught his grin.
And she kissed him again.
He changed his mind, and they did their celebratory fuck first.
Because, hell yes.
It was an aye.

#teamblairforever

The End

The River Rain Saga will continue…

SECONDARY (BUT NO LESS IMPORTANT) DEDICATION

To E and G
If you read this, you'll know why.
#TheOG3Forever

ACKNOWLEDGEMENTS

If you know, you know that I write the books in the River Rain saga with my River Rain team on Facebook, and as ever and always (I mean, it's a little scary, I think at this point they know these families better than I do!) for Blake and Dair's story, they didn't disappoint.

Therefore, giving credit where credit is due, many heartfelt thanks not only to the whole team who pitched in, but to these particular members whose contributions made it into the book:

Nikki Brunke for the idea behind Alex allowing her bridesmaids to wear what they want.

Kim Bourdages for Blake's beige lounge outfit she wore after waking up that first morning with Dair.

Angel McDougal for how Blake does her nails.

Elizabeth Connell Nielson for the outfit Blake wore when she made dinner at the Sharp Family house in Prescott.

Jessica Browning for giving me the name Sorcha for Dair's pupper. Jessica also suggested Effie, which I loved, so I gave it to one of Dair's fur babies who passed.

Sarah Crumplebottom offered up the name Nessie for Dair's dog, and it was popular (and I thought, funny), so I found a way to wedge that in as well.

Janine Machado suggested the hat Blake wore to Helena's funeral.

Nanette Willems suggested the hat Alex wore.

Adele O'Neill gave me the hat Blake wore to the little girl's funeral.

And Kristal Dalgetty gave me the one Alex wore.

Again, it is so freaking fun to work on these books with all of you. Thank you so much for jumping in with such verve yet again! The Holloways, Pierces, Sharps, Oakleys, Wheelers, Cohens, Ellingtons, and now the Wallaces all send their love to you.

Oh, and if you want to see pictures of all this inspiration, head to the River Rain section of my Pinterest page.

I also need to note that a reader emailed me about the idea of putting a family tree or something akin to that with the River Rain books, and I thought that was a smashing idea. Which is why that's included in this book. I also specifically wrote down this reader's name so I could acknowledge her awesome idea. I then, as is woefully my way, somehow lost my note with her name, and because of that, could not give credit where credit is deserved. I believe you know who you are…and I'm so sorry I'm not naming you here, but thank you for the fantastic idea!

And I would be remiss if I didn't share my undying love and gratitude to the team at Blue Box Press who puts their all behind these books and are a joy to work with, full stop.

So here's that love and gratitude for these folks:

Liz Berry

Asha Hossein

Kim Guidroz

Jillian Stein

Stacey Tardif

And posthumously, MJ Rose

DISCOVER MORE KRISTEN ASHLEY

AFTER THE CLIMB
A River Rain Novel, Book 1

They were the Three Amigos: Duncan Holloway, Imogen Swan and Corey Szabo. Two young boys with difficult lives at home banding together with a cool girl who didn't mind mucking through the mud on their hikes.

They grew up to be Duncan Holloway, activist, CEO and face of the popular River Rain outdoor stores, Imogen Swan, award-winning actress and America's sweetheart, and Corey Szabo, ruthless tech billionaire.

Rich and very famous, they would learn the devastating knowledge of how the selfish acts of one would affect all their lives.

And the lives of those they loved.

Start the River Rain series with After the Climb, the story of Duncan and Imogen navigating their way back to each other, decades after a fierce betrayal.

And introduce yourself to their families, who will have their stories told when River Rain continues.

Chasing Serenity
A River Rain Novel, Book 2

From a very young age, Chloe Pierce was trained to look after the ones she loved.

And she was trained by the best.

But when the man who looked after her was no longer there, Chloe is cast adrift—just as the very foundation of her life crumbled to pieces.

Then she runs into tall, lanky, unpretentious Judge Oakley, her exact opposite. She shops. He hikes. She drinks pink ladies. He drinks beer. She's a city girl. He's a mountain guy.

Obviously, this means they have a blowout fight upon meeting. Their second encounter doesn't go a lot better.

Judge is loving the challenge. Chloe is everything he doesn't want in a woman, but he can't stop finding ways to spend time with her. He knows she's dealing with loss and change.

He just doesn't know how deep that goes. Or how ingrained it is for Chloe to care for those who have a place in her heart, how hard it will be to trust anyone to look after her…

And how much harder it is when it's his turn.

Taking the Leap
A River Rain Novel, Book 3

Alexandra Sharp has been crushing on her co-worker, John "Rix" Hendrix for years. He's her perfect man, she knows it.

She's just not his perfect woman, and she knows that too.

Then Rix gives Alex a hint that maybe there's a spark between them that, if she takes the leap, she might be able to fan into a flame This leads to a crash and burn, and that's all shy Alex needs to catch the hint never to take the risk again.

However, with undeniable timing, Rix's ex, who broke his heart, and Alex's family, who spent her lifetime breaking hers, rear their heads, gearing up to offer more drama. With the help of some matchmaking friends, Rix and Alex decide to face the onslaught together…

As a fake couple.

Making the Match
A River Rain Novel, Book 4

Decades ago, tennis superstar Tom Pierce and "It Girl" Mika Stowe met at a party.

Mika fell in love. Tom was already in love with his wife. As badly as Tom wanted Mika as a friend, Mika knew it would hurt too much to be attracted to this amazing man and never be able to have him.

They parted ways for what they thought would be forever, only to reconnect just once, when unspeakable tragedy darkens Mika's life.

Years later, the impossible happens.

A time comes when they're both unattached.

But now Tom has made a terrible mistake. A mistake so damaging to the ones he loves, he feels he'll never be redeemed.

Mika has never forgotten how far and how fast she fell when she met him, but Tom's transgression is holding her distant from reaching out.

There are matchmakers in their midst, however.

And when the plot has been unleashed to make that match, Tom and Mika are thrown into an international intrigue that pits them against a Goliath of the sports industry.

Now they face a massive battle at the same time they're navigating friendship, attraction, love, family, grief, redemption, two very different lives lived on two opposite sides of a continent and a box full of kittens.

Fighting the Pull
A River Rain Novel, Book 5

Hale Wheeler inherited billions from his father. He's decided to take those resources and change the world for the better. He's married to his mission, so he doesn't have time for love.

There's more lurking behind this decision. He hasn't faced the tragic loss of his father, or the bitterness of his parents' divorce. He doesn't intend to follow in his father's footsteps, breaking a woman's heart in a way it will never mend. So he vows he'll never marry.

But Hale is intrigued when he meets Elsa Cohen, the ambitious celebrity news journalist who has been reporting on his famous family. He warns her off, but she makes him a deal. She'll pull back in exchange for an exclusive interview.

Elsa Cohen is married to her career, but she wants love, marriage, children. She also wants the impossibly handsome, fiercely loyal, tenderhearted Hale Wheeler.

They go head-to-head, both denying why there are fireworks every time they meet. But once they understand their undeniable attraction, Elsa can't help but fall for the dynamic do-gooder.

As for Hale, he knows he needs to fight the pull of the beautiful, bold, loving Elsa Cohen, because breaking her would crush him.

Sharing the Miracle
A River Rain Novella, Book 5.5

Elsa Cohen has everything she ever wanted.

A challenging career. A bicoastal lifestyle.

And an amazing man—the kind, loving and handsome Hale Wheeler—who adores her and has asked her to be his wife.

She isn't ready for the surprise news she's received.

And she doesn't know how to tell Hale.

Once Hale discovers that his future has taken a drastic turn, a fear he's never experienced takes hold.

He just doesn't understand why.

Family and friends rally around the couple as they adjust to their new reality, and along the way, more surprises hit the River Rain crew as love is tested and life goes on.

Please note: This is a slice-of-life novella in the River Rain series. It was written to be read after *Fighting the Pull*.

Embracing the Change
A River Rain Novel, Book 6

That Kiss…

Gorgeous New York socialite, Nora Ellington has been waiting a very long time for her happily ever after.

So long, she's given up on it and has decided, even though she's the plus-one friend without benefits to a man she's head over heels in love with, an HEA will forever be out of her reach.

Handsome billionaire Jamie Oakley thought he'd had two happily ever afters in his life. However, neither lasted long, and both ended in tragedy. He's not about to try it again or put his children through the trauma Jamie has learned from experience undoubtedly will come their way.

And he's made this decision even if the woman who's become his constant companion is a woman he loves straight to his soul....and wants with everything that is him.

But then, one night, Jamie loses control and kisses Nora.

He can't go there.

She can't go on without it.

They'll never be the same.

Or will they?

Gossamer in the Darkness
A Fantasyland Novella

Their engagement was set when they were children. Loren Copeland, the rich and handsome Marquess of Remington, would marry Maxine Dawes, the stunning daughter of the Count of Derryman. It's a power match. The perfect alliance for each house.

However, the Count has been keeping secret a childhood injury that means Maxine can never marry. He's done this as he searches for a miracle so this marriage can take place. He needs the influence such an alliance would give him, and he'll stop at nothing to have it.

The time has come. There could be no more excuses. No more delays. The marriage has to happen, or the contract will be broken.

When all seems lost, the Count finds his miracle: There's a parallel universe where his daughter has a twin. He must find her, bring her to his world and force her to make the Marquess fall in love with her.

And this, he does.

Wild Wind
A Chaos Novella

When he was sixteen years old, Jagger Black laid eyes on the girl who was his. At a cemetery. During her mother's funeral.

For years, their lives cross, they feel the pull of their connection, but then they go their separate ways.

But when Jagger sees that girl chasing someone down the street, he doesn't think twice before he wades right in. And when he gets a full-on dose of the woman she's become, he knows he finally has to decide if he's all in or if it's time to cut her loose.

She's ready to be cut loose.

But Jagger is all in.

Dream Bites Cookbook: Cooking with the Commandos
Short Stories by Kristen Ashley
Recipes by Suzanne M. Johnson

See what's cooking!

You're invited to Denver and into the kitchens of Hawk Delgado's commandos: Daniel "Mag" Magnusson, Boone Sadler, Axl Pantera and Augustus "Auggie" Hero as they share with you some of the goodness they whip up for their women.

Not only will you get to spend time with the commandos, the Dream Team makes an appearance with their men, and there are a number of special guest stars. It doesn't end there, you'll also find some bonus recipes from a surprise source who doesn't like to be left out.

So strap in for a trip to Denver, a few short stories, some reminiscing and a lot of great food.

(Half of the proceeds of this cookbook go to the Rock Chick Nation Charities)

Welcome to Dream Bites, Cooking with the Commandos!

Wild Fire
A Chaos Novella

"You know you can't keep a good brother down."

The Chaos Motorcycle Club has won its war. But not every brother rode into the sunset with his woman on the back of his bike.

Chaos returns with the story of Dutch Black, a man whose father was the moral compass of the Club, until he was murdered. And the man who raised Dutch protected the Club at all costs. That combination is the man Dutch is intent on becoming.

It's also the man that Dutch is going to go all out to give to his woman.

Quiet Man
A Dream Man Novella

Charlotte "Lottie" McAlister is in the zone. She's ready to take on the next chapter of her life, and since she doesn't have a man, she'll do what she's done all along. She'll take care of business on her own. Even if that business means starting a family.

The problem is, Lottie has a stalker. The really bad kind. The kind that means she needs a bodyguard.

Enter Mo Morrison.

Enormous. Scary.

Quiet.

Mo doesn't say much, and Lottie's used to getting attention. And she wants Mo's attention. Badly.

But Mo has a strict rule. If he's guarding your body, that's all he's doing with it.

However, the longer Mo has to keep Lottie safe, the faster he falls for the beautiful blonde who has it so together, she might even be able to tackle the demons he's got in his head that just won't die.

But in the end, Lottie and Mo don't only have to find some way to keep hands off until the threat is over, they have to negotiate the overprotective Hot Bunch, Lottie's crazy stepdad, Tex, Mo's crew of frat-boy commandos, not to mention his nutty sisters.

All before Lottie finally gets her Dream Man.

And Mo can lay claim to his Dream Girl.

Rough Ride
A Chaos Novella

Rosalie Holloway put it all on the line for the Chaos Motorcycle Club.

Informing to Chaos on their rival club—her man's club, Bounty—

Rosalie knows the stakes. And she pays them when her man, who she was hoping to scare straight, finds out she's betrayed him and he delivers her to his brothers to mete out their form of justice.

But really, Rosie has long been denying that, as she drifted away from her Bounty, she's been falling in love with Everett "Snapper" Kavanagh, a Chaos brother. Snap is the biker-boy-next door with the snowy blue eyes, quiet confidence and sweet disposition who was supposed to keep her safe…and fell down on that job.

For Snapper, it's always been Rosalie, from the first time he saw her at the Chaos Compound. He's just been waiting for a clear shot. But he didn't want to get it after his Rosie was left bleeding, beat down and broken by Bounty on a cement warehouse floor.

With Rosalie a casualty of an ongoing war, Snapper has to guide her to trust him, take a shot with him, build a them…

And fold his woman firmly in the family that is Chaos.

***

Rock Chick Reawakening
A Rock Chick Novella

From *New York Times* bestselling author, Kristen Ashley, comes the long-awaited story of Daisy and Marcus, *Rock Chick Reawakening*. A prequel to Kristen's *Rock Chick* series, *Rock Chick Reawakening* shares the tale of the devastating event that nearly broke Daisy, an event that set Marcus Sloane—one of Denver's most respected businessmen and one of the Denver underground's most feared crime bosses—into finally making his move to win the heart of the woman who stole his.

***

Rock Chick Rematch
A Rock Chick Novella

In high school, Malia Clark found the man of her dreams.
Darius Tucker.
But life hits them full in the face way before it ever should. Darius makes a drastic decision to keep his family safe and Malia leaves town with a secret.
When Malia returns, she seeks Darius to share all, but Darius finds

out before she can tell him. At the same time, she finds out just how much Darius has changed in the years she's been away.

She just refuses to give up on him.

Until he forces her hand.

Secrets come between Malia and Darius, at the same time Malia has to worry about weird things going on at the law firm where she works, her kid wants a car and she's stuck in slow-cooker hell. Luckily, her ride or dies have her back.

And in the meantime, she might just learn she never should have lost hope in Darius Tucker.

ON BEHALF OF BLUE BOX PRESS,

Liz Berry and Jillian Stein would like to thank ~
Steve Berry
Benjamin Stein
Kim Guidroz
Chelle Olson
Tanaka Kangara
Stacey Tardif
Chris Graham
Jessica Saunders
Grace Wenk
Ann-Marie Nieves
Dylan Stockton
Kate Boggs
Richard Blake
and Simon Lipskar